THE FIELD OF DREAMS

ISBN: 1450595634
EAN-13: 9781450595636

THE FIELD OF DREAMS

PHILIP SWATMAN

Dedication

For Rosemary – my muse and many other things.

Chapter 1

THE WATCHERS ON THE SHORE

Smudges of smoke punctuated the skies above the Hormuz Strait, one of the busiest shipping lanes in the world, and one of the global oil industry's most sensitive bottlenecks, while it shimmered in the forty degree heat haze.

Mohammed Al-Kazaz took a photograph using the tripod mounted Nikon with the special five hundred millimetre lens, turned away from his binoculars and entered down the usual details on the computer log running on the laptop on his desk.

Time, date, name of tanker, line, flag, Plimsoll line position and the photographic exposure number. He, and three others, working round the clock in shifts, had been keeping this watch for nearly a year now. Their look out post was high up in a tall building in Saudi's principal tanker port, Ras Tanura. Thankfully, Al-Kazaz thought, it was well air conditioned, otherwise the repetitive and tedious task would have become pretty much unbearable.

They were closely supervised, these watchers on the shore. At least twice a day the young, English speaking, university educated Saudi supervisor would come to their office, check their entries and download the photographs onto his own laptop. Once or twice he had been accompanied by another man of about forty, a Geordie, very tough looking, called, thought Al – Kazaz, Dyer, who said little but when he did appeared to have fluent Arabic.

There were four teams of these watchers on the shore, one for each Saudi oil port and one at the end of each of the Saudi pipelines – Yanbu on the Red Sea, at the end of the East — West and Sidon in Lebanon at the seaward end of the Abquaiq-Sidon pipeline.

None of them knew what their work was for or when it would end.

'So you're out here as a journalist, Mr Doyle?' asked Omar Faisal, flicking an imaginary speck of dust off the fabric of his sharply tailored Italian suit.

The two men were in Faisal's gleaming high tech office in the heart of the new Arabian Oil Corporation centre of technology excellence. Faisal was head of production at the Ghawar complex, Saudi's most important oil field grouping, which produced almost two thirds of Saudi oil and met five per cent of world oil demand. He was in his late thirties, having been educated in the US and then with Arabian Oil since he graduated. He was a high flier, with the easy charm of the educated Saudi elite.

They were sitting in low chairs in front of a coffee table with a large screen laptop in the centre of it. Glasses of water and cups of coffee were to one side.

'Yes, that's right,' Doyle replied. 'I'm commissioned by Vision Magazine to do a big piece on modern Saudi Arabia, its industrial and social development, the growth in population and all the challenges that poses, and of course, a review of its oil industry. I've been out for about two months actually, travelling pretty much everywhere, but I thought it was time to tackle oil. Your oil industry is so important for all of us.'

Doyle looked blandly enthusiastic.

'Do you know much about oil, Mr Doyle?' queried Faisal; his beautifully kept teeth gleaming politely.

'Not much,' lied Doyle easily.

Faisal relaxed. He could easily deal with this kind of visitor. He switched on his laptop.

'This is a presentation on the history of our oil, Mr Doyle, and, of course, its prospects for the future.'

Doyle nodded and effortlessly assumed a posture of polite interest.

Doyle spoke French and German fluently and had reasonable Arabic. He had, over the last three hard, dusty months, posing as a journalist, and sponsored by BMW, visited, by motor cycle, just about every part of Saudi Arabia. Officially he had had two aims. One was to create, for BMW, an elaborate marketing travelogue which could be used to further boost the Middle Eastern sales of their already wildly successful off road bike. The second was to research and write a major piece for Vision Magazine — a commission rather more easily obtained as a result of Doyle being one of its shareholders — on Saudi as a whole.

Both those aims were real. But they were blinds.

Doyle had begun to take an ever increasing interest in oil. He had long been convinced that there was a looming global crisis in oil supply and that such a crisis would decimate global economic growth. This belief had been reinforced by the enormous spike in the oil price which occurred at the tail end of the 2007 credit boom.

His affair with a very sassy girl called Philippa Davos, who ran her own boutique advisory firm advising Middle Eastern sovereign funds on international investments, had introduced him widely, in the guise of a publisher, to the upper echelons both of the Saudi royal family and the increasingly sophisticated technocracy which supported the crucial Saudi oil industry. Then, as he moved among the Saudi elite, he had begun to hear just the faintest whispers questioning the long term reliability of Saudi oil supply.

Doyle wasn't the first person to embark on a mission to get at the truth about Saudi oil. But with his dual cover he had slipped in under people's radar. And he had been lucky with his timing. There was a willingness to talk more openly. Saudi's at every level sniffed a wind of change. The internet, the pressure to provide employment for a rising population, the challenge of creating a sustainable long term economy apart from oil, the growing demands for emancipation of women and the need for higher education to drive development of an industrial society were all proving a potent cocktail for reform and development.

Faisal went smoothly through his material. It was predictable stuff. Saudi could pump oil at virtually whatever level it liked, he maintained, for the foreseeable future. If there had been fall offs in production in the past they were either

5

to handle cut backs agreed with their friends in OPEC or had been designed to rest their great fields after a period of enhanced production. One should, he thought, pay no attention to scaremongers who had penned books and articles along the lines of 'Twilight in the Desert' or 'From Bourgeoisie to Bedouin'. Besides, Saudi had the finest oil field technology in the world, and had had no trouble maintaining consistent levels of production from even its largest and oldest fields. Saudi reserves were still twenty five per cent of the global total, so it was easy to see that there was no risk of a shortfall in Saudi oil. Had the country not been, for the last nearly forty years, a stable and friendly bedrock of the oil supplies depended on by the West? Global oil consumption was running at eighty five million barrels a day and Saudi had consistently provided about ten per cent of that with the scope to increase production by fifty per cent if required.

Doyle lured Faisal on with flattering and respectful questions. Eventually Faisal leaned towards Doyle and said: 'My friend, you make such a good audience, I can see why you are such a successful journalist.

Of course,' said Faisal, tapping the memory stick on the side of his laptop, 'there's an awful lot more I could tell you but we have had to become very careful as to the information we release these days.'

Doyle thought how much he would like to inspect the contents of that stick. He also thought of the intelligence that had come out of his long and costly investment in the watchers on the shore. The story there was clear. The output from the old Ghawar complex was steadily dropping, and probably had been for a couple of years. It was being made up by more and more production from the newer fields.

But the Saudis had been clever. The number of tankers leaving port had been much the same — those were watched by a lot of people. But the tankers serving Ghawar had been sitting higher and higher in the water. They weren't being fully filled.

Faisal's secretary put her head round the door.

'Omar, I'm terribly sorry to interrupt but the Chief Executive is on the phone and he says he must see you urgently.'

Faisal excused himself and made towards the door. Halfway there he seemed to stop and look back, first rather longingly at his laptop and then, concerned, at Doyle. But Doyle already appeared engrossed in his Blackberry and Faisal evidently reached a decision to leave him to it. However almost the second the door closed behind him Doyle sprang to it, put his head round it, flashed a smile at Faisal's severely attractive secretary and said: 'Do you mind leaving me on my own for a moment? I've just had an important message and need to make a confidential call.'

'No problem,' she replied, 'just stay in the office. Omar will be some time, he always is with Ghafar, I'm afraid.'

Doyle went back into the room, opened the laptop, hoping the password protection had not yet kicked in, and quickly closed down Faisal's plain vanilla presentation. Then he inspected the other files on the stick. He started to open and copy material, slipping Faisal's stick out of the computer and substituting his own, keeping a low and fictitious conversation going into his Blackberry microphone. Doyle couldn't believe what was on the file. It had production figures, water content trends, and a myriad of stuff that Doyle knew he would never have time to copy. Most intriguing of all was something called a 'Draft Report to the Cabinet on Production Sustainability', marked 'Highly Sensitive, for Cabinet use only'. Doyle raced through the most interesting files. He felt no compunction. In his book being told lies was the quickest way for a journalist to lose reputation, or, he reverted to his more usual perspective, for an investor to lose money. Finally he slid out his memory stick and replaced it with the original, re-opened the presentation, concluded his artificial Blackberry discussion and sat back in his chair.

Three weeks later Doyle's eyes were screwed up against the glare of the early evening sun glinting on one of Arabian Oil's expatriate compounds. He looked across at the old Scottish engineer who had been in charge of Ghawar maintenance for twenty years.

Bill Isles, a red faced Scot of seventy, was the oldest expatriate staffer at Arabian Oil. His moustache quivered with emotion.

'You ain't no petroleum engineer whatever you might be cracking yourself up to be,' Isles spat casually over the rail of the veranda, 'or,' he went on suspicion grating in his voice, 'what you might really be.'

He relented and went on: 'See, a petroleum engineer knows the sign of a field running out. You can go on pushing more and more water into fields and building bigger and bigger downstream water separation plants but eventually you can just get overwhelmed and the whole equation goes bad on you. Saudi oil is dependent on a tiny number of huge fields and they've been pushing most of these fields harder and harder for nigh on seventy years. What no one understands is that when the end comes it can happen suddenly. I know that from working out some of the smaller fields at the end of the eighties. But no one wants to believe it about Ghawar — they call it the King of King's around here you know.

What's more,' he went on, 'all the older Saudi fields are under threat. And at least ten per cent of their total productive capacity is at serious risk from acute low pressure – it could be lost at any time.'

Doyle was acutely interested. He took another sip of whisky, though it was far from his favourite drink, leaned forward and said: 'How long do these stages last?'

'It varies,' said Isles, 'from field to field.' He refilled his whisky. He went without ice even in forty degree heat.

'Take Ghawar. It's been the noblest oil field in the world. It's regularly pumped over five billion barrels a day. It's the finest type of light oil and for the first ten years it pumped purely on natural pressure in the field. Then they had to start pumping sea water, first one or two million barrels a day, then in the last twenty years at increasing rates and now it's absorbing nearly seven million barrels a day. They then had to build a huge water separation plant. Now even that's under pressure and I'd say the output falls at Ghawar — which have been about five per cent over recent years, though some say greater — but whatever it is has been a ruddy engineering miracle- will start to drop really sharply any time now.

All the tell tale signs are there,' Bill said ruminatively.

This was too vague for Doyle.

'Bill,' he interrogated, 'just what kind of an output drop do you envisage for Ghawar?'

'You don't give up, do you?' Isles expostulated, 'what you got? All your savings in oil?'

'No, Bill, I just want to get things right for my piece,' soothed Doyle.

'Well, it's hard to say but I reckon we could soon see a drop of twenty per cent and if that happens we could see a total drop of fifty per cent over the next two years.'

Isles knocked out his pipe.

Doyle knew the slightest glitch in oil production could send global prices soaring by twenty or thirty dollars a barrel. The removal of two and a half million barrels a day from Ghawar alone would have a catastrophic effect on global oil prices and the global economy, let alone the comparable impact from other old, tired, Saudi fields going the same way.

Doyle said he couldn't understand how the Saudis, even now, could be pumping at stable rates overall or claiming the same level of reserves.

'The production side is simple,' said Isles. 'They just over pump the smaller newer fields – and by doing that they are shortening their lives and storing up problems for the future.

And as for reserves,' he said, 'those figures have, ever since Arabian Oil lost its foreign owners, been based on some pretty speculative assumptions as to how much oil can be recovered – their recovery assumptions are way higher than anyone else.

The whole thing,' Isles shot dottle out of his pipe onto the sand outside his bungalow, 'is shaping up to be a complete house of cards. I as sure as hell don't want to be here when the balloon really goes up. Anyhows,' he said comfortably, 'I retire at the end of this year and by next summer I'll be growing tatties in Fife — away from this heat, the sand, the flies, and,' Isles grinned wickedly, 'some of the people.'

Doyle had some feel for the kind of pension arrangements Bill might have secured after fifty years with his employer and made a face.

'I don't think you'll be reduced to growing your own potatoes, Bill.'

Bill grinned slyly.

'Bill,' said Doyle slowly, 'I don't understand why more people aren't aware of these issues?'

The desert, hot, empty, shimmering, disappeared into the horizon in wave after wave of ochre sand dune. Even at six o'clock in the evening the glare and heat outside the bungalow were oppressive.

'Because bloody few people are told about it, that's why,' Isles said belligerently. 'You've been out here nearly three months, you said, and look how hard you've found it. They give out less and less official information on field performance.

Now all the production figures are controlled by a tiny team which reports directly to the Chairman of Arabian Oil and he in turn passes the figures to the Energy Minister. It's all in code. And anyone who leaks anything tends to disappear.'

The meeting with Bill Isles had almost been Doyle's last.

Doyle had travelled thousands of miles. He had slept under the stars, in remote local and expatriate bungalows, with the Bedouin and in cheap hotels. He had waited endlessly during his days for appointments. Meetings had frequently been postponed or delayed. He had spent evenings and nights socialising, sometimes with Saudi's, mostly with expatriates, during which he had drunk either no alcohol or bad alcohol. He had drunk no fine wine, his diet had been monotonous, and he had grappled with motor cycle repairers and occasionally with camel keepers. He had spent days and days, as part of his cover, interviewing people with very little or no relevance to his main quest. His love life had been nonexistent and his sex life had been commoditised.

But Doyle had come away with the material for the biggest financial coup of his life. He was certain that no one else, in the entire global financial system, could have quite the same level of his convictions about the outlook for Saudi oil production and reserves or that outlook's potentially disastrous impact on global oil supply, price and global economic confidence.

But he was very tired. He flicked open his Blackberry and punched a speed dial.

'This Friday, Chuck', he said, 'USAF Riyadh, 7am. Touch and go. Back to London.'

'Good to hear you boss', drawled his pilot, 'goddamed plane's damn near rusted up.'

'Let's hope you haven't forgotten how to fly the brute,' said Doyle laconically.

Thirty six hours later Doyle watched the first fires of the sun etch themselves into the hills surrounding the USAF Riyadh Air Base. The runways were still pools of darkness with the barest pinpricks of blue lights stretching away into the distance.

Doyle was waiting on the apron, in the shelter of a refuelling truck, his parka pulled around him as the early morning desert wind lowered the temperature to just above freezing. He carried his attaché and laptop cases, and a small overnight bag. They were the sole remnants of his kit. A slight lethargy hung over him, the legacy of a farewell dinner the night before with the British ambassador. Doyle generally had little time for Foreign Office officials, distrusting both their intellectual arrogance allied to a disagreeable air of ineffable social superiority, while despairing of their lack of commercial flair.

However the unaccustomed pleasures of the Ambassador's wine cellar and the beguiling presence of his eldest daughter, combined with his fatigue, had nearly caused Doyle to drop his guard. He had had to exercise supreme self control in giving the Ambassador a strictly edited version of his travels and findings, focussing on the wider political, economic, social and religious issues, while quietly congratulating himself on a promising start as a rookie investigative journalist. At least, he felt, he hadn't let down his fictional editor at 'Vision' magazine. In fact his measured political positioning seemed to strike an Ambassadorial chord and they parted on good terms with the daughter's telephone number firmly in Doyle's pocket.

Doyle shivered again. A black dot, sinking fast, suddenly appeared in the Western sky and enlarged itself into an aeroplane with breathtaking speed. Doyle stiffened. No matter how many times he saw his plane materialize literally from thin air it caused the hairs on the back of his neck to prickle uncontrollably.

Suddenly the plane's landing lights blazed and for the first time Doyle heard its shattering roar as it came in down the flight path at what seemed an incredible speed. It touched down with a spurt of smoke from the tyres which mingled with the flames from the after burners as Chuck applied full reverse thrust and taxied over to within fifty metres of Doyle. The engines died and in the almost deafening resultant silence the canopy slid back and Chuck poked his head out. 'Pretty darned good,' he guffawed, 'just over an hour and a half from Northolt.'

Chuck eased himself down the tall ladder and walked across to Doyle. His familiar rolling gait, his shaven head and granite features were welcome reminders to Doyle of his normal life.

'Hope I've time for a cup of coffee and a pee, boss,' he said. 'Cabin service in that thing isn't all it should be.'

While the plane was refuelled Doyle and Chuck had breakfast and looked at the flight plan for the return journey.

Doyle offered no excuses for the plane. It was his magic carpet.

Two years before he had completed a very sensitive project for the US State Department. Concorde had been taken out of service and the US were retiring the second generation of SR 71's, originally known colloquially as Blackbirds. This second version was a significant improvement on the first and far easier to adapt to civilian use. It was smaller, looked more conventional, used standard jet fuel, cruised at the same height, eighty thousand feet, and was slightly slower, Mach 3, had a greater range and was much more fuel efficient. It would also self start without elaborate ground handling equipment. The fuelling problems caused by the need to handle the extraordinary in-flight fuselage expansion had been eliminated, as had the fuselage cooling problems on landing. The overall result was a plane which could now be flown more or less like any other although, as Chuck frequently reminded Doyle, it was a handful to fly and especially to land. Finally, and best of all, the need for elaborate crew pressure suits had been eliminated by the incorporation of superior cabin cooling and pressurization systems and revised bail out procedures.

Doyle had thought he could see a charter market for the uber wealthy businessman. The USAF had let Doyle have three, de-militarised them and removed in each case nearly two tons of reconnaissance equipment. This had allowed Doyle to put in more fuel tanks and the planes now had a range of four thousand miles. One of Doyle's companies ran two under the 'Mach Four' brand, though for passenger safety reasons they ran at Mach 2 and flew at fifty thousand feet. Doyle had persuaded the US military to re-engine his own plane, which, using the air inlet technology now applied to the spy plane which had replaced the second generation Blackbird, gave more than Mach 3.5 for a brief period at a height of ninety thousand feet. They had also allowed him to retain some of the radar jamming facility which they had insisted be removed from the charter fleet. The US had given him free servicing and fuel for five years on his own plane — and worldwide use of US air bases – they had been very grateful for his efforts. For his own part Doyle had acquired and replanted a million acres of South American rainforest to off-set its still spectacular emissions.

Twenty five minutes later Doyle was being pushed back into the co-pilot's seat as the relent-less, never ending thrust of the pair of forty thousand pound Pratt and Whitney ram jets pushed the Blackbird up to fifty thousand feet. A tidal roar of sound engulfed Doyle as he watched the altimeter and speedometer compete with barely comprehensible numbers.

Finally the plane levelled out, the roar of the ram jets abated, and the scrolling of the map under the flight path arrow on the nav station suddenly quickened as the Blackbird, its wings remaining a dull metallic grey even in the glinting morning sun, began to haul in waypoints over Iran, Turkey, Austria, Germany and France at what seemed like warp speed.

By nine thirty that morning Doyle was at Northolt and shortly after was en route to London in the Ghost, the new baby Rolls, with his driver Frank at the wheel. Doyle sank back into the cushions. He could feel the luxury of his normal life beginning to seep back over him like warm scented water.

Chuck's final words to him as he left the plane had been: 'Well, it runs into fuel a bit but it certainly gets you about.'

Doyle had told him to make the most of it while it lasted.

Chapter 2

THE CARDS OF THE GAMBLER

Doyle left the Assassins Club shortly after one in the morning. He had been playing Texas Hold Em with his regular Monday evening group. But there had been one new face there who he thought he recognised and who had introduced himself as Alexander Lutin. Medium height, blonde hair, baby faced with rather cold pale blue eyes. A banker apparently, according to Doyle's regular bridge partner, George Nutting. Normally the betting at the weekday games at the Assassin was relatively modest but Lutin had persistently tried to ratchet it up. Doyle had gone with him and had ended up losing several thousand pounds. Outside the club Doyle had moodily lit a cigarette and reflected. He must have lost his touch after his months away. But there had been something utterly nerveless about Lutin's play which had systematically undermined Doyle's self confidence. His smoke curled up towards the old streetlight outside the club's Duke Street portal. There was a shadow at his shoulder and the caustic tones of the tall thin hard bitten man Doyle always called Uncle George intruded on his uneasy thoughts.

'Blimey', Uncle George muttered. 'You need to sharpen up, matey.'

George Nutting clapped Doyle on the shoulder: 'That chap joined the Club while you were away and he's had an extra-ordinary run. Most of the high rollers have been hurt by him in the last few months. It's even got to the point where people are beginning to ask some questions.'

Nutting loped off into the night.

Doyle's mobile rang and he listened to a message. Alec Cowan.

Cowan was a small eager man of seventy or so, bright eyed and voluble. A private and highly successful stock market investor who had married into a very wealthy family with big interests in land and media, Cowan specialised in tracking down interesting investments in smaller companies. Doyle always listened to him very carefully.

'I need to see you urgently, James. Please call me as soon as you can.' Doyle made a mental note to ring Cowan first thing, walked down the street into St James's Square and looked for his car.

Doyle was the only son of a Nottinghamshire telephone engineer. His mother had died in a car crash when he was eight. He had left little mark on the Nottingham comprehensive that he attended. However very early on in his school career he had developed an obsessive interest in all forms of gambling. Immediately after school he had sent himself on his gambling winnings to Yale and had then spent three years with the Special Forces knocking about the world on various assignments, using, in his spare time, his bridge and poker skills to finance his lifestyle and build some capital. After that he spent a short time on an MBA course at Harvard.

But early on at Harvard, Doyle had realised that he would much prefer a freewheeling existence, living on his wits, to mainstream corporate life. After spending some time working for a couple of New York hedge funds, he had so impressed one or two of their backers that with their support he had decided to base himself in London and carve out a career as a financial adventurer. In his mid twenties, with his New York backers and some London ones he acquired from networking the cream of London's card clubs, he had put together the beginnings of an investment partnership called the 'Sphinx', a loose affiliation of some leading hedge funds attracted to one off investment exercises outside of their principal strategies.

For the last decade he had developed the Sphinx with a series of daring financial coups.

One of his more recent successes had been exploiting the credit crisis through the very early and ultra aggressive short selling of Asiabank, one of Britain's biggest, and now one of its most troubled, financial institutions. He had followed this with a play on recovery by taking very heavily leveraged long positions in some of the most damaged banks. Before that there had been the corner of a large part of global uranium supplies and mining capacity not locked away in the major mining houses; a position which he subsequently sold on to the US Government at a very substantial profit. Then there had been a major thrust into top end London housing; at one point the Sphinx had owned over five hundred multi-million pound central London properties; and there had been investment plays in German real estate, in wheat, oil, large gem diamonds, and some rare metals linked to the manufacture of solar power equipment.

The Rolls eased along the Embankment. From the back seat Doyle could see the dark mass of

Frank's massive shoulders and his afro haircut forcing its way out from under his traditional Igbo hat. Frank had been a Biafra war orphan and had had a tough upbringing with a so called auntie on one of London's worst sink estates. Doyle had caught him one night breaking into his house but, rather than call the police, had taken him under his wing and trained him as a mechanic, driver and bodyguard.

Doyle reached his house at Southwark Place shortly after midnight. He climbed the silent stairs and sat in his darkened first floor office overlooking the Thames. The bank of computers set in a semi circle round his desk whirred gently. Doyle called up the Bloomberg screen and switched it over to the Hong Kong market. For the last three nights he had been completing the slow building of a position in a company called Emerging Minerals which, amongst other assets, owned a mine producing Tulsamite, a metal critical to the manufacture of electric fuel cells. The yellow line of the stock price had jumped sharply upwards in opening trading. Doyle called up the stock page for Cellor, the Australian company which was Emerging's principal competitor in Tulsamite. It contained a one line newsflash to the effect that Cellor's Tulsamite mine had had to be shut because of overwhelming flooding. Doyle had visited both mines in the last year and he was well aware of the bad weather risks to Cellor. He was also a subscriber to a global private weather forecasting service which had been advising for several weeks of the risks of torrential storms reaching Western Australia, compensating for many years of drought.

Doyle closed his position in Emerging, and went down another set of stairs sealed off at the bottom by hydraulic doors. As they hissed open he felt the warm air waft over him and confer an instant sensation of luxurious well being.

Doyle was a bachelor, aged thirty five, dark haired, just under six foot in his socks. Although he had just conceded the need for a personal trainer he was still nearly as fit and muscular as in his Special Forces days, his weight still the same at some eighty five kilos.

His deep blue wide set eyes, easy going smile and firm jaw made him attractive to women. However the wariness, detachment and steely reserve of the professional gambler in Doyle had killed off many budding relationships and the time consuming intensity with which his various projects were pursued allowed little time for those which did penetrate his reserve to flourish. Doyle was charming and persuasive, but he could be terrifyingly abrupt and had no patience for fools.

But the two characteristics he had which really cemented the loyalty and belief of his team beyond any other were that he always seemed to be one jump ahead and exhibited absolutely zen like calm in moments of tension and crisis.

They had all seen markets move heavily against the Sphinx and seen no more reaction from Doyle than if he had lost five pounds in the street.

Doyle's London accommodation was predictably unconventional. He had bought a small office block just downstream of Southwark Bridge, converted part of it into a home, kept part as an office, put a swimming pool and gym in the basement and retained spaces for a large number and variety of vehicles which Doyle, who loved cars, justified to himself on account of his work.

The pool which Doyle now entered was spectacular. It was twenty metres long and ten wide, lined entirely in peacock blue tiles. There were black tiles on the pool hall floor and the hall ceiling was covered by inverted waves of mirror tiles. Lighting bounced off the tiles into myriad watery reflections. Luxurious settees and some perspex tables and chairs completed the furnishings with a bar concealed behind mirrored doors at one end.

Doyle loved this very private place. He kept the water temperature at a cool twenty five degrees — anything more inhibited serious swimming — but the hall itself was superheated. For

Doyle it was a totally secluded oasis conferring spiritual, mental and physical well being, a continuous source of sensuous pleasure and exercise and a profound stimulus for creative thought.

Next morning he slept late. On waking he stretched luxuriously and swung himself out of bed grabbing a silk dressing gown embroidered with extracts from the markets pages of the Financial Times, a leaving present from a particularly exasperated girlfriend.

He called Fred, his ex army batman, on the internal phone, for breakfast.

'By the way, Fred,' he said, 'two here for dinner tonight. Eight o'clock. And for God's sake keep lamb and goat off the menu.'

Doyle did not charge the Sphinx with regular management fees, instead taking an abnormally large share of profits on any project. These profits, together with his own private trading activities, enabled him to pay his small team exceptionally well.

Doyle had been back in London for three days and was now joined for breakfast by Matthew Fleming, who ran trading and corporate finance.

Matthew had a double first in mathematics from Cambridge, had gone on to Chicago's business school, and had then worked with

Morgan Stanley and Goldman Sachs, initially in commodities and later in proprietary trading.

Something had drawn Fleming to Doyle. Perhaps it was the thought that at twenty eight he had plenty of his life left to work in big, highly regulated institutions. It was certainly the lure of being a part of a more buccaneering environment, even more so after the regulatory and bonus backlash that had been a consequence of the credit crunch. Matthew had developed a great feel for markets and more importantly had a network of contacts amongst broker dealers and commodity traders that provided invaluable intelligence to the practical execution of the operations of the Sphinx.

Doyle had an obsessive need for hot, fresh coffee at breakfast; as long as he got it he was quite happy to base his breakfast on cheese in Denmark, croissants in Paris and dates in Morocco.

'So, what's going on in Saudi, James?' quizzed Matthew, happily pouring himself a helping of coffee from the large silver pot which nestled at Doyle's side.

'Matthew', said Doyle, 'what is going on in Saudi is that their oil really is running out. And much faster than expected. The new and pretty devastating information is that there is about to be a major and completely unexpected contraction in their oil output. Over the years they've sat on this situation, they've dried up the flow of detailed information about field performance and they've maintained that their reserves are undiminished despite finding very little new oil. One day it all had to blow out on them and I now know that that day is very near. Basically they have pushed their old fields to the very limits and a number of them including the largest, Ghawar, are about to break down. This will lead to a sudden and irreversible decline in global oil output.'

Fleming twisted his elegant fingers together.

'But we are at the bottom of the economic cycle now James; oil demand is about to start increasing again.'

'Exactly, Matthew' replied Doyle, 'it is and this news, when it comes out, will have cataclysmic consequences both for markets and for that embryonic economic recovery that everyone is banking on.'

'As you asked during your trip,' said Fleming, 'I've unwound most of the long positions we had in global equities but I've kept the long oil positions which were designed to exploite higher global economic activity. Now we keep them and also put on a play on industrial shorts?' Fleming's brain was whirring fast.

'Exactly,' said Doyle. 'The initial reaction will be total panic with endless predictions of the end of the world. At the moment oil is still very much the basic engine of the global economy. Do you remember, as the last price rise went on and on, that everyone convinced themselves that despite its negative effect the world could probably live with oil at $100 a barrel because of improving productivity? It's very hard to see how the same arguments could be made it oil went to $200 or even $300. People will think another deep global recession is a certainty.'

Fleming said: 'Will there be an official announcement from Saudi? And what about the Sphinx — this is obviously one of the biggest trades of a lifetime?' He looked slightly flushed.

'Something will break shortly,' said Doyle, 'but I have to find out the exact timing. And, yes, of course we should bring in the Sphinx, but they are going to want proof of my findings before they commit.'

Fleming was flabbergasted.

'What, even after your three months in the desert and the Arabian Oil stick they are going to want more?' he queried.

'Fraid, so, Matthew. Given traditional Saudi secrecy they will want chapter and verse on the certainty and timing of an announcement. They are very careful people, especially where really big positions are concerned.'

'Anyway, Matthew,' concluded Doyle, 'for our own funds I suggest we treble our long oil exposure and take some big positions in the more highly prospective junior oils. With the oil prices we are going to see soon a lot of the prospective resources of those companies will be developed far more quickly.'

This was said casually but already twenty per cent of Doyle's liquid resources was margined against oil futures and now he had proposed it be increased to sixty per cent.

Fleming returned with a spring in his step to his office, doing some quick mental arithmetic.

He knew Doyle's spare cash resources were about five billion sterling. Applying three billion to margin requirements, and assuming a margin as low as five per cent, would mean exerting leverage over sixty billion dollars worth of oil. And if the oil price doubled — to a hundred and twenty dollars — or, Fleming's eyes dilated — trebled to a hundred and eighty dollars? He reached for the phone. He knew that to Doyle all these things were now just a game of chess, and that Doyle was increasingly motivated by making money for his various philanthropies. But Fleming had an expensive lifestyle and big ambitions. He talked precisely and earnestly into the phone.

In the afternoon Frank drove Doyle down to Bisley where he was due to fire in a pair of new twelve bores. The pair had been specially designed and made for him by Scaglietti, a little known firm of Italian gun makers situated up in the hills behind Lake Maggiore. Signor Mario Scaglietti, the second generation proprietor and a wiry little Italian of forty five, was waiting for Doyle at Council Camp, the most remote of the extraordinary collection of wartime wooden and Nissen huts that are scattered over Bisley's undulating sandy pine woods.

'Ah', he said, with a huge smile that creased his features, 'James. Delighted, James, how are you keeping?'

Doyle had been waiting two years for these guns. He shook Scaglietti's hand warmly and said : 'Mario, it's been so long I'd thought you'd forgotten all about me.'

'Forget an important customer like you, James, ah, impossible,' laughed Mario.

'But, James, perfection, takes time to achieve, eh?'

'Certamente,' said Mario happily to himself.

'We have followed your instructions to the letter', he said, turning his attention back to Doyle, 'using all those German tests. I must say we all found the process very interesting James, and I thank you, we have all learned a lot from it.'

Doyle was a keen game shot and had become obsessed with improving shotgun performance. Like many other products which had been around for a long time shotgun technology had remained in a traditional backwater for decades. Doyle had seen heavier and heavier loads being used for high bird shooting but he preferred not to go down that road. He had set out to produce a faster gun. Faster in the sense of faster handling — achieved through a lower gun profile — and through reverse striker technology faster in reaction through reducing lock time-the interval between pulling the trigger and the firing pin hitting the cartridge. Improved chokes and ported barrels had tightened shot patterns and reduced barrel flip while a re-designed cartridge developed superior pellet hardness and improved retention of high velocity right up to the point of impact. His aim was to cut down the lead required on shooting high birds and to improve the effectiveness of cartridges of average load.

He had obtained the services of a leading German technology institute which had worked both with Scaglietti's people and a leading German cartridge manufacturer to produce the package of improvements Doyle had wanted. The trigger response time had been halved, the powder had been improved, ignition time had been accelerated and the pellets had been made harder by using a mixture of bismuth and lead and adding a space age Teflon type coating.

Doyle admired the pair of guns lying in their new leather cases. The engraving was not particularly elaborate — Doyle's belief was that fancy engraving didn't kill any more birds – but the stocks — of Austrian walnut — were beautifully figured works of art.

'You will see James,' said the little Italian ecstatically to Doyle, who was trying the guns for fit with the Bisley head instructor, 'the results are amazing.'

Doyle smiled at his enthusiasm, loaded a couple of the new twenty eight gram cartridges and gave the signal for a clay sequence to start.

When it finished, fifty clays later, Doyle had missed the first three clays as he adjusted to the parameters of the entirely new set up. Then he hadn't missed a single clay. Doyle carefully put down his gun and walked over to Scaglietti.

'Mario,' he said, 'you were right. Those guns are amazing. On the high birds I reckon the lead is more than halved and for everything else you can more or less shoot straight at it. For a shotgun it's absolutely uncanny.'

Four hours later the firelight was flickering in the elegant dining room on the top floor at Southwark Place.

Doyle inspected his champagne flute carefully — the glass was from Pauly in Murano and dated from the late nineteenth century. It contained 1985 Krug which Doyle happily regarded as his house champagne. Doyle felt relaxed. He was dressed in a dark blue linen suit with an open necked white linen shirt. He had completed an initial expansion of his personal exposure to oil futures and Fleming was working on a presentation to the Sphinx.

Opposite him Alec Cowan, more formally dressed in Prince of Wales check and a club tie, was excitedly shifting in his seat and fingering and re-fingering his glass, although he had touched very little of its contents.

'James,' he said eagerly, 'have you heard of a company called Kunene Resources?'

'It's a small AIM listed explorer isn't it?' said Doyle.

'Yes,' replied Cowan, 'it was put together about two years ago primarily to look for oil and gas in the coastal strip at the very Southern tip of Angola, just above the Kunene River which marks the border.'

Doyle swirled his white burgundy round his mouth ; he really must finish the 1996's he thought, even though their sulphur problems had not yet impacted his own cellar. He took a compensating mouthful of smoked salmon.

'Has it found anything yet?' he inquired.

'Nothing,' said Cowan.

'Make me excited,' murmured Doyle.

'I've asked Fred to set something up for me,' said Cowan.

Fred slid noiselessly into the room and raised and fired up an enormous digital plasma screen from the bookcase which lined one half of the room. He clicked a couple more buttons and handed a remote control to Cowan.

A large scale map of the south western coast of Africa appeared on the screen.

Alec Cowan hovered the pointer over the Skeleton Coast just a little distance above the Namibian/Angolan border.

'You remember those Geoffrey Jenkins thrillers set on this coast, James?'

'Yes,' said Doyle, 'a sort of Hammond Innes on steroids. I read them all — enjoyed them.'

'Well, a little above that is pretty much where Kunene is operating. It takes its name from the river on the Namibian/Angola border. They have drilled a couple of wells and, like a lot of AIM exploration companies in this market environment, have just about run out of funds to do any more exploration.'

Cowan explained — over a delicious lasagne and even more agreeable 1999 Armailhac — that the concessions granted to Kunene were a small sublease of Angolan concessions owned by Rangoon Oil. But at the same time as the Angolan rights had been granted to it Rangoon had acquired a one hundred and fifty year lease over a vast area of onshore Namibian exploration rights. This had happened just after the Second World War, when Namibia was basically being run by the South Africans. Rangoon had apparently done some shallow test drilling in Namibia after the war but found nothing and had turned its attention elsewhere.

'So no one's ever found anything there?' Doyle persisted.

'Well, not apart from some gas offshore a little way out from the coast. You have to appreciate that Namibia is very under-explored, James. Of course there's been a great deal of oil already found offshore Angola,' said Cowan, 'but look at this.'

He flashed up an even more detailed schematic of the geology running down the African coast line and the equivalent on the eastern seaboard of South America.

'These are both classic oil bearing structures James,' said Cowan, 'and they may even run right across the South Atlantic. They go back to the original supercontinent of 'Gondwanaland' which joined South America, Africa, Australia and Antartica. Then tectonic rifting occurred which has parallels in the Great Rift Valley in East Africa. After that a series of deep lakes formed which eventually resulted in the opening up of the South Atlantic. But while the water was trapped the saline build up led to massive salt deposits which sit on top of the organic shales and they in turn became oil bearing rock. Look,' he pointed to a spot off Brazil, 'this is where Twenty First Century Gas made its great Tiger find and these are the equivalent structures off the Angolan coast where oil has already been struck. The finds on both sides of the South Atlantic are in sub salt basins. Originally they never found much oil at shallow depths in Brazil but they did find Diamdod structures in the crude which indicate a blending of two types of petroleum, one of which must have been formed at great depth. Then the Brazilians were persuaded to drill much deeper into the pre salt layer and they think they may eventually find that the resource there reaches half a trillion barrels.

As I mentioned earlier there's been quite a lot of oil found off the West African coast extending down into Angola. Most of it is offshore except for one or two notable finds in the Congo including M'Boundi. The first point is that these offshore structures may run further south into Namibian waters. That's the golden rule in exploration, James. The best place to find oil is next door to where you've already found it. But for various reasons there hasn't yet been intensive prospecting activity offshore Namibia. Secondly the only real find there has been gas — and it frequently happens that gas rather than oil is found where the temperatures at depth have been too hot for oil deposits to survive long term, so there is a risk that there is only limited oil there. The third point is that no one's really focussed on the coast or further inland, either where we are on the border, or further south in Namibia itself. But geologists with whom I've spoken now believe these offshore structures could also be replicated onshore, and run for hundreds of miles inland parallel to the Skeleton coast.'

Doyle expostulated: 'That's all very well Alec but how the hell can it mean anything for us? I mean Rangoon must be able see that geology — it sticks out like a pair of dog's balls.'

Cowan swirled his Suduiraut around his glass and scooped up the remains of his crème brulee.

'Well, that's the final point. It's not quite that simple James', he said. 'As I said Rangoon lost interest in that area — hardly surprising as they had other fish to fry elsewhere and of course they never drilled sufficiently deeply – and when I said Kunene haven't found anything that's not quite true.'

Doyle sat up.

'We have told the world what we have or haven't found within the limits of what is possible under stock market rules in relation to hydro carbon discoveries. But those rules do not allow for results obtained through use of the latest ultra seismics — it's called Seismic X – which are a revolutionary development of the commonly used 3D seismic — the chaps at the London Stock Exchange evidently think this Seismic 'X' technology needs to be tested further before its indicators can be used as a basis for announcements. But Kunene has a link to Twenty First Century and has used the same technology that Twenty First used in making its own finds in South America. We've drilled to six thousand metres and all the indicators are that what might be there and its free flow reservoir characteristics are identical to the finds made so far in the Tiger basin.'

Doyle said, 'so this could be pretty big then Alec?'

'For Kunene, huge, James, yes, but we have only a small area under concession. But the real prize is Rangoon. If what we have found extends south into their area they could be sitting on one of the biggest oil finds ever made. The really extraordinary thing about their concession, James, is that its very old — it dates back to the time when Persia granted the D'Arcy concessions – and at that time oil rights, globally, were virtually given away. In Rangoon's case, the Namibian Government, in exchange for virtually nothing, leased it the mineral rights, subject to a royalty scale which was fixed in money terms, not a percentage, so by now, with the rise in the oil price, it's completely out of date. And, as you know, those kind of rights just don't get granted nowadays.

James', said Cowan, 'You should have a look at this. If it pans out you should bid for Rangoon.'

Chapter 3

RIVERS OF BLOOD
AND RIVERS OF GOLD

Doyle woke early. There was no hint of the February dawn filtering through the heavy curtains. He propped himself up on the pillows and thought.

He was obsessed with the Saudi oil play and long experience had taught him to concentrate on only one project at a time.

Yet he couldn't escape from the previous evening's conversation with Alec Cowan.

It could be nothing, he told himself. The world was littered with exploration companies pursuing their dreams. The very reason the incipient

Saudi oil disaster was so compelling to an investor was precisely that so few of these dreams ever came anywhere near realisation. Less and less oil was being found even as more and more resource was being applied to the search. Oil wasn't the only industry with this problem, Doyle reflected. The same applied in new drugs, and probably in metals. Yet even in oil some spectacular successes had occurred, often produced by smaller companies working over concessions abandoned by the majors. Idly he wondered why Rangoon had done so little to explore their interests in Namibia.

That was another thing. He had got to know certain African countries pretty well although he knew little of Namibia. But something stirred in his memory. Something way back when he had spent a brief time at Harvard, something before he had concluded that large scale corporate life was not for him. There had been someone there with a Namibian connection. Then it came to him. One of the people in his class had been Joseph Barula, a young, idealistic Namibian, much the same age as Doyle. He had had some big dreams for Africa, recalled Doyle, thinking fondly of parallels with some of his favourite reading, John Buchan, and Prester John.

Doyle wondered idly what he was up to now.

He didn't have to wait long to find out. Within an hour of reaching his office his head of research,

Becci Malone, ex Cabinet Office, tall, blonde, statuesque, blue eyed and Irish, had unearthed a mountain of information on Namibia including the rather startling revelation that Joseph Barula had been elected President the year before.

Doyle wasn't superstitious but he did believe in acting when the stars seemed aligned in one's favour and, later that day, after a friendly conversation with Barula, he was on his way to Windhoek.

Before he left he tried to piece together what he really knew about the detailed process and logistics of oil exploration and, despite his lengthy trip to Saudi, he realised it was absurdly inadequate. He instructed Fleming to make himself an expert and identify the best operators in the business while he was away.

Just before he left for his plane he received a call back from Barula. Listening to his deep warm friendly tones Doyle wondered to himself, again, why he hadn't kept up with him since college.

'Hey, Doyle, you mentioned oil and I've had my people look out the current concession agreements. The major one by far was awarded to Rangoon in the middle of the last century and they've never done anything with it. But apparently in those days the concessions were all issued as bearer documents so they could be freely transferred. So if you got one,' Barula chuckled hugely, 'you needed to make sure you looked after it!'

A tiny little warning signal flashed across Doyle's mind. He called Becci in.

'Becci,' he said, 'I want you to find out who has left Rangoon in the recent past who had worked in the company secretarial or legal departments. Preferably someone who either didn't want to leave, or who left under a cloud. We may need some information from them.'

It was three hours in the Blackbird to Windhoek, including a brief refuelling stop in Lagos. Doyle dozed for most of it but in his more energetic moments he flicked through the briefing provided by Becci.

He was appalled. Namibia's history seemed to be the outcome of the very worst kind of pen and ruler decisions inscribed, in a vacuum of indigenous representation, on a map of Africa by a gaggle of colonial powers. Doyle thought that the title of one of the books on Namibian history in the early twentieth century summed it all up – 'Rivers of Blood, Rivers of Gold'. For the native population there had been much blood spilt and never any gold. Their lands had been annexed and the prosperity from the burgeoning diamond industry had passed them by. Since independence, some twenty years ago, the mining of many different metals had continued, together with diamonds, to account for about twenty five per cent of GDP and there were some particularly promising uranium prospects. The stunning scenery, pristine wilderness areas and outstanding wildlife provided scope for a sustained growth in tourism.

But, Doyle noted, there was still a large trading dependence on South Africa and massive disparity in income between rich and poor.

At seven in the evening the lights of Hosea Kutako airport were glowing faintly against the fast deepening orange and purple African sunset. Barula had been unconvinced that Doyle would be in Namibia in time for dinner — the President had obviously thought that either Doyle was pulling his leg or had made some elementary mistake about time zones –and it had been a bit of a struggle for Chuck to get landing consent and a suitable spot to park up the Blackbird. Doyle had taken a taxi to the rather impersonal Kalahari Sands Hotel, had a shower, dinner and a couple of Windhoek lagers, forewent the hotel's associated night club and turned in.

Barula had said he had a Cabinet meeting the next morning and asked Doyle to present himself at the State House at midday. Doyle was seldom at a loss in his clothing selections but he had puzzled over what to wear for this meeting. He had rejected a formal suit while a safari jacket and trousers seemed faintly ridiculous so he settled for what he thought of as the standard financial adventurer wear of a linen suit and open necked shirt and some pleated moccasins which were cool in the humid rainy season heat. On being shown into Barula's sprawling office, with its panoramic view over the beautiful bougainvillea decked trees interspersing the terraced lawns, Doyle was slightly dismayed to find the President rather splendidly attired in a Savile Row suit.

'Hello, there, James,' he said smiling broadly, 'sorry about the formality, have to try to keep standards up at Cabinet meetings.'

Barula made an imposing figure. Standing over six feet he was a little heavier and broader than Doyle remembered, but his pleasant, open face, wide set eyes and easy smile were unchanged. Barula was a year or two older than Doyle. He retained a slightly academic, serious air enhanced by his round gold rimmed spectacles and earnest manner. Before Harvard he had been educated in Paris. His background, and his easy confidence, was beginning to make him a favourite of Western politicians.

'So,' Barula's deep voice was relaxed and friendly, 'what have you been doing with yourself, James, since our little sojourn at college?' Despite the gap of twelve years or so since they had met Doyle found it easy to talk to Joe Barula, and he felt that the longer they talked the more a friendly easy intimacy was developing between them.

'Well, James,' grinned Barula, after Doyle had given him a sanitised version of his commercial history, 'you're not out here for the good of your soul, or maybe even my soul, eh? Besides my chaps tell me you arrived in a rather unusual plane — I bet they don't grow on trees – and I can see I should have taken your availability for dinner more seriously.'

Barula continued: 'I'd like to regard you as a fairy godmother, James. Lord knows, I certainly need one out here. I was elected on a clean, ticket, promising development and reduction in corruption, not that it's as bad here as elsewhere in Africa. It sounds good but actually the first effects of trying to reduce corruption in a country like this is that a lot of people find that their living standards actually go down while foreign investors manage to keep a bit more of their investment returns. The theory is, of course, that in the long run such investors are encouraged to invest more and that fans out and replaces the lost income from graft. But,' Barula said rather wearily, 'we've only got about two million people in the country and that hardly makes it the first port of call for the Chinese and such like who are making such a run at investing across Africa. Most of our mineral wealth has apparently been identified so there's not much to go for there, apart from the uranium, but I understand from my American friends that you already know quite a bit about that. We need an X factor, that's for sure.'

'But,' Barula continued, 'what makes you all of a sudden interested in oil in Namibia? It's never been much on our radar and we haven't been exactly inundated with requests for concessions. Anyway Rangoon have got concessions over nearly the whole of the area just inland and have done absolutely nothing with it for over sixty years.'

Doyle spoke in earnest for about ten minutes.

'All I would like,' said Doyle finally, 'in the first instance, is permission to make an aerial survey.'

'Well, I can't see that the Rangoon concession precludes a third party overflying their territory,' said Barula, jovially, 'in fact I think you can do anything apart from actually drilling. I'll get the necessary permits for you and you can go ahead.'

'Of course,' said Doyle, 'if we find some promising geology we will want to get on the ground.'

The President crossed the room to a table and came back carrying a cardboard canister.

'These are copies of the original documents relating to the Rangoon concessions,' he said. 'I haven't the time or inclination to delve into them so I'll leave it to you. And I don't want to involve my people in this as that tends to produce complications. Make what you can of it. Keep me informed of your progress on the aerial survey, but I'm not dreaming oily dreams just yet.

By the way, how much do you actually know about oil exploration, James?' asked Barula. 'I'm not going to get too many plaudits from allowing some unknown adventurer into some prime assets if there really does turn out to be something here worth going for.'

'Relatively little,' replied Doyle, cheerfully, 'but, Joe, the difference is this. You can go and get all the heavy hitters in the world to look for your oil, such as it might be, but I've never failed in something I've set out to do and what's more, if I succeed, while I've got to keep my backers sweet, after that I'll be on your side.'

Barula stared hard at him.

'Yes,' he said reflectively, 'I really think you might be. Well, good luck — and happy hunting, James.'

Doyle returned to London, feeling rather flat. Was he wasting his time? The whole thing was a large and tiring distraction from planning for the Saudi coup.

His mood was not improved by a conversation with Fleming, who had been calling oil exploration companies all round the world to get a take on the best exploration teams and consultants.

'It's a very complex picture, James,' Fleming began as they sat opposite each other in Southwark Place's river room very early the next day. The morning sun was slowly forcing its way through the late February mist and beyond the balustrade great shadowy black and gold pools swirled in the flood tide. Shafts of sunlight glinted on the sparse lighter traffic, some edging their way painfully downstream, others racing up river.

'I've spoken to about forty oil exploration companies and they have all had wildly differing experiences. By the way, you have to get a licence from the US State Department to use that new seismic X technology Cowan referred to. As to the results, I won't weary you with the detail, as there is one very clear conclusion. There's a consulting company called Oilfac which is privately owned by a guy called Jock Millar. He's the one they all want but he's very difficult to get. He's a Scotsman who has spent a lifetime in the business but now he only works for the very top end international companies. He did the work for Brazilgas and was pretty much responsible for the Tiger find. He also worked for Castle Petroleum on their big finds in Iran. Everyone I've spoken to says that even despite the drop in the oil price he's booked up for years ahead and you'd have to be the Crown prince of some heavy duty Middle Eastern State even to have a conversation with him about new contracts. 'The rest of the field is very mixed. There are one or two recommendations but no one with Oilfac's record.'

'Where is Millar based?' asked Doyle.

'He's got an office in Mayfair but he's hardly ever there.'

'Well, Matthew, find out who else we know who knows Millar or who has anything to do with his company,' instructed Doyle.

Doyle had more luck with Becci Malone.

'I've had some fun,' she said. Doyle tried not to be distracted by her long legs clad in skin tight black jeans which she was now folding under herself as she sat in the chair vacated by Matthew.

'I went along to the HR department of Rangoon pretending to represent a new counselling company which specialised in providing support for employees who were to be terminated or who had been terminated but who were kicking up a fuss.'

She fished some cards out of a tiny black handbag.

'See, I even had some of these printed specially.'

Seeing the look on Doyle's face she laughed.

'Don't worry, James, you're not billed as a director — yet.'

'They said they had a panel of similar firms doing this kind of work. I said I'd do one case for free and begged them for a chance to show what we could do. I said we were especially experienced with people who had been in the legal and administrative areas. I think I may even have made myself out to be a qualified lawyer, I'm sure I made some quite dreadful claim,' Becci grinned to herself.

'Anyway, to cut a long story short,' she went on, 'they said there was one person – an assistant company secretary – who had got himself, very late in his career, into the most frightful trouble. It's quite a tragic case actually,' her face softened. 'Apparently his wife became terribly ill with some rare skin disease and the only effective treatment was in the States. Well he was absolutely devoted to her but he just couldn't afford the treatment so he, well, he embezzled the money he needed.

Of course Rangoon found out and he was sacked and now he's got a court case hanging over him. He's incredibly bitter about the way Rangoon handled the whole thing. His wife recovered by the way, but their lives are going to be ruined if he ends up in gaol. But apparently he keeps threatening Rangoon to sell his story to the newspapers and even though they are in a strong legal position they just don't want that in today's climate.'

Doyle rotated his chair round so that it faced out over the river. The lighters making downstream were beginning to travel faster now as the tide eased.

He turned back to Becci.

'Becci, tell this man that we want him to give us some information on some of Rangoon's old concessions and where and how the documents relating to them are stored. In exchange we will fund him to repay his debt to Rangoon and help get the company off his back.'

Becci unfolded her legs, stood up and said: 'That sounds wonderful James, but what exactly do I tell him we want?'

'Get him to agree to help us, Becci, and then get him up here and I'll tell him what we want and give him a cheque if we get it.'

Fleming appeared with a dossier on Oilfac. It wasn't a small company. It had a turnover of getting on for a billion dollars and fairly eye watering profit margins. It appeared that Millar was nearly sixty five, yet he seemed to take very little out of the business. Doyle wasn't surprised. He had known quite a few Scottish entrepreneurs who were quite happy to walk round in woolly jumpers with holes in the elbows. There didn't seem to be any junior Millars working in the business either. Fleming confirmed that, while there were two sons, one was an Edinburgh surgeon and the other was a high flyer with the investment bankers Whitehills and living in New York.

Doyle thought that it couldn't be long before Millar examined the sale or flotation of his business. Everything in his industry was going his way and he had no obvious management succession.

'Matthew,' said Doyle, 'find out from your contacts at Whitehill's if there are any plans to bring Oilfac to the stock market. If there are I'll bet they'll be using Whitehills, blood's even thicker than oil with these Scottish companies.'

Fleming disappeared and before long returned to say that not only were there plans to float Oilfac but that they had advanced to the stage that Millar and his management team were making preliminary presentations to institutional investors.

'Matthew,' said Doyle, 'tell your contact that the Sphinx partnership would be interested investors and that we would like a presentation from Millar himself on the business. Oh, and get a copy of the preliminary prospectus.'

A couple of days later Millar and two of the Whitehills people were sitting at the boardroom table in the river room.

Millar was a red faced, dour, rugged Scot from a very poor background in Glasgow and was obviously firmly convinced that the City and all its inhabitants were a complete den of thieves.

'I'm only here because of these friends of yours at Whitehills, 'Millar began. 'I've never heard of you fellows, haven't got much time for any of you actually. Fortunately I'm advised that I can sell the company many times over.'

It was heavy going. Eventually they had ploughed through the presentation, and Fleming and Doyle had asked some decent questions which slightly thawed the atmosphere.

Finally Fleming had asked the Whitehills team how much stock was going to be offered and its pricing range.

After that Doyle asked to see Millar privately.

Doyle took Millar into his private office and offered him a Scotch, which was accepted.

'What are you going to do with the money?' asked Doyle pleasantly.

'I'm thinking of an educational foundation, with the focus on the major cities in Scotland,' replied Millar.

'Perhaps we could work together,' offered Doyle. 'I've got my own interests in that area.'

Doyle spent about fifteen minutes running Millar through his charitable activities. They included sponsorship of a new academy for headmasters — Bighead.com — Doyle was passionate about the need for improved leadership in schools. Doyle also took Millar through 'Doyle's Den' — an investing group led by Doyle which provided two to three million pounds a month in seed money to budding young entrepreneurs. Doyle had been surprised to find himself among many other things the co-owner of a Hackney tattoo bar, but the one that really sparked his interest was an eighteen year old Asian schoolboy with a search engine that might compete with Google. The Whitehills people fretted outside, hating to lose any control over a client.

Millar thawed visibly.

'Look, Jock,' said Doyle, 'I'll be frank with you. I happen to have a piece of knowledge about the global oil industry. When that becomes public, which I think it will in the next few months, the value of your business will soar. Any price attached to a flotation now will seem completely inadequate and your new foundation will be the loser.'

'Those are just words,' grunted Millar. 'All you guys are the same.'

'No, they are not just words, Jock. I'm giving you a piece of advice of enormous value. I can't give more details I'm afraid. But I'm not going to ask you just to trust me. The people I represent are asking you to put your flotation plans on hold for a few months and are prepared to buy a stake in your business now at a much higher value than you will get from the stock market. If we are wrong it is we who will lose, not you.'

Millar looked somewhat mollified.

'But, Jock, there will be a condition attached. And that is that Oilfac, led by you personally, does a job for us in Africa.'

'Africa,' grunted Millar again. 'I'm far too committed elsewhere even to think about going there. But everyone has dreams about Africa, what are yours?'

Doyle spoke to him for about twenty minutes.

'I'm not convinced,' said Millar. 'You see, I'm not sure you really know a thing about this game. Just for example, if you wanted an effective exploration programme over that kind of area in double quick time you'd have to access this new Seismic X technology and I can't see an unknown bunch like you standing a chance of getting State Department consent to get it issued to you.'

Doyle refilled Millar's glass, leaned towards him and for five minutes spoke quietly.

'Christ, man, you don't give up easily do you?' Millar expostulated.

'I'll let you have an answer in the morning. You're an interesting man, Mr Doyle, that's for sure.'

Chapter 4

MOSCOW

Alexei Mordakov inspected his nails and lit an Egyptian cigarette. He was sitting at his desk on the twelfth floor of the Petrogaz headquarters in Moscow overlooking Europe Square.

Alexei was a large dominating man, beautifully dressed, who stood well over six foot with a frame to match. Now in his early forties he had spent a lifetime with Petrogaz and had been appointed Chief Executive at the beginning of the year. Petrogaz was by far the largest Russian oil and gas company, listed on the New York and London Stock Exchanges, but still forty one per cent owned by the Russian State. Mordakov flicked off some ash into a silver tray and reflected not without bitterness that at times that forty one percent felt like a hundred per cent. It was the fourth largest oil and gas company in the world in terms of proven and probable reserves. That in itself was an astonishing statistic given Petrogaz's short history.

The company was also, reflected Mordakov with a genuine sense of grievance, the chosen instrument of the Russian State for exerting its natural resource based hegemony in Europe — and he had no doubt that that process would not stop there.

Mordakov reflected on the astonishing series of moves which Petrogaz, orchestrated by its puppet masters, had made in the previous ten years. Supplies had been withheld from the old Russian satellite states pending punitive re-pricing, pipelines planned by Western companies had mysteriously been aborted and Petrogaz pipelines with different routes had been laid instead. Gradually a nexus of control over the European distribution of Russian oil and gas — and, come to that, supplies from other European countries – had been tightened and tightened.

But there was one urgently sought Holy Grail that these steps did not address. That was finding – and exerting Russian control over — additional global oil and gas supplies. Within Russia itself the economic kleptocracy so feared and scorned in the West had been at work, both in the annexation by the State of Russian companies controlled by oligarchs who could be pushed about and in the extraordinary pressure exerted on foreign companies such as Great Western Desert and Rangoon Oil to sell their share of Russian joint ventures at below market value. As one banker involved in such negotiations remarked on behalf of his client — 'actually any proceeds greater than zero would be a result.'

But the really big prize of finding — or securing — major new sources of oil and gas outside Russia had eluded Petrogaz and this failure had become progressively more frustrating to its masters.

Mordakov blew a cloud of fragrant blue smoke towards the ceiling of his office and turned down his hands in a gesture of despair.

The really dispiriting thing about his position, Mordakov reflected, was that whatever progress Petrogaz made he knew it would never be enough to satisfy those masters. For the current generation of Russian leaders the aftermath of the cold war, the dismantling of the wider Russian State, and the subsequent years of being outgunned and out-influenced by the West had bred an almost insatiable appetite to find an alternative battle ground upon which Russian power could be restored to its former glory.

Mordakov reflected dismally that both the men he regarded as his masters were due to arrive shortly.

His beautiful blonde secretary, Lubya, came into the room, wearing a very short skirt, and he instantly felt his pulse quicken on two accounts.

'The Prime Minister and Chairman are here, Alexei. I've put them in the Siberia room, I hope that's alright. I've got coffee for them — would you like some?'

Mordakov thanked her, put on his jacket and his bear – like frame bore itself down the corridor and into the Siberia room, which was adorned with some extraordinarily good photographs, prints and original paintings from Siberian artists and several wildlife sculptures of sinuous power.

Prime Minister Orlov was standing looking impassively out of the window at the Moscow River, rippled by the wind and gleaming in the sun. He was about five foot nine, in his early fifties, with a medium build that exuded strength while his tanned face with its trim grey beard radiated a relaxed air of power and control. But it was his eyes, watchful, grey and cold, that inspired an air of tension, even menace. People who had frequent dealings with him knew to focus on those eyes, and their ever changing shades, and to be particularly wary of grey green, a sign of great anger, the only signal discernible from Orlov's carefully cultivated poise. He was, as ever, immaculately dressed by Anderson in Savile Row, with shirt and tie by Charvet; there was an unsubstantiated rumour that he regularly bought three months supply of shirts at a time and invariably discarded each one after wearing it once. Orlov was a bachelor and there was a rumour that he applied the same policy to his women.

Orlov turned away from the window and extended his hand to Mordakov in a wintry greeting.

Mordakov muttered some words in response and turned away to shake hands with Dimitri Karlkov, his Chairman at Petrogaz. Karlkov was a huge shambling man, over six foot three with a massive frame which with even with expensive tailoring barely managed to disguise his excess weight. Karlkov looked like a larger and more jovial version of Joseph Stalin. He was a dedicated pipe smoker and now he re-lit an enormous carved and curved pipe decorated with three silver bands. Clouds of smoke billowed around his luxuriant moustache and over his ample shoulders.

It was dangerous to underestimate Dimitri Karlkov. Despite his avuncular looks — the attendant instinct was almost to dismiss him as a throwback to yesterday's generation of Russian leaders — he was in fact extremely well connected to the ruling elite. This impression was reinforced by his Chairmanship of Russian Universal Export, a virtually unknown private company through which were channelled all exports of Russian oil and gas regardless of whether they were sold by state controlled or privately owned businesses. The identity of the shareholders in this business was a perennial topic at higher levels of Russian society; Mordakov thought rather sourly to himself that he would be very surprised if they did not include the two people in the room apart from himself.

'Beautiful day,' remarked Karlkov, without addressing anyone in particular.

'Glad you are enjoying it,' said Orlov in the unusually deliberate tones he had cultivated over the years; he had long realised that whatever the strength of your argument the fact of it being transmitted in a extraordinarily precise, measured and quietly emphatic way gave it great power.

Julius Orlov sat down, looked at his watch and beckoned to the others.

'Come, gentlemen', he said, 'to business.'

'Gentlemen, we have a problem,' he began. 'For the last ten years of steadily rising oil and gas prices Russia has enjoyed a fantastic resource. We have had very large export revenues, which we have applied' — Mordakov turned his face away to hide his expression — 'in various ways including the long term strengthening of Russia's industrial infrastructure, and have gone some way to reclaiming the political and economic influence that Russia so richly deserves. But now the severe reduction in revenues currently being experienced due to weak oil and gas prices is threatening to put all that at risk, and,' his tone became dangerously silky, 'is leading to disaffection among our people who were by and large very happy with the resource imperialism we were developing in better times, and not too worried about how we achieved it provided a little of the largesse percolated down to grass roots level.'

'We are, as you know,' Orlov continued, 'making good progress with growing our control over European gas distribution even to the point that we can begin to consider some kind of Russian led 'Gas Opec'. This will not happen overnight. But the real prize is finding or controlling more of the world's oil resource.'

Karlkov raised his great head in agreement.

'Prime Minister,' his deep voice growled, 'we have made good use of our existing assets and have punched far above our weight in terms of controlling gas distribution but, I agree, we need to control or access more oil to obtain the real market power we require.'

Orlov said rather coldly, ' Dimitri, you are on the same wavelength as me but the difference between us is that your organisation is actually charged with this task of resource expansion and so far the results have been frankly poor. We have made the most of Russian resources, principally by our normal methods but we have shown no flair for the real value added in this business which is finding new sources of oil and gas. Perhaps we should ask your chief executive what he has to say about it.'

Alexei had been anticipating this.

'Prime Minister, Dimitri', he began, 'we must not forget what we have achieved in Russia in the last ten years and we must remember the international factors which make this success difficult to replicate internationally. Firstly the main problem in world oil supplies in the short term is actually not a shortage of unexploited reserves but the finance to develop them, the availability of technical expertise, very often the cost of investment in transport infrastructure and sometimes political disputes about ownership of rights. In the longer term, yes, there is a huge problem in terms of oil in the ground running out, but simply solving the four issues I highlighted above would go a long way towards improving global oil supplies in the medium term.'

'Alexei,' said Orlov heavily, 'your speech would be what I would expect from some economist at the World Bank but may I remind you that as CEO of Russia's largest oil company your job is to make sure Petrogaz is involved and has a stake in these solutions.'

'Yes Prime Minister,' said Mordakov, 'we all want that. But the resource nationalism you pioneered in Russia is now mirrored all round the world. Every developing country wants to control and develop its own reserves rather than hand them over to the West. They much prefer to use the technology and service companies to advise their own national oil champions rather than simply hand the whole task over to a foreign integrated oil major. Then they are generally all fairly corrupt regimes, so a large amount of current oil cash flow gets siphoned off rather than being re-invested in producing more oil so there is a shortage of cash resources with which to fund the service companies. Our problem at Petrogaz is that, like many other companies, our cash flow is often diverted, even though we are an internationally listed company. We don't have an oil services division which might give us entry to projects outside Russia. Finally we also have to remember that the Russian State is viewed with caution after the experiences some international majors have endured at its hands.

That leaves us with two options, gentlemen,' Mordakov was warming to his own defence, 'either we find more oil in Russia — and I would remind you that, for instance, in Saudi, they have been looking for over fifty years and have found nothing substantive – or we have to muscle in to overseas opportunities, probably in the new frontier areas.'

'Alexei', said Orlov icily, 'you of all people hardly need reminding that everyone and his dog want to do the latter.'

'Yes, Prime Minister, but some are markedly more successful than others. Take Twenty First Century in Brazil for instance, or Cortez in Uganda, or Castle in Kurdistan.'

'Well', interjected Karlkoff who had got his pipe going again and was wreathed in fragrant blue smoke, 'what has been their secret? We must emulate it.'

'Broadly choosing the right geology and being perceived as desirable partners,' concluded Mordakov. He lowered his voice and became more precise and deliberate: 'Gentlemen you must see that we have played a zero sum game. Traditional Russian kleptocracy has enabled us to build a very powerful position at home, but very much weakened trust in us as partners overseas.'

Orlov remained impassive although the colour of his eyes had changed.

'So Alexei, what is the answer?' he said with no trace of emotion.

'I don't think we can quickly alter our perception by the international community, Prime Minister,' said Mordakov. 'Frankly we are going to be regarded as pariahs for some time to come. But there are two factors of huge importance that could start to work in our favour.'

Orlov stroked his beard slowly and repetitively, gazing into the middle distance. Mordakov waited until he had Orlov's full attention. Karlkoff used the opportunity to pull out his pipe's twin and charged it noisily from a large tin he carried in a side pocket. He lit up using an equally capacious box of matches in the other pocket.

'The first is that many of these oil finds are being made in some very unstable parts of the world; areas where it is possible for Russian involvement in the production phase to be perhaps more profitable for the home State and its rulers than with more conventional — shall we call it more straight laced — international partners. Of course, initially those kind of more generous sharing arrangements are not so profitable for us but, as you gentlemen well know, the trick is to get in. Later on there are ways and means of improving the arrangements.

The second is to make use of the new Seismic X technology which was so successfully used by Twenty First Century in identifying its huge success in Brazil.'

'This is all very well Alexei.' Karlkoff shifted his vast bulk around in his chair. 'We can have all the superior oil finding technology in the world but we have to first be invited in as exploration partners and, as you have pointed out at such length, that will pose a difficulty for us.'

Mordakov's face became energised: 'I don't propose we use it ourselves, gentlemen, but I do propose we use our surveillance skills to monitor its use. Once we have become alerted to a potentially sizeable find we then evaluate our leverage with host governments and seek a role as one of the production partners.'

'Alexei,' said Orlov cheerfully, 'at long last you are beginning to sound like a proper Russian businessman and a true servant of Petrogaz rather than a Harvard educated boy scout.'

'How the hell are we going to exercise surveillance on a whole bunch of seismic kit all over the world, Alexei,' muttered Karlkov. 'Most of the time our intelligence people couldn't even work out what type of tobacco I'm smoking.'

Mordakov pressed a buzzer on the table between them and the beautiful Lubya entered the room, wrinkling her nose at the atmosphere.

'Send in Sergei Popaloff would you in a couple of minutes please.'

Mordakov quickly outlined that Popaloff had been the star graduate in his class at the Moscow State Technology Institute, and had made a study for his special subject of the potential industrial and mining uses for seismic technology. In his third year he had spent a year on secondment to Mining Technologies in Texas and had actually worked on the development of the

Seismic X technology that Twenty First Century had used in its Brazil finds.

A few seconds later a tall, thin, rather saturnine bespectacled man of about twenty seven walked in dressed in smart casual clothes.

'Sergei,' said Mordakoff, after introductions, 'please tell these distinguished gentlemen about Project Spyware.'

Popaloff began a little nervously. 'I'm sure you are aware of the relatively crude processes hitherto deployed for establishing the potential of hydro-carbon bearing structures'. Everyone nodded.

'Well,' he continued, 'there is only one company worldwide that has made any real progress in developing more refined technologies and that is Mining Technologies based in Houston. They have developed Seismic X, an advanced seismic detection process which is a considerable advance upon the old Seismic 3D techniques. I won't bore you with the technicalities but, in summary, it's far more sensitive, has far higher quality images and has greater range than 3D. It's also much cheaper to operate — it requires less equipment and staff. It enables a company to explore a very large acreage much more quickly and economically than before. As it produces such reliable results it also saves on abortive drilling cost.'

Orlov drummed his fingers quietly and asked: 'How much practical success has this had so far?'

Popaloff explained. 'Mining Technologies have tested the technology extensively in on-shore US basins with incredibly good results and the only thing stopping the wildcatting community ordering it in bulk is price. But the real break-through offshore came in offshore Brazil when Twenty First Century found the Tiger field. You will recall that they discovered astonishing quantities of oil at 6,000 metres. The equipment not only helped them identify a productive basin very quickly but was also extraordinarily helpful in identifying the right locations for exploratory drilling programmes. Without the equipment Twenty First Century would never have been able to explore so effectively or so quickly.'

Orlov rose and paced catlike and silently around the room.

'Who can access this technology?' he asked brusquely.

Popaloff hesitated and answered: 'No one, Prime Minister, at least not without a license from the company and that has to be approved by the US Government.'

'What is the usual basis for approval?'

'You must understand, Prime Minister, that whereas Mining Technologies manufactures the equipment it is distributed only through a company jointly owned by Mining Technologies and the US Government. You will not be surprised to hear that to date it has only been licensed to

Western companies. A further complication is that once a lessee is approved the equipment is hired on conventional lease terms but there is a rather unusual kicker in the shape of a production royalty on any oil and gas derived from a field originally identified with the help of the equipment.'

'Hmnn,' pondered Orlov out loud. 'It's always good to know that we have taught the Americans something about energy imperialism. But', he continued, glacially, 'it's also very disappointing to see that yet another technology driven segment – energy — in which we might have achieved dominance — is being led by one of our traditional enemies.'

Orlov remained impassive. But Karlkov could see the outward signs of volcanic mental activity.

Popaloff continued. 'All production of the Seismic X equipment is prioritised towards US exploration and production companies but Twenty First Century and its Brazilian partner were licensed the product as a deep sea test bed, with lower royalties. All the equipment is fitted with software and digitised data bank collection which transmits material direct to the joint distribution company owned by Mining Technologies and the US Department of Energy. Actually,' he went on, 'the level of sophistication on those Seismic X rigs makes even the technology on an F1 race car look quite prosaic.'

Orlov looked at him speculatively. 'How,' he said with great deliberation, 'can we use this?'

Popaloff had been bracing himself for this moment. 'Prime Minister,' he replied, 'I don't think we can copy the technology, nor do I think we can steal it as the US have taken enormous steps to protect it.'

Orlov ceased his pacing. Karlkoff took his cue and lit an already re-charged pipe. Blue smoke swirled up in heavy clouds to the elaborately carved and painted ceiling.

'As I see it Russia needs two things from this.' Orlov began. 'One, it needs the actual equipment to help speed its own discoveries, either in its backyard or elsewhere. Secondly we need early warning as to discoveries by other companies so that we can ensure that we have an opportunity to play a part in exploiting those new reserves. The first is more difficult as I cannot envisage the US would readily make such vital technology available to us. We will have to find somewhere where this equipment is being deployed, steal it and copy it. It will not be easy and there could be software codes and barriers to hinder us, eh, Mr Popaloff ?' Orlov smiled at Sergei.

'Quite so Prime Minister.' Popaloff was relieved he hadn't been asked a more searching question.

'The second,' continued Orlov, 'is a question of finding out which countries or companies are having the equipment made available and of somehow intercepting the results. We need to infiltrate Mining Technologies and access such information on a regular basis, and we need to attach some kind of monitoring device onto Seismic X equipment in the field that lets us know what users of the equipment have found.'

'Dimitri,'he said softly, 'we all know what has to be done. All necessary resources are of course at your disposal. Come to me by the end of the week with a plan please.'

Orlov rose, inclined his head to the company, and left the room.

Chapter 5

TIERRA DEL FUEGO

Apart from a steady low pitched growl behind his head and the odd crackle in his ear phones Doyle's world was peaceful.

The steady green digital display in front of him indicated airspeed of just over two thousand knots and a height of eighty thousand feet. In the limited vision he had out of the cockpit canopy the world was pitch black apart from the stars and the remaining glow of the setting sun in the Western Hemisphere. The land mass of South America on the GPS screen crawled surprisingly quickly under the southerly facing arrow that denoted the Blackbird's position.

As Doyle watched it lazily the Northern Venezuelan coast crawled under the arrow and the map started to veer down towards the Amazonian rain forest. Suddenly Doyle's headphones crackled into life.

Chuck muttered: 'Boss, just got a call from the US Defense department monitoring our flight plan. They said they are glad to see the thing is still running well.'

'Tell them that if it ever lets us down we'll sell it to the Taliban,' responded Doyle laconically.

Doyle reclined his seat and reflected. They had a short time before a refuelling stop in Rio and then it was well under two hours to Uschuaia, the southernmost town in South America and on the planet.

Doyle had decided that he had to go to his backers. He now knew that he potentially held a double set of cards which could be the key to one of the largest financial coups in history.

Doyle knew that the largest source of the world's established sources of oil was running out and more acutely that that decline was about to accelerate in a shocking way, far faster than the markets currently anticipated. He was also aware of the strong potential to find new oil fields that could massively enhance world oil supplies, potentially more than reversing the decline.

Anyone with real conviction in these assumptions could put on a massive range of trades in large and liquid markets. With the application of sufficient leverage returns could be made which would make the normal profits of the global hedge fund industry since it began – in the late nineteen forties — look like a children's tea party. It wasn't just the oil play, large as this was. There were associated plays in global stock market indices, interest rate futures, and metals and these plays could be conducted through physical ownership and derivatives and with varying levels of financial gearing. The possibilities for a group of well capitalised aggressive hedge funds were literally limitless, a once in a lifetime opportunity.

But Doyle was doubly reflective. At the end of the day the world, after these seismic events, would go on much as it always had. But the short term shifting of the global financial tectonic plates would hugely reward some, and massively disadvantage others. Doyle thought back to the so called banker induced recession of two thousand and eight and nine — and the public anger against the banker breed that was perceived as having wrought such havoc and misery on the population as a whole.

Doyle had always kept a low profile. He had worked for intellectual stimulus and financial reward. But increasingly he didn't really need more than a fraction of the money he earned from his trades — nor, he reflected, did his backers as individuals, although they had a business to run and stakeholders to whom they were accountable.

He felt a cold shiver running down his spine. He had never thought of himself as any kind of master of the universe, that arrogant, materialistic, self obsessed icon of greed that stalked first the pages of financial fiction and then the real world in the last quarter century.

Instead he now felt unpleasantly responsible. What had started, for him, as just another financial game, was in danger of becoming something much darker, much more visceral with unpredictable consequences for a huge number of people. He shuddered.

Almost, he caught himself thinking, it was almost too good for his normal backers — people and firms driven by an obsessive focus on short term returns and an unhealthy interest in enjoyment of the trappings of success.

The refuelling stop broke his thoughts. After it his own trapping powered on with a steady rumble. The moving arrow on the GPS passed over Buenos Aires and started to enter the narrowing cone of Patagonia.

Anyway, he thought, he was getting ahead of himself.

He 'knew' – a comforting phrase — but what did he really know?

In fact, Doyle knew that he only really knew one thing — which was that as far as his backers were concerned –and despite the copied Saudi files, which had been a goldmine — that he didn't have enough indisputable intelligence that would induce them to put on anything other than minor positions. They were tough guys, used to taking very large but very calculated risks, and would need a great deal of convincing to put on the sort of exposures that Doyle believed the opportunity warranted.

He ran through the thumbnail impressions he carried about in his head.

There were four of them.

Patrick Myers, an ex Australian army officer who controlled White Waters, a ten billion pound London based hedge fund which ran a dozen strategies and had a consistent record. Myers, unlike most of the breed, was also a noted philanthropist. Then there was the aggressive Christopher Bulstrode who ran Bullsec, a fund specialising in global macro and long short equities. There was Charles O'Neill, a beautifully mannered American, who had been a professional tennis player in his youth and who ran one of the largest East Coast funds with some twenty five billion dollars under management. Lastly Michel Weill, an affable Frenchman, who was a commodity specialist, and ran one of the largest funds in Europe.

Together these four men probably controlled funds under management of fifty billion sterling. In addition to this they had the power to put together so called 'sidecars', sponsored by the backers of their own funds, which could significantly enhance their firepower. They had been an integral and loyal ingredient in Doyle's deal flow over the last ten years and slowly a significant trust had been built up between them all.

Nevertheless, Doyle reflected, an acquisition of Rangoon — which would involve an outlay of up to a hundred and fifty billion sterling – would seriously test this group, notwithstanding the additional resources which might be provided by the side cars. While it might be possible to fund a good part of the acquisition with debt, the process of obtaining that debt would involve bringing a great many other people into the loop, with all the attendant risks of leakage and speculation which could easily drive the Rangoon price to a level where a bid became much less economically attractive to the Sphinx and its backers.

Doyle started to run through other sources of capital. Then he was struck by a thunderbolt. If the Namibia resource was as massive as he thought it might be, any new owner of Rangoon would in reality become the controller of a second OPEC. That meant that at least four governments were going to interest themselves in the outcome — the UK, (he mentally bracketed it with the US), China, Russia and India.

He started to adjust his mental perspective. Would the fate of such a resource really be allowed to be decided by a group of hedge funds, or would they simply be seen as people who had primed the takeover pump, perhaps made some money on stake building, and at the right time moved or been pushed aside by some kind of global takeover battle?

Doyle decided that these questions were too difficult and drifted off to sleep.

Doyle had tried to get the group together in London but, led by Bulstrode, who was one of the most passionate fishermen on the planet, they were all staying for a week in the luxurious Kau Taupen fishing lodge on the Rio Grande in Terra del Fuego, one of the most prolific sea trout rivers in the world. The sea trout — so called because they migrated back to the sea for part of their year — had originally been imported from the United Kingdom, and now, in the fresh clear waters and rich nutrients of the South Atlantic, grew up to a weight of over twenty five pounds and made for some of the most exciting game fishing in the world. Doyle was pleased to be able to get his group together all in one place with, he hoped, an attention span that might be both undivided and rather longer than normal. However Bulstrode's reply to his e mail had

contained the characteristically brusque coda —
'Yes, we can discuss, but not in fishing time'. Doyle
thought wryly, knowing Bulstrode's intense approach to everything, but particularly fishing, that
any such discussion was likely to be well into the
night.

The rumble of the Blackbird engines became
muted and the great plane started gently to lose
height. Doyle stared out of the cockpit at one of
the most romantic sights in the world. The Beagle
channel was gleaming far below, the southern
ocean winds whipping its surface into endless
white capped rollers, framed by the dark brood-
ing backdrop of the Andes to the West and
South. The Blackbird sank lower, cruised east-
wards along the southern bank of mountains
and finally banked dramatically onto its final approach towards the tiny airstrip that jutted out
from Uschaia into the channel.

'Goddammit, boss,' rasped Chuck. 'We'll only
just be able to get down here. It feels like the
bloody end of the world.'

'It is the end of the world, Chuck,' said Doyle
evenly, 'just make sure you don't put it in the drink.'

Chuck's reply was inaudible.

The Blackbird came in on full flaps at three hundred knots and Chuck had activated reverse
thrust and the brake chute the instant the plane
touched. They were greeted by a couple of

open mouthed attendants who were promptly despatched for some more serious ladders. Doyle grabbed his bags and fishing tackle, and climbed stiffly down to the tarmac.

He strode across to the bleakly utilitarian airport buildings, noting the large raft of tough looking yachts and fishing vessels in the small harbour, and muffling himself against the wind which relentlessly bored and clutched and tugged at any loose clothing or equipment.

After a few minutes clearing immigration and customs, a quick cup of coffee and a fairly disgusting cheese sandwich he was on his way out again to a waiting Squirrel leaving Chuck to guard and go over the Blackbird which was towed off to the small air force compound; Doyle's final wry injunction to him had been to enjoy the night clubs.

The chopper spiralled up into the cloud cover over the Andes. The pilot shouted that it was two hundred miles to the lodge or about two hours.

The scenery changed from the snowy dark mass of the Andes to a vast rolling pampas interspersed with hills and gorges. After about an hour and a half Doyle caught his first glimpse of the Rio Grande coiling its way westwards as they flew upstream from the estuary and a few minutes later the Kau Taupen lodge came into view, its roof a mass of aerials. A couple of Toyota trucks were parked outside.

Carlos Bandera, the extrovert Colombian lodge manager, came running across to greet Doyle. 'They are all on the river now Mr Doyle, but they will be back for lunch in the next twenty minutes and in between I will show you to your room. If you want to fish we start fishing again at five o'clock and go through till ten tonight and then there is dinner. Most people try and sleep a bit after lunch.'

Doyle said he thought he could see why and agreed he would do the same and join the evening fishing. Doyle had been down to the Rio Grande once before and, despite the inevitable increase in lodges, numbers of anglers and intensity of fishing methods, the average number of fish caught (and of course returned) by each rod and their average weight remained mouth – wateringly attractive to the average British sea trout fishermen who were battling with dismal sea trout runs in many hitherto prolific rivers at home.

And what fighters those fish were! Doyle remembered his first ever Rio Grande fish — a fourteen pounder hooked in the fast gathering dusk and played on a ten foot trout rod. It had taken out two hundred yards of line and backing, not once but several times before being brought to net. Doyle thought of all the hours he had spent fruitlessly engaged on the Spey and the Findhorn and grimaced.

The rumble of Toyota trucks outside the lodge announced the arrival of his 'hedgies' for lunch and Doyle braced himself for the apparently endless supply of schoolboy banter and joshing which seemed such a social trademark of the breed once they had left their trading screens behind and were esconced on a grouse moor or river bank.

'Doyle, you're wasting your time,' opened up Bulstrode. 'A useless fisherman like you won't be able even to cast across the river in this wind. But we caught ten this morning, the biggest twenty and twenty two pounds.'

Myers interjected: 'Don't listen to the bugger. There's the hell of a run of fresh fish down there and your great aunt could walk across the river on their backs and help herself to whatever she wanted.'

Michel Weill grinned, held out his hand and said: 'Well, James, I know it's not just the fishing that will have brought you here, nor the pleasure of our company, so I look forward to hearing more about your *vrai agenda* later tonight.'

O'Neill grunted: 'S'pose you came in that ridiculous plane of yours –surprised our military are still subbing you on that.'

And so it went on over drinks. Bulstrode was at pains to point out that while he was prepared to drink the finest Argentinian Malbec at lunch he had brought his own supplies of first growth

Bordeaux for dinner. Doyle thought this was a ridiculous affectation but it was so typical he could see no point in commenting on it. He also remembered that Bulstrode had private interests in at least three classed growth Bordeaux properties. He was privately thankful that the river was fishing well and that the mood of the party was upbeat.

That evening Doyle was put into a pool called Blue Flash, so called because of a mineralised streak of blue in the rocks on the far bank that marked the exact taking spot in the mid height water that prevailed on the river. Mostly the opposite bank, under which the big fish lay, was a peat cliff of up to four metres high; the art of fishing the river was to get your lure to within at least a metre of that bank. The fish would then react, turn to follow the lure and take as it swung round into the centre of the stream. But if the cast across fell short the potential catch was greatly diminished.

Doyle watched his guide put up his eleven foot single handed rod with a weight forward line, idly looking up from time to time at the great open skies. The occasional condor circled lazily high up above the level of the cliffs that rose half a mile or so back from each river bank. The banks themselves were almost treeless, gravelly with light scrub. The wind blew incessantly, a quartering wind that relentlessly took the power and distance out of a cast. It was warm at five o'clock but Doyle knew it would get much colder as darkness set in.

Doyle's guide Randy, a mad keen fisherman recently graduated from Montana, suggested he use one of the traditional black 'woolly buggers' as a lure. Minutes later Doyle was working his way slowly down the pool, revelling in the peace of the moment and absorbed by his total concentration. Slowly the complex, interlocking, high tension financial edifice he had been building in his mind started to recede, blur and disappear in the most welcome way. He vaguely became aware that he had reached a point about twenty meters above the blue flash and was idly wondering whether the fabled taking spot would live up to its name when there was an explosion on the end of his line which started to rip off the reel as if there was a shark on the other end.

'Let it go,' drawled Randy, unnecessarily. 'It's a really big one actually James, don't start to put pressure on him too early.'

The sequence of run, return, and increasing pressure was repeated four times before the fish started to tire and eventually allowed Randy to net, weigh and gently return it to the river.

'Twenty four pounds, James, wow, that's the biggest for a while.' Randy was enthusiastic. Doyle pocketed his little camera and thought of the ribbing this achievement would earn that evening. How, he thought exasperatedly, had he ever thought it would be possible to get the undiluted and serious attention of these guys on a boys' own sporting outing like this?

Doyle caught six fish that evening and returned to the lodge tired but ecstatic, all the while bracing himself for the post dinner discussion.

The mood at dinner was cheerful and there was an optimistic atmosphere for Doyle's presentation.

Finally Doyle concluded: 'So gentlemen, that's the scenario and I'd like some feedback from you all tomorrow if possible as I have to be back in London the next day.'

O'Neill quipped: 'Oh, so you do have to allow for travel time in that thing of yours, James; it's not a real time machine then?'

Bulstrode gave his great braying laugh: 'I think we should all get one. Now, James, we need to think about this. Can we have an hour after lunch tomorrow with you?'

The hedgies drifted off to bed. Doyle lingered over the remnants of some particularly delicious Haut Brion. He should have felt tired after thirty six hours with very little sleep. He should have been dismayed by the ultra low key reaction to what was in anyone's language potentially one of the greatest financial coups in history. But he didn't. These were guys who wouldn't evince any emotion if they found a million pounds under their feet. Their belief was that displays of enthusiasm were unnecessary and undermined their negotiating position; like all very rich people they were paranoid that the world's greatest ambition was to remove or diminish their wealth, even, in this case, thought Doyle caustically, before they actually had it.

The door opened and Michel Weill put his head round it, smiling.

'C'est enorme James, mon ami,' he grinned, 'absolument enorme. Mes felicitations, mon ami, mes felicitations'. He disappeared.

Doyle went to his room. It was amazing he thought, how little could make you happy.

But the next day was a different story.

Black, cold, a howling wind, the South Atlantic weather shot through his five layers of clothing and numbed him to the core. The big sea trout run of the previous day had come and gone, up river. Doyle found himself forced to use a sixteen foot rod but even with that and three casts he was failing to get across the river. He flogged away for three hours without success. No one else had anything to show for their efforts and it was a cold and disconsolate party which returned to the lodge for lunch, a meal at which intemperate amounts of the lodge's Malbec was consumed.

Bulstrode, a little flushed, opened up without any preliminaries.

'Look Doyle,' he said, 'this all sounds good but there's absolutely no proof either that the Saudi's are running out of oil or that there are these huge reserves in Namibia. On top of all that, bidding for something like Rangoon is just a fantasy. It's just not something any of us would normally do. It would absorb all our resources, and more, and we would just get trampled in the rush and mangled by the politics. It's not a runner for me.'

'Even if we fancied it,' drawled O'Neill, 'there's the question of timing. The whole scheme depends on a manicured flow of information; if it came out in the wrong order we'd all be blown away and we'd none of us ever recover. We'd never work again. This so called Saudi shortage has been around in the market ever since I was a kid and it's never, but never, been confirmed or broken out into market action. Confirming such a big reserve in Namibia could take years and we can't possibly tie up our capital like that, we'd be mad.'

Myers grated in his Australian twang: 'It's all very well talking about bidding for Rangoon but we can't do that on our own and going to the banks would be lethal for our security.'

Weill commented: 'It is of course a fantastic scheme but in addition to all these points, James, there are regulatory issues, are there not, trading on inside information, market abuse and all your other charming little British pre-occupations?'

Doyle cursed the weather and the fish. There were good answers to all these points but the art of persuasion was to have a receptive audience and he felt that to go on digging on this occasion would simply hasten a full burial.

'Gentlemen', he said, 'now is not the time to fully cover these points and I suggest we do that in London. But very briefly these are a few headers for you think about for the rest of the week and take back to London at the end.

Firstly, proof of the Saudi position. The Arabian Oil memory stick referred to a forthcoming Saudi cabinet meeting to which I hope to gain access. There will be a full presentation of the position and I am told the Cabinet will reach the view that, for the first time ever, they will have to make a full press release on the situation. They are under immense political pressure to do so and there will also be international pressure given the leaks that are bound to occur very soon. As to Namibia, we have access to remarkable new exploration technology that will enable the field to be checked out on a very large scale in a fraction of the time normally required. In fact, it is now February; we would hope to have done this by the end of May. As for financing the take-over of Rangoon you are quite right, we cannot do it yourselves. But I have in mind a rather

special debt solution, far more secure than looking for conventional bank debt. It will mean some
dilution of your equity but as you have already
acknowledged you expect that.

Finally the important question of regulation which is not, Michel,' Doyle smiled at him,
'an optional extra in the United Kingdom as it
may be elsewhere. In terms of speculation in
commodities and oil futures there are no real
regulatory issues to worry about, unless you dis-
seminate false information. Bidding for or buying
shares in Rangoon based on information that is
not proprietary to Rangoon is not a problem. For
instance Rangoon's ownership of these old Namibian rights is a matter of public record, albeit
dusty, and our knowledge that the fields may be
oil bearing has been won as a result of our own
efforts.'

Myers grunted: 'Well all that doesn't sound
too bad to me James. You'd better work it up
and we'll have another session in London.

And by the way,' he went on, 'let me speak
for all of us when we say we appreciate this opportunity and the work that has gone into it'.

One by one the others muttered similar ap-
preciations and Doyle went to get his bags
packed.

Chapter 6

RIYADH

'James, what you are asking is very difficult. But I will try to help you. Talk to you later.'

Doyle put his feet up on the desk and fervently hoped he had invested enough energy in the past in looking after Philippa Davos. He knew that there was no one in London who had a better insight into how Saudi government really worked.

Fleming appeared and said: 'We are about halfway to putting on a long oil position with a gross equivalent exposure of about fifty billion dollars and there is no sign of anything untoward in the market at all.'

It was two days after Doyle had returned from South America. The phone rang again. Philippa.

'There's an Iranian girl called Persia Mansour who was mistress to Ghassan Quaraishi, the Saudi energy minister. But they had a huge row and she's been kicked out. She's also a close friend of Ali Koury who is vice chairman of the main political pressure group angling for reform, Mahdi Mahdi.

I think you should talk to her James. This is her mobile number.'

Two days later Doyle was back in Saudi staying at the Rose Petal, a small boutique hotel off al Masmak Square in old Riyadh.

Persia Mansour sat in a highly brocaded easy chair across the other side of a low table supporting a brass tray on which were set out Arabic coffee and iced mineral water.

Persia was one of the most stunning women Doyle had ever met. She was about five foot eight with a voluptuous yet subtly toned body. She had long jet black hair which perfectly set off her dusky skin. Her eyes were deep brown, her mouth was wide and sensual and she had brilliant teeth. Her dark purple Prada sheath with low heeled Manolo Blahnik shoes wilfully dismissed local dress codes; she wore a plain necklace of brilliant white diamonds and a pair of large diamond clustered earrings, with gold and diamond bracelets on her right wrist and a small gold Patek Philippe on the left. Her scent wafted over him leaving him almost helpless with desire.

'So, James,' Persia spoke low, 'what is it you want of me in Saudi Arabia?'

At that moment Doyle nearly put the whole Saudi project into the bin, or at least on hold, in favour of answering this question in the simplest possible way.

'I'm a political journalist,' he said. 'I'm fascinated with Saudi politics. In fact I'm doing a book and a large piece for Vision magazine on the political tension in Saudi and how the ruling elite are responding to popular pressures for change, especially now that the low oil price has reduced Saudi revenues.'

Persia's flawless features clouded over.

'Oh, but this is so dangerous James,' she whispered, 'it's not like Britain here you know, you could get into real trouble for pursuing something like this. And we should not discuss it in the open,' — she waved an imperious and jewelled arm towards the lounge — 'is there somewhere more private that we could go?'

Doyle grasped the moment.

'I could offer you lunch in my suite – it has a beautiful balcony looking out over the square.'

Persia looked at Doyle carefully with a sweeping glance that took in his dark hair, blue eyes, handsome open face, white linen shirt, dark blue cotton chinos, black Cole Haan loafers and gold Breguet.

'Let's go,' she said simply.

On the balcony there was a semi circular cane settee facing a low mahogany and glass coffee table beneath a large dark blue awning. Two large fans rotated silently underneath the awning and, added to the little wind blowing gently round the pretty square, made the balcony refreshingly cool.

James handed Persia the room service menu and asked her what she would like to eat and drink.

'Fresh orange juice, please James, followed by grilled fish of the day and mixed salad.'

Doyle picked up the phone and ordered a limejuice and soda for himself and the same food.

Persia kicked off her shoes and stretched luxuriously in the sunlight.

'This is nice, James,' she said, and chatted away about her time in London.

'Now,' she eventually gave him a disturbingly direct look, 'you know, you look much more like a financier than a scruffy journalist. Why don't you tell me why are you really here?'

Doyle took a deep breath and decided to commit.

'Persia,' he said, 'the truth is that what I am really interested in is oil. I want to find out what's going to happen to Saudi oil in the longer term, and its domestic political implications. What I particularly want to find out is what is happening currently to Saudi oil output and what kind of reserves they truly have left.'

Persia leaned towards him and put a finger on his lips.

'I know the answers to these questions, James,' she whispered with a teasing smile. 'Wouldn't you like to know?'

Doyle felt a soft sensuous pressure on his knee and felt his self control begin to slide.

At that moment, to his relief, the bell rang announcing the arrival of their room service.

Their food and drink were delicious. They talked more of what they had done in the past and their personal backgrounds. Doyle was surprised and impressed that Persia had gained a double first in classics from Cambridge and done post graduate study in efficient market theory before spending time with Michael Godov in his New York fund of funds operation. What had drawn this highly intelligent modern woman back to the Middle East and especially Saudi? Doyle enquired.

'The usual things, James,' she replied. 'Roots, family, my father lives here now, the desire to settle down, wanting to make a contribution.'

She told him she was in the early stages of establishing a financial advisory business to capitalise on her international contacts and financial training.

Doyle ordered coffee and offered her an Egyptian cigarette.

She edged a little closer to him on the settee and playfully blew smoke rings at him.

'Shouldn't we get to know each other a little better, James,' she breathed in his ear, 'then,' she gave him a wicked smile, 'I can make up my mind whether to help you or not.'

Doyle told her sternly that he never slept with girls on a first date. ' Unless they are exceptionally beautiful,' he added hastily.

Her body was exquisite. Her breasts were deliciously full and her long strong thighs disclosed a beautifully cut Brazilian which was perfectly in line with Doyle's tastes. Above all she smelt wonderful, was incredibly energetic, inventive and utterly uninhibited. After two hours they drew breath in favour of China tea and more Egyptian cigarettes. As they smoked she toyed idly with his member.

'You can tell me one thing, James,' she said. 'You are well provided for' — she gave it an added tweak — 'but why do more Englishmen not do what so many Arab men do from so early in their youth — and exercise them to enlarge them?'

Doyle said it wasn't really a question to which he had given much thought.

'There's a culture that it doesn't make much difference, I suppose,' he said, 'and that it's not really possible to do much about it.'

Persia got up, tossed her cigarette end into one of the sand filled pots on the balcony, and, returning to the bedroom, said scornfully: 'Come back as a woman next time James and see if you say that.'

Doyle watched her intently, letting his smoke curl lazily upwards towards the carved cedarwood ceiling. Finally he swung his legs out and looked at the sunlit square with its row of taxis, their drivers leaning against them, smoking, eating and reading newspapers.

He leant over to Persia and kissed her on the cheek.

'Shall we stay a little longer, James ?' she smiled at him eagerly.

Doyle interrogated his own satiety and concluded that, yes, he would definitely come back as a woman next time. 'Persia,' he said, 'have I passed the test?'

'Yes' she said softly, 'I think you have James, and,' she went on langourously, 'in any case you can apply for a re-sit at any time.'

'The answers to these questions, Persia,' Doyle mused, ' it's not so much the answers I need as proof of what I already think I know — or have found out on my travels.'

Persia wrinkled her nose: 'The Saudi Cabinet meets once a week James, but once a quarter it has a sort of longer session where it reviews production, reserves, exploration and development in more detail. Once a year, coming up quite soon I think, it has a full dress session, a sort of summit, generally with consultants, where it looks intensely at Saudi and global peak oil, technical issues, the trend in production economics and the medium term outlook for Saudi and OPEC production, the global oil price, and the impact on the Saudi economy.'

'God,' groaned Doyle, 'what wouldn't I give to be able to listen in on that.'

'If you listen to me James,' said Persia, intently, 'you could. But I warn you that it will be difficult, dangerous, and expensive.'

'Now listen,' she said. 'The annual oil summits are always held in the drawing room in the oldest Royal Palace in Riyadh, right in Al Khobar, the heart of the old city. That drawing room is on the first floor. The whole Palace is heavily protected inside and out by guards, and last year they fitted digital cameras everywhere in the interior. Very discreet, you can hardly see them. But underneath all this old part of Riyadh there is a huge network of tunnels between all the old palaces. No doubt they were used in the past for all manner of political, social and amorous intrigues but now they are hardly used at all.'

'Are they actually useable?' asked Doyle.

'Well, I was coming to that. Mahdi Mahdi have been using them and have installed some listening devices in one or two palaces.'

'Aren't these tunnels patrolled or guarded in some way?' said Doyle, cautiously.

'No,' said Persia, 'but, even better, a company run by the brother in law of one of the leaders of Mahdi Mahdi – who happens to be a member of the ruling elite – has got the contract to maintain them in safe condition — we have health and safety here too James, you know.' Persia smiled at the incredulous look on Doyle's face. 'And so they have unlimited access at all times.'

'And what did you mean by it being expensive?' quizzed Doyle.

'Well, James, opposition parties have to be paid for and Mahdi Mahdi is always in need of funding; obviously they are not able to cream off oil revenues in the same way as the Royal Family.'

The setting sun made a crimson splash over the white houses across the square and the shadows lengthened in its far corner. The flickering lights of street sellers started to slowly bob about in the dusk.

Doyle grunted acknowledgement, offered Persia another cigarette and asked as lazily as possible how matters might be progressed.

Persia said she would need to introduce Doyle to Ali Kouri, the deputy head of Mahdi Mahdi, and that Doyle would need to come to an arrangement with him.

Persia stood up, dressed, gathered up her things and pressed her body against Doyle's. 'That was such a nice lunch James,' she breathed, 'perhaps we can do it again some time'.

The door closed gently and Doyle was left with a waft of Chanel and a mixture of utmost fatigue, satisfaction, anticipation and a little hint of fear.

He went for a swim in the cunningly back- lit black tiled pool the bottom of which had the outline of the Gulf States picked out in gold leaf while all their major cities winked soft red.

He was lying on his sun bed watching the first stars in the deepening night sky when his mobile rang and the rough and ready tones of George Nutting intruded on his thoughts.

'Watcha, cock,' intoned George, 'ow's it going then?'

'Where are you and what the hell are you doing George?' said a startled Doyle.

'I'm still at the old office, cock,' George replied.

Doyle reflected that George must be making himself more useful to MI6 than he had imagined.

'Well, I'm lying peacefully by a pool in Riyadh,' said Doyle evenly.

'Yeah, peaceful you may be at the moment matey,' breezed George, 'but it may not last, if you get my drift.'

'Really?' said Doyle laconically.

'Yes, really, you cocky so and so. I hear you are messing with some big wheels out there and, what's worse, messing with their women, you stupid git.'

'I need big wheels to get to my destination George,' said Doyle calmly.

'Destination. Bloody journey's end more like, cock,' George rasped.

'Look mate, I can't say any more on this line but take care eh?' George rang off.

Doyle was mulling over this conversation in his room when the room phone rang. Persia.

She told him to go to an address for 10pm and ask for 'Baba'.

'Oh, and James,' she hesitated, 'do be careful. It may not be quite what you expect. Call me tomorrow please James. Good night.'

There was a click. Could Doyle really still smell her perfume? He wrenched his mind back to the task in hand.

Doyle made some more calls and ordered some food up to his room.

He changed into a pair of lightweight black Armani jeans, a black cotton shirt, and some black trainers. He consigned his Breguet to the hotel safe and replaced it with a luminous waterproof Swatch. He strapped a flick knife with a six inch stiletto blade into a sheath on his right leg and slipped an extendable cosh into a specially tailored pocket inside his trouser waist band where it could remain hidden at all times. Finally he put three powerful CS gas sachets in his jean pockets.

After a couple of cups of Arabian coffee he approached a cab from a rank outside the hotel and gave the address. The driver told him he was waiting on another job and directed him to a cab standing a little way back from the rank.

The driver was a young Saudi who introduced himself as Danni. Doyle asked him if he knew the place. There was a monosyllabic reply. Doyle was slightly surprised at the length of the journey and that they seemed to be plunging into some industrial area a long way away from the centre of town. After some time they drew up outside a large warehouse in a back street.

It had a sign in blue neon over a small black studded metal door with a heavy central grill. The sign read 'Heaven's Gate.'

'This isn't where I asked for,' said Doyle.

'This is where I'm taking you. The arrangements have been changed by Mahdi Mahdi,' said Danni.

'All the same I'm a bit surprised they would want a meeting here,' observed Danni.

'Why?' said Doyle. 'What is it?'

'It's a club.' said Danni. 'A gay club, highly illegal.'

'Full of gays,' he added, unnecessarily.

Doyle felt something in him tighten.

'Well, at least they can't make you pregnant,' said Doyle with apparently impervious jocularity.

'You want to be careful going there mate. All sorts.' advised Danni. 'It can be a bit rough.'

On impulse Doyle handed Danni a wad of riyals and told him to wait for him in a side street.

'If I'm not out in three hours ring this number,' said Doyle.

'Hope you get out,' said Danni with a sardonic smile, taking the money.

Doyle and Danni drove round the building once and fixed on the side street where Danni would wait. It was 9.50 pm. Doyle left the car and walked slowly round the building; most of which seemed to be offices of distributors and transport agents and all of which were shut. It was impossible to see from street level how extensive the Heavens Gate premises were, or what the roof layout was like. Otherwise there was nothing of note. There weren't many cars parked but Doyle noted, far up one of the adjoining streets, a Chrysler Voyager. He couldn't see if it was occupied but it seemed quite low on its springs.

Then right at the last minute before he rounded the final corner to the club entrance he noticed — parked deep into an alleyway — two dark blue unmarked vans, again it was impossible to see their contents. The sensation of walking into a trap became more acute.

Shrugging his shoulders Doyle strolled to the studded gate and pulled the old bell hanging by its side. It was opened by a very large Arab with a luxuriant moustache, dressed in a militaristic brown uniform.

Doyle said: 'Is Mr Baba in the club?'

The large Arab said nothing and beckoned Doyle inside the door which closed with a soft click behind him. The Arab looked at Doyle and an almost imperceptible smile crossed his features. He went behind a desk and pulled out a large cash box. 'Fifty riyals,' he intoned. Doyle handed him the notes and the Arab pressed a bell.

Another attendant of similar size but in white fatigues appeared and, handing over two white towels, instructed Doyle to follow him. He padded off up a long featureless corridor. Doyle became conscious of how warm the club was.

He began to imagine likely future scenarios and fished out one of the tear gas sachets from his jeans and secreted it in one of the towels. Bending down he quickly furled the hunting stiletto in the same towel. Two young Saudi's in uniform, who both looked very fit, suddenly appeared and fell in behind Doyle.

The attendant stopped by some lockers and handed Doyle a key. 'Change here please,' he said gruffly. The two younger men seemed to have disappeared. One or two young Arabs just wearing towels pushed past Doyle, one letting his hand trail across Doyle's lower back.

Doyle did as he was told, putting one of the towels round his waist and keeping the other, loaded, towel, rolled up under his arm.

The large Arab re-appeared and indicated the showers. Doyle managed to take a shower and dry himself without using the second towel and then the Arab jerked his head towards a further dimly lit corridor. This led to a large room at the end which contained only a plasma TV screen and two rows of slightly raised beds — so arranged that anyone on the beds had an overall view of the room — and what might be going on in it, Doyle reflected gloomily. The Arab flicked a switch and the plasma screen became full of the graphic image of a lean young Arab fellating another very fat Arab who was leaning back with a look of total enjoyment. Doyle marvelled at the massive size of the fat Arab's member; he really must remember to tell Persia. The idle thought seemed to slide around his nerves which were on a knife edge.

'I really want to meet Mr Baba,' he said to the large attendant who simply nodded impassively and went out.

After about fifteen minutes the door re-opened and an Arab in a bath towel, in his mid forties, stockily built with rather cruel features, introduced himself to Doyle.

'Saddam Ibrahim,' he said, extending his hand. 'You probably don't know this but I work for Istikhbarat, the Saudi Secret Service, and we have been interested in your movements.'

'Perhaps, Mr Doyle,' he went on, 'you would care to explain to me what you are doing here.'

Doyle re-iterated his story of being a political journalist. Ibrahim listened politely.

The features of the large Arab on the screen contorted grotesquely as he achieved orgasm and the young Arab stood up wiping his mouth. Doyle struggled to concentrate on Ibrahim.

'How would you describe yourself, Mr Doyle?' Ibrahim's tone was edgier now. 'That is when you are not engaged in peddling these imaginative fantasies?'

'A cross between an entrepreneur, a trader, and a secret agent perhaps? Strange balconies and strange women can make uneasy bed fellows, Mr Doyle.'

'If you say so,' said Doyle, unruffled.

'I do, Mr Doyle.'

'But come, let me show you round the club. It's the best in Riyadh'.

It probably was, thought Doyle, if you liked that kind of thing.

'Actually', Ibrahim smiled, 'I am one of the owners.'

He led the way out of the plasma room down the corridors which twisted and turned in semi darkness. They passed a myriad of back rooms mostly with their doors closed, Doyle trying not to let his imagination run riot as they emanated a rich mixture of grunts, groans, slaps and screams. They passed on into a large swimming pool hall with a Jacuzzi — fairly full — and with double loungers scattered about its periphery. Then they plunged down some rubber covered stairs into a large room below.

'You'll need a strong stomach for this,' indicated Ibrahim. To Doyle the room looked like a huge dungeon, about sixty feet long with a grill running all the way down it. The lighting in the room was very dim but when they paused Doyle's eyes grew accustomed to the murk.

Doyle drew his breath. He had never seen anything like the scene which the dim light eventually presented to him. The room was covered in low beds with narrow corridors running between them. Most of the beds were occupied by a swirling, sucking, crawling, crouching, thrusting pack of male humanity. Male body sprawled over male body like huge spiders while others looked on in ghoulish fascination. There was no conversation. As Doyle watched, repelled, a young boy was passed down the line of beds, each occupant handling him roughly and intimately before he was finally roundly abused by two men at the end of the row.

Ibrahim looked at Doyle and gave a thin smile.

'We call this the common room,' he said quietly. 'It's not to everyone's taste, of course'.

Heads turned and stared at them. He added: 'They are all interested in you, they don't get many white foreigners here and certainly not in this room.'

'Now,' he continued, 'you and I need a chat.'

He led the way to a back room which was far more elegantly furnished. It had an enormous oval double bed with rich tapestries and furnishings, some homo erotic paintings and an elaborate bar and several comfortable chairs. It was very hot.

'Please,' said Ibrahim, 'what will you have?'

Doyle asked for whisky and water. Ibrahim poured himself some fruit juice.

'I know why you are here and I also know who you were due to meet tonight. He has, I'm afraid, been unavoidably detained. The sort of questions you have been asking, Mr Doyle, are not helpful to Saudi. We have spent years drawing a veil over delicate matters such as oil production and reserves and the last thing we want, frankly, is an adventurer like yourself upsetting that situation for the sake, no doubt, of purely personal gain.

The best situation for you is to leave Saudi as soon as possible in that ridiculous plane of yours, and not to return seeking any further specialist and confidential information. And, Mr Doyle, if you were to be doubly wise you would desist from intimate relationships with well connected women.

I can facilitate all these outcomes for you Mr Doyle — at a price. Alternatively I can make life considerably more difficult for you.' Ibrahim spoke easily and appeared utterly relaxed and in command.

Doyle sipped at his Laphroaig. He didn't like the direction in which things were moving.

'The price?' Doyle enquired.

Ibrahim's hand came to rest on Doyle's knee.

'You have a fine body, Mr Doyle. All I want is simply that you and I get to know each other a little better, here in this room, and that afterwards I escort you to the airbase. You can call your pilot now to warn him if you like.'

'You know, I think, from your previous remarks that I'm not that way inclined,' said Doyle smoothly, 'so what you suggest is not really much of an option is it?'

'My dear Doyle,' Ibrahim's voice had the edge back in it, 'your own preferences scarcely come into this. I find you attractive and I find the thought of screwing you very compelling. I can assure you,' he went on, gently rubbing a growing tent in his towel, 'that you will remember every bit of it as well.'

'What's the alternative?' asked Doyle, betraying no hint of concern.

'I take you to the common room and after a few hours I will collect you in whatever condition you are then in. After that I will have you incarcerated in Damman Central prison and ensure that in due course you go on trial for attempted espionage – which, you won't be surprised to hear – carries a death sentence.'

Neither prospect seemed at all compelling to Doyle.

'You had better take me down to the room then,' said Doyle equivocally.

'Are you mad Doyle?' said Ibrahim, his face darkening with rage and frustration, 'you have no idea of what you are letting yourself in for.'

'Well, I'm not going to be fucked by you for a start,' said Doyle.

Without a word Ibrahim got up, angrily yanked Doyle to his feet, and with a vice like grip took him towards the stairs.

Doyle thought quickly.

'Can I go to the lavatory?' he asked.

'I suppose so,' Ibrahim relaxed his grip and thrust Doyle into the next doorway.

Doyle urinated and found the handle of his stiletto in his spare towel, unbelievably not searched by Ibrahim. On the knife were two buttons set flush into the handle. He pressed the uppermost one twice.

Rejoining bin Ismail he went down the stairs — and the two young officers reappeared and stood guard either side of the door. A stirring of anticipation rippled down the room behind the grating. Ibrahim pushed Doyle roughly into the room behind the bars.

'Good luck,' he said sourly, 'see you later'.

The room smelled fetid with human sweat and other even more personal odours. A large exceptionally hairy Arab lumbered towards Doyle, a massive erection preceding him and with a wolfish leer on his face in which surprise and lust were working equally hard. Two other equally bear like specimens loomed close behind him.

Doyle felt the handle of his knife. He was in a quandary. He didn't want to kill or wound anyone.

Anyway there were too many men in the room to make taking them on a viable option.

He had just reached that conclusion when the lights, such as they were, went out.

Doyle shrank back towards the inner wall of the chamber. Chaos and confusion reigned. Doyle started to move towards the door, bumping in to men as he went. At each contact he mentally weighed the man involved. Finally he made contact with someone about his size. He put his left arm round the man's throat and jerked it back, whipped out his knife and pressed its blade against the man's ribs.

'Move,' he ordered in Arabic. The man stumbled in front of him making muffled protests. Doyle felt his way along to the door, thrust the Arab through it and leaped for the floor, shooting under the legs of the two guards who eagerly arrested the progress of his erstwhile companion. Doyle shot up the stairs and into one of the back rooms which he prayed would be unoccupied. He leaned against the wall just inside the door and got his breath and his bearings. He had to get his clothes and get out. Doyle had made a few more preparations than it might have appeared. Tony Dyer and a team of four had been instructed to follow him and had been based in the side street in the Voyager. They had reconnoitred the back of the club and put out the lights at his signal. Doyle pressed the second button on his stiletto. A pencil thin beam of intense light swiftly guided him to the locker room. He seized his clothes and quickly dressed. He switched off the torch and cautiously put his head out. He detected a slight cold draught and followed it. He hoped it would take him to the back entrance and a getaway with Tony. Suddenly he ran into what he guessed correctly was one of the two secret servicemen. He punched him very hard in the stomach, pulled the tab on his tear gas sachet and dropped it on the prostrate form. Doyle went swiftly on, down a short flight of stairs, round a corner and encountered Dyer.

'What's been keeping you man? Jesus, what a place.' Dyer spoke low into a mouthpiece, recalling his team and summoning the van. Soon four beams of light converged on the door and the van drew up with a screech.

'Better get going sir,' he said. 'Where to now?'

Doyle looked at his watch and was surprised to find it was only half past midnight. How time flew when you were having fun. He needed little time to think.

'I need to get out of here fast,' he said. 'Call Chuck. Make for the base. You can recover my stuff from the hotel — here's the key. You're all ok but lie low for a bit and junk the van.

'Oh, and thanks,' said Doyle. 'I really can't recommend that establishment.'

Chapter 7

DOWNING STREET

Harvinder Singh eased off his Lobb loafers and rocked back gently in his chair. His Downing Street study was quiet. The antique ormolu clock above the mantelpiece showed 6.05pm. His large George VI desk was covered with red boxes and buff files.

He ignored them all.

They were, he felt, symbolic of the problems faced by all of his predecessors since Margaret Thatcher left office. It was very simple. They had all, for years, confused activity with achievement.

Singh thought there was very little that governments could do well. His premiership had followed the astonishing Tory Party coup which had seen Singh replace the deposed David Argyll months before the election. Right from the start of his administration he had been appalled at the utter mess which had been bequeathed to him by governments of the last twenty five years.

Government expenditure, inherently inefficient, had become a travesty of waste. Education was in a dire state with literacy levels at the lowest for twenty years. Healthcare spending had grown like a giant hogweed and the resultant bureaucracy seemed to have lost all sight of the requirement, and certainly all ability, to deliver the basic services required of it. Government debt had expanded to a record proportion of national product. Manufacturing was confined to a few high end firms gravely handicapped by lack of a decently educated workforce. The social consequences flowing from all of this were plain to see.

Britain's infrastructure was creaking. The motorways were worn out, the railways still absorbed massive subsidies, Heathrow was operating way beyond its capacity and it would be years before a much larger modern nuclear power capability could be built. Meanwhile the primeval planning system meant that any improvements took years to get off the ground. There were too many people in Britain and the quality of life was deteriorating, but the budget deficit and pension problems meant that anything other than an expanding workforce would be a financial disaster.

Then, Singh reflected, there was the question of oil and gas supply. The sudden boost from North Sea oil which had first saved then become political life blood for Mrs Thatcher had long since dwindled to a relative trickle. The oil and gas hegemony pursued by Russia had put the whole of European energy supplies at risk and any sustained growth in economic activity drove the oil price to levels which swiftly resulted in recession and which did long term damage to the economic and social fabric.

Singh sighed heavily. Why oh why had he ever accepted this job? He ruminated. Oil and gas had saved Thatcher. Only something similar, he felt sure, would allow him to escape from the straightjacket in which a warring Tory party and expectant electorate had placed him. But where the hell would it come from?

Singh was a businessman first and politician second. He had come to Britain in nineteen eighty, become a British citizen and had made a huge fortune in consumer electronics in the Thatcher years. Gradually he had been drawn into the fringes of the Tory party as a treasurer and as a fund raiser — and major donor — and later had become involved in various policy think tanks. In a fit of enthusiasm he had stood for a Westminster seat and his growing popularity and philanthropic profile had eased him into Parliament. Then he had sold his business to the Chinese and entered the shadow cabinet. His pragmatism and experience had steadily increased his popularity. When the coup had come against Argyll he had been a natural choice as replacement leader.

His private secretary buzzed him and told him it was time to leave.

He slipped his shoes back on, slung his jacket over his shoulder and walked out to his waiting Jaguar. Even that, Singh thought wryly to himself, was mainly made in India now.

At the private back entrance to the Bank of England the Governor, Sir Robert Melchett, greeted him warmly.

'Prime Minister, welcome, do come on up, everyone is here.'

They stepped into a lift which rose silently to the Governor's new penthouse meeting suite.

In the fast fading light Singh saw the whole of the City of London spread out before them with glimpses of the sunset reflected on the Canary Wharf complex downstream. A magnificent blue and gold patterned Persian carpet covered the floor with deep cream silk wallpaper adorning the walls, the governor's huge desk filled one corner and soft leather sofas and glass tables another.

Melchett effected introductions.

'Prime Minister this is Lord Fettes, Chief Executive of Rangoon and likewise Mr Bjorn Stavenuiter of Great Western Desert, Sir Thomas Mannering, Permanent Secretary to the Department of Energy, Matthew Konig his deputy and Niall McNeil the historian and economist.'

Singh inclined his head. He had deliberately asked for a small meeting to precede dinner.

'Prime Minister, as you requested Mr Konig is first going to give an overview of global oil and gas resources and the strategic positioning of major European companies in relation thereto. Lord Fettes and Mr Stavenuiter will then give their perspectives on how their own companies are responding to that scenario. Then we shall have time for some questions and hopefully answers, and then we have drinks and dinner. Chatham House rules of course.'

Singh again inclined his head.

'Thank you, Governor.'

The group sat in easy chairs, the lights dimmed and a plasma screen glowed at one end of the room.

Singh had to admit to himself that Konig's presentation was excellent. It showed the increasing energy cost of extracting oil, a cost in itself a major inhibitor of economic growth, the fact that peak oil — the point at which oil and gas production peaks and then declines – had occurred in many countries and was soon to occur in many more; the accelerator effect on growth in oil consumption induced by rapid development of emerging markets; and finally the dramatic effect of predicted population growth and increased oil and gas consumption per capita combining with the slowing rate of increase of global energy production and the predicted eventual decline in global aggregate production. Above all Konig focussed on the stark failure of many large long established worldwide oil companies to find a significant number of new oil and gas fields in the last fifty years.

Harvinder Singh knew all of this. It was the single biggest problem facing the industrial world.

Now Konig was talking about future prospects.

'However,' he continued in his dry precise tones, 'there are new projects due to come onstream in the next decade which may defer the predicted lurch into reduced overall oil production. But much of this new potential production – even if it happens — will be far more expensive and technically difficult to access than before. Nationalisation of natural resources has also meant that many countries have applied inadequate investment to exploration and production in favour of short term expenditure elsewhere in their economies. Moreover very few potential large new resources are in countries which allow free access to Western companies to assist in extracting it.'

Singh shot a glance at the Governor, who said smoothly: 'Thank you so much Matthew. I think it's now time that we heard from the great industrial titans we have here tonight. Lord Fettes, perhaps you would make a start.'

Lord Fettes was a tall, greying, sixty year old, with a lifetime's experience in the industry. Apart from his business his two passions were women and horse racing. He had been expensively married three times and had spent the last twenty years in search of a Derby winner. When he spoke it was in the precise mannered tones of a person whose overwhelming confidence in their intellectual abilities brooked no opposition and stifled debate.

'Prime Minister, Governor, Sir Thomas,' he began with a quick inclusive sweep round the rest of the participants, 'let me assure you that Rangoon is doing and has always done everything in its power to overcome these issues. The situation we find ourselves in is that induced by the parallel decline of imperialism and colonialism which has been at the root of Britain's economic problems over the last hundred years.'

Singh looked indifferent.

'It is hardly surprising that we at Rangoon have been unable to escape from the global march of self determinism and nationalism which has also affected so many of our other industries. There is also another factor. We and our friends at Great Western account for an important percentage of all dividends paid by the top hundred European companies. Continuation of that dividend policy, despite low oil prices, has been a most vital support for the financial health of pension funds with billions under management, and, of course, our shares are especially widely held in Britain. But,' a wintry smile crossed Lord Fettes's features, 'it has meant that we have had to be very careful with capital expenditure in recent years.'

Harvinder Singh thanked him and turned to Bjorn Stavenuiter.

'Ja, yes,' started Stavenuiter in his surprisingly heavily accented English, 'very much the same things as Lord Fettes, I fear.' Stavenuiter was a huge Viking figure of a man who had dabbled in all in wrestling before rising through Great Western Desert on the finance and petrochemical side. 'There is so little we can do under the circumstances, and of course, Lord Fettes has made a very good point with regard to dividends.'

The big man sank back into his seat, clearly believing this contribution was sufficient.

Singh struggled to contain an overwhelming tidal wave of frustration. These seemed to him to be men who had spent a lifetime accepting the status quo and were now desperately covering up their failure to replace, let alone augment, the oil and gas reserves of the great companies for which they were responsible. They both seemed to be in a time warp.

'Gentlemen,' said Singh softly, 'that all seems rather depressing. Are you comfortable that you are covering all the ground available to you and in particular using all the new exploration technology – I hear that the big finds made by Brazilgas in South America were greatly assisted by the new Seismic X equipment which they sourced from the US.'

'Lord Fettes?'

'My technical people believe this technology is of limited value, Prime Minister. Perhaps the very deep water conditions offshore South America made it more relevant.'

'Another thing,' probed Singh, 'is that some of the junior oil companies seem to have found quite material reserves and built quite big market capitalisations on the back of successful exploitation of areas which both Rangoon and Great Western had abandoned at an earlier stage.'

'Ah, yes, Prime Minister,' said Stavenuiter, rousing himself, ' but, you know, companies of our size really have to devote themselves to elephant hunting, these smaller finds cannot, how do you say, move our needle enough.'

'So', said Singh, 'when, my friends, are you going to find some elephants, for your companies and your country?'

'Ha, Prime Minister, very good,' chuckled Stavenuiter, 'but you have to remember – as Mr Konig told us earlier — that no company, worldwide, has found, in the last fifty years, an oil field remotely comparable in size to the large fields upon which the world presently depends.'

'Have you no areas in your portfolios which you believe might be the source of such fields?' queried Singh.

'I wish I could say we have,' the replies came almost in unison.

At this juncture the Governor's butler glided into the room and whispered a few words deferentially to Sir Robin.

Melchett rose from his chair.

'Prime Minister,' he said, 'I think perhaps we should take a break for drinks at this point. We have some of your favourite Pol Roger on ice. May I thank all those who have contributed so far to this most interesting discussion.'

Singh was angry. These people were complacent. He had heard nothing new. But far worse, in his book, was that he had not seen in either of the protagonists that evening the slightest hint of genuine ambition or burning desire for change.

He masked his feelings as he sipped his cold champagne. What was it that his hero Winston

Churchill had said about finding excuses to drink it? 'In victory you deserve it and in defeat you need it.'

Those that had worked for him in business would have been fearful of the anger and resentment in his eyes and the studied cool of his demeanour. In business Singh had been used to getting results. One of the things he had learned in that career was that if things did not get done the only solution was to change the people.

Singh gave Mannering, who lived in Whitehall Mansions, a lift back after dinner.

'Rather frustrating, Sir Thomas,' observed Singh as the Jaguar glided along the Embankment.

'Quite so, Prime Minister.'

'Who is doing better than Rangoon and Great Western?' asked Singh.

'Oh, there's Twenty First Century, the exploration and production arm of Empire Gas which was spun off a few years ago. As you know they have found, in conjunction with the Brazilians, very large quantities of oil and gas off the coast of Brazil. Of course it's in deep water and expensive to produce, and they are in partnership so the net benefits to us are not that great, but it shows what can be done. They have managed very easily to finance the huge investment required through the London market, too.'

'You amaze me, Thomas,' replied Singh. 'Who would have thought that an archaic bureaucracy like the old Empire Gas could have spawned such a successful business? How have they done so well?'

'It's all down to management, Prime Minister. For the last ten years or so they have been blessed with the most charismatic chief executive.'

'Well who is he and why the hell didn't you invite him tonight?' asked Singh irritably.

'Not available, Prime Minister, abroad on business.'

'Well, get him in to see me, one on one, would you, and now I think this is your front door. Good night.'

A few days later Singh was looking carefully at the man who sat across from him in an easy chair in his study. Tall, dark, spare, Michael Walsh looked more like a film star than an oil company executive.

'Tell me what you have achieved and how you have done it Michael,' said Singh.

'We've always been a new company Prime Minister. The upstream arm of the old Empire Gas hadn't been set up long before it was spun out to the stock market as Twenty First Century. And the upstream arm had recruited new people anyway.'

'So the cancer of the old bureaucracy never infected you,' summarised Singh.

Walsh chuckled. 'Well that's one way of putting it Prime Minister. Our approach has been simple,' he continued. 'Our culture has been to explore, find, and produce or we die as a business. We had no legacy of producing assets, no historical associations or pre conceived ideas about our status or who might be desirable partners. We started with a clean sheet of paper, we focussed ruthlessly on the most promising geologies world-wide, and the best exploration technologies and we partnered up whenever oil nationalism was an issue. And, as we've got luckier with the drill bit, partners have become easier to find.' Walsh flashed his film star grin at Singh.

'Another factor is that we were very early to spot the potential of the liquefied natural gas market, in which we are now global leaders.' Walsh added.

'Give me generals that are lucky,' commented Singh. 'Now tell me why Rangoon and Great Western have underperformed.'

'Just the inverse of these factors really, Prime Minister. They have been around since the year dot, they have been used to an imperialist ap-proach, they find taking partners difficult, and they have big dividend yields to service, which cuts their ability to invest.'

'If you were running either of them what changes would you make?' asked Singh.

'I'm quite happy where I am Prime Minister.'

'I appreciate that but give me an answer.'

'You would have to bring in a raft of outsiders at the top level to change the culture, and sell some mature assets to fund a much greater exploration effort,' responded Walsh.

'But frankly it would be a gigantic task.'

'Could you find the right people?' queried Singh.

'Yes, at a price, possibly some would come from outside the industry,' said Walsh.

'Why don't you get Twenty First to bid for one of those two dinosaurs and solve my problem?' said Singh mischievously

'They are too big, they would dilute our growth, and distract our management; our shareholders would be up in arms,' said Walsh flatly.

'Thank you for coming in, Michael'.

Singh's private secretary, a young Indian Insead graduate, called Anita Mohan, was at the door.

'Prime Minister, you know that hedge fund fellow you wanted to see?'

'No, who, what?' floundered Singh.

'James Doyle, Prime Minister. He's linked to something known as the Sphinx partnership.'

'Oh, yes.'

'He's here.'

'Show me that briefing note,' Singh pointed to a sheet of paper dangling from Mohan's hand.

Singh speed read it.

'OK, show him in.'

Doyle entered the room.

'Prime Minister,' he said, 'James Doyle, I'm here at your request.'

'I'm pleased to meet you. I'm trying to familiarise myself with the oil and gas business and understand you have extensive interests in the sector. I also am told by my American friends that you have been very helpful to them in recent years.'

'Well,' said Doyle, 'it's true we have traded oil, among many other things. But then so do plenty of other firms some of which are both much bigger than us and trade all the time — we tend to have one off projects in a variety of sectors which our backers support on a discrete basis.'

Singh looked carefully at Doyle and made a snap decision to trust him.

'I'll be frank with you Doyle. You have the reputation of being a financial adventurer but I understand you also have some pretty significant philanthropic interests.'

Doyle inclined his head.

'This country is in a mess, Doyle, and I need all the help I can get to straighten it out.'

'That would seem to be a need which cannot be met from private philanthropy, Prime Minister.'

'I'm not asking you to write out a cheque to redeem the National Debt, Doyle.'

'I'm not quite clear what you do want, sir'.

'We need more oil.'

'Even if you got it,' Doyle replied, 'it would be overseas and you couldn't tax it as they did North Sea oil.'

'I agree, we need to find something in which the British Government can be more directly involved.'

'With respect, Prime Minister,' said Doyle, 'the average British Government hardly seems able competently to discharge its basic functions, let alone turning itself into a successful oil explorer.

Anyway,' continued Doyle, 'the current management of Rangoon and Great Western aren't likely to find much more oil and the independents haven't got the financial or political muscle to get a big share of any field even if they were lucky enough to find one.'

'I agree,' responded Singh, 'and there's a limit to what I can do about the management of the bigger companies from where I sit'.

Doyle reflected for a moment. He liked Singh. He made a decision to compromise the ultimate returns which the Sphinx partnership might make operating entirely on their own.

'I may be able to help you, Prime Minister, but first we need to have a discussion about certain issues'.

'Tell me how you can help', said Singh.

'I know quite a bit about the potential oil resources which might be available to one of the majors if it were properly handled,' said Doyle.

'How can they possibly have valuable resource assets of which they are unaware, Doyle?' Singh's eyes glittered in the study firelight.

'Because they are very big companies, Prime Minister, and inevitably opportunities get lost. You've met them, I understand.'

Singh nodded.

'As far as our Sphinx partnership is concerned,' said Doyle, 'we have no interest in dealing with this by changing the board of these companies. You know the form. A large scale proxy fight organised by us and other activist investors followed by a trip to some heavy duty headhunters to replace management. That isn't what the Sphinx is about, sir. That is a route you could go down yourself by putting some discreet pressure on certain disaffected investors, perhaps through your City Minister who seems very fond of telling everyone how to run their business. There is more you can do from your position than you might think. But we have something else in mind.'

Doyle leaned forward and spoke quietly to Singh for perhaps twenty minutes without interruption.

Finally he concluded with the words: 'To make progress with this we may need some help. I don't want to go down this route without some cover from you sir. The trade off is that UK plc might through partnership with us acquire a uniquely valuable position in these new assets.'

'Something of a Faustian pact, Doyle, if you don't mind me saying so.'

'Yes, Prime Minister.'

Chapter 8

ARABIAN NIGHT

The stench and heat were indescribable. Doyle, wearing nothing but shorts and t shirt and trainers, followed Tony Dyer's torch which flickered over the concrete beams, tunnels and pathways of one of Riyadh's main sewers. Out in front of Dyer Ali Koury and his team quietly picked their way forward.

Doyle watched Dyer's muscle packed frame, constantly amazed that such a powerful man could have such a light tread. Dyer was highly intelligent with unexpected linguistic skills, but had a history of violence and alcoholism. He had been cashiered out of the Army for beating an Iraqi to pulp after one of his best mates had been shot in a sweep through some Basrah backstreets. With two failed marriages behind him before he was thirty, Dyer was now stable, with an older partner and was the key member of Doyle's security team.

Kouri had been sprung by a combination of Dyer's team and the Mahdi Mahdi security section from the high security private house in which he had been held. The Mahdi team had had a contact there working as a member of the domestic staff who had provided an accurate picture of the internal lay out, the room where Koury was held and the movements and rotations of the guards. Two of the guards had been laid out after they had gone off duty and had been substituted by Mahdi Mahdi team members who had tear gassed the entire house when they returned on the next shift and, using oxygen masks, escaped with Koury.

The party had gone through the sewers for about a kilometre before the leaders halted and Ali Koury called them together for a briefing.

'We are now close to the palace. We have had a rough listening post in this palace for years. It's been good enough to pick up snippets from meetings and casual conversation. But in the last week Dyer and his team have installed a state of the art web cam system which is focussed on the large room they use for the cabinet meetings held here. The sound quality is extraordinary. Unfortunately because of the distances and the amount of concrete around in these sewers and foundations we cannot get remote transmission at any distance so we have built a listening and viewing post in part of the original lower basement of the house next to the palace which happens to be owned by my brother in law. You will be pleased to know that it also smells better than this.'

Doyle was relieved. Conditions in the sewers were appalling. He put it down to a combination of the Riyadh heat and the spicy diet enjoyed by its inhabitants.

They clambered up some steps, through a couple of heavily re-inforced and apparently soundproof wooden doors and into a hot and dusty room about twelve foot square. There was some makeshift seating, a large wall mounted plasma screen and about a dozen sets of Senna headphones cabled into a stack of audio visual amplifiers and tuners. One of Ali Koury's team busied himself making Arabic coffee in a small kitchenette just off the main room. Koury told them there was a toilet in a small room off the listening post if anyone needed it. A last unpleasant whiff assailed Doyle; he thought that a toilet was something of a superfluous facility given the proximity of one of the largest sewers in the Middle East.

Dyer switched on the camera system. The screen glowed and seconds later an amazing sight greeted them.

As Dyer wielded the remote control, and as the camera panned round it disclosed an enormous room lit by floor to ceiling mullioned windows across which heavy net curtains had been drawn — probably bullet proof, Doyle thought. Some daylight filtered in but the main illumination came from pools of light from a large number of antique standard lamps and chandeliers. Those walls of the room not decorated with tapestries depicting desert landscapes and Bedouin life were covered with the most exquisite oak panelling carved with classic Islamic motifs. The floor was covered by one of the largest Persian carpets Doyle had ever seen. There were about half a dozen low settees around the periphery of the room on which the most richly decorated silk cushions were scattered. Many bronzes were displayed on chests and tables spread around between the settees, mostly abstract but some distinctly erotic while others depicted racehorses. Doyle thought they were pretty accurate representations of the principal obsessions of their owners; he was also amused to see that Islamic rejection of representational art appeared to have little currency among the top strata of Saudi society.

In the main window bay, gathered round a huge oval table inlaid with every conceivable variety of rare tropical hardwood, were the Saudi Chief Minister, the Saudi Finance Minister, Persia's former lover – the Energy Minister – together with half a dozen officials. The ministers were all dressed in Arab robes and all wore sunglasses. Unnecessary dark glasses were a particular bugbear of Doyle's; he pondered that this must either be sheer force of habit or borne from a desire to conceal their emotions. In contrast the officials were in their thirties and were dressed in immaculate business suits, they all looked like products of American business schools.

Dyer explained that half the headphones were equipped with a simultaneous translation facility. Koury's had a transmitting facility so that he could interject comments as the party watched. The plasma screen showed the Chief Minister urging his colleagues to take their seats and the watchers in the cellar room all donned their headphones as they did so.

Suddenly the buzz of conversation coming through the phones ceased and the seated party round the great table stood up. A party of three entered the room. Ali Koury looked excited and in a whisper said: 'It's the King, and two of his brother's sons. That's unprecedented. It means this must be a really unusual and important meeting.'

Elaborate greetings were exchanged and the King and the two sons took seats opposite the Ministers. The lights were dimmed and a very large screen rose from the far end of the table.

The Chief Minster welcomed the Royal Party and went on to address the meeting as a whole.

'Gentlemen, as you all know we have an annual summit to review our oil industry and its prospects, the wider global oil supply and demand balance and the interaction with that of OPEC and our own relationship with OPEC. For many years now Saudi has been the backbone of Middle East oil production and the Middle East in turn has been the most important component of global oil supply. Gentlemen, that situation is about to change most dramatically with untold consequences for our economy and our people; on an international scale what is about to happen is also likely to cause a most profound global slump. As you know we have been pumping our main fields relentlessly for upwards of seventy years. As time has gone on we have to use more and more devices to maintain the flows of these old fields, principally ever increasing water injection but also many other techniques. The rest of the world has always speculated that this cannot be maintained. Yet for years we have managed to maintain and indeed increase production as needed to cater for global growth; for years we have confounded the pessimists, and, I think I can say,' this with a glance towards the King, 'that we can be proud of the consistent and statesmanlike way in which our oil industry has served both our country and the global economy and the work of Allah. Allah be praised.

But, as you also know, despite much expenditure and persistent exploration effort over many years we have not succeeded in finding new producing fields remotely on the scale of fields such as Ghawar. The legendary American investor Warren Buffett once coined a phrase – 'when the tide goes out you find out who has been wearing no clothes' — well, gentlemen, our oil tide is about to go out and we risk swimming naked.'

He pressed a button and a servant motioned a truly extraordinary looking man into the room. He was about six foot four inches tall, broad to match, but looked incredibly muscled and fit. His tanned face seemed to be hewn out of some kind of deep brown granite and his piercing blue eyes to have spent a lifetime shading themselves from the glare of the sun. That face was creased into a smile – as well it might be – for Hank Harriman was the highest paid oil consultant in the world. He wore cowboy clothes, cowboy boots and carried a large cream Stetson hat. A huge hand held a large Cuban cigar whose blue fumes slowly rose and lazily wrapped themselves round the chandeliers in the centre of the room. With a regretful look he parked the cigar on the edge of an ash tray made out of an old howitzer shell case and began to speak.

'Good morning gentlemen.' The massive confidence of his Texan drawl radiated through the old room.

'May I introduce Hank Harriman, everybody,' said the Chief Minister. 'He has been our lead oil consultant for the last twenty years and a very good friend of Saudi Arabia.'

'Pleased to be of service,' drawled the Texan, bowing to the Royal party.

He motioned one of the young men.

'Gentlemen,' he began, 'it's been my privilege to advise you folk for many years. I like you people, you've treated me well, and I don't enjoy telling you what I've got to tell you. I've been telling you plainly for the last five years that you will have a problem and now its time has come.'

'This slide' — he extended a long arm toward it- 'shows the rolling average monthly production of each of your top six producing fields, which together have produced about seventy per cent of Saudi output for as long as records show. As you know we have been using every tool in the box to maintain those outputs but in very recent months we have been struggling more and more, first at Ghawar and then one by one in the other main fields. We have tried everything we know but the truth is these fields are quite rapidly coming to the end of their economic lives. There is still oil there but the cost of injecting water on a sufficient scale to pump it out and the resultant chronically high water content are simply un-economic. It is really bad luck — and quite un-expected – for all these fields to exhibit the same sharply declining output at more or less the same time but that is what has occurred.

When something like this happens to a field the rate of decline is not gradual — it is sudden — and the recent weekly statistics on the next slide show what I mean. And finally we have tabled a projection of Saudi output over the next twelve months. You will see that it is projected to reduce by twenty per cent over that time and then de-cline by a further fifty per cent over the follow-ing twenty four months. Gentlemen, you stand to lose nearly two thirds of all oil revenue within three years. Any questions?'

The King spoke.

'Mr Harriman we have been deeply grateful to you for your work on our behalf. I have two questions. Firstly the world will surely tell us we must have seen this coming, and blame us for it. And secondly is there nothing we can do?'

'I can help with the first of those, your Highness. It is absolutely inevitable that fields eventually run out or at least become sub – economic. Every-one realises this will eventually happen here. But we have been almost too successful in massag-ing the rate of slowdown, and putting back the onset of a serious decline. When that happens, as it now has, it will, as a result, be even more of a shock to the world at large. You are of course uniquely unlucky that all your major fields have run into the last stage of life at the same time.'

'Allah is angry with us,' murmured the King, twisting a heavy set of ornate worry beads on his lap.

'As to your second question I'm afraid there is nothing more that can be done, your Highness.'

'Your only choice is to explore outside of Saudi Arabia. I truly do not believe that there are more large oil fields to be found here. You have explored as thoroughly as is humanly possible. But there are many possibilities elsewhere. However to take advantage of them you would have to re-orientate your thinking and resources in a way which would be completely unfamiliar to you.'

Hank Harriman recovered his now defunct cigar from the lip of the old brass shell case and waited for further questions.

The King said :' Thank you Mr Harriman, your advice is welcome.' After Harriman was shown out, the King turned to the Chief Minister, and asked: 'What are the implications of these developments?'

'They are very grave, Your Highness. I need hardly spell out the economic implications for us and for the rest of the world. We need to grapple with these but they are not for this meeting. The most important issue we have to focus on now is that in the very near future we will need to make some kind of announcement about our situation to the world at large. To date we have managed to conceal the production shortfalls through over pumping the newer fields and with the help of our friends in OPEC. But,' he turned to the Energy Minister, 'we have had discussions with them as to the long term prospects and there is no way they can in increase production over the long term to compensate for our shortfalls. For years the West has been cynical about our true reserve position and we have managed to preserve a united and confident front; the sudden loss of production on this scale could mean a very significant loss of face and credibility for us, a great pity given the high reputation we have patiently amassed over the last decades.

In fact this is such a serious issue that I have taken the step of asking one of London's top public relations advisers to give us his views. You may be open with him gentlemen, he has the trust of many of the world's top business people.'

An energetic, vital dark haired man of medium height in his early fifties entered the room and smiled at the party.

'Gentlemen, this is Roderick Maguire who is founder and senior partner of Cataclysm

Reputation Management. Mr Maguire, you had the opportunity via the screen in the annex outside to follow our discussion so far?'

'Perfectly, thank you, Chief Minister,' said Maguire bowing to the Royal Party. He continued: 'I appreciate being asked to advise you. May I say, first of all, that I think you have shown great wisdom and foresight in seeking such advice. History shows – most recently with our banker friends – that when society is disadvantaged in a major way by one group within it that it tends to lash out wildly at that group without much discernment.

The one thing you must do here to minimise the risk of a similar response is to avoid dropping the equivalent of a nuclear bomb on public opinion. What I mean is that any initial announcement must be low key. I would favour something along the lines of encountering a slowdown in production in one or may be two fields, a technical task force allocated to look at all means possible to restore production, and finally OPEC examining ways of a compensating step up in their production.

Then as the months elapse I recommend you make further announcements to the effect that more fields have become affected, that technical measures have not worked as well as had been hoped and that OPEC has struggled to compensate.

After about a year the whole story will have unfolded but of course many people will have adjusted their expectations long before.

But a slow release mechanism will pre-empt embarrassing charges of having deceived oil consumers, covered up information and created the most violent shock to market and economic sentiment that the world would ever have seen.'

'Thank you, Mr Maguire,' said the Chief Minister. 'Does anyone have any questions or comments on that advice?'

No one had.

The King and the two sons rose.

'I am content that we have the position under control', said the King. 'Keep me informed.'

He shook hands with his Ministers and swept out of the room. Maguire was dismissed. The Chief Minister summed up briefly, and said he would organise some follow up meetings. Coffee was brought in and the conversation became broken up and general.

Dyer switched off the equipment and gave Doyle a memory card.

'Guard it with your life, there aren't too many copies.'

Well, thanks everyone', said Doyle, 'that was a really fantastic show.'

'Now,' he went on, 'the really hard part starts. I'm out of here. I want the rest of you to clear up and for Tony and his team to take the next flight out. As that team was all blacked up and disguised I don't think anyone saw their faces in the raid which got Ali out and they've been underground a lot of the time since then. Ali, you will have to lie low, I'm afraid, until they decide it's not worth hounding you any more.'

With the memory stick taped firmly to his abdomen Doyle began to hurry back down the sewers, one of Koury's men preceding him. He felt the air tasted a little sweeter this time. He wanted to speak to Fleming on the satellite phone, wanted to steam clean himself in the shower, and wanted to get out of Saudi before the Saudi authorities worked out that he was in it. He had actually arrived by borrowing a helicopter ride to the US air base from one of his Texaco friends working on a rig offshore, and had then taken a taxi to a backstreet flat in central Riyadh owned by a friend of Koury's.

Back in that flat he completed his tasks, giving Matthew an agreed set of codes for a huge raft of trades for his personal accounts. He instructed Matthew to send an encoded message to the Sphinx which read as follows;

'We have to move very fast. We have full conclusive proof. Announcement soon. I need to make an immediate draw down of ten billion sterling to support the agreed range of positions. My trades will be rolled into yours on a pro rata basis if you confirm, otherwise they will be stand alone.'

He told Matthew to take his time getting the trades on –he didn't want any noise in the market before they were all complete.

Doyle called a taxi. When it arrived in the street below he called Chuck who had the plane at an air base in neighbouring Abu Dhabi and said he would be airborne in minutes.

In the taxi he leaned back and reflected. In his wildest dreams he could not have imagined such a stark trigger of a massive change in global economic conditions. The speed of the Saudi production collapse would be beyond the comprehension of any investor, however sophisticated, and however it was massaged by the flamboyant Mr Maguire.

What was going to happen was an economic shock equivalent to Hiroshima.

The Sphinx were the only group of investors — apart from the Saudi's of course — able to use this knowledge; knowledge which could make the Sphinx profits of tens if not hundreds of billions.

But the Sphinx partnership had some unusual provisions. On any trade a proportion of profit made above a certain percentage return on capital was ceded to the Sphinx Foundation and this proportion increased geometrically as returns rose.

Doyle speculated that the ironic effect of the incipient melt down could be to make the

Sphinx Foundation one of the largest of its type. As with all investment it was, in the short term, a zero sum game, a simple mechanism for transferring wealth from the smart to the less smart.

Was it smart? he reflected. Or did it simply prove the old saying, 'All sensible investment is done with the benefit of inside information, all other investment is pure speculation.'

He just needed to get out of Saudi now.

Suddenly he stiffened. The taxi driver had been consulting his rear view mirror with increasing frequency and now he gesticulated to Doyle and muttered something in Arabic about 'police'. Doyle swivelled round and saw two black Toyota Landcruisers with police markings about fifty metres behind them. Doyle switched his Blackberry to the GPS function; the US base was about five kilometres away, very close to the end of the smart suburbs presently on either side of them. He speed dialled Chuck on his satellite phone.

He could hear the low rumble of the Blackbird engines behind Chuck's muffled response.

'Yes, boss, what is it?' Chuck was laconic but Doyle sensed his tension.

'Things are getting a bit hot here. I'm about twenty minutes away and need to really run when I get there.'

'On the ground in five, boss, no worries. I'll brief my mates at the base.'

Doyle got the base commander on the phone. He was sympathetic but cautious. The last thing he wanted was to be seen to be helping adventurers who seemed to have fallen foul of local police but he was equally conscious of the extraordinary support Doyle seemed to attract at the highest levels at home.

Suddenly one of the Landcruisers pulled in front of the taxi with its lights flashing, while the other closed up behind. Doyle caught a glimpse of at least four police officers in each vehicle. He tensed –this was not going to be easy.

Doyle's driver started to gibber with concern. Doyle told him to slow down and stop. Doyle opened a compartment in his case and removed two large tear gas canisters and a can of CS spray. He extracted his gun from its shoulder holster under his jacket and swiftly changed the clip.

The taxi stopped. Men jumped out of the Landcruisers and swarmed round it. They ordered the taxi driver to get out of the car and approached its near side rear door, gesticulating at Doyle to get out.

Doyle looked relaxed. He had locked the door. He opened the window two inches and chucked out an activated tear gas sachet. He swiftly crossed the back seat and opened the off side door, using it as a shield. He took careful aim at the offside rear tyre of the Landcruiser in front which exploded in a cloud of dust. He repeated the exercise with the front tyre of the Landcruiser behind. The tear gas had created havoc on the far side of the taxi. Two of the remaining police rushed at him. He pulled out the CS spray canister and shoved it in their faces and they collapsed at his feet. He slid into the front seat of the taxi praying that the driver had left the keys in the ignition. He had. He tossed two more tear gas sachets out of the passenger door window, started the engine and roared up the road. Something clanged very loudly off the boot of the taxi.

He hoped any police reinforcements were some distance away. Minutes later he swept into the base noting with satisfaction the elaborate security pantomime the commander had laid on to deal with the police. He briefly stopped at the checkpoint, explained the position to the adjutant and was waved on.

The Blackbird was right at the end of the runway. A long lightweight ladder was propped against the cockpit coaming. A US air force jeep was drawn up below the plane with a couple of airmen lounging by it.

Doyle drove the taxi up to the ladder, grabbed his cases and climbed up. The Americans grinned and one of them said, removing the ladder: 'Bit of a hurry today, eh sir?'

Doyle smiled down at him and nodded.

'Do me a favour and take the cab back will you mate,' Doyle shouted.

Then the familiar deep roar of the Blackbird engines drowned out all his thoughts and emotions.

The Blackbird shot off into the shimmering afternoon haze, banking so steeply that Doyle nearly blacked out, and went into a near vertical climb.

'Think they'll put anything up, boss?' Chuck grunted, who was clearly enjoying the opportunity to run the plane at full chat.

'I can't see them getting very far,' said Doyle, for the first time feeling that he was not going to disappear through the back of his seat as at fifty thousand feet and two thousand knots Chuck eased the Blackbird into a more gentle climb, 'but let's get out of their airspace as fast as we can.'

'Yes, boss.'

Doyle leaned back and tried to compose his thoughts. This second Saudi episode had not been helpful — nor had the first. He hated leaving a mess. He could see the Americans becoming exercised about the diplomatic repercussions. He was going to have to cultivate some more goodwill in the structuring of the Sphinx deal to recover lost ground. At least he hadn't killed anyone — unless that tear gas was stronger than he thought.

What concerned him was what had put the secret police on to him in the first place. First 'Heaven's Gate' — he grimaced — and now this.

A crackling of the intercom cut into his thoughts.

'Something on the radar, boss,' muttered Chuck.

'Where? '

'Ahead and below – about fifty miles away.'

'What's our closing speed?'

'That's the funny thing, boss, there isn't any.'

'Don't be silly Chuck, there has to be,' said Doyle.

'I'm not sure, boss. One of the guys at the base was saying that the US have lent the Saudi's one of the new generation of spy planes which re-placed these, just to have a look at.'

'With an American pilot I assume, Chuck.'

'Of course, boss.' Chuck thought only Ameri-cans could possibly fly something like a Blackbird.

Doyle swore.

'How far to the border, Chuck?'

'Just over five hundred miles.'

That would have sounded bad to most peo-ple but to Doyle it meant fifteen minutes even at their current speed.

'Chuck,' said Doyle, 'what do these new planes do?'

'Nearly Mach three point eight. Just over two and a half thousand knots boss. They have uprated engines and the latest ceramic technology on the leading edges.'

'What's our ceiling height?'

'Ninety thousand.'

Doyle knew that his heavily modified plane, with the twin sets of after burners and additional ram jet could nearly match this speed for a short period. The radio started to crackle.

'It's the Saudi's sir, want to escort us down.'

Doyle thought rapidly. He had promised the Americans not to use his radar jamming it unless absolutely necessary.

He decided that this was one of those occasions. He really didn't want to be found in possession of the Royal Palace memory card. He thought, very briefly, of Saudi gaols.

'Put on the radar jammer and take her up to ninety thousand feet with the second afterburners.'

'Ok, boss. We will have to watch our range if we use them for longer than a few minutes.'

There was a truly deafening roar and a jolt as the twin afterburners flared into life. Doyle watched fascinated as the plane angled into a steep climb and the altimeter and air speed indicator flickered upwards.

Christ, this thing was powerful, he muttered to himself under his breath.

The universe seemed to shrink as a layered kaleidoscope of colours rotated endlessly before him, each layer in turn sharpening and magnifying before receding and another effortlessly sliding into its place. The radio went silent and the radar blanked out. They were flying flat out in a total communications black hole.

Doyle hoped they wouldn't drop off the end of the world.

'That'll do, Chuck. Level her out and bring the speed down to Mach three. Leave the jamming on for five more minutes.' The plane levelled out and the background roar receded. A few minutes later the instruments flickered back into life.

The radar glowed again.

'Any sign, Chuck?' said Doyle.

'Seems to be heading back, boss.'

Just over an hour later they were in Northolt.

Chapter 9

ALEXANDER LUTIN

Viktor Bezkov, head of oil and gas trading at Petrogaz, stared moodily out of his window at the park below. Spring was still several weeks away and the remains of the last heavy snowfall of winter glistened in the feeble sunshine.

There was a knock on his door. Bezkov said 'come' and his senior dealer walked in.

Bezkov offered him a cigarette – there was no Western nonsense in Russian offices about not smoking.

'Well, Roman, what is it?' asked Bezkov pleasantly.

Roman Borletti, a thirty year old Italian who had moved to Moscow when he married a Russian girl three years before, and who had previously worked in the same capacity for the great Italian utility ENI, did not answer at first but looked calmly at Bezkov.

'There has been huge buying of spot oil and the near term oil future in London,' he said.

'The price has edged up from thirty five to thirty seven dollars.'

'Who?' asked Bezkov simply.

'It's been coming from London brokers, principally Berri Bros.'

'But why?' queried Bezkov, 'and who's really behind it?'

Bezkov was puzzled. The world was still in recession. Oil demand had been in reverse.

Borletti drifted his smoke up to the ceiling.

'It's only rumour at this stage. But some say it's that investment vehicle backed by a few major hedge funds in the UK and US — they have runs at things from time to time. Have you ever heard of the Sphinx partnership?'

'No' said Bezkov uncertainly. But something had stirred in the back of his mind.

'But, again, why?' he said again to Roman. 'There isn't even a sign of a floor being reached in the global economy.'

Borletti again evaded the question.

'Another interesting thing is that the trading volumes have been huge, and all the trades have been on an ultra thin margin. According to my sources at Berri it's all been done on a very highly leveraged basis.' Roman threw his cigarette but into the bin beside him.

Bezkov thought to himself that these were the trades of someone who knew something, or at least had an unusually high level of conviction.

Bezkov's phone rang. He listened intently. His normally impassive face gradually became more animated. Finally he spoke.

'Yes, thanks, very helpful. Yes, that too, very puzzled by it.'

He turned to Roman.

'That was my counterpart in Total, Francois Berthon. He has also seen the volumes in the spot markets. But,' Bezkov leaned forward and jabbed a sheaf of contract notes at Borletti, 'they have also noticed a tightening of physical supply, which they think is coming out of Saudi.'

'But the Saudi's only recently agreed with OPEC to maintain volumes,' objected Roman.

'And the other thing,' said Roman, looking pleased with himself at his element of surprise, 'is that the six and twelve month futures have been sold off and are looking much weaker.'

Viktor Bezkov was now extremely puzzled. This was a pattern of trading he had never seen before. Short term speculation in spot oil was usually in response to short term shocks such as Middle East political instability — and that was no worse than usual. The story about Saudi production shortfalls seemed incredible — those guys had delivered solidly for fifty years and had some of the best technologists in the business running their kit. Anyway they had a spread of giant fields. It was inconceivable for them to experience a material level of production volatility. Finally the weakness in the longer term future suggested that these traders – if they were the same people, Bezkov's brow furrowed – believed that short supply would be temporary. Yet economic recovery was round the corner and Bezkov thought you could go to a thousand people before you found one who thought that that would not put up the oil price over a period of several years.

He got to his feet.

'OK, thanks, Roman,' he said,' I'll do some more digging and then I'd better take this stuff to Karlkoff.'

Three hours later Bezkov and the Chairman of Petrogaz were lingering over coffee in a basement restaurant round the corner from the Petrogaz office.

Karlkoff's face betrayed his concerns,

'Unless we can find out the basis for these deals we cannot position our own trading. Do you think we have reached the limit of intelligence we can get from the market?'

'Everyone's asking the same questions, Dimitri,' said Bezkov, 'whether they are in New York, Rome or London. And no one's got the answers.'

Later that afternoon Karlkoff was taking tea with Mordakov and Orlov. Delicate bone china cups of Lapsang Souchong were perched on the round glass table between them.

Orlov spoke.

'I don't need to remind you gentlemen about the parlous state of the Russian economy. We have endured oil prices which scarcely cover our production costs. We have cut back maintenance because of cash flow pressures and that has resulted in a further drop in production and national income. Going back to our previous conversation, we have been unable to find serious new oil fields, either in Russia itself, or,' he coughed discreetly, 'in our so called satellite states.

The resultant economic and social instability,' Orlov continued heavily, his eyes cold, 'is resulting in some serious political strains. Now we find that we are unaware of potential future events of which our speculative friends in the West are apparently firmly convinced.

It's not good enough, gentlemen.

Karlkoff, you have offered some potential explanations for all this. But let us cast our minds further afield. Let us suppose not that there is some temporary glitch in Saudi production but rather a systemic decline. After all we have long been suspicious of their claimed reserve levels. That would be good news for Russia. Conversely the trade causing the weakness in the longer term future could be speculation on the development of a very large new oil resource which would outweigh even the Saudi problems and be sufficient to cope with future economic growth. That would be bad news for Russia, unless of course we were clever enough to involve ourselves in that resource in some way.'

Karlkoff and Mordakov looked discomforted. Experience had told them that Julius Orlov was very often one jump ahead.

Orlov drained his cup. 'My friends,' he said, 'you had better find out the answer to these questions, quickly.'

He watched with amusement as spasms of concern flitted across the faces of his colleagues.

'That's the bad news,' he said. 'The good news is that I am going to help you as you have clearly reached the limits of your capabilities.'

He pressed a buzzer on his intercom and as it crackled into life he said into it, 'Send in Alexander Lutin, will you.'

Lutin looked in all respects like an archetypal international investment banker. He was thirty five, sandy haired, stood just under six feet, with a slim build. He had wide set eyes, a ready smile and an air of easy self confidence. He was immaculately dressed in a two piece Richard James dark blue pinstripe, cream silk shirt, and dark blue Italian silk tie. His shoes were handmade Cleverly's.

A close observer would have noticed that his eyes were an extraordinary shade of violet and that they didn't smile as much as his mouth, that his skin had a distinctly Mediterranean colouring and would have remarked on the scar running under his left jaw line. The son of a Russian father and Lebanese mother he had lived in Beirut until the age of thirteen when he had gone to Eton, followed by Oxford and Harvard. He had read Arabic and Mathematics at Oxford and spoke six languages. Thereafter he had been recruited into investment banking, first on the commodity side at Morgan Stanley, then in mergers and acquisitions at Lehman. He had wound up at the age of thirty in the Saint Petersburg Bank, where for the last couple of years he had been Chairman of its London operations.

During this period Alexander had been recruited into Russian intelligence and received training at the highest level. He was a brilliant shot with almost any weapon, a trained killer with particular expertise in chemical killing, a computer software expert and, going back to his investment banking role, was a considerable expert on commodity trading with a speciality in oil and gas.

Lutin was a well established figure in London banking and social circles. He was a member of White's, he raced old Aston Martins, he was a habitué of many leading shoots, and appeared infrequently but with careful calculation in the London gossip columns. More than anything he was a well known lady killer. There had been the odd whiff of sexual scandal, said to involve some unusual practices, but these stories were always swiftly repressed and, if anything, added to the aura surrounding him.

Over the years Lutin had become almost a second son to Julius Orlov, who had no children of his own. The two shared many intellectual interests, the same deep rooted appreciation of Russian culture and history, the same ambitions for the country, and above all the same cold emotional detachment from the sometimes distasteful practical realities required to realise those ambitions.

Lutin, although nominally responsible to the Head of the FSB in Moscow, possessed a significant autonomy in London under the patronage of Orlov. Orlov used him for a variety of tasks, mostly intelligence gathering at the senior levels of British politics and business. But there had been other assignments.

There had been the unexplained death of the controversial oligarch Egorov in a car crash – his Mercedes had been completely destroyed in an explosion on the M1 while he was travelling at a hundred miles per hour. Another was the horrific death by radiation poisoning of a maverick Russian journalist, Anna Safina, all the more shocking as it appeared to have occurred in a famous London restaurant.

Orlov visited London more frequently than many people, including British officials, appreciated, and he regularly stayed at Lutin's town house on Cheyne Walk where Lutin had equipped himself with a Ramsay trained chef and an excellent wine cellar.

'Good morning Alexander,' said Orlov cheerfully, 'are you enjoying your stay in Moscow?'

Lutin smiled and replied that as ever he was glad to be on Russian soil and that at least his trip had helped keep one or two of his girlfriends in Moscow from becoming too restless.

'Alexander,' Orlov lit a cigarette the offer of which Lutin refused, 'have you ever heard of the Sphinx partnership?'

'Yes, of course, it's a partnership of some London and New York hedge funds which focuses on extracting significant value from certain one off situations. Probably the closest comparison would be Maxos but of course the Sphinx only operates on discrete projects and doesn't have a permanently drawn fund.'

'Who is the moving force behind it?' asked Orlov.

'Ah, well, there you have a very interesting man. James Doyle. He moves in some of the same circles as I do, but,' Lutin laughed in a self deprecatory way, 'rather like me I suspect that he is not quite exactly what he seems.'

'What do you mean?' interjected Mordakov, puzzled.

'Well, nominally he runs the Sphinx which from time to time draws funds from its backers and takes extremely highly leveraged positions based on Doyle's extensive intelligence systems. But Doyle is more than a financial adventurer. He has done some special work for the US government who regard him very highly and he has a coterie of freelance people with a wide range of skills who he can pull together for different assignments.'

'I'm still not clear what he does,' muttered Mordakov.

'I don't know all of it, certainly,' said Lutin, 'but I do know that it has included putting together a uranium corner for the US Government, some work sorting out the leadership of one or two African states and he has dealt with one or two high profile kidnap situations. But you never see the Sphinx or Doyle visibly linked to any of this stuff. Doyle also has big philanthropic interests. All in all he is a very difficult guy to pigeon hole.'

Orlov knew all this from an earlier breakfast he had had with Lutin. 'Now,' he said briskly, 'Alexander, we need you to get to the bottom of what the Sphinx are doing at the moment and why. There is a full report on your desk dealing with current trading and rumours in the oil market. The reasons we need to know more are obvious; we think there is something — or things – going on, which are pretty big in the oil world and of great significance for Russia and how it positions itself. In particular if the rumours of a major new oil find are right we need to evaluate how we can involve ourselves in it. You report directly to me on this.'

Alexander Lutin caught the 7pm British Airways flight to Heathrow and from there was driven to his house in Cheyne Walk.

Next day he was at his Saint Petersburg city office at 9am. He was immaculately attired in a Timothy Everest single breasted suit in chalk grey pinstripe, a Turnbull and Asser shirt and Berluti shoes. He wore a very rare antique Tissot.

He told his personal assistant to get a list of all the hedge funds known to have supported the Sphinx and to obtain from the UK regulators a list of people working for them. Then Lutin settled down to the report which Orlov had left for him. After several minutes he lit a Balkan Sobranie – his family had bought the factory and still made its products to private order – and watched the blue smoke drift up to the elegant plasterwork above his desk.

Lutin flicked the pages of the report. Two things really interested him. The first was the size of the positions. They were many times greater than even the larger hedge funds would have contemplated, even allowing for several funds being involved. He drew slowly on his Sobranie. He wondered idly which prime broker — the intermediary who provide the derivative instruments and debt to hedge funds and who executed their transactions – was behind the Sphinx. The second feature which attracted his attention was the asymmetrical nature of the trades. The short future position was many times smaller than the very large long spot and near term future position. Lutin was puzzled. The first, very large, position was clearly one put on by people who were extremely sure of their ground. They knew something, thought Lutin, and they knew something big. Lutin was inclined to believe the rumours about a weakening in Saudi supplies. As to the alternative theory of incipient political instability he didn't really see how the risk would repay trades of this size; if a really major Middle East spat — nuclear based? — broke out all bets would be off as far as economic recovery was concerned. And a simply minor affray wouldn't produce enough impact on the oil price to justify trades on this scale.

Yet, Lutin reflected, the second, short position, although much smaller, was extremely dangerous. If the oil price continued to rise, rather than a fall which was the apparent assumption behind the trades, the Sphinx could be exposed to loss without limit. Lutin reflected that long term rises in the price of oil had to be a default assumption for any oil trader; no one thought the global economy would move away from oil dependency that quickly and the recession seemed to be coming to an end. Moreover many other factors could unzip that short trade – instability in the Middle East for example. Again, he concluded, the Sphinx had to know something big to justify putting that trade on, and the more Lutin thought about it the more he felt it had to be a major source of new oil supply. Yet he remained puzzled. A new find on this scale would have had to be announced by any company with a stock market listing. He supposed it might have been a find made by an unlisted state owned oil company, but, even so, many of those would have listed partners.

He stubbed out his Sobranie, and, exceptionally, lit another.

There were clearly, potentially, two independent pieces of new information, but the Sphinx was obviously much more confident of the one supporting the long position. But what was increasingly clear was that both trades were based on information that the Sphinx had found out for itself and which could not easily be accessed by others. Even this conclusion bewildered Lutin. How was it conceivable that a bunch of hedge fund managers had somehow made an oil find the like of which the rest of the world had not seen in fifty years? And how was it possible that the same people had somehow penetrated the deepest secrets of Saudi reserves, over which in recent years a thicker and thicker veil had been drawn?

His personal assistant brought in a tray of coffee, and said she hoped to have the information he needed by lunchtime. Lutin smiled at her. Girls. His mind ran free.

Suddenly he sat up and removed his feet from the desk. The other day, he remembered, had he not met a girl who worked for the Sphinx? How could he have overlooked this? She had been with Arianna Loizou, the wife of one of his shipping clients. What had been her name? Rebecca something? He racked his brains. How had she reacted to him? He cast his mind back. She had been tall, statuesque even, blonde, with very striking blue green eyes and a wide inviting mouth. He recalled a tight fitting black skirt, cream blouse and a most inviting posterior. He could feel his interest stirring. Had there been a point of common interest? Ah, yes, Italian food.

Her mother had lived in Italy for several years. He returned to the key question. Had there been some chemistry? He was sure of it, had there not been a lingering touch on the arm?

He called Arianna on his Blackberry and within seconds had Rebecca Malone's mobile number.

A voice with an immediately beguiling Irish brogue responded immediately.

'Rebecca', Lutin smoothed, 'it's Alexander Lutin here. We met the other day when you were with Arianna, do you remember?'

Did he detect a slight eagerness in her affirmation?

'I was wondering if you would like dinner?'

'Yes, anytime, even tonight if you were free,' said Lutin.

'You would? That's splendid. Listen, I'm right next door to Ceccolios — I think you mentioned you were fond of Italian food? Come and have a drink at my house first — say seven thirty? I'll send my car for you — you're where? Dolphin Square? He'll be there at seven fifteen; you're at number ninety, you said? I'm looking forward to it very much.'

Lutin sat back, buzzed his secretary to book the restaurant and asked her to find out all she could about Rebecca.

Lutin then invited himself round to Len Kravitz at Berri Brothers; fortunately Saint Petersburg was, in its proprietary trading activities, quite a significant user of Berri's so Lutin knew Len well enough to get a least a moderately respectful reception.

Len Kravitz had been a trader for thirty five of his fifty two years. Even now he had an alertness and a poise which belied his years but his grey-ing temples and lined face betrayed a sagacity burned in by years of tension, anticipation, disaster and relief endured in the trading trenches at Ralli Bros, Merrills, Goldman's and finally Berri's.

Len didn't particularly like Lutin and he certainly didn't trust him.

'What can I do for you mate?' Len breezed as he shook Lutin's hand and gesticulated towards the coffee.

Lutin knew that he had a difficult hand to play. Simple inquisitiveness about the Sphinx wasn't going to get him very far.

Lutin decided to lead with his most alluring cards.

'I've had a meeting recently with Julius Orlov and Alexei Mordakov,' he began smoothly. 'They are trying to make sense what is happening in the oil markets and so far our normal counter-parties haven't managed to shed much light.'

Out of the corner of his eye Lutin saw Kravitz slightly alter his posture and some of the cocki-ness drained almost imperceptibly from his face.

Lutin decided to consolidate his gains. Berri's only did Saint Petersburg business; they had no share of the really big volumes traded by Petrogaz.

'The recent weakness in the nine and twelve month future is causing the Russian State very serious concern. You know, Len, that the whole Russian economy is underpinned by oil and gas revenues. We simply can't understand how these futures can be so weak when everyone expects an economic recovery. Obviously we are concerned less about the big long spot position, but we are still very curious about the genesis of it.'

Kravitz's features seemed to grow craggier by the minute.

'Obviously our conclusion is that the short position has been taken as a punt on a renewed global recession possibly generated by some large scale military conflict,' continued Lutin, 'and that might fit with both trades.'

Kravitz's face betrayed an internal struggle. He poured some more coffee for both men and took a gulp. He seemed to come to some kind of personal resolution.

'As, you know, Alexander,' he said, 'we are execution only prime brokers. We don't trade on our own account nor do we have much insight into the thought processes which drive our client's positions.'

'Could you give me some insight into the pattern of trading,' asked Lutin quietly. 'Is it the product of a large number of different traders or is it down to one?'

'More of the latter, Alexander,' muttered Kravitz grudgingly.

'It must be an enormously leveraged position for one trader, Len. I can't imagine who would have the balls to put it on — could be Maxos, I suppose,' Lutin hypothesised.

'They are some of the biggest trades I've ever seen,' admitted Kravitz.

'It's hard to see who could have that level of conviction outside of major oil companies and they mostly have disclosure obligations,' pursued Lutin.

Kravitz nodded. Lutin had got something.

'Most of the hedge funds are pretty bombed out after the last three years and I can't see them stepping out on a risk of this size,' said Lutin, 'I suppose there are a few who still take exceptional positions.'

'Yes, there are,' Kravitz stonewalled.

'Well, Len, thanks for the chat and the coffee. I'll let the powers that be know you've been helpful.'

Kravitz allowed himself to relax.

'Nice to see you, Alexander. Give us some business, we all need it.'

Becci Malone was looking at herself in the mirror, naked. Her long blonde hair cascaded round her shoulders and weaved over her proud full breasts. Her gaze travelled down to her flat stomach, generous hips, and the neat triangle which was atop her long strong toned thighs.

Not bad for twenty nine she told herself. She allowed a flicker of annoyance to cross her face as she thought of her love life, or rather the lack of it. It was simply incredible, she told herself, that a girl of her age with her looks — well they did at least seem half alright –had gone since Christmas, four months, without a boyfriend or even a lover. What the hell was wrong with London and its men, she asked herself angrily. Time ticked by, and on a recent trip to her mother's for the weekend she had endured an unwanted lecture on the risks of sudden declines in her fertility as she got into her thirties. Damn fertility, she thought. First things first!

Still, there was tonight to look forward to. She remembered Alexander from that chance meeting with her best friend Arianna. She had a mental picture of a very good looking, beautifully dressed, smooth, urbane individual — seemingly very British yet definitely a bit foreign.

She mused. He was a little too perfect to be quite her type — she didn't like her men to be too narcissistic — but he had been very charming.

She grabbed a towel and headed for the shower. What the hell! A date was a date. Now, what was she going to wear?

At seven fifteen she was ready. She wore a short black dress with moderate cleavage, black and purple flattish Jimmy Choos to disguise her height, and a striking designer pendant and matching earrings. She took a final look in the mirror. Attractive and sexy, she thought, but not over the top.

The car was a dark blue Maserati Quattroporte, driven by a solid cockney chauffeur who looked as though there was nothing he might see or hear that could ever surprise him.

Lutin greeted her warmly and showed her up to the first floor living room overlooking the Thames. She instinctively wandered over towards the window. You could just see upstream to Chelsea Bridge, Chelsea Reach and Whistler's view. Lutin cut into her thoughts.

'I'd like to offer you a Cabaret.'

'Goodness me, Alexander, what's that — a drink or a performance?'

'It's a drink which might lead to a performance, my dear,' he said, a little too unctuously she thought.

'No, seriously, it's a mixture of champagne and sauterne, Rebecca, and I really didn't mean the bit about the performance – I always mess things up,' Lutin said, self deprecating and charming.

She felt warm again.

'That sounds very intriguing, Alexander', she said. 'I'd love to try it.

By the way,' she added, 'most of my friends just call me Becci.'

'It's a drink that used to be all the rage in Nazi Germany,' Lutin added, throwing her off balance again.

Lutin disappeared into the small high tech kitchen and took a bottle of 1999 Pol Roger and 1997 Suduiraut from the fridge and mixed the drinks — two thirds champagne to one third sauternes. He dropped two different coloured phials into Rebecca's frosted glass and swirled them round with a swizzle stick. The result was invisible. He tasted both drinks — there was no trace. He topped the glasses up and took them into the living room on a silver tray.

She was sitting on one of the two enormous cream sofas which flanked the period fireplace. The last of the gold and black shadows of the late spring evening stole into the elegant room and mixed with the soft light thrown by the enormous dusky pink shaded lamp beside the sofa.

She looked very beautiful. Lutin bent down and kissed her very gently and told her so, and handed her the drink.

Rebecca took a sip of her drink, then another, and after a while she slowly eased her left foot half out of its shoe.

'You know, I'm enjoying this,' she confided, smiling.

'My dear, it's lovely to have you here,' said Lutin. 'I've so much wanted to see more of you since we met.'

Two cabarets later they walked round the corner to Ceccolio's where Lutin was greeted with deference by the maitre'd.

Rebecca was feeling very relaxed, and rather strange. How did she find it so easy to talk to such a comparative stranger, she wondered. Still, she felt, it hadn't really mattered and all the talk so far had been on neutral ground, her home, her family, her interests outside of work, travel and finally her love of music, a topic on which she had been pleasantly surprised to find Alexander apparently very knowledgeable. Then he had really bowled her over by playing — rather beautifully — some Chopin preludes on the exquisite Steinway he kept in a corner of the large living room.

All in all by the time she got to the restaurant she was beginning to feel that the evening was going rather well and had even begun to let her mind race ahead. Too far ahead, she told herself sharply.

Dinner was perfect. Antipasto followed by penne amatriciana for them both, afterwards veal escalopes for Rebecca and sole for Alexander. The delicious meal was accompanied by some outstanding Frascati from an estate apparently owned by a friend of Lutin's.

The conversation during dinner became slightly more probing about her work and the Sphinx. She did feel that Alexander was very interested in James Doyle and what he was currently doing but she thought she had batted him away as much as was polite. Hadn't she? Eventually she did indicate gently to him that they seemed to have wandered off the point and he immediately became all charm and solicitude and apologised profusely for being carried away by business.

Then after even more delicious desserts and some Muscat it was time for a final nightcap back in the living room. Then – Rebecca flushed at the memory – she had an impression of Alexander showing her over the rest of the house and somehow she had ended up in his bedroom with the king size bed and full length mirrors around the curved walls — and she had some impressions of one or two other strange things as well.

And that was all she remembered.

Chapter 10

THE JUNGLE OF YOUR MIND

'Another beautiful spring day, sir.' Doyle had overslept and Fred was drawing the curtains back. Doyle blinked into life.

'I hope so,' grunted Doyle, 'but I had some weird dreams and I've got a bad feeling about this morning.'

After his swim and breakfast Doyle felt more cheerful. He went to his office and ran through papers and engagements with Julie Walters, his ruthlessly efficient private secretary.

Suddenly the door opened and a pale faced and obviously stressed Becci Malone put her head round it.

'Sorry to butt in,' she said in a strained voice. 'But I can't remember what happened last night.'

Doyle grinned and asked her if she had tried drinking less when she went out.

Rebecca looked peeved and said: 'It's nothing like that at all actually, James. I know from my diary that I was due to go to dinner with someone called Alexander Lutin. I can remember being taken to his house in his car, and I can remember his driver, and I can remember being offered a drink called a Cabaret. After that I can't remember anything at all.'

'Is there any evidence of what happened after that?' asked Julie Walters.

Rebecca flushed. 'Well it's obvious that I must have ended up going to bed with him and', she flushed even more deeply, 'I seem to have been used by him rather comprehensively.'

Doyle looked mildly embarrassed and cleared his throat. 'Becci, I'm very sorry to hear that and obviously you may want to think further about how you deal with this. But was there anything in this episode which affected your work at all?'

'Well,' said Rebecca, 'I didn't think so but this morning I got a call from a girlfriend who happened to be sitting close to me at the restaurant.' She looked flustered again. 'Ceccolios,' she said the restaurant was. I now can't remember if I did notice her at the time – I must have been too wrapped up with Alexander, I suppose. Anyway she said Alexander seemed to spend the whole evening pumping me for information about the Sphinx and about you, James, and what you were doing.'

Doyle now looked concerned.

'And did she tell you what you told him in response to his questions?'

'No, she said she could hear snatches of his voice but not mine.

The thing is, James, he must have drugged me because she said I seemed incredibly relaxed and laid back, which for a first date just isn't me. Secondly there's this complete, and I mean complete, loss of memory which I never normally suffer from at all — no matter how pissed I get,' she added, concluding defiantly, 'and I didn't actually.'

She burst into tears.

'James, I might have told him everything.'

'Becci, I'm really sorry about all this,' he said quickly. 'Would you very much mind going with Julie to the doctor to get some blood samples done so that at least we can try and work out what he gave you? And the doctor could also help with the other stuff,' he trailed off.

'Becci, if you feel strong enough to come back here after that perhaps you could tell me everything you know or can find out about this new boyfriend of yours.' Doyle was grateful for the chance to return to something analytical. Rebecca nodded and thanked him. Doyle told Julie to get the samples to a contact at Scotland Yard, and to get someone called Malcolm Murdoch at the Foreign Office on the phone for him. Doyle called to Fred for some strong coffee for them all and received the usual muffled response.

Then he sat looking at the river and thought back to the evening at the Assassins Club. That had been the first time he had met Lutin — and it had been expensive. This could be infinitely worse. He felt a twinge of fear.

An hour later Doyle had had a long conversation with Murdoch and was a very troubled man.

Murdoch had told him that the Foreign Office view was that Lutin was basically a Russian agent using the Saint Petersburg Bank chairmanship as cover.

'He does a super job in the UK maintaining that cover, but the reality is he's always over in Moscow and our lads there say he's very close to Julius Orlov — I've even heard him described as a second son to him.'

Doyle swore long and freely. Then he spent a concentrated quarter of an hour reviewing just what Rebecca actually did know. The answer to that was quite a lot.

She certainly knew the basis of the dual trade strategy although not the precise details of the Saudi crisis or the exact location of the potential Namibian finds. She didn't know the exact breakdown of all the futures positions — that was Fleming's preserve. But, Doyle concluded, she certainly knew enough to have made Lutin aware of the genesis of the trades, and the Sphinx strategy, which Doyle thought would be all he was after at this stage.

Finally, and worst of all, Doyle thought, Rebecca knew all about the Rangoon title deed issue in Namibia.

He groaned.

Murdoch had also told Doyle that it was well established that Lutin had a very extensive knowledge of pharmaceuticals. Finally he told him that he also had a reputation for certain sexual fetishes, and that there had been a few issues with the numerous London society girls who had passed through his hands although none had taken matters to the stage of a formal complaint.

Doyle had convened an emergency meeting of the Sphinx at 1pm. Now he sat, ostensibly relaxed, at the head of the table in the meeting room adjacent to his office. Inwardly he braced himself. Members of the Sphinx were an articulate lot and apt to be fairly acerbic when they felt their interests were being threatened.

Charles O'Neill looked morosely into his diet coke and toyed with his chicken ciabatta.

'So, James,' he drawled, 'now we're stuffed because some Russian agent disguised as an English public schoolboy slips one of your girls a truth drug and the next thing we know our strategy is beamed right round the world.'

There was a muffled chorus of grunts of approval from Myers, Bulstrode and Weill.

'Well, basically, yes,' said Doyle, looking completely relaxed.

There was an excitable buzz round the table.

'Except for one thing, gentlemen, we are not stuffed — yet. We have in place massive futures positions supporting the trading strategy agreed by you all. If our assumptions pan out — no matter how public they are — nothing can stop us making a most monumental killing,' said Doyle quietly. He continued: 'However the real risk posed by this development is that it in theory makes it possible for the Russians — or others who get to know — to foul up the smooth realisation of our plans. For instance they can steal the Rangoon title lease, they can pressurise the Namibian government to tear up the Rangoon agreement and substitute it for one in their favour in exchange for God knows what corrupt deal, they could even beat us to the punch on a bid for Rangoon.'

Myers glowered and shot back in his Australian twang,

'Jesus, Doyle, just those things alone would be enough royally to stuff us, and there must be a load of other things we haven't even thought about yet.'

Doyle was unruffled. 'We can take care of most of these, Patrick. For instance it certainly means speeding up the move on the title lease. I'm confident about the Namibian Government. My good friend Joseph Barula is one of the very few non corrupt leaders in Black Africa, but we will have to cut a pretty good deal for the Namibian state that reflects his loyalty to us. What's more I frankly I don't believe that the Russian Government have the money or the balls to bid for Rangoon, certainly not in a competitive situation with us or the Chinese for instance. Their forte is quietly stealing stuff and breaking a few bones en route until they get what they want. Putting a high cash price on Rangoon and finding – what is it? – a hundred and fifty billion sterling, plus, just isn't their bag. The international financial community won't lend them anything like that — their credit rating is shot — and anyway the antitrust people here would probably invoke national interest arguments anyway.'

Myers simmered down and muttered his assent.

Weill said softly, 'James, these are convincing responses but of course we really need a comprehensive risk assessment of all the factors which might throw us off course.'

Doyle agreed, saying that he would issue something the next day.

Doyle summed up: 'My view is that we need to accelerate the safe storage of the title lease and we need to start acquiring Rangoon stock. We need to start building a significant position. At the end of the day gentlemen, if our plans work out, we will not be the only people in the world interested in the ownership of Rangoon.'

Doyle said quietly: 'Just a few more words, gentlemen, about where we are. We are playing for high stakes here. When we started this it was as a highly developed and highly leveraged play based on some hard won special intelligence. A normal operation for us. Right?'

Everyone nodded assent.

'But what we are heading towards is a global power struggle for a massive new energy resource. This is not something we shall acquire simply and easily, shove into our back pockets and head off with into the boondocks. It is going to be very public, very political and probably very competitive. We shall have to work with and accommodate a lot of other people. We already have a highly secret and unusual arrangement with the British Government for security and legal protection; there will be a price for that. We will have to deal in the Namibians. Then there is the whole question of financing the deal — I have some ideas on this but they will involve a price and that will probably include significant dilution of our equity.'

'At the end of the day,' Doyle surveyed his group, 'if this resource turns out as large as we hope it might get caught up in a whole new era of global resource and power sharing which is a million miles away from our freewheeling approach. The important thing, though, is to make sure we are properly rewarded for our time, intelligence and capital.'

'Impressive speech, James,' smiled Weill.

Bulstrode banged the table angrily.

'Well, I don't think so,' he said aggressively, his face reddening. 'I don't see why we need to co-operate with all these people or even give them the time of day. They have universally fucked up and been asleep on the job. Rangoon management either don't know what they own or don't exploit it properly. The Namibians don't know what day of the week it is. They've sat on a huge underexploited resource for decades without catching up with it; they could have been one of the wealthiest countries south of the Sahara and a leader of the region. Russia is a kleptocracy and I won't deal with them.

We've done all the work, committed bucket loads of our equity in very highly leveraged plays, and taken all of the risk. I damn well don't see why we shouldn't have the whip hand.'

'Christopher,' Doyle soothed, 'if we all lived in the jungle of your mind you would be right, but unfortunately we do not. We are in the world of sophisticated geo politics and, using your jungle speak, all we are doing is sticking a very sharp, very long financial spear up these people's arses and hoping that when we see it again it'll be gold plated from top to bottom.

Christopher, if this turns out to be a resource on which a second OPEC can be based you may rest assured it will not be controlled by a bunch of financial adventurers like us.' Doyle was getting impatient with Bulstrode posing as a financial equivalent of one of Britain's most politically incorrect journalists.

Bulstrode grumbled to himself.

'Should have been a hedgie in the eighteenth century, Christopher,' said Myers unhelpfully.

O'Neill asked how much capital Doyle wanted to commit to the Rangoon stake.

'I think,' said Doyle, 'that we want initially to aim to acquire about ten per cent, but of course we can do most of it on margin through contracts for difference ('CFD's') which means we won't need more than about five hundred million pounds.'

'Don't forget that the Saudi news is still not out so we will be buying at market prices based on forty dollar oil, it certainly won't be as low as it is now once that announcement is made.'

Myers said heavily: 'There are just two things which give me concern James. One is whether we could be held to be trading on inside information. I don't want to end up in gaol however much money I make. And the second — and I know we've been over this before – is whether we can rely on this Namibian field without a more extensive drilling programme.'

'I share your concerns,' said Doyle. 'I've fixed a meeting with counsel at 6pm this evening here. That should deal with the first of your points. You are all very welcome to attend but I will distribute a settled opinion in due course. As for the second I have organised a conference call with Jock Millar for two fifteen which is about now so I will get him on the phone.'

'Jock', said Doyle minutes later on the encrypted satellite phone, 'I've got the members of the Sphinx here and they would like to hear from you on progress and try and gauge your comfort level with what you think you've got hold of out there.'

'Och aye'

'Aye, well, all ye gentlemen ken that what we started doing after James had squared away yon President, was flying aerial surveys. We flew these across the whole of the Namibian coastal strip, aye, nearly wore a plane out doing it. It's never been done before, ye ken, by anyone. What these surveys can tell ye now is a quantum leap from what they could even ten years ago.

Just to put this in context, aye, there are four ways of exploring for oil. Aerial survey, mapping magnetic fields, 3D Seismic mapping and Seismic X, and drilling. You're looking for oil bearing rock. So you need to find a way of mapping underground strata and determining the shape and size of geo physical structures underneath the surface of the earth. Aerial magnetic surveys detect minute variations in magnetic fields when interrupted by oil bearing rocks, which are non magnetic. Seismic and Seismic X send manmade vibrations into the rock from which ye can measure recovery of wave energy reflected from features underground to create a visual imagery of the sub surface rock. And then ye can check it all out by drilling.

To get back to the aerial work. I think you gentlemen ken all about Saudi oil. You know that the biggest field in Saudi is Ghawar. Well, Ghawar is based in what is known as Arab D Zone rock which often not only contains huge reservoirs but also layers of rock of much higher permeability known as 'Super K'.'

'These are the two ingredients which have formed the backbone of Saudi oil production for the last decades. And however hard they have looked the Saudi's have never found any other instances of similar formations in the country.'

Jock dropped his voice.' In a nut shell gentlemen, what we have identified in Namibia, on the basis of the aerial magnetic and subsequent seismic surveys, is a geology which produces comparable grades of crude oil and in similar quantities. Our surveys indicate a potential oil field of truly extraordinary size.'

There was a momentary silence from the Sphinx.

'That's shut you up, gentlemen,' said Jock jovially.

'That's the basis for our medium term short oil future and long equity positions,' Doyle reminded the group.

'It's all very well,' Bulstrode spoke crisply, 'but we have taken some very big bets, and now we are talking about starting the ultimate bet, and we still haven't seen a drop of actual oil.'

'Where we've got to,' said Jock, 'is that we have now analysed the preferred locations for exploratory drilling. If we drill there and see the flow rates we have computed we can have about eighty per cent confidence in our projections of field size. If we doubled that programme our confidence would rise to ninety five per cent.

We believe the field could be twice the size of Ghawar, easily. It could possibly be five times the size.

Either would absolutely transform the prospects for world oil supply for the foreseeable future. We have used the most sophisticated new Seismic X in each of four locations, which pretty much replaces drilling for accuracy, and had our expectations confirmed. It was a hundred per cent accurate in Brazil. We've done a little bit of drilling, though we're not really allowed to drill, and that's produced oil exactly as we had anticipated. But to allow us to drill properly James needs to pay another visit to yon President to secure permission and thereafter it will take about eight weeks to complete an expanded programme.'

'Thank you, Jock.' Doyle cut the satellite phone link.

'I'd really like to see some more oil,' said Bulstrode mulishly.

Doyle summed up: 'Gentlemen, I believe we have enough to go on to justify building a ten per cent position in Rangoon, but we need to secure these leases as soon as we can. Before we bid we will need to have completed the drilling. I accept that. Is everyone comfortable?'

They were. Doyle closed the meeting.

Two hours later Doyle was having a cup of tea with his doctor. At least Doyle was drinking Lapsang Souchong while his doctor cradled a large whisky and soda.

'James, Scotland Yard is very interested indeed in the blood sample that your poor girl provided. It contains traces of two extremely rare drugs which have only ever been seen coming out of Russian laboratories. One was a drug inducing rapid loss of extreme short term memory — it literally erases it for a few hours — and the other a truth drug and relaxant known as Veritol. The latter is extremely effective — some say even the Americans tested it, at Guantanamo Bay. No side effects have ever been recorded, I'm pleased to say, especially for the sake of that poor girl — she's alright in every other respect though even though the fellow does seem to have made rather free with her.'

Doyle raised an eyebrow.

'So she could have told him anything? Everything?'

'Oh yes,' said the doctor cheerfully. 'Veritol works as a compulsive desire to empty the mind on any topic towards which it is specifically directed by the interlocutor.'

'Very helpful', grunted Doyle.

The doctor left and Doyle put his feet up on the desk, poured another cup of Lapsang Souchong and lit an Egyptian.

A phone rang. Doyle glanced at his desk and was intrigued to see that it was the encrypted satellite phone.

It was Jock.

'Was that alright sir? 'quizzed the old oil man. 'I hope they went away happy.'

'It was perfect, Jock', said Doyle. 'I'll come out and fix the additional drilling permits in the next few days.'

Jock coughed. 'Actually, the drilling's already been done, sir. I didn't like to mention this on the call with your friends, ye ken.'

'What can you mean Jock, done? I thought you hadn't done much yet?'

'Aye, sir, but it's not been done by us. I was making good friends with a very old civil servant in a bar last night and he told me that long ago, before even Rangoon got the lease, that an Australian company had drilled, way back in the nineteen – thirties, in some of the places almost exactly where we want to drill.'

'And?' said Doyle.

'They only drilled a couple of wells but very deep by the standards of those days. They found huge flow rates but went bust before they could check the size of the field. The wells were capped and no one had enough resource to do any more. All the records all went missing. Rangoon were quite unaware of this early success. But this chap had some retirement job in the energy ministry sorting out old papers and he found them there.'

'Where are those papers now, Jock?'

'Och, he lent them to me, he has a pension problem and I said we could help him.'

'I think you should come out and have a look.'

'I will,' said Doyle, 'and Jock, this could get a bit hot shortly. Don't lose those papers will you? And thanks for your help.'

'Do ye ken what the boys out here are calling this field, sir?'

'No – tell me.'

'The Field of Dreams', said Jock.

Doyle replaced the handset and picked up the internal phone.

'Fred, glass of the best champagne we've got, in here fast please.'

'Very good, sir.'

Chapter 11

POSSESSION IS NINETY PERCENT

Sir Nigel Higgs QC was a man in his late forties of just under medium height. He had prematurely greying hair, and large extraordinarily intelligent eyes slightly obscured by horn rimmed spectacles. He was the leading commercial silk of his day and combined massive intellectual authority and a fair dose of intellectual arrogance with a very puckish sense of humour. In his spare time he wrote immensely erudite books on the Renaissance.

'So, Doyle,' he said, his glance raking round the table and taking in the members of the Sphinx sitting round it, 'what devilment are you lot up to now? I must say that was a pretty extraordinary brief I got from your lawyer.'

'It's a pretty extraordinary story, Nigel, but I am not proposing to tell you all about it just now. We may need your help again later, though, and if so I'll expand then.'

Sir Nigel inclined his head.

'As I understand it you want to know if you will contravene the insider dealing laws if you deal in the securities of a major corporation having acquired knowledge about their assets which is not publically available?'

'Well, yes and no, Nigel, if I can put it like that,' observed Doyle.

'Yes, we wish to deal in the securities of a major plc based on non public information about their assets. No, in the sense that not only is the non public information not known to the public but the plc itself is not aware of it.'

'What on earth do you mean, James?' expostulated Higgs.

'I mean that the plc is unaware that areas over which it has exploration and exploitation rights actually contain very significant amounts of oil.'

'Why are they unaware of that?' said Higgs

'Because, Nigel, they have not troubled themselves to explore them,' said Doyle.

'We,' he continued, 'have taken that trouble and believe we have established the existence of a very major resource which would have a massive impact upon the value of the plc were it to become public knowledge.'

'But Nigel,' Doyle continued relentlessly, 'that knowledge is proprietary to us and does not belong to the company, excepting of course the fact that it is germane to company property.'

Sir Nigel Higgs sighed.

'You hedge fund people, whatever will you get up to next?'

'Hopefully, making a lot of money,' said Doyle, laconically.

'Well,' said Sir Nigel in the practised, clipped and deliberate tone for which he was both feared and famous, 'the actual wording in the Act is ....'

Doyle cut him off.

'Spare us the grisly detail, Nigel. Just tell us whether we're good to go.'

Higgs sighed. These hedge fund people really had no manners, and no sense of the theatre of professional advice.

'I think it fairly obvious,' Higgs's voice had a slight edge. ' The Act was designed to apply only to trading based on non public information which is the property of the company concerned, and of course being information of which it itself is aware, so I think you rascals are in the clear.'

'Incidentally,' he continued, 'would you be acquiring these securities with a view to trading or acquiring control?'

'Control,' replied Doyle, 'unless someone else fancies their chances of course.'

'I wouldn't like to be the plc's lawyers,' said Higgs enigmatically.

'Now, I'm going to leave you before you get me into more trouble. I take it you want a written opinion?'

'Please,' said Doyle, 'the stakes are rather high here.'

Sir Nigel's smile disappeared. He gathered up his things, shook hands with everyone, and headed for the door with a 'good evening, gentlemen' as he went. After a short further discussion the Sphinx left. Doyle had decided not to reveal the drilling results recorded by the Australian company until he had seen the evidence for himself.

Doyle summoned Fred. 'What menu are you thinking of for dinner tonight?'

'Just the two, isn't it, sir?'

'Yes Fred,' said Doyle, 'but bear in mind that the guest is the Prime Minister.'

'I'm conscious of that, sir,' Fred said stiffly. 'I've laid on some fusion food with Indian and Malaysian themes and also some Middle Eastern desserts which I know you like.'

'What about the wine?' asked Doyle.

'Does the PM drink, sir?' Fred questioned.

Doyle guffawed. 'Is the Pope a Catholic, Fred?'

'I just thought that being Indian, sir, he might not.'

'No, Fred, Mr Singh is a Sikh, a member of the great warrior class, and they can drink like no one else on earth.'

Doyle scribbled down some suggestions on a pad.

Fred left the room.

An hour later Doyle was sprawled on a sofa in jeans, a white open neck shirt, a dark blue silk jacket and pair of Lobb loafers with black silk socks. He inspected the glass of old Dom Perignon in his hand.

The phone rang. Damn, he thought, the Prime Minister, cancelling.

'Hi, James, its Persia here, do you remember?'

Her clear, bell like tones and underlying warmth made his stomach tighten.

'Of course I remember, darling.'

'Why haven't you called me, James?'

'We left it that you would call me when your people had found out the date,' Doyle said, weakly.

'You know what I mean, James,' she said silkily.

'I have no excuse,' brazened Doyle, 'except that we've had rather a busy time here.'

'That is no excuse, James.'

Doyle said contritely that he knew it wasn't.

'Well, James, I've got the date.'

'But you're going to have to come and get it,' she said, playfully.

'What, come and see you in Saudi?' Doyle's heart sank.

'No, not Saudi, James, I'm at the Ritz in London.'

'Could I give you lunch tomorrow?'

'What's wrong with dinner now, James?' Persia's voice was at its most seductive.

'I've got the Prime Minister coming in a couple of minutes and after him I've got a meeting with my team.'

'James, you don't love me any more.'

'I love you so much, Persia, that I must have enough time with you to really show my feelings.'

'James, you are such a beast. Make it dinner, then, tomorrow.'

'I'll send a car for you at six fifteen.'

'Good to hear that le cinq a sept is not dead yet, James.

I love you.' She rang off, satisfied.

Doyle called Fleming.

'Okay, Matthew, it's full on with Plan A. We need to move fast to build our oil futures position out to the maximum, we need to build the Rangoon stake and we need to get our global equity shorts in place before this Saudi news breaks.

I'll know the exact date by the close of play tomorrow but get as much as you can on as soon as possible please.'

'The Prime Minister, sir.' Fred was at the door, enjoying the moment.

Harvinder Singh, dressed casually in black, greeted Doyle warmly.

'You know, Doyle,' he said, 'there aren't many people I'd do this for, and I'm still not quite sure why I'm doing it for you.'

Doyle handed him a glass of champagne.

'It's very simple, Prime Minister,' he said, 'together we have made one of the best kinds of deals. I am going to help you become one of the most successful Prime Ministers ever seen in Britain, and you are going to help my business pull off a great financial coup.'

'And,' continued Doyle, 'if one word of any of this leaks to anyone all bets are off for you, one half of our bets are off, and together we will be consigned to the dustbin of history.'

Singh chuckled. 'I like your style, Doyle, and what's much more important I like you and I trust you — those have always been big things for me in business.'

'Politics must be a bit awkward for you, Prime Minister,' said Doyle.

'That's why,' Singh chuckled again, 'we are dealing directly with one another.'

'Wasn't it Churchill,' asked Doyle, 'who said that during the war all he wanted from his Cabinet colleagues was compliance with his wishes after a reasonable period of discussion?'

'Yes, he knew what he was doing,' agreed Singh.

Doyle thought Fred had excelled himself. Dish after delicious dish arrived and the wines were perfect — an old Alsatian, and an Haut Brion from the most wonderful claret vintage of all – nineteen fifty nine. Harvinder Singh, who told Doyle that he had a wonderful cellar himself, mellowed visibly.

'I have to be careful, James,' he chuckled after a while, 'I have to keep my wits about me with you as I'm never quite sure what you might want next.'

Quietly Doyle took Singh through the imminent Saudi announcement, its likely effect on global markets, and the turmoil which could result.

'It's going to produce absolute panic,' Doyle concluded. 'The oil price will go through the roof and stock markets will crash round the world. There will be an immediate wealth effect on consumer spend and central banks and governments worldwide will have to pump a massive amount of liquidity into the world economic system to prop things up. And all this will happen just as the world is struggling to recover from the long after effects of the credit crunch. If it's not well handled it could trigger a global recession that could last for years.'

Singh told him that the earlier intelligence he had received from Doyle had enabled him to run some serious economic war games which had resulted in a set of very clear optimum policy responses and a blueprint for Britain leading the subsequent worldwide economic co-operation.

'You'll look like you are on top of things to a greater extent than any other leader,' observed Doyle. 'However you should also know that there are some developments which are more problematic for us.'

Doyle explained the Rebecca Malone affair and told Singh that in his view the Russians would try to strong arm events.

'Their first move will be to try to steal the bearer leases covering the Namibian rights from Rangoon's offices. If they are foiled in this their second will be to put intense pressure on the Namibian Government to withdraw that concession and re-allocate it to themselves. Our top priority is to remove those leases from Rangoon. We will leave them with excellent copies but deposit the originals with the Bank of England.'

Singh said: 'It's all very well Doyle but you can hardly expect the British government to enter into some kind of competitive kleptocracy with the Russians in relation to the property of a major blue chip company.'

'Not even my expectations run that high, Prime Minister, but I would appreciate some back up when we remove them.

We shall be ultra discreet, of course. Modern copying technology is so good that the copies we leave behind will be indistinguishable from the original without forensic tests. But I don't think the Russians will act until we have the originals in transit. I don't believe they will opt for a pitched battle at the storage site — it's too high profile. But bumping a car and its inhabitants off in a country lane is right up their street.'

'I cannot have the UK military on that site either, Doyle, I hope you understand that. Given that tell me what you need.'

'I need two small detachments of SAS to accompany the road party and an SBS unit on the shore. And I need a very discreet police guard round the perimeter of that site for the next four nights, starting tonight, just in case the Russians go it alone.'

'SBS?'

'Don't ask, Prime Minister.'

'Very well,' said Singh. 'I am going to give you a contact number in the Ministry of Defence who will give you all you need. Don't tell him anything about the wider scheme. And here's the Scotland Yard number. Give me fifteen minutes after I leave and you can use that to put your police cover in place.'

'And Doyle,' Singh drained a glass of nineteen ninety Climens that had been served with the sticky Middle Eastern desserts, 'don't embarrass me. If anything goes wrong we will have to put our activity down to terrorist counter measures — so think about that.'

'One last question,' said Singh. 'You said you were going to store the originals in the Bank of England. That's pretty sensitive for us.'

'I have a personal bank account there, and a walk in vault accessible at all times,' said Doyle blandly. 'It need never be associated with Government.'

Shortly after Singh left, Doyle was in his study with Dyer, his security chief, and Frank, who ran his transport. Doyle reflected on their contrasting characters. Dyer had a crew cut, three days growth of beard, was dressed in black jeans and black sweater; power and menace oozed from every pore. Frank's laughing, good natured face sat on top of a bear like frame decked out in a Rastafarian t shirt and yellow jeans; he wore heavy gold jewellery round his neck and his wrists.

'So it's very simple, guys,' Doyle smiled, 'we just get in, copy onto aged paper, substitute the copies for the originals, clear up, get out, and deliver the originals to the Bank of England.'

'Jesus, man,' growled Tony Dyer, 'it's not that simple at all, you devious bugger. We don't know how to get in, we don't know where the documents are or even what they look like, we don't know what the copying facilities are like and we know nothing about the alarm systems.'

Frank laughed: 'Just give me the documents and I'll get them to the Bank.'

'Alright,' said Doyle, 'here is what you need to do and what is going to happen. Today is Tuesday and I want to lift on Thursday night as I have to go to Namibia for the weekend.'

He spoke for about twenty minutes and gave them three telephone numbers.

'We'll meet first thing Thursday morning to review your detailed plan,' he concluded.

Amidst clouds of steam swirling around the ornate tiled interior of the Sandinov bathhouse Julius Orlov dimly saw the Stalinesque figure of the chief attendant shuffle towards him. Twisting a large and luxuriant moustache he advanced to a respectful distance and said:

'Comrade Lutin is here for you sir.'

Orlov reflected that some old habits took a long time to die.

'Oh, good, Dimitri, show him in and then leave us in peace for half an hour would you.'

'Yes, sir.' The fellow bowed respectfully and the slap of his large feet echoed away down the corridor. He soon returned accompanied by Alexander Lutin swathed in a large white towel with another draped carelessly over his shoulder.

Orlov smiled a welcome.

'Late as usual, Alexander.'

'Sorry, something came up.'

Orlov reflected that this phrase probably concealed a multitude of sins.

'You wanted to see me.'

'Yes,' said Lutin. 'I've found some interesting information.'

Lutin stretched himself and adjusted his towels.

'You were absolutely right, Julius.'

Orlov showed no emotion. He had expected to be right. He then listened to Lutin's report of his dinner with Rebecca Malone.

'She told me that this fellow Doyle, and the Sphinx, are working on one of the biggest things the partnership has ever attempted. Basically they have found out that there is a looming crisis in Saudi oil production and that that fact will become public very soon, she didn't know exactly when. They have also been exploring for oil in Namibia and believe they have potentially found a world class resource of incredible size. She thinks they have put in place an extremely sophisticated trading strategy to take advantage of all the consequences of these developments.'

'How did you manage to get such information out of a presumably trusted and loyal employee, Alexander?' queried Orlov.

'My charm, and judicious use of some of the chemicals which our boys are so good at.'

'Alexander,' said Orlov, 'be careful, you have built up such a good cover in London.'

'You wouldn't have this information without those things,' observed Lutin drily.

'Did you get any feeling for the timing of these facts becoming public?' asked Orlov.

'No, but I think the Saudi news is relatively imminent while the Namibia scenario needs to be confirmed by further drilling.'

'So who actually owns the development and exploration rights on the Namibia land?' asked Orlov. For the first time a rare, but tiny, hint of excitement and tension had entered his voice.

'Well, she didn't reveal that. I got the impression that she didn't know.'

Orlov pursed his lips. He thought that the Sphinx would be most unlikely to have acquired exploration rights for itself. They had to be working someone else's rights. He picked up his mobile phone, flicked it open and spoke low and rapidly into it.

He turned to Lutin.

'The first step, Alexander, is to find out to whom those rights belong; I'm dead sure it won't be the Sphinx.'

Lutin stretched himself again. 'Even if you find that out,' he said, 'I'm not sure if it takes you much further forward.'

'Alexander,' said Orlov, 'you can be one of the most complacent individuals I have ever worked with. Let me explain. There are several options for the Russian State here. One, the most costly and hence least desirable, is to find out who owns the rights and simply acquire the company concerned, if that is possible. A second is simply to get those rights withdrawn from whomsoever owns them at present and ensure that they are re-allocated to us.'

'Julius,' Lutin's tone was conciliatory, 'the issue with the first is our financial resources – they are very limited at the moment. I don't see how we could assemble the funds required to bid for a major Western oil company and I very much doubt if these Namibian rights are owned by any of the smaller modern oil juniors – they sound too old for that. And as to your second idea, we all know that we can play at being Robin Hood inside Russian borders but doing it overseas, even in a place like Namibia, is bound to have repercussions.'

'That's where you are wrong Alexander,' said Orlov, 'look at what the Chinese have been doing all over Africa. Look at the indifference the Southern African States have shown towards Mugabe's regime in Zimbabwe.'

Orlov stood up.

'With right incentives,' he concluded flatly, 'my view is that you can do whatever you like in Africa.

Alexander,' he said, 'I will find out who owns these leases. Then you have to deliver one of those two solutions, whatever it takes.'

The two men concluded their bath house routine and Orlov's black Mercedes dropped Lutin back at his large office in the foreign ministry.

Five hours later Lutin was scanning a list of Russia's major corporations and the top twenty oligarchs. That list set out a schedule displaying their estimated near cash or net cash resources plus a note of assets which could be readily sold to international buyers. It wasn't a promising picture. Russian corporations and oligarchs had been hit hard by the credit crunch. Some of the oligarchs with more liquid assets, Lutin knew, had spent ridiculous amounts on foreign football clubs and building more super yachts than they could possibly need. He made a mental note that Orlov should have a word with some of these; most had been labouring under the delusion that as long as they kept their noses clean in Russia and spent most of their time abroad they were untouchable. Lutin thought he would see about that. Most of the corporations were based on commodities and oil and the lack of any sizeable more broadly based companies demonstrated the poor development of Russia's industrial infrastructure.

Lutin thought it be very difficult to raise much more than thirty to fifty billion sterling in terms of 'mandatory' subscriptions to a syndicate formed to take a tilt at a major Western company. Even to raise that would take considerable arm twisting while a great deal of debt would still be needed on top.

A little later he was in Orlov's office. Orlov was sitting behind a large desk. His eyes were focussed on a wall mounted screen which had a digital display of international date and timelines. He was adjusting an old Rolex Daytona on his left wrist.

Orlov's face was impassive.

'Our intelligence people have come up with the goods on Namibia. Even better than I thought. The leases are actually in possession of Rangoon and have been for over sixty years. Rangoon has never done anything out there. But the really good piece of news for us is that these leases are bearer leases, i.e. anyone who is in possession of them can exercise all the exploration and exploitation rights that they confer. I gather this was quite common in the early days of the oil industry when companies came and went like confetti.

Alexander, I would imagine that Doyle and his team are planning to bid for Rangoon. All his culture, background and education means that he will do the decent thing, even if it costs. But as you know, we are not constrained in quite the same way.

However now that Doyle knows his plans have leaked, he will recognise the risk that we pose and he will realise that our first step will be to try and lay our hands on the leases.

My message to you is very simple. You have to get these leases before he does.'

The next evening Doyle was looking deep into Persia's fathomless dark brown eyes. They were laughing steadily back at him and at their combined reflections in the massive gilt ceiling mirror above the king size double bed. A second bottle of vintage Dom Perignon sat in an ice bucket on a side table. A pair of delicately pink shaded bed side lamps lit the whole room with a soft shimmering glow. Persia's dusky, voluptuous, eager body was partially sheathed in the cream silk sheets. Doyle's mouth went slowly down onto hers. She writhed under him. After several minutes he pulled away and breathed: 'Persia, my darling is there anything else I can do for you?'

'Oh, James,' she whispered, 'you mean before I give you that date?'

'Something like that, you minx,' he laughed, playfully slapping her rump.

'Well, maybe, in that case, just one more thing.'

Doyle made his way slowly and sensuously down her body.

'Do you know James,' she said appreciatively after a while, 'I really think you do deserve that date now.'

She breathed in his ear.

'Persia, darling,' said Doyle, 'I honestly think I'd exchange all the oil in the world for you.'

'You say the nicest things, James. I suppose this is a prelude to kicking me out now.'

'Yes,' said Doyle, 'I've got a plane to catch, or rather take.'

'Can't I come with you?' Persia wheedled.

'It's not really that sort of plane I'm afraid.'

'Well it's high time you got a bigger one,' she pouted.

Much later she lingered at the front door before getting into the Ghost.

'I really love you, James.'

Doyle kissed her goodnight.

The Ghost eased away from the kerb.

Chapter 12

TUNNEL VISION

It was just past one in the morning on a cloudy night on the Suffolk coast. Occasional gusts of a warm early summer wind brought a spatter of rain. The moon was half full but frequently obscured by the scudding clouds. The ornamental gates, now pinned back, disclosed a wide driveway sweeping round a corner and onto a gravel apron in front of the flight of double steps which led up to the front door of an Elizabethan country house. Beyond the driveway was a further tarmac road which led to some modern garages and workshops. The door to one of these workshops was open and parked just inside was a large black van. No lights were visible.

A side door opened in the main house and a dark figure, carrying several stainless steel tubes each about a metre long, and closely followed by another figure, not carrying anything visible save a revolver, made their way carefully through the trees to the van.

Two miles away Frank was leaning, chewing gum, against the driver's door of a Porsche 997 GT3, painted, unusually, in black, save for a thin gold line running from front to back a few inches below the windows of the doors. He wore a black race suit and boots. Both seats of the GT3 were fitted with four point harnesses. It was parked in a clearing deep in a wood up an obscure country lane; no one passing would have seen the car. Frank hoped the rain would not get much heavier; there was a limit to the off road capabilities of the two wheel drive Porsche.

Dyer's chiselled features looked even more rugged in the glow from the huge photocopier in the van.

'Easier than I thought, so far,' he observed.

Doyle was watching as Julie Walters fed into the machine the last of the twenty documents that made up the totality of the Namibian title leases. There was an infra red light poised over the copier; a cable ran out of a side hatch in the van to the power supply in the garage. The forcibly retired assistant Rangoon Oil company secretary who had helped them locate the leases was already on his way back home in transport organised by Frank and with a guard organised by Dyer.

Doyle was leaning against the wall of the van, also watching.

'I'm not so sure, Tony,' he said. 'I have a funny feeling that we are not alone, here, tonight.'

Dyer looked unconcerned.

'Well, very soon, we'll be out of here, and then it won't matter,' he concluded.

Doyle continued to look uneasy.

'There's something else going on here besides the storage of old documents,' he persisted.

'I'm sure I heard movement in the cellars,' he added.

'Well,' said Dyer, 'when you and I come to use the tunnel we'll see what we see.'

Dyer watched Julie as she drew the final document out of the machine and placed it in the last of three tubes.

'Right, Julie,' he said. 'Here's a final briefing. The original documents are being split between tubes one and two in a way which means that neither set have full legal validity. The third tube, which you will take back to London, is a blind. You will travel back to London in the van, with Frank's driver and the two guys I've got here, Fabian and Carlos. There is every possibility that you will be held up by our Russian friends. There should be nothing to worry about. You will have an SAS unit in front and behind and you will be in a bullet proof passenger compartment. You have your lady gun with you?' Dyer didn't really rate anything with a calibre less than point 44.

'The third tube will be in the van with you but as we all know while it contains some very interesting plans and leases they in fact relate to an Iranian oil field which has nothing to do with Rangoon. So the van is clean except for the photocopier and we will wipe all records off that.

Doyle and I will make our exit through the tunnel we reconnoitred earlier in the week which goes down from the house to the creek. Once we get to the end I will run cross country with the second tube accompanied by two men from the detachment at the end of the tunnel and rendezvous with Frank; he is in a wood which is only half a mile away from the creek as the crow flies. Doyle will get taken off by the SBS with the first tube. Then Frank and I will take a different route to London from the one taken by the van, but both have been cleared with the police. Once we have deposited our tube at the Bank we will swap cars and pick Doyle up from the waste wharf below Southwark Bridge and take the first tube up to the Bank. We will then re-group at Southwark Place. Before any of us leave the house here Carlos and Fabian will remove all our traces. Is there anything that's not clear?'

Walters looked nervous. It wasn't often that she was dragged into the rough stuff, as she put it to herself, but she had to admit to being thrilled by it. If only men could operate photocopiers, she thought idly, she might never have had the opportunity.

She was locked in the bullet proof compartment, together with one of the stainless steel canisters. Doyle and Dyer went back into the house to find the tunnel entrance and Fabian and Carlos began to obliterate all evidence from the ground floor document storage area. Frank's van driver, Derek, armed, hovered between the van and the house. Everyone carried a secure mobile operating on an encrypted private frequency, to which the leader of the three SAS detachments, Lieutenant Andy Horner, also had access.

Dyer led Doyle through the house and down the backstairs to the cellar door. It appeared a perfectly ordinary door such as you would expect to find in a very old country house. Except that it wouldn't open. Dyer scoured around with his flashlight. High up on the wall was a red lever which appeared to control some hydraulics. Dyer pulled it. Nothing happened. He beckoned Doyle away from the door and whispered urgently to him.

'Either this thing's not working or you're right. Someone the other side of the door has locked or disabled it. We've no choice but to blow it. If the people the other side are about some different business from ours I think they'll lie low and let us go through to the tunnel. But be prepared for fireworks. Going back upstairs and going down to the coast in the open simply isn't an option for us.'

Dyer opened a pouch he had strapped to his waist. Working incredibly quickly, while Doyle held the torch, he gauged the positioning of the door hinges and fitted small charges. Dyer motioned Doyle back.

'Thirty seconds,' he said gruffly. There was a small explosion and a lot of dust. The 'door', in reality a three inch thick safe door with a false wooden front, gaped open.

Doyle and Dyer passed quickly through into brilliant light.

Doyle gasped. He had expected to find himself in a damp country house cellar and had been speculating on its potential contents. What confronted them both was a gleaming laboratory, about forty by thirty feet, with work tops set out under blinding white light in the centre of the room and storage units all round the walls. As Doyle was hurried through the room by Dyer he saw that these were no ordinary storage units, more like a series of the highest security safes. There were, he noticed, two doors, shut, leading off the room. Dyer led the way to another opening in the wall, this time the hydraulic door which controlled it was fully open. As he half ran behind Dyer Doyle ran his fingers over the nearest work top and quickly looked at them, then smelt them, then tasted them. The scales fell from his eyes.

After entering the tunnel, Doyle noticed with surprise that something like miniature railway tracks appeared to have been laid on its floor. Doyle stopped for a moment to call the SBS unit, which he hoped was waiting for him, offshore, and warn them that his arrival was imminent; Dyer did the same with the SAS unit which should have been at the end of the tunnel.

Neither received a reply.

The tunnel wasn't straight and it wasn't dark. It was lit at a low level in its walls by a series of lights. It curved and twisted for about the first two hundred yards. Then it ran straight for a while. The two men could see, way in front, that there was some kind of junction. When they got nearer they could see that the railway lines ran away to the left, into what looked like a much more recently constructed tunnel. 'Their' tunnel carried on, from that point without lights. Suddenly Doyle felt a slight change in air pressure. Then he heard a low rumble coming from way down the new tunnel. He tugged at Dyer and whispered to him. They looked around frantically. Then Dyer motioned towards a break in the wall of the tunnel, just before the junction, which gave on to a brick built ventilator shaft housing an iron ladder. They rushed towards the ladder and saw that it led up to a grill about twenty five feet up. They shot a few feet up the ladder and craned their heads downward. The rumble became louder and louder and suddenly a battery driven electric drogue came into view. It had a driver, a dual seat and controls at the front and a flat load area of about six feet behind. This was piled high with what looked like ten kilogram dark blue plastic sacks. Behind the load area was another dual seat upon which rode two unmistakeable South Americans, dark, swarthy, with banderos and ammunition belts round their bodies, each armed with an AK 47.

The drogue rolled on out of their sight.

'What the bloody hell!' exclaimed Dyer. Doyle motioned to him.

'Come on,' he said, 'we've about three minutes to get out of here before we're history. Try that grating, if it won't move get down and bloody well run for your life.'

The grating proved immoveable and Doyle got down and started running down the old tunnel in front of Dyer. He again called the SAS unit which had been posted at the mouth of the tunnel.

Again there was no response.

They ran on as fast as the uneven floor of the tunnel would permit.

When they neared the entrance Doyle motioned Dyer to slow, and told him about the non response from the SAS unit. Listening intently for noise from their likely pursuers, they crept forward to the mouth of the tunnel which was about fifty yards from the high water line of the creek.

The creek was looking very beautiful. The rain had stopped, the tide was ebbing fast and the faint moonlight gleamed on the mud flats and on the ripples left by the now dying night breeze. The small jetty further down the creek was black against the night sky.

Apart from an old Thames barge at anchor the creek was completely empty.

There were no SAS at the mouth of the tunnel. There were no SBS in the creek.

Dyer left Doyle on watch and went for a scout over the ground. He was some time and came back to Doyle looking grim.

'There's every sign of a struggle here,' he said. 'The grass is crushed badly and what's worse is that there's blood, – and quite a lot of it – on some of the rocks. But there's nothing and no one here, so bodies – or prisoners – must have been removed', he added, 'but there must have been quite a posse to catch the SAS napping like this.'

'You'd better get on,' said Doyle urgently. 'Those fellows could be here any minute.'

'I can't leave you here after all this,' objected Dyer, 'you could be dead meat if the SBS aren't here soon.'

'There's no two ways about it,' said Doyle, 'you must get off. I'll hole up somewhere close to here. There are only two of them.'

Dyer thrust Doyle his gun. 'Here, sir, take this magnum. You may be needing it more than me. I'll take your gun.'

Dyer loped off effortlessly – he had been a triathlon champion in his army days.

Doyle was in a tight spot. He knew there was every chance that the two South American gunmen would come down the tunnel to look for him very soon. If not them, he reflected, it might be the posse that had dealt with the SAS unit. He had taken Dyer's night glasses. Holding them he scouted for some cover. There was a ramshackle and very disused Nissen hut about a hundred yards down the shore. He quickly took up a position in it from where he could command the mouth of the tunnel and the shore line.

What the hell had happened to these SBS guys? So far the support meant to be provided by these crack units had been distinctly uninspiring. He focussed his night glasses on the barge and immediately drew back into the entrance of the hut. There had been a solitary figure on deck apparently looking at him with similar equipment. The Thames barge might not be as innocent as it had seemed. He looked again. Now there seemed to be quite a bit of activity on deck. Two more people had appeared and seemed to be busying themselves on the far side of the barge.

Doyle's phone vibrated. It was the skipper of the SBS boat. They were on their way from the creek entrance. Doyle focussed his glasses; he could just see a line of phosphorescence being carved close inshore about one and a half miles away. He asked the skipper to pick him up a couple of hundred yards down the shore from the hut, gave him some details about the security position and started towards the shore. He looked back for a last time at the mouth of the tunnel. Then he looked at the barge. A very powerful RIB was nosing its way round its stern and seemed headed towards the beach further up the creek. Doyle reckoned that that was where the newer tunnel began and that the RIB was going to pick the returning gunmen up.

Doyle briefed the SBS skipper, and eased himself back into the shadows in the mouth of the hut.

His phone vibrated again. The SBS skipper came on;

'They are bound to have seen us but if they don't come looking for us straightaway I suggest we pick you up when they are busy loading their men on the shore. As soon as they get close to land we'll open up and be with you at the jetty in under a minute and get a bit of a start.'

The SBS boat came flying in in a cloud of spray, Doyle was hauled aboard by strong hands, the skipper reversed violently and then opened up both engines. Doyle was pleased to see he had a pair of two hundred and fifty horse Honda's fitted and, listening to their deep steady growl, he relaxed a little. He got his precious cylinder stowed in a relatively secure spot and turned round to watch what was going on astern.

Through his night glasses Doyle could see that the RIB from the barge had set off from the shore again and was already about a five hundred metres from it. But it wasn't headed back to the barge; it was tracking the SBS boat's wake. Doyle reckoned it was a kilometre or so behind them. Doyle knew that they had at least a hundred kilometres to run. He got the skipper on his own in the tiny cuddy.

'Our job is to get you to London, sir. That's what we've been told. We're fully armed to deal with your Russian friends, I think they were, but we hadn't anticipated an unrelated enemy. It's hard to see what they've got in terms of speed. We're good for fifty knots in flat water but they could have a bit more. We don't really want to start shooting with people we know nothing about so I'll guess we'll just have to lose them.'

'Lose them?' echoed Doyle. 'We're at sea, how the hell can we do that?'

'You leave that to me sir,' said the skipper, 'my old man was a Thames lighter skipper himself and what he didn't teach me about channels in the Thames estuary isn't worth knowing.'

'But these things barely draw anything,' said Doyle.

'You'll see,' said the skipper sagaciously.

Doyle thought for a while on his own in the cuddy. It was at least an hour to Southwark Bridge, and probably more, he thought, as they wouldn't be able to carry full speed right up the Thames. Even if the pursuers were only a few knots faster, the SBS boat needed a margin of several kilometres now to be able to rely on being ahead at the end.

Doyle talked again with the skipper and rang the coastguard. They had an armed corvette at Southend which had nearly forty knots and which could be scrambled in thirty minutes. Doyle calculated that this might not be much use as they would be off Southend in less time than that — that is if they were still in one piece. He passed on his analysis to the coast guard, asked him to mobilise their vessel in any event and poked his head outside.

The pursuers were still the best part of a kilometre away but seemed to have started to close the gap. Doyle asked the skipper what arms he was carrying.

'Machine guns, revolvers, and a rifle,' he responded.

Doyle was interested.

'What kind of rifle?' he asked.

'It's a sniper rifle, actually' came the response, 'got some decent sights on it but,' the boat jerked and swayed, ' almost unusable at this speed.'

'They're gaining,' Doyle said quietly. 'How soon can you implement your escape plans?'

'In about fifteen kilometres there is an old breakwater which runs several hundred metres out from the shore, part of the old World War Two defences. At this tide it's less than thirty centimetres under the surface and it'll rip their engines off if they are unaware of it. There's a twenty five metre gap in it – but it's very hard to spot at night, only identifiable by two unlit and unmarked poles. That's our chance,' the skipper concluded.

Ten minutes, thought Doyle. The SBS boat could almost be in range by then, assuming the pursuers just had AK47's.

'Won't they follow you straight through the gap?' queried Doyle.

'We won't be going through the gap,' said the skipper. 'This boat is fitted with optional jet power. Cuts our top speed by about ten knots but you can lift the whole S drive hydraulically which takes the props out of the water and then she draws virtually nothing.'

'Sounds good,' said Doyle, relieved to have underestimated him. 'By then, if we are still out of range, that has to work, or if not we have to shoot his boat up — and that will mean slowing right down for the best chance of using the sniper – so we virtually only have one shot. Either that or it's a running machine gun battle and the attrition could be very high.'

The skipper nodded agreement. Doyle scanned the tiny GPS which now had the breakwater set as a waypoint and was showing ten kilometres and seven minutes to go.

There was a rattle and a spatter on the water about three hundred yards behind them.

The SBS crew unslung their weapons. At a glance from Doyle the skipper signalled to them to hold off. Doyle asked for the sniper rifle and lay down straddled awkwardly across one of the hulls. He looked through the sights. The pursuers swung into view, out of view, back into view in a crazy pendulum motion. It was impossible to aim the gun for more than a split second. But, he thought, slowing the boat would be a giant gamble, immediately bringing the pursuers right into range.

Doyle concentrated on his breathing. Suddenly he had them in the sights. He aimed at the gyrating rubber hull and squeezed off two rounds.

Meanwhile Dyer had reached Frank and the Porsche without incident. Seconds later they were strapped in and the GT3 was being hurled by Frank down the country road which, in about ten miles, gave on to the A12. Dyer concentrated on keeping his stomach in touch with the rest of his body as the GT3, already travelling at nearly a hundred miles an hour, wound back and forth through a series of sharp bends. In less than seven minutes from leaving the clearing they were on the main road. Dyer watched as the Porsche screamed up through the gears and the orange tipped speedometer needle climbed to over a hundred and twenty miles an hour.

After about ten minutes Frank, who looked as cool as a cucumber, said;

'Something in the rear view mirror, Tony.'

'You have got to be joking,' muttered Dyer.

'It's not police,' said Frank. 'I've got their traffic coming into my earphones.'

'It must be our friends, unless it's some wide boy out for a late night burn.'

Whumpf! Whumpf! Whumpf!

There was a heavy clang off the offside rear.

'Well,' said Frank, wittily, 'its not a wide boy, at least not as we know them.'

He flicked a switch and suddenly there was a low menacing growl accompanied by a shrill whistle and both occupants felt a kick in the back. The speedometer needle edged gradually upwards and briefly hovered at a hundred and fifty. Dyer watched fascinated. Even the longest curve now felt like a hairpin.

'They've dropped back', said Frank. 'Lucky there aren't many supercharged GT3's around,' he added with the quiet satisfaction of the true petrol head.

'Time for some real countermeasures,' shouted Frank. The noise inside the car was now spectacular. 'Really all we've got apart from the speed is the chaff'.

'I'm going to wait for a long sweeper, let them close up, and then drop it.'

A long sweeping left hander was next. Dyer felt the car slow minutely, then saw Frank pull a lever down on the floor to his right, there was a thump at the back, then another 'Whumpf!' as the GT3 got within range of its pursuers; this time something clanged from the back and an appalling screeching noise set in as part of the bodywork of the Porsche was dragged along the tarmac at a hundred and twenty miles an hour.

Frank was scanning the rear view mirror.

'That's done it,' he said. 'They've bought it.'

Dyer craned his head round and saw what looked like a Maserati just finishing a last cartwheel about four hundred yards from the road. Suddenly it erupted into a fireball. Dyer watched fascinated as a massive explosion rocked it. Frank braked to a halt out of sight round the next bend.

'I'll just hack away this bodywork,' he muttered, 'then we'll get on. Call the police will you?'

Doyle watched as the front section of one of the hulls of the pursuing RIB exploded. It swerved madly behind them, corkscrewing first one way then the other. Finally it slowed and went into an ever tightening turn, only violent avoiding action by its crew prevented it rolling over. After it stopped Doyle could just see its crew thrown together in the bottom of the boat while one of them crawled forward to inspect the damage. Soon the attackers had dropped way behind them and were very soon lost to view.

The SBS boat carried on at a more relaxed forty knots. In a short while the skipper slowed the boat right down, switched to jet power, and whipped over the top of the breakwater. Then the skipper said he was going to keep using the jet power and go right inshore through the unmarked Thames Estuary shoals.

Forty five minutes later they were cruising at a sober pace past the Thames Barrier en route to Southwark Bridge. The dawn was beginning to break over the Thames and the great river was a glorious swirling mixture of black and gold pools with the buildings of Canary Wharf bathed in a soft pink glow. It was going to be a beautiful day.

Doyle deposited his documents at the Bank, pleasantly surprised to find that the special opening of the vaults which he had requested was supervised by the same immaculately uniformed attendants habitually on duty throughout the rest of the day.

A very tired group assembled at Southwark Place for breakfast.

The photocopier van contingent had run into a highly professional roadblock set up by Lutin's men between the house and the A12. But this was swiftly dealt with by the SAS and its protagonists handed over to police custody. There had been no sign of Lutin himself.

There had been no further reports as to the fate or identity of the occupants of the crashed Maserati. Doyle wondered if Lutin had been in it; he caught himself hoping in some bizarre way that he had not.

That left the mystery of the operation being carried in the basement of the house and the fate of the SAS contingent at the mouth of the tunnel.

For a variety of reasons Doyle was extremely keen to keep these matters as private as possible and two hours later he had made calls to Singh, and then at his direction the Commanding Officer of the SAS and the head of security at the Inland Revenue and Customs.

So far, thought Doyle, so good. Lutin's attempts to access the Namibian assets and derail the Sphinx project had been reasonably determined and predictably murderous but there hadn't been displays of overwhelming force.

Doyle thought such a display was probably not far away.

Chapter 13

NAMIBIA FIRE FIGHT

Two immaculate black Hummers stood outside a dingy café in the back streets of Windhoek. Every other car in the street was old and dusty; most were on their last legs. An overwhelming tawdriness hung over the street with its filling station, a builder's yard, and some ramshackle offices. The early morning sun was just beginning to chase away the chill shadows while the freshness of the African dawn was replaced by a composite smell of wood smoke and cooking, decaying rubbish and burnt rubber.

Several African guards in incongruous white uniforms lounged over the bonnet of one of the Hummers. Heavily armed, they were laughing and bragging. From time to time a radio in one of the Hummers crackled inconsequentially and was ignored.

In the otherwise deserted inner room of the café sat two men. One was Doyle in jeans, a bush shirt and desert boots. The other was President Joseph Barula, dressed in a black tracksuit and jogging shoes.

A door opened and a very large beaming Namibian lady waddled through it bearing two huge plates of bacon, eggs and hash browns.

'I'll bring the coffees in just a minute,' she lilted, 'and is there anything else that you good gentlemen would be wanting just now? If you do, just ring the bell. I'll be right outside.'

She beamed at them and waddled out.

Barula forked some food into his mouth and spread out the front page of the 'Republikein'.

Its headline was as unwelcome as it was unequivocal.

'NAMIBIA OIL EXPLORATION FAILURE' it screamed. Below the headline sat the words, 'Your paper has learned that Namibia has huge and potentially enormously valuable oil assets. Assets that would be of huge benefit to the people of this country. Namibia could become another Saudi Arabia with free public health services, free telephones, and prosperity for all. But what has this government, the government of President Joseph Barula, done about realising this wealth? The answer, friends, is ABSOLUTELY NOTH-ING. About sixty years ago most of the oil explo-ration rights over Namibia were granted to an imperialistic company, Rangoon Oil, which has NEVER done anything with them. Meanwhile it is thought that other foreign companies, including Russian and Chinese, are queuing to take ad-vantage of these opportunities.

The Republikein asks WHEN will newly elected President Barula act to enable his citizens to take advantage of their own natural wealth?'

Barula tapped the paper.

'This is pretty unhelpful, James. Pretty soon I'm going to have to be seen to be doing something. Something a lot more than giving an old college mucker the chance to mess about on someone else's rights. I should be stripping Rangoon of these rights and auctioning them off to the Rus-sians and Chinese. As a matter of fact I've actu-ally got a Russian booked in to see me tomorrow from Petrogaz, I think.'

'What's his name?' Doyle asked.

'Alexander something, something musical? Lute? No, Lutin, that's it.'

Doyle took a sip of his coffee, pushed his plate away, and lit a cigarette.

'Joe,' he said, 'there are some things you should know.'

After about fifteen minutes Barula interrupted him.

'Yes, I can see all of that James. But I have a bottom line. And my bottom line is, is there oil in Namibia, if so, how much, and can I get the Namibian State a good deal on its extraction?'

'Joe,' said Doyle, 'I understand your priorities completely. I can promise you one thing. There definitely is oil here, probably quite a lot, and there is the chance that it could be one of the biggest fields in the world. It could make Namibia one of the leading Black African economies.'

'When, James, when, can all this be fully checked out and made public?' Barula was urgent.

'Joe, we need to do some more drilling. We've done the minimum so far, as you were rightly sensitive to the effect on your reputation of treading on Rangoon's toes. If we can do more we need about another two months to have an eighty to ninety percent confidence level in the ultimate size of the field. Then we'll bid for Rangoon and we'll do a deal with you.'

Barula's brow furrowed.

'Two months is a long time out here, James, and when they've got a bone this size they never let go, you know.'

'I doubt if they've got any proof that there's a dicky bird of oil out here, Joe. Why don't you find out what the editor thinks he's got and if there's nothing announce you are commissioning a strategic review addressing how the mineral resources of Namibia can be optimised, which will report in say three months?'

'This bloody well isn't Whitehall you know James. You can't feed the people here la di da reviews,' said Barula. But he looked happier.

'You can tell that to Mr Lutin, too,' added Doyle as they parted company.

Doyle flew up to Jock's operation centre, based on the coast at Terrace Bay towards the Northern end of Namibia, about one hundred and fifty miles west of Kamanjab. The little Cessna crossed miles of arid plain on the way West to Walvis Bay and then headed north up the Skeleton Coast, flying at about five thousand feet. Doyle was lost in his thoughts as the towering rolling dunes unfolded steadily beneath them.

Lutin was going to be a very frustrated man. Doyle had been absolutely certain that the Russians' basic instinct would be to try to obtain the original leases. He had put one spoke in their wheel in relation to that. This newspaper piece was exactly what he would have predicted by way of follow up. It was a blatant attempt to pressurize Barula into strong arming the rights away from Rangoon into more pro- active hands. It would have worked in nineteen out of twenty other African countries. But not with Joe Barula, one of the very few principled African Heads of State who had a passionate interest in doing the right thing for his people and not freely helping himself to the spoils en route. Doyle felt for him and the agony that headline must have caused — the charge of inertia would have been bad enough, to actually be doing something and yet not be able to make it public could only have twisted the screw.

No, thought Doyle, Lutin would continue to put the pressure on. But Barula's establishment of the mineral rights commission, while a win, of a kind, would frustrate him yet further. He would have no progress at all to report to Orlov and he would be deeply uncomfortable with that.

He would contemplate something more forceful, Doyle was sure. Lutin and his masters wouldn't think that getting Petrogaz into some kind of level playing field auction with a whole bunch of other heavy duty global oil players was a win at all.

Doyle reflected. Now he saw glimpses of the sea interspersed with the golden dunes — so much had been written about this treacherous coast.

Doyle mulled that Lutin would want to find out just how big the prize might be before he calibrated his next response. So far Lutin's efforts, he reflected again, had been competent but no more.

But if Lutin were to get a feel for the potentially monstrous size of the prize he might adopt some much more muscular tactics.

Doyle watched as the Cessna waggled its wings on its final approach to the dusty strip.

He expected a visit from Alexander Lutin before very long.

Jock Millar looked across the large table in the saloon in the old schooner. He had just taken James Doyle in microscopic detail through every bit of work he and his team had done in the last four months since they had first come to Namibia. The table was strewn with aerial survey photographs, seismic drilling reports and logs and the actual drilling results he and his team had obtained in the last two months. The original drilling reports of the Australian company, now rather faded and dog eared, lay to one side.

Doyle was tired. He had spent the afternoon flying with Jock in the twin engined Cessna, over about a quarter of a million square miles of Namibian desert and scrub. Then he had spent four hours with Jock in the saloon, with the old schooner's distinctly primitive air conditioning struggling to keep pace with the evening heat.

'Time for a beer I think, Jock,' muttered Doyle.

They went up on deck and Doyle drank in the beginnings of the night time breeze. A delicious smell of cooking wafted up from the schooner's galley.

'So what is it tonight, Jock?' grinned Doyle. 'Lion curry?'

He took a long drink of ice cold Windhoek lager and luxuriated in the sight of the last rays of the setting sun illuminating the giant dunes The night sky was unbelievably clear. A mile further out the sea fretted and clawed at the bar.

Millar cracked a grin. He was a rock hard Glaswegian who had spent the last thirty years knocking about every kind of god forsaken hole where his masters thought oil might be found. His considerable reputation had been built on the fact that he had been party to many of the most important finds made in that time. But for the first time in his life his grizzled features betrayed the hope that this time, maybe this time, and quite contrary to all his initial instincts, he was onto something that he, his kids, and his grand kids, would remember forever.

The Field of Dreams. Where had the boys got that name from? He couldn't remember. Something out of childhood reading he supposed. Anyway, James Doyle seemed happy enough with it.

He filled and lit an ancient pipe and watched Doyle open his packet of Egyptian cigarettes.

James Doyle was something of an enigma to him. He was neither one thing nor the other. Or was he a combination of every boss he'd ever had? He wasn't an out and out hard dealing hard talking serial entrepreneur. He wasn't a hood. He wasn't a professional softie consultant.

Millar gave it up.

Doyle's satellite phone rang. The deep tones of Joseph Barula came through,

'How are you getting on there James? Thanks for breakfast, by the way, and for your thoughts on the commission. Something to that I guess. I'm happy for you guys to drill on more extensively for a couple of months but then I really have to have something I can use.

One piece of information for you though. My guys down at Tshabong on the South African border have reported a posse of trucks heading north. Seemed to be Russians and some South Africans. Looked like a pretty tough lot. Had some weapons — not unusual round here, I admit, but they just seemed to my people to be a cut above most of the players we get round here. They let them through – only had a one week visa and said they were on their way to deliver some spares for one of the fishing fleets at Walvis. They had a lot of kit with them. I just thought it seemed a bit co-incidental, seeing as how I've got that Russian friend of yours pitching up tomorrow.'

'Joe,' said Doyle. 'It's probably nothing. But coming up here today I thought our friend's next move might be to pay us a visit. Any chance you could let me have some help?'

Barula chuckled.

'I need to keep you alive I guess James. I'll see what I can do.'

Doyle groaned. What a pity Lutin hadn't been in that damned Maserati after all.

Jock Millar looked disconcerted.

'Would you care to tell me what's going on here, James?' he asked a touch peevishly.

The curry was brought up on deck and over the strongly flavoured and nutritious meal Doyle gave Jock a thumb nail sketch of recent events.

'The thing that really worries me,' said Doyle gesticulating towards the cabin as he ate, 'is Lutin getting hold of all our work.'

Jock waved his hand at the bleak landscape.

'There's not a lot of hiding places here,' he said. 'I suppose we could bury it, but these sands shift the whole time and if we left it any length of time we might never find it again.'

He thought for a moment.

'Wait a minute,' he said, 'there is another option. There's an old wreck on the reef about two miles from here. That would make a good spot — and you need a RIB to get to it. But what the hell would we store all the data in? The conditions on that reef can be horrendous.'

'Got any lead?' asked Doyle.

'A few sheets, just in case we damage the schooner hull.'

'Why don't we make a chest out of that?' Doyle said. 'It's fairly easy to solder.'

Within the hour Millar had called his maintenance team from their huts onshore and a lead case was being constructed.

Doyle had another call with Barula. He was sending two Landcruisers, each with four men from his special forces. They would be on station by dawn. Barula also estimated that the Lutin trucks, if such they were, would not be likely to arrive before the later part of the next day.

'We'll hold them up a bit for you,' he laughed.

After dinner they loaded the chest into Jock's RIB, not without difficulty, and with two extra men set out for the wreck. Doyle had got them to build four lugs into the case and they took some lightweight Kevlar rope from the schooner in order to lash the box onto the wreck together with some rope ladders and lifting tackle.

Once they were out of the shelter of the creek the wind rose dramatically and Doyle was mesmerised by the huge seas which had built up during the day and which were now still running offshore outside the reef. Millar navigated on a course just inside the jagged line of rocks which marked it and soon they were within sight of the wreck. This was an old coaster, lying on the reef well down by the stern and listing heavily to port. Her black paint had nearly all gone and streaks of rust covered nearly every surface. Doyle thought grimly that she made a poor burial ground for all his expensively acquired intellectual property. Under the RIB's floodlights he caught a glimpse of her name – 'Ali Baba'- very appropriate, he thought.

They closed the wreck and Jock and another man got some grappling irons and a ladder onto her and shinned up it. Then the lifting equipment was taken aboard and set up rather awkwardly on the listing deck. Jock shouted down that there was a perfect hiding spot inside one of the old deck lockers, which, miraculously, still had a lid which hadn't rusted on.

After a considerable struggle, Doyle with his heart in his mouth as his precious cargo swayed above the bouncing RIB and grated on the flaking side of the coaster, the deed was done, the case firmly lashed and no evidence was visible of the intrusion into the old coaster's death throes.

They returned to the schooner at three am and Doyle snatched a few hours sleep.

The first of the Russian trucks was spotted by one of Barula's men who had been posted high up on a ridge two miles to the South. After a while he could see, through the midday heat haze, three more trucks moving slowly behind in a loose, dusty, convoy.

Doyle had been in two minds about how to play his hand. He had considered simply deserting the camp and the schooner and letting the raiders comb through them and eventually go away empty handed. He had rejected this out of concern for potential damage to their kit and equipment and the fact that the raiders would be bound to return if they were thwarted on a first visit.

He decided that the camp and the schooner, which were about six hundred yards apart and joined by a dusty track, would present themselves as operating entirely normally. The Cessna would be flown upcountry. He, Dyer and his team of Carlos and Fabio, who had flown up from Johannesburg that morning, and the eight men sent by Barula, would arm and conceal themselves, splitting their forces between the schooner and the camp. Concealment in those arid treeless dunes was extremely difficult; fortunately Barula's men had brought a good deal of desert camouflage gear.

The trucks were arranged in something of a V formation in front of the camp. Individual dug outs had been built on the hill behind the camp behind some of the large boulders strewn on it. When covered with camo they were pretty much invisible at least to the naked eye. The team guarding the schooner were split between the sail locker in the forehatch and underneath the pontoon to which the old yacht was moored. Arms had been split; Barula's men would not be parted from their AK's while Doyle favoured a hunting rifle, others had revolvers and shotguns. Dyer had managed to smuggle in three Kriss Super V's; God knows, thought Doyle, how he had managed to do that.

At about three o'clock in the afternoon the Russian trucks roared into the camp. They were all ex South African Army Toyotas. Their engines died and there was complete silence apart from the ticking of hot metal. For a while no one got out and to his concern Doyle saw that they were minutely scanning the surroundings with binoculars. These people meant business, thought Doyle, and they meant harm. He tightened his grip on his rifle. Eventually a figure emerged from the rear passenger compartment of the leading truck. He was a tall white South African. Doyle scanned him with a glass. He had the most unpleasant features Doyle had seen for a long time. His thin lips turned down at the corners of his mouth, his bloodshot eyes were close set, a scar ran down one cheek and under his chin. He wore old army fatigues and had a revolver tucked at his waist and a hunting knife strapped to his right leg. Doyle thought he looked a professional killer.

He called out in a very heavy Afrikaans accent to Jock Millar, who was pretending to work on one of the Sphinx trucks.

'Hey, man, I'd like to speak with you.'

'Who are you?' asked Jock.

'I ask the questions round here, man,' came the clipped response.

'You can ask all the questions you want, mate', said Jock in his dour Glaswegian accent, 'but I canna say you'll be getting any answers. It's nae business of yours, anyway.'

'I think I need to make myself clearer,' said the South African.

'We understand you've been up here for months doing surveys and seismic work and some drilling. I've got some experts in the trucks who'd like to go over that work with you and just check how you are getting on.'

'Why would I want to do that?' Jock was at his most dour.

'We are security, working for the Energy Ministry, my friend. You're probably out of touch here but you should read this. By the way, I am Jan Baster.'

He handed Jock the two day old copy of the Republikein.

'You can see from that there are folk who might want to know exactly what you're doing here to justify the licences you've been given. The President wants everyone prospecting resources on Namibian land to become more accountable.'

'We're here to help you do that,' Baster concluded shortly.

'Have ye papers? Ye are not in Government vehicles I see,' Jock looked openly sceptical.

Baster's face darkened.

'Listen,' he said. 'There are two ways of doing this. Either you co-operate, you speak to our people, and you keep your licenses and get on with your work. Or if you don't help us we'll forcibly search this camp for your data, and you may lose your licenses and all your investment. There are plenty of other people standing ready to help Namibia look for its oil.'

'Prove who you are,' said Jock, 'and then we'll have something to talk about.'

'I'll let this,' Baster dug his revolver into Jock's ribs, 'do the talking if you don't mind. Now we'll search your camp.'

Baster jerked his head at the trucks behind him and some fifteen men, some white South African, some who looked Russian, and some black South African, all uniformed and heavily armed, left the vehicles and ranged round Baster.

Baster led them forward into the huts.

Doyle flicked his radio on and said: 'Let's wait till they come out, guys. They'll be empty handed and then they'll start to beat up Jock. That's when we'll let them have it. I'll give the order. Everyone take the man closest to them. Shoot to disable first. Don't miss, we are outnumbered, it's got to be very quick and very clinical. Don't close with them until we re-group after that first round. If they shoot back shoot to kill second time round.'

Muttered voices of assent crackled back to him.

They waited for about an hour in the searing heat and flies. Doyle's throat was dry and his eyes were sore. He was puzzled. Where was Lutin? He scoured the raider's vehicles; he couldn't see right inside them all. He cast his mind back. How many people had got out of the last truck? He thought it might only have been two.

Eventually the men re-appeared. Baster's face was like thunder. He walked straight up to Millar, put his revolver to the side of his head, took him by the collar and pushed him down in front of the first of their trucks. He gave an order and Millar was soon strapped to the front bumper of the truck.

'It's already pretty hot here my friend and for you it's about to get a whole lot hotter unless you prove capable of answering some simple questions.

And my first is,' Baster kicked Jock hard in the balls and he doubled up, 'where have you hidden all your papers? The camp is bare, you bastard.' He kicked him again with real force.

Jock was doubled up, straining at his bonds.

'Right, start her up,' Baster ordered a subordinate, 'we'll see how you like some real heat.'

Baster stood back to one side. Doyle looked at the rest of the men who had begun to converge on the truck in goulish anticipation of the spectacle.

Doyle readied his rifle, picked his man and said into his radio: 'Go'.

A volley of shots rang out. Baster's men started to drop like flies. A return burst of machine gun fire sprayed the sand to the left of Doyle's dug out.

Then Doyle felt a heavy blow on the back of his head and lost consciousness.

When he came to he was lying bound in the forepeak of the schooner. His head felt appalling and he had a raging thirst. Judging by the light which filtered in it seemed to be early morning. The schooner didn't appear to be moving and Doyle concluded it must still be made fast to the pontoon. Doyle wondered dimly what had happened after the fire fight started.

The hatch opened and an African whom he did not recognise came down the ladder.

'Water,' croaked Doyle. The African disappeared and came back with a water bottle which he helped Doyle drink.

'Is he conscious?' came familiar, confident tones. Lutin, thought Doyle.

'Bring him up,' Lutin continued.

The bonds which bound Doyle's feet were released and with the aid of the African he staggered to his feet and was pushed out on deck. He walked unsteadily to the cockpit where Lutin, in safari kit, was lounging imperiously.

'Ah, Doyle,' he said breezily, 'how nice to have the chance to have a chat with you in a more leisured, more civilized environment.'

'You have been getting in my way,' he said pleasantly, 'and now this has to stop.

I have admired the enterprise and initiative you and your, er, Sphinx, partnership, have shown in your oil and other dealings. You really have, as I understand it, achieved a great deal.

But I'm sure you understand the energy agenda of the Russian state. In simple terms it seeks dominance, firstly in European gas, where it conceives of itself leading a second kind of OPEC, a gas OPEC. Secondly, if an opportunity arose to greatly extend its oil interests internationally, that would give an impetus, together with its already massive domestic oil reserves, towards a second oil based OPEC along with some of our traditionally good international friends. Those two new bodies would set the seal on Russia's truly imperialistic energy ambitions and restore to the Russian state the international weight and respect it deserves and which so many Western governments have persistently sought to belittle.

I understand that you have been doing a lot of work out here and have potentially identified very large reserves. In fact we are better informed than you may think. Through industrial espionage via devices installed at the factory on your new Seismic X equipment we have been able, in Moscow, to monitor your test results. We share your view that this could be a world class or even top of the class resource. But we have not been able to access all your other data and especially your drilling results. We also know Doyle, that the leases to this resource are bearer leases which were in the possession of Rangoon, which, in a typically incompetent way, have done nothing with them.

We know that you removed the originals of these the other night from the possession of Rangoon.

I have been guilty of underestimating you, Doyle. I admit it. I focussed on your financial record and not your other abilities.

But what you have to understand is that in the long run there is no way that a bunch of financially literate traders such as the Sphinx are going to be allowed to own or control this kind of resource. That is for big boys like us I am afraid.

Russia means to control these reserves, Doyle. Nor do we propose to bid for Rangoon or follow any of those other boy scout procedures to which you and your friends are so attached. We want those leases and we want your data and your drilling results.

Do I make myself clear?'

'Perfectly,' muttered Doyle.

'So, are you going to tell me where each of them are? ' asked Lutin silkily.

'No,' said Doyle.

Lutin disappeared and came back moments later flourishing a rhino hide whip.

'I love those old stories of naval floggings don't you?' Lutin cracked the whip savagely.

'It seems so boring simply to use a truth drug on you Doyle, especially when you've given me so much aggravation.'

'Give me some answers, you bastard, quickly, or you get this.' Lutin's feature's were contorted into a vicious leer.

Doyle said nothing.

Lutin ordered the African to bind Doyle to the mainmast. When this was done Lutin stepped forward and ripped Doyle's shirt off.

He stepped back. The whip cracked across Doyle's back and an immediate huge weal appeared with blood rising from it.

Doyle was almost faint with pain. He had never experienced anything like it. Another savage blinding pain engulfed him as Lutin gave him a second lash.

He made up in his mind.

'Stop.' He could barely utter the words. 'I'll take you to the records. And the leases are in the bank. I can get them for you.'

Lutin put the whip down, regretfully.

'Well, that didn't take long. A pity really,' his grin was wolfish. 'I was really rather enjoying myself.'

He instructed the African to take Doyle below.

When Doyle returned stiffly to the deck, in handcuffs, he was offered a cup of coffee.

His mind was still working through the pain. He wished he knew how the shore battle had ended.

'So where do we go?' asked Lutin.

'We can't go anywhere without the captain,' said Doyle. 'Where is he?'

Dyer didn't mess about. His first shots took out Baster, crippled in the knees. He watched as eight other men folded. Four men ran off behind the Sphinx trucks. Dyer cursed long and freely. Why the hell couldn't the people sent by Barula shoot accurately?

He kept his head right down. He tried to remember how many there had been to start with. Fifteen he had counted. He wasn't sure if there were others in the trucks who had never got out.

He hadn't seen Doyle's capture and he had no idea where the remaining men had got to.

He was most worried about getting to Jock Millar who was still crumpled in front of the radiator of the idling truck. He would be burned beyond redemption unless he could be released very soon.

He spoke quickly into the radio.

'We're going to disarm these people one at a time. I'm going to ask them to surrender and then we will remove their weapons, one by one. I want two of the Namibian men to help me. Fabio and Carlos and the rest of you will provide covering fire.'

He cupped his hands and shouted: 'Everyone put their hands up and drop their weapons. Anyone who fires their weapon will be shot dead.'

Six pairs of hands went up slowly. Dyer shouted: 'All of you, right.'

Another pair of hands went up, and, slowly, the last pair.

Dyer got slowly to his feet. A vicious burst of machine gun fire kicked up the sand round him. Like lightening he returned it. There was a scream of pain.

Dyer sprinted weaving madly down the hill towards the truck which had Millar attached to it. Another burst of fire came from the Sphinx trucks. Fabio silenced it. Dyer and two of Barula's men reached the back of Millar's truck and took cover behind it. Dyer told the Africans to cover the truck. He crawled under its rear bumper, inching his way forward under the heat and rumble of the engine, feeling for his hunting knife. He reached Millar, who was groaning in pain. The heat was intense. Dyer rolled onto his back and felt for the cords. He quickly slashed them and Millar's body slumped to the sandy floor.

'Play dead,' he snapped.

'I am fucking dead, you stupid bastard,' groaned Jock.'

With a herculean effort Dyer dragged Millar's frame further back down the truck away from the engine and left him.

'We'll be out of this in a minute,' he re-assured.

Dyer crawled back to the rear of the truck. He reckoned there were two men unaccounted for and he knew he had first to disable them and then disarm the wounded as quickly as possible. He gestured to the two Africans and pointed them at the two nearest fallen men, whose arms were beginning to slump down.

One of the remaining eight had let his hands completely drop to the ground. Dyer shot him dead with his revolver.

'Keep your hands up,' he yelled.

Seven pairs of hands straightened up.

Tony Dyer got down under the truck once more and peered past the recumbent Millar to-ward the Sphinx trucks. There were two pairs of legs showing underneath the far truck. Dyer flat-tened himself on the sand and taking very care-ful aim loosed off a burst of the Kriss at each. The legs gave way and were joined by the bodies which belonged to them.

'OK, guys,' he yelled at his two Africans, 'let's disarm the rest.'

THE FIELD OF DREAMS

Minutes later there was a surprisingly large haul of automatic weapons on the sand in front of the huts and ten minutes later they were joined by a row of ten bound attackers and three dead bodies.

Even Dyer felt faintly sickened by the spectacle.

There was no trace of the two remaining men who had originally got out of the trucks.

Dyer assumed they must have made for the schooner.

But there was no sign of the yacht, and no sign of Doyle.

Dyer felt a wave of desperation. He was savagely loyal to Doyle.

He reconnoitred and was pleased to see that the RIB, which had been tied up in front of the schooner, was still moored there, apparently undamaged.

Dyer told four of Barula's men to load the injured and the dead into the trucks in which they had travelled and to take them back to the nearest military post at Outjo.

Miraculously the Sphinx team, apart from Millar, who was in a bad way, and two of Barula's men who had sustained bullet grazes, were uninjured.

The sun's rays were almost extinct by the time they had all eaten some food and drunk some cold beer.

They were all dog tired and Dyer ordered sleep. He concluded there was no point in trying to search for Doyle in the dark in unfamiliar waters in a RIB which could be shot out of the water at the leisure of whatever attack team was on the yacht.

But Dyer couldn't help himself taking a lengthy trawl round in the RIB in the blackest night he'd ever seen. The wind was rising and he couldn't see any silhouette resembling the schooner, even with his night glasses. Eventually, and with much foreboding, he reluctantly packed it in.

Dyer woke early with a lingering revulsion at the previous day's events. He went quickly down to the jetty. Still nothing. He cast his eye out to sea and was pleased to see a heavy bank of fog rolling in from far out beyond the reef.

He went back to the camp, fiddled with the radio and caught up with the Barula drivers. They would be back later in the morning. The Namibia police wanted a full report. Dyer groaned at the thought. Doyle was the man to talk their way out of this situation, he thought.

There was an odd regular beeping sound on one of the more remote radio frequencies. He went to see Millar, who, if the amount of swearing and demands for tea had anything to do with it, was recovering fast.

Millar was puzzled.

'Schooner's gone you say?'

'Could be that they've chucked the EPIRB overboard to indicate their position, the Emergency Position Indicator that most yachts carry to indicate their position if they get into difficulty.' Millar picked up a large mug of tea.

'Could mean they are aground somewhere,' he concluded.

'There's quite a useful fog coming in,' said Dyer. 'I suggest we have a quick breakfast and get out there in the RIB. We're going to need some arms, some food and drink and some warm clothing — we'll take the portable shortwave.' He summoned Fabio, Carlos and two of Barula's men.

When they got to the RIB a sudden instinct made Dyer get the five man rubber dinghy ready, with its oars, to be towed behind the RIB.

'That RIB's a noisy beast,' he said, 'and we may need to be stealthy.'

There was very little wind. They got out into the open sea and cast about, constantly testing the signal strength of the EPIRB.

'They're North,' said Dyer decisively, 'that means he led them away from the Ali Baba.'

After two miles of cruising up the inner edge of the reef, going slowly as the fog was coming in thickly, the signal strength increased markedly. The wind had dropped away and it was very cold and uncannily quiet.

'I'm dead sure they're not far away,' said Dyer, 'let's switch off.'

They drifted gently on the swell. There wasn't a sound. Dyer listened intently. After a while some snatched phrases came very faintly over the water.

'I think she moved. Let's have another go in reverse.' The words tailed off.

'They must be aground inside the reef,' muttered Dyer, 'and I can only hear two voices.'

'Three of us into the dinghy with our guns,' continued Dyer. 'Fabio, stay with the RIB. As soon as you hear a shot move in close to the schooner, belay alongside and get stuck in.'

They rowed steadily off in the rubber boat, following such snippets of chatter as there were. Dyer prayed that the fog would remain thick. Suddenly voices sounded, very very close. The sides of the schooner suddenly loomed high above them. Dyer gave the signal for complete silence. Holding themselves off the sides of the schooner they poled round it looking for some access. There was nothing, neither a fixed ladder nor a rope ladder. Again Dyer's foresight paid off as he unrolled a small rope ladder lying in the bottom of the rubber boat. Dyer poled to the bow of the schooner and indicated to Carlos that he should shin up the massive bobstay which controlled the bowsprit. Carlos took one end of the ladder with him and within seconds they were all taking cover behind the sail bags in the bows. Listening intently they could hear four voices, the deep rolling tones of the old African skipper, the familiar tones of Doyle, the impeccable English of Lutin with that indefinable Mediterranean accent, and one of the Africans from the raiding party.

The conversation seemed to be about the remaining options for getting the schooner off the sandbank on which she seemed to be very firmly lodged – Dyer had detected no movement in the hull whatsoever.

There was a fore hatch open just in front of them. Dyer gathered Carlos and the African and whispered: 'I'm going below to see if there's anyone there. I'll deal with them if I can and continue down to the main companionway. As soon as you hear me say anything I'll want you in the stern — remember the only enemy seem to be Lutin and his African mate. We want to take them in one piece if we can. If any shooting starts wing them.'

Dyer disappeared down the hatch. There was silence for a moment and then an ominous clunk from a cabin aft. Suddenly there was an exclamation of voices. Carlos and the African moved aft surreptiously but were almost knocked off their feet by Lutin running like a hare towards the bow. He crash dived into the rubber boat and within seconds had been swallowed up by the unrelenting fog. When they got to the cockpit the remaining African had his hands up.

'Am I pleased to see you,' said James Doyle.

Chapter 14

LONDON CAPITAL

It was the day after the Saudi announcement. Oil had risen from forty dollars a barrel to over a hundred and was still climbing. Major stock market indices around the world had tumbled up to thirty per cent. Newspapers and television stations were predicting the end of the civilized industrial world and heralding a new dark age. A great deal of interest was being taken in the political stability of lesser oil producing nations and their disposition towards the West. The Saudi Arabian Government was being vilified. All manner of Islamicist conspiracy theories were rampant, imperilling the delicate progress towards a new relationship between Islam and the West which had been one of the pre-occupations of the new American President, Den Leopold.

Yet in Doyle's headquarters in Southwark Place all was calm.

The Sphinx had gathered to count its spoils from what Doyle referred to as Phase One.

It was ten in the morning. Fleming was making his report.

'All in all, not counting our strategic investment in Rangoon, but including all the sidecars, we laid out some ten billion pounds on margin on a wide variety of oil futures, oil stock futures and related equities, global equity shorts, and foreign currency futures. Very roughly this margin gave us leverage over something short of two hundred billion pounds of the underlying assets. The gross value of those exposures has increased by about fifty per cent since we incepted them. The gross Sphinx profit from this exercise, on paper, net of expenses, is just about a hundred billion pounds, gentlemen, of which about half or fifty billion is attributable to our own funds.'

It generally took quite a bit to coax a smile from the faces of the members of the Sphinx. Doyle was pleased to see that this number had done it.

'Have we realised any of this profit yet?' asked Bulstrode.

'We have started to do so,' replied Fleming, 'we are about twenty five per cent realised in the last two hours and the process is continuing. We should be completely liquid within forty eight hours.'

'What about our investment in Rangoon?' asked Michel Weill.

'Hey guys,' said Patrick Myers, 'I know we are a pretty mean bunch but let's just take a second to express our appreciation to James for the success of Phase 1; it's far and away the single biggest financial coup any of us have pulled off in our lifetimes, right?'

There was a warm buzz of endorsement around the table which passed for appreciation. Doyle shifted cautiously in his seat; enjoyable as these moments were they seldom lasted long.

'Well, as you know,' began Doyle, 'we have built up a holding in Rangoon of some twenty nine point nine percent, largely through using CFD's. That is the largest holding which can be built without incurring an obligation under the European Takeover Directive to make an offer for the rest of the shares. It is vital that we do not trigger that obligation as it will impose on us a requirement to finance such an offer which at present we cannot meet; I will come on to that later. Rangoon is up some twenty per cent on our average entry price which reflected a gross cost of some thirty billion pounds though we have had to lay out less than two billion pounds on margin to secure the CFD position. What I propose is that we convert our CFD's into actual stock, which will absorb an additional twenty eight billion pounds of our profit. That will make our holding appear to the market to be much more substantive and vastly increase the speculation that already surrounds it. Then we have to be ready for the balloon to go up and we have to have a very disciplined approach to what we say about that holding to the outside world.

I have Graham Makepeace from our lawyers Death and Maiden coming round at eleven to brief us on all these issues. But the most important issue now facing us is our strategy to take over Rangoon and the financing requirement imposed by that. Not surprisingly the steady build up of our Rangoon holding has attracted enormous speculation in the press combined with considerable agitation on the part of the Board of Rangoon. The fact that we have persistently refused to discuss the reasons for the accumulation of our stake either publically through the media or privately with the Chairman of Rangoon has added fuel to the flames. The more sophisticated commentators are at a loss to work out why we would want such a large holding in a mature, almost moribund, oil major, and have concluded that it is a completely counter cultural investment for such a group of aggressive hedge funds to have made. They cannot see any upside in it, apart from the rather prosaic possibility of further cost cutting, generally the last refuge of major corporations with a failed growth strategy.

Meanwhile the Board of Rangoon have become ever more agitated over our refusal to engage with them. Let me read you the last letter we had from their Chairman, Sir Adrian Melrose.'

'*Dear Mr Doyle,*

The Board of Rangoon Oil have noted the steady increase in the interest in Rangoon held via CFD's by the entity we believe you collectively refer to as the 'Sphinx.'

As you are aware Rangoon is a most important constituent of the FTSE Euro 100 share index and has a long and distinguished history in oil and gas exploration and trading. It has played a major part in the development of the oil and gas resources enjoyed by the world today.

Despite our many attempts to engage with you and your organisation to discuss the future of your shareholding we have been surprised and disappointed to receive no response.

It remains our policy to establish and maintain a continuous dialogue with our major shareholders.

Once again I would re-iterate our interest in meeting with you in order to obtain a better understanding of your interest in our company.
Yours etc.'

'In other words,' said Doyle, 'get your tanks off our lawn before you ruin the grass.'

Fleming continued: 'Rangoon is now capitalised at one hundred and twenty billion pounds after the rise in the last two days induced by the oil price. In addition it has fifty billion pounds of debt on its balance sheet.

Our advisers, Petersons, have told us that we will need to pay one hundred and fifty billion pounds in a public bid for the equity. Of course Petersons know nothing of the contingent value of the Field Of Dreams. Neither do the Rangoon Board. This will produce complications which I will come on to in a moment.

Of that hundred and fifty billion pounds of equity, we already own some forty five billion pounds worth, so in a bid we would have to find a further hundred and five billion just for the equity. In theory, as Rangoon is not that highly borrowed at present, we could use more debt to finance some of the amount required for the rest of the equity. But we also have to be prepared to refinance the debt that Rangoon already has on its balance sheet, as much of that will have loan agreements that trigger repayment on a change of control to us, or to anyone else for that matter. That means a debt requirement of over a hundred and fifty five billion pounds with costs on top.

We have consulted the debt specialists at Rotherstein and they are telling us that the debt markets, which were pretty fragile before this Saudi news, are now locked in a panic stricken state. Rotherstein say there is no way we can get actual or standby debt on anything approaching the scale needed, gentlemen. Things might improve when the initial shock of this Saudi announcement blows over but they advise not to the massive extent that we need.'

'All dressed up and nowhere to go,' murmured Charles O'Neill.

'Come on James,' said Myers, 'you've got us stuffed with thirty billion pounds worth of Rangoon stock and we can't do a bloody thing with it.'

Doyle smiled wryly. He had known it wouldn't last long.

'Gentlemen,' he said, 'as I think I've indicated to you before this is not just going to be a nice little party to which we can invite ourselves and no one else.

As you know we had some adventures in Namibia,' Doyle continued.

'Yeah, James, we heard you were put through the ringer a bit,' said Bulstrode. 'I suppose your biggest problem is deciding which girl is going to kiss it better,' he added crudely.

'Before I left Namibia,' continued Doyle, 'I had a long review with Millar. He has done quite a bit more drilling – he managed to get about six extra rigs, which will cost us by the way – and he has more to do.

But the key point is he has come to some more definitive conclusions about the size of that resource.

In summary, gentlemen, it is absolutely massive. Millar reckons the Field of Dreams could produce at up to twenty million barrels a day, nearly one quarter of entire global oil demand. He also reckons the reserve base could last, even at that rate, for nearly fifty years. There's never been an oilfield like it in the history of the world. The controller of this resource will be a kind of one man second OPEC.

My message to you, I've said it before, but I'll say it again even more strongly now, is that it is inconceivable that we are going to be that controller.

We are going to have to either sell our Rangoon stake on once it has reached a market value which truly reflects the Field of Dreams or we are going to have to share it with others.

Because of the size of the equity required to fund the bid, and the international politics of control of such a resource, those others are not likely to be conventional institutions or even more of our friends in the hedge fund industry. They are likely to be governments, gentlemen, or state controlled companies. And one more thing is that the debt problems we face in financing this deal can actually only be solved by government.'

'Well, I'm bloody well not getting into bed with this Government, Doyle, so just forget that will you,' blustered Bulstrode.

'Christopher, it is almost certainly too big for the UK Government. It probably means the US Government, maybe even the Chinese.'

'This is all very different from how you made it out to be,' grumbled Bulstrode.

'It's not actually,' said Doyle, 'but what is different, Christopher, is that the size of the asset we have found is vastly different from what we expected. We are far better off than any of us ever dreamed. It just gives us some added problems in how to exploit it.

Any bid for Rangoon will produce controversy at the best of times,' continued Doyle, 'but what makes our bid potentially far more controversial is the question of value.

We have found out, through our own efforts, that Rangoon is sitting on a resource of such size that it would utterly transform its value. But, as I indicated earlier, its Board and shareholders presently are completely unaware of that fact. Were we to bid now, at a conventional premium to the Rangoon price, that bid would reflect the recent rise in oil prices, and a premium for control which, as we know is usually twenty to thirty per cent. But that bid would not reflect even one iota of the value of the Field of Dreams. Were the real value of the Field of Dreams to become appreciated either during the bid process or after the offer had gone through, there would be the most monumental row. We would be accused, together with our government backers, of trying to steal the business, and the Rangoon Board and its advisers, who have a responsibility to advise on the fair price for Rangoon in a bid, would be accused of being massively incompetent.'

'Well, that's what they are,' spluttered Bulstrode.

'However, since the Board of Rangoon has no information to go on in valuing that resource it makes it extremely difficult for them to respond to a bid,' finished Doyle.

'I can't see the problem,' said Patrick Myers. 'People have always bought companies with undervalued assets and made money out of them, while selling shareholders have been disadvantaged. It's simple Darwinism to me.'

'Well, that's true Patrick,' said Doyle, 'but hardly on this kind of scale.'

'In a way,' said O'Neill, 'why should we care?'
Everyone looked at him, askance.

'You're not thinking straight, guys,' he said. 'Don't forget we already own twenty nine point nine percent of this company. Thanks to James's work we bought that at much lower prices even than today, let alone the real value. At some point the value of that stake will reflect the true value of Rangoon. This situation only worries us if we want to get an even bigger share of the Rangoon pie at the same kind of undervalue.

As I see it, we have two choices. We commit more resource, we bid, and then there is this monumental row about which James has waxed eloquent. Or we sit on our stake and we leak the Field of Dreams information to the market and watch, fat and happy, while the value of our stake rockets.'

Bulstrode was incandescent.

'What, just give it to the Rangoon Board and its shareholders? Make those muppets a present of all our work?' He could scarcely contain himself.

At that moment Julie Walters came in to the room and said: 'Graham Makepeace is desperately keen to see you, James.'

'Get him in here, then Julie please.'

The avuncular features and large and slightly podgy frame of Makepeace, one of the most careful and sagacious lawyers in London, filled the doorway.

'Morning, Graham,' said Doyle cheerfully, 'the boys are just deciding whether to bid for Rangoon or sit on their hands.'

Makepeace shook his head sorrowfully. In his hand he held a large brown envelope.

'I've been going through those Namibian leases you were given by President Barula, and comparing them to the copies you made of the documents you removed from Rangoon,' he said, sucking his teeth at the memory.

'Don't you think that's over the top, Graham?' Doyle said jovially. ' Surely impugning the accuracy of modern photocopiers is one step too far even for you?'

'No, no, not that,' said Makepeace wishing his client's sense of humour would for once desert him. 'The point is, you didn't photocopy everything.'

'There's this,' he flourished the envelope dramatically.

'What's that?' Several voices spoke at once.

'This is a supplementary deed to the main leases, but signed about ten years later. As you know the leases confer mineral right ownership for a hundred and fifty years together with unfettered rights to explore and extract on certain royalty terms. Those terms are now way out of date really, because of the rise in the oil price in the last fifty years, but this additional agreement,' Makepeace said with emphasis, ' restricts the right to extract to twenty five thousand barrels a day.'

'Bloody hell, that stuffs us,' said Bulstrode. 'You mean that instead of Rangoon owning the rights to what could produce twenty million barrels a day it's actually twenty five thousand.'

'What can we do?' asked Doyle, temporarily stunned.

'Well,' said Makepeace, 'you're matey with the President down there. You'd better go and see him in that ridiculous plane of yours and sort it out — you need a bit of an extension to that agreement to put it mildly. Obviously years ago someone smart in the Namibian Government realised, late but not too late, that Namibia had given Rangoon too good a deal. Quite why Rangoon signed the additional agreement remains a mystery but their signature is clearly there. Of course in those days even twenty five thousand barrels a day would have seemed like a lot.

'But any extension would have to be in favour of Rangoon wouldn't it?' asked Doyle.

'I don't see why,' said Makepeace, 'he let you explore, and even more, drill, which was pushing against Rangoon's rights quite hard. The fact is Rangoon's extraction rights run out at this tiny production level – in theory he can do a deal on the rest with anyone he likes.'

'The other very interesting thing,' went on Makepeace, 'is that Rangoon are now probably unaware of this additional contract as there was no version of it in the documents you copied — unless you missed it, that is. It's probably years since any of their people looked at this stuff anyway.'

Doyle spoke slowly,

'First of all I'm sure we copied everything, unless, that is, that additional agreement was kept in a separate place – we'll have to talk to our assistant company secretary friend again.

But secondly, if we got something out of Barula in favour of the Sphinx it could be incredibly valuable for us. We wouldn't have to bid for Rangoon.'

'No, no,' said Makepeace. 'Rangoon's title gives it a leasehold interest in all of the mineral resource. You, the Sphinx, know what is there but can't extract something you don't own whereas they are in the position of owning it, albeit not knowing what they really own, without being able to extract more than a teaspoon full of it.'

Doyle thought it was beginning to sound like Alice in Wonderland gone mad.

'It would make a bid even more interesting, James,' said Weill. 'If we bid and the Namibia news leaked Rangoon would make a great play for the value conferred without realising that it really wasn't all there at all.'

Makepeace groaned.

'If only you people had a more sophisticated ear for the myriad of legal implications that that simple statement entailed,' he said resignedly. 'I suppose I'll have to go away and write a paper for you.'

'Good idea, Graham,' said Doyle breezily, 'I'd better go and see Joseph. We should better discuss between ourselves the parameters of the terms we would accept, always supposing he is inclined to deal with us.'

'By the way,' asked Myers, 'what happened to that Lutin fellow?'

'We don't know,' said Doyle, 'the last we saw of him was him disappearing into the rubber dinghy. He had oars but was nearly a mile from the shore in a strong current and in thick fog with no navigational aids. Maybe Barula's men can tell me more.'

Makepeace left, grumbling to himself, and the Sphinx had a discussion about the potential structure of a deal with the Namibian government. To Doyle's mind this was largely academic. The value of the Field of Dreams, even after payment of royalties, the operating costs of extraction, and allowing for the massive capital costs of establishing the infrastructure to extract, process and transport crude oil on this scale, was unimaginably vast. Even if a large part of the value was ceded back to the Namibian State the investment returns for the Sphinx would be beyond spectacular.

But the members of the Sphinx seemed purblind to all this. As far as they were concerned the Sphinx had done the work, at its own expense, and had the vision and drive to create an opportunity out of nothing, and they saw no reason why they shouldn't achieve almost limitless reward for it.

Doyle thought hard and long about Barula's psychology. He became convinced of one thing.

Barula, however he felt about the distribution of rewards, would be unlikely to sign anything at all unless he had the confidence that the end result could be delivered. It was no use, he concluded, telling Barula that the Sphinx might bid for Rangoon, might be able to raise the funds. He simply had to be able to guarantee that they could do it. Without ownership of Rangoon and the consequential ownership of the Namibian mineral rights any piece of paper in the possession of the Sphinx would be of no use at all.

Doyle went to see Harvinder Singh.

Downing Street was bedlam as the economic crisis rolled over it.

'You do pick your moments, Doyle,' muttered Singh as aides, civil servants and the odd minister cleared out of his study, 'but I'm more than grateful to you for putting me on notice about this crisis. We've been able to look pretty coherent in our response at home and I've been able to make a good fist of leading things internationally, thanks to the preparation we put in.'

Doyle took Singh through the position in detail.

'So, Prime Minister,' he concluded, 'will you back us? We need a commitment on the equity and the standby financing.'

'I really need Cabinet approval for this,' muttered Singh uneasily.

Doyle said nothing.

'I'll have to take it to them at some point,' mused Singh.

'I'll tell you what. I'll give you a commitment on twenty five percent of the equity and the same proportion of the standby debt. God knows how this poor bankrupt country will pay for that.'

'Prime Minister, it'll pay for itself in spades. The gross cash flow from the Field of Dreams alone, even if it pumps at only five million barrels per day and the oil price re-sets at only thirty dollars, will be over fifty billion dollars a year, from which you have to knock off operating costs and royalties.'

Singh's businessman's eyes gleamed.

'Doyle,' he said, 'aren't there some things missing from what you've told me? What about the equity that Barula will want for the additional extraction rights? And what about the reward for the Sphinx? Let alone the cost of any production sharing agreement that might be negotiated?'

'Ah, yes, Prime Minister, those are very good questions. Let's assume Barula wants half of the ownership back of the field back as a quid pro quo that for extending the extraction rights — the value of that half would still be equivalent to much more than the value of Rangoon at the likely bid price. You can't lose actually.'

'Well I'd be happier with the detailed answers James,' grinned Singh.

'The blunt truth is that there aren't any at the moment, Prime Minister. You'll just have to trust me to get you a good deal.'

'Well, you had bloody well better not let me down, James.'

'There's one further thing I need and that's an introduction to President Leopold.'

'I thought you were pretty well connected in the US, Doyle?'

'I am, but I don't know the new President.'

'I'll fix it for you,' said Singh, smiling.

Doyle's next port of call was Ratan Bata, the well respected Indian Chairman of the huge Bata conglomerate with commercial interests that spanned dozens of emerging economies. Bata was on the Board of one of Doyle's charities.

Doyle knew that any bid for Rangoon would have to be through a new corporate vehicle partly owned by the Sphinx and partly, if his financing requests were met, by the UK and US governments. The last thing Doyle wanted when the bid started was to have to spend his time fighting the furore that the press would put up about the dangers of a group of unregulated hedge funds bidding for a priceless national asset. He thought that appointing a well respected industrialist as Chairman might deflect at least some of that.

Doyle told him just enough to whet his interest although Bata knew Doyle too well to be confident that he had been told everything.

With Bata in the bag Doyle flew to Washington. He stayed a couple of days in Washington's Willard Hotel, seeing some of his old friends and contacts before his scheduled meeting with Leopold. One of the other reasons he did this was to get rid of jet lag; the Blackbird was fast but nothing could eliminate the effect of time differences. Doyle idly thought he must ask the new President for an upgrade to a time machine, he was sure NASA or the Pentagon would be wasting some of their money on a scheme like that.

On the third day he was asked to wait in the White House library. Doyle was dressed formally; the new President was renowned for his taste in elegant suiting.

With great difficulty Doyle had secured a one on one meeting. He knew the appalling tendency to attract gagglers that beset so many American meetings; it had taken all Singh's influence together with some intervention from his own friends in Washington to produce that commitment. Now Doyle was profoundly hopeful that it would be delivered.

Widely regarded as a second Kennedy, Den Leopold was riding on a tidal wave of popular confidence and hope for the future. A brilliant

Yale graduate, he had already shown a hugely sophisticated grasp of international issues and great ambition for solving some of the most complex and persistent global conflicts, as well as attacking simultaneously a wide range of pressing domestic problems. Beyond an already legendary reputation as a speech maker, he had shown a superbly deft diplomatic touch in actual negotiation.

Doyle thought he almost sounded too good to be true. But even so, he was a little in awe of such charisma and popular power. Besides, Doyle knew that, if Leopold would not back him, he did not have many alternatives. He was also well aware that Leopold was moderately left wing and had no innate sympathy with financiers, bankers or hedge fund people.

Suddenly Leopold was in the room flashing the smile that kept front page photographers virtually fully employed.

'James Doyle?' he said, 'I'm pleased to meet you. Heard a lot about you from my people, all of it favourable. You've been a good friend of ours I understand.'

Doyle found Leopold very easy to relate to and get along with. He quickly recognised a master in the art of persuasion. Leopold seemed to have all the time in the world. Doyle was his sole focus of attention. Everything else seemed to be blotted out, or to be of no importance.

Nevertheless Doyle didn't waste time. He took Leopold through the whole story including his Saudi travels, the arrangement with Barula and the finding of the Field of Dreams.

'Goddam,' exploded Leopold, 'I'd like to have had the same phone call about the Saudi issue as you made to Singh. We've been making policy on the hoof for the last week since this thing broke.'

Leopold looked thoughtfully at Doyle.

'You really do believe you've found something big here don't you,' he said quietly.

Doyle nodded: 'Yes, we are as sure as we can be.'

Then Leopold uttered the words that Doyle dreaded.

'Gee, I'd really like to have this thing checked out.'

Doyle knew what that meant, from all his friends who had spent time working with big American corporations. Hundreds, literally hundreds, if not thousands of people, would descend upon him and his small team in a well meaning yet utterly chaotic, clumsy and worst of all, public way, until the entity being checked had almost been submerged under the weight of due diligence. That, Doyle thought bitterly, was nothing compared to the time it took, not to mention all the follow up work that could absorb yet another army. He felt weak at the thought of it.

'I'm afraid that won't be possible, sir,' he said as calmly and as decisively as possible.

'Mr Doyle,' said the President, heavily and slowly, 'how the hell do you expect me to put one hundred billion pounds on the line without it being checked out? It would be political suicide – and I can't afford that.'

'I want you to trust me, sir,' said Doyle calmly.

'I've only just met you,' expostulated Leopold.

'That's your business, sir, deciding who to trust. By all accounts you're pretty good at it,' said Doyle.

Leopold looked at Doyle long and hard.

'Alright,' he said. 'I don't quite know why I'm doing this. Part of me says this could be just a dream. But if the Field of Dreams does become a reality we could have a new world order, and that's very consonant with so many of my wider ambitions.'

Turning to face Doyle directly he said: 'I'll do one hundred billion pounds, split proportionately between equity and debt standby. The terms of the Rangoon and Sphinx deals with Barula have to be okayed by me; and, be warned, Doyle, I won't support your industry getting a free ride to eternity at the expense of the rest of the world simply because you've gotten your knees brown.

And one more thing, Doyle. At the end of the day I'm going to want the US to have a big say in the outcome of all this.

Finally I'll have to take it to Congress, but I can fast track it there; at long last I've sorted those guys out.'

They shook hands.

'What are you doing now?' asked the President.

'Flying down to Namibia to see Barula.'

'Give him my best. That plane of yours running ok?'

Doyle said it was.

'Goddam it, pull this lot off and we'll build you a replacement to your own specification.'

Chapter 15

THE FIELD OF DREAMS

Doyle took the Blackbird to Windhoek and then was ferried by helicopter to President Barula's beach house in Swakopmund, Namibia's summer playground on the coast.

The house was long and low, built in classic colonial style. Lawns and palm trees surrounded it and Doyle noticed a sophisticated communications mast which had been cunningly encased in one of the larger trees. It was six o'clock, the sun was fast dropping into the Atlantic and the wind had died. Doyle found it a strangely ambivalent scene. It didn't have the soft warm tropical feel of the Indian Ocean yet it wasn't full on Atlantic grandeur – and all the time there was a consciousness of the huge African desert stretching away behind the town to the East.

It was a peaceful place, though, and Doyle began to unwind a little.

He found Barula lounging on his veranda dressed in shorts, t shirt and sandals, whittling away with a pen knife at a carving of a desert lion.

'Hello, James,' said the President, gesticulating at the lion with his knife, 'need all the help we can get, I guess. Still, it's good to see you here and welcome back to Namibia. I hope you're not going to create a mess on quite the same scale as on your last visit.'

Doyle apologised and thanked Barula once again for his men.

'They were invaluable, Joseph. By the way has there been any sign of our friend Mr Lutin? The last I saw of him was him disappearing in our rubber dinghy a mile or so offshore.'

Barula let out a short laugh.

'Yes, he turned up, worse luck. The coastguard found him in a rather dishevelled state about three miles further down the beach. It turned out that he had left some kit in his hotel in Windhoek so we got him back there and put him on a flight back to London. Glad to see the back of him. There's been nothing more in the press and the Resource Commission has been established and is working away.'

The president cracked open a couple of celebratory beers and they were joined for dinner by Barula's charming American wife, Michelle.

The next morning the two men gathered again on the veranda while a small posse of security men patrolled the lawns and the curtilage of the house.

'Joseph,' said Doyle, 'we believe we have found in your country possibly the greatest single oil resource in the world. Later today I want you to come with me and Jock Millar in the Cessna and we will show you the full extent of it and all the technical data which supports our conclusions.

This find will of course utterly transform your country and will massively underpin global energy security. You will become, at a stroke, one of the most important people on the planet and Namibia will go from being a poor developing African State to being the effective headquarters of a second OPEC. It will be utterly transformational.'

Barula looked completely shell shocked.

'I hadn't expected this, James,' he muttered.

'None of us expected it, Joseph. We expected to find some oil but nothing like this.'

'I have to thank you,' said Barula.

'Nonsense,' said Doyle. 'The reality is that it was there for anyone to find. In fact we have become aware that way back in the nineteen thirties an Australian company found oil here but it went bust before it could develop it. After that nothing much seems to have happened until Rangoon obtained the exploration and development rights over pretty much the whole country.

And,' went on Doyle, 'those rights are what I need to talk to you about Joseph. We are in a sticky situation. The mineral, exploration and extraction rights are leased to Rangoon and no one else is entitled to extract oil from that land. That lease agreement was for a one hundred and fifty year term, in other words it lasts another ninety years until the end of this century which is not much use to you or anyone else. The agreement contains some terms, which are now commercially out of date, covering the basis upon which oil might be extracted and the royalties payable. But there was a later separate agreement in the papers you supplied although it does not seem to be in the possession of Rangoon. That separate agreement – we don't even know if Rangoon are aware of its existence – doesn't change their leasehold ownership of the mineral rights but restricts their right to extract to twenty five thousand barrels a day, a mere pinprick in the context of the amount of oil we have found. Of course, back then, even twenty five thousand barrels a day must have seemed to be a significant amount of oil.

So we have the bizarre situation that there is a vast amount of oil, that Rangoon have lease-hold ownership of all the mineral rights, but they are only entitled to exercise them to the extent of extracting a relatively tiny amount.

You could of course simply negotiate a new agreement with Rangoon that covers royalties on far higher production levels, possibly with an upfront sum. Then they continue to control all the oil and pay you royalties together with whatever production sharing agreement you negotiate on signing. Obviously you would set terms which require them to invest in amounts and on a time-table which ensures your huge resource is exploited and developed in a timely and efficient way. But that world class resource of yours would remain, at least for the next nine decades, outside your ownership and control; in fact it would be Rangoon who became the home of the second OPEC and not Namibia.

The problem for you is that you cannot do a deal with any other company on the right to extract at levels above twenty five thousand barrels a without you or that company doing a deal with Rangoon for access to the mineral rights. They hold you – over an oil barrel.

But the good news is that Namibia now has a chance to claw back from Rangoon part of the value inherent in the Field of Dreams which was ceded to them in the original agreement.'

Barula looked troubled. He sipped the coffee which Michelle had brought and fiddled with his lion. A flock of seabirds rushed over their heads and the lawns on their way up the coast.

'I don't feel any appetite to deal with them, James. They have done nothing with our land whereas a, well, maverick like yourself, has come in out of the blue and pointed the way to a future which I am still trying to get my mind round.'

'Joseph, we want to deal with you. We are prepared to bid for Rangoon to get it under our control and access the oil rights. But we will only do that if you sign an additional agreement with us granting increased extraction and production.'

'You are prepared to bid for Rangoon, James? Isn't that rather large even for your Sphinx people?'

'Poetic licence, Joseph. Of course it's too big for us. We would have to have equity partners. But at the moment it is extremely difficult to find partners on the scale required. However an even bigger problem is the debt — Rangoon has about fifty billion pounds of debt that we would need to cover – and the debt markets just aren't open at the moment, let alone in those amounts.

The other issue is geopolitics. Once it becomes known that Rangoon has this fabulous asset the company will become a global political football.

It will become a strange hybrid — an owner of a resource that is vital to world economic security but with private shareholders and management who are accountable pretty much only in financial terms.'

'So you can't do it,' said Barula, his eyes disappointed, 'and Rangoon could end up anywhere — even in Chinese hands.'

'We can do it Joseph. Don't forget we already own twenty nine point nine per cent of it. But we can only acquire the rest in partnership with government. I have just been to see Prime Minister Singh in the UK and President Leopold in the US. They will back us to do it — but only if the Sphinx can get an agreement with you.'

'I need to think about all this, James. We're going out in the plane at eleven am, you said? Let's meet then.'

Barula returned to his study. Doyle lit an Egyptian cigarette and watched a flock of flamingos pour over the trees en route to Walvis Bay. Twenty minutes passed. Doyle made a big mental effort to put himself onto African time.

There was a rustle of a silk dress and Michelle Barula appeared on the veranda. She smiled brilliantly at Doyle as she bent down to clear away the coffee tray.

'Joseph's just told me something of your chat together, James.'

'We're both so excited.'

'He's not had an easy time, here, you know,' she confided, sitting down opposite Doyle and re arranging her long legs.

What was it, Doyle thought, about these tall statuesque black women? He wrenched his mind back and smiled at her.

'This could make it easier,' he said.

'He's really wanted, you know, to break the mould, of African leaders,' she went on, 'but he just hasn't had the raw material to do it.'

'This could make him a world leader, Michelle, you know, not just an African one.'

'I know, I know,' she said, flustered, 'but it's all just so huge, coming all at once.'

'Cometh the hour, cometh the man.'

'I do hope so, he's wanted so much to really be able to do something for his people, for Africa. You know the history here. So much that has been horrible for our people, so much imposition from outside, such little basic respect.

I understand,' she went on, 'that you'll need to involve the British and the Americans to pull this thing off. I think that will worry Joseph. It's sort of out of the frying pan into the fire, in a way. I worry that he'll lose control. It's so big, he'll end up getting pushed around, and it'll be just like the past. He's got so many people trying to do that.'

She looked at him beseechingly.

'He says you're a very unusual man, James. Can't you think of something that will protect him, us, give us some independence for once? It's obviously about money,' she fluttered slightly, 'but it can't all be about money can it?'

She said she would bring more coffee, the silk dress rustled again and Doyle was left alone with his thoughts.

There was a way, he thought after a while. Why hadn't he thought of it before?

Then he knew why. It was her phrase. All about money. That, he thought to himself summed up the primary weakness of Western capitalism. Namibians had virtually no money but they had other things equally important to them.

Michelle re-appeared with fresh coffee.

'Joseph will be with you in half an hour,' she said, 'he's had some phone call that seems to have upset him quite a lot.'

Doyle looked at her. It was impossible not to be moved by such honesty and integrity.

'I think I can offer Joseph something that will satisfy him,' he said.

She came up to him. For a moment he felt blown away by her overpowering womanliness and by wafts of some exotic perfume which he couldn't place. She kissed his cheek gently.

'That would be so good,' she said. And she was gone.

An hour later Doyle, Barula and Jock Millar were in the twin engined Cessna at two thousand feet with thousands of square miles of desert underneath them.

'We're going to show you your oil, Mr President,' said Doyle jovially.

Millar carried on.

'Here is the map showing all the drilling locations, Mr President,' he said. Despite injunctions to the contrary a President really was a President to Jock and he couldn't bring himself to the familiarity of Christian names.

'You can see the outline of the predicted fields and their anticipated reserves and flow rates,' he went on, 'and the really unusual thing is the persistency of these in your territory. They are far more uniform, as well as being several times the size, of the Saudi equivalents.

We've drilled in about twenty five locations now, which give us a really high confidence level that the oil bearing rock is endemic throughout the area, and the oil in every location has been not only at an economically accessible depth but has also been top quality sweet light oil which commands the greatest premium on world markets. You've an absolute gold mine here,' said Jock, cheerfully mixing his minerals.

After two hours aloft they had covered the larger part of the Field of Dreams and they flew back to the President's beach house for early evening drinks.

There followed a two hour presentation by Jock on drilling results and production issues and Doyle then gave a thumb nail sketch of the economics of the field in terms of capital investment required, operating costs and returns at various oil pricing and royalty levels.

Barula, Michelle and Doyle wound up with a late supper together.

'You know,' said Barula, 'I find it hard to adjust to this. It's just too stark a contrast with the course of this country's history.'

Doyle said he supposed it had been no worse for the Bedouin in Saudi Arabia.

Actually,' Doyle went on, 'for them it's not been adjusting to the cash flow from oil that's been the biggest problem. The real issue has been a burgeoning population and a failure to build an industrial infrastructure which creates the employment required to give social stability to their growing numbers of young people.

Anyway,' said Doyle, 'that's all down the track for you in Namibia. We can discuss the financial proposal tomorrow and hopefully we can move forward from there so at least we can start getting your oil out of the ground.'

Barula looked troubled.

'It's not going to be quite as easy as that James. I've had a proposal from the Russians and the

Chinese Energy Secretary wants to come and see me at the end of the week. Let's talk about all this tomorrow. Good night.'

Doyle woke early the next morning and went for a jog in the morning sun down the coastal path. A procession of four by fours passed him, most carrying heavy duty sea fishing rods. At the deserted Reef Bar he stopped to watch the great curling Atlantic breakers sweeping in from both the North and the South, meeting in the middle in a great arced wave and dispersing onto the beach. The coast line stretched away to the south, the palm trees soon ran out, massive golden dunes rose on the Eastern side of the coast road while the horizon became smudged by the low lying buildings supporting the fishing fleet at Walvis bay.

Doyle jogged back to State House. Then the pit of his stomach brought him back to the reality of the President's final words the night before.

He saw something protruding under his door. He pulled it out and his stomach gave a further turn.

'Russians ready to bid for Namibia oil,' screamed the headline.

'*The Russian State, led by Prime Minister Julius Orlov, is ready to table a huge cash offer for the privilege of being allowed to explore for and produce oil from Namibian fields,*' it went on, 'this will bring to an end months of shilly shallying by President Barula and his so called Resource Commission, which has always seemed to us to be simply a device for further inactivity. Apparently the Russians are very confident that huge oil reserves can be found and exploited in Namibia, all for the good of the poor and suffering Namibian people.'

It ended, 'We call upon the President to take action NOW to capitalise on this generous Russian offer, and to open talks with any other countries interested in helping the people of Namibia enjoy the wealth that is rightfully due to them.'

The article was studiously short on the details of the offer and Doyle was relieved to see that it make no reference to any current exploration rights.

Doyle returned to his room's veranda although he was now no longer conscious of the view.

Unless Barula decided simply to strip Rangoon of its rights, Russian style, Doyle didn't see how the Russians could be invited in on any other basis than that of the Sphinx; in other words to bid for the right to lift surplus production over and above the first, nugatory, twenty five thousand barrels. But, and Doyle kept returning to this, only Rangoon had the right to actually lift any oil, so, like the Sphinx, the Russians would first have to bid for Rangoon. Doyle knew they would never do that.

Doyle also just couldn't see that Barula would act like an old fashioned kleptocrat – it went right against the grain of everything his career so far had stood for.

One more thing had bothered him overnight.

The Russians might not, out of a mixture of inadequate cash resources and distinct lack of inclination, bid for Rangoon. But the Chinese could easily afford it and were desperate for strategic oil and mineral resources. They had already shown the West that they were quite prepared to bid on commercial terms for world class assets and the Field of Dreams had to be the classiest asset of all.

Doyle went out to breakfast on the dining room veranda with an uneasy mind.

Barula had already finished his breakfast and was leafing through Cabinet papers, supported only by a large cup of black coffee. The hazy morning sun was percolating through the bougainvillea which grew rampantly up the veranda's pillars. Doyle noticed that the President had already discarded his copy of the Republiklein onto a side table.

'Help yourself, James,' he gesticulated at the breakfast table. Doyle noticed, rather regretfully, that there was no sign of Michelle Barula, instead a rather pretty maid was hovering to see if they wanted anything more.

'Seen the news, James?' Barula gesticulated towards the newspaper.

Doyle nodded.

'The Russians have been very clever,' added Barula, 'they've gone for the soft underbelly of the beast.'

'I have had a letter,' he continued, 'from Prime Minister Orlov, suggesting I cancel Rangoon's rights on the grounds that they have not met their obligations and re-allocate them to Petrogaz in exchange for a new class of securities in Petrogaz and a royalty.'

'What is more each member of my Cabinet has received a letter from an agent of Petrogaz offering them a commission in cash of five million pounds, paid offshore, if Petrogaz successfully enters an agreement with us.'

How typical, thought Doyle. Very little hard cash involved but all of it aimed at the venial and whatever value was on offer for the Namibian State diffused in some hard to value security with easily alterable rights.

'I can see they've gone for the jugular,' observed Doyle calmly, lighting a pre breakfast Egyptian, 'but unless you welsh on Rangoon I don't see them getting any further. But what's that bit in Orlov's letter about 'obligations' – there aren't any in the original lease, as you know.'

'That's where the worst news comes in,' replied Barula.

'One of my civil servants in the Cabinet Office has been digging out all the documents relating to the original grant of the exploration and development rights. He has found this.' Barula tossed a three page agreement over to Doyle.

'Basically', said Barula, 'this is an original of a supplementary agreement which gives the Namibian State the right to withdraw the rights granted to Rangoon should no exploration be carried out by the bearer of that agreement in the first twenty five years since they were granted.'

Doyle drew on his cigarette and studied the document minutely. One of Doyle's friends worked in the British Museum and was an authority on old documents. Over the years some of his knowledge had rubbed off onto Doyle.

'This is a fake,' said Doyle sharply. ' It's been put together using some old paper and a manual typewriter but they can't disguise the freshness of the ink or the fact that there is no way this paper is more than ten years old – it's got a structure that comes from impregnation techniques that simply were not around fifty years ago.'

'I'd ask your civil servant how much he is being paid by your Russian friends if I were you,' Doyle concluded.

Barula looked discomforted, then a little mollified, then more relaxed.

'Look Joseph, there are three issues in relation to the valuation of the Field of Dreams. The first, and most central, is the relative value of the mineral rights held by Rangoon Oil versus the value of actually being able to lift and sell oil up to the output capacity of the field. It's really hard to evaluate that scientifically but we estimate the life of the Field of Dreams at a hundred and fifty years, assuming an extraction rate of five million barrels a day. Rangoon have ninety years remaining on their lease. A simple horse-trade would ascribe some kind of fair split between Rangoon Oil and the Namibian State in ownership of the field. It's a horse-trade because neither you nor Rangoon Oil can produce oil without squaring the other. Having established that the second question is what kind of return an international oil company would want in order to make the capital commitments required to lay down the extensive infrastructure required to develop the field. That's often called a production sharing agreement and frankly it will be much easier to auction that once we have control of Rangoon.

The third issue is that the Sphinx would like a share of the Field of Dreams as a payment for our work and entrepreneurism in getting this far.

Joseph,' Doyle knew that the next phase of his negotiations were crucial,' we need, before we bid for Rangoon, to agree between us the first and third points. The second, as I indicated just now, can be left until later.'

Doyle knew that you could never test the first issue, the horse-trade, by asking third parties to bid on the split. The whole thing was just too hypothetical, even fantastical. Worst of all any approach to the international oil industry indicating the reserve and production potential of the Field of Dreams would produce a furore of international speculation just before the Rangoon bid, the very last thing Doyle wanted. A deal had to be worked out between him and Barula in such a way that the final settlement looked generous to Joe and could be underpinned if possible by third parties.

'James, James,' said Barula, heavily, 'to me all those thoughts sound sensible. But this is Africa. My Cabinet has smelt money now. If each of them can get a sum like five million in their pockets offshore they won't care if we do a good or a bad deal for Namibia.'

Doyle felt innate sympathy for Barula. How was it possible for anyone to remain clean in an environment where just about every counterparty was corrupt and was prepared to corrupt others to achieve their goals? He had no feel for Barula's ability to control his Cabinet under these conditions.

Michelle Barula appeared on the verandah, another shimmering vision, this time in tight black jeans with a floaty cream chiffon top.

'Call for you, Joseph,' she said, 'in the study.'

Barula grumbled to himself and left the veranda.

'How's it going?' she flashed her smile at Doyle.

'A few complications,' Doyle grinned back.

'I'm sure you'll get through them.' She bent down and gathered the last of the breakfast things onto a tray. 'I hear you usually get what you want,' she added rather flirtatiously.

Barula returned heavily onto the veranda.

'That was the Chinese Energy Secretary,' he said, 'wanting to give me an outline proposal ahead of our meeting later in the week. He is talking unbelievable numbers, in cash. He seems completely convinced that there are massive oil reserves here.'

Doyle thought, the Chinese are spying on the Russians who have the seismic spy gear.

'Here's what you should do, Joseph,' said Doyle. 'You should appoint an investment bank to advise you on the appropriate value split between mineral right ownership and the right to extract. Once they have reported we will make you a proposal and try to agree a deal and you will have the comfort of their opinion.'

Doyle knew he wasn't giving much away. Any investment bank would value the ownership of the mineral rights more heavily than the right to extract – the longer the right to extract was denied the more political pressure there would be on the Namibian political leadership to break the log jam and start to get some oil out of the ground. Doyle was confident that the Sphinx and its UK and US government backers would be able offer Barula more generous percentage of the Field of Dreams equity than any bank would suggest as a fair deal.

'We'll negotiate our position from what comes out of that exercise.'

Barula looked more cheerful.

'What about these Cabinet Ministers, James? They could give me endless problems if they're deprived of their take'

'This is your chance to have a show down – and you've got the trump card of the prosperity from the oil. You'll be fine if you're brave.'

Chapter 16

GROUSE

James Doyle brought his Range Rover to a halt at the highest point of the B6278 between Eggleston and Stanhope. The wild moorlands of the Pennines, some of the finest grouse shooting in England, lay before him in a magnificent vista. It had been a hot August day and now the evening shadows were just beginning to create a kaleidoscope of light and shade right down to the bottom of the Bollihope valleys.

He lowered the windows. It was absolutely quiet except for the rustle of the light breeze and the utterly distinctive, 'go-back, go-back', call of the young grouse about the hillside.

Doyle breathed in the moorland air, reflecting on his good fortune. For him, as it was for many sportsmen, grouse shooting was the very king of shooting sports. The birds were wild; most attempts to breed them in captivity failed. They were fast, capable of flying at seventy miles per hour, or even more with the wind behind them. To shoot them you had to mount and pull the trigger on a bird almost as soon as you saw it. Above all they were unpredictable. The birds would jink, weave and swerve, often only skimming the moor; coming over the guns in singles, pairs, or a great covey. In some years they were prolific, in some sparse, their populations had a natural, almost biblical, cycle of waxing and waning. They had a dense plumage, nothing but a direct hit would get through it and bring a bird down. Grouse were quite unlike any merely reared game bird. They needed intense conservation by a team of keepers dedicated to the elimination of the many predators which threatened their stocks. Yet at the end of a season too many birds left on a moor could stimulate disease and paradoxically reduce rather than increase stocks for the following year. That was when the call went out from moor owners to the so called 'A' teams to come and clear up stocks, with shooting often given free or at much reduced rates.

Most of the big moors on the Pennines had changed hands in the last fifteen years. This had

had the consequence that many of them, on account of their huge capital value and the staggering annual costs of intensive management, were owned by members of the hedge fund community or proprietors of successful private companies. These people tended to shoot amongst themselves, the last in a combination of factors that had made the sport ever more wildly exclusive in recent years.

Doyle was headed for Teviotheads as the guest of Alan Mann, a self made investor who had built up a personally owned private equity business and with whom Doyle had from time to time invested his own funds. Teviotheads was a large, very pretty and incredibly productive moor with a myriad of drives; you could shoot for three days without re-covering ground.

In fact Mann, a short, dapper, fit looking fifty year old, was the first person he met as he entered the hall of the lodge.

'Who have we got then, Alan?' asked Doyle, keen to establish the identity of his fellow guests.

'Oh,' said Mann, 'the usual rogues' gallery. Your mates Myers and Bulstrode, the diamond dealer Richard Schrager, the game artist Ken Holloway, and Madeleine Fenwick, she's head of a new public relations outfit. Oh, and it was going to be my mate the tailor, Benjamin Everett, but he can't come so he's invited someone else.

Normally I wouldn't let that happen but Ben's a good mate and I'm sure his guy will be alright. Some kind of foreign banker, I believe. Apparently a good shot. His name's on the locker over there, actually. Do you know him?'

Doyle managed to look unconcerned as he read the name, beautifully inscribed in italics in Mann's major domo's hand.

'Alexander Lutin.'

'Yes,' said Doyle, forcing unconcern. 'I think you could say that I do know him a bit.'

'Is he alright?' Alan Mann showed traces of worry.

'I'm sure he'll behave himself on your beautiful moor,' said Doyle enigmatically.

Mann looked more than a little disconcerted.

Grouse shooting could be incredibly dangerous. The butts from which guns shot were generally not more than forty or fifty metres apart, a range at which a twelve bore was unlikely to kill a man but at which it could still maim or blind. Because the birds flew so wild, and often so low, inexperienced, and even experienced, guns could easily be tempted into taking a shot which could harm their fellow guns, the most dreaded being the 'swing through the line.' Loaders, though their primary function was to load the next gun of the pair – grouse shots invariably used two guns – also had an unwritten function as 'minders' and were briefed to put their masters straight if they showed dangerous tendencies. In bad cases guns could suffer the ultimate social embarrassment of being asked to leave the moor.

'He's brought his own loader,' Mann said cautiously. 'Mostly people are using our locals. His is a rather sinister looking chap, apparently he's Albanian. Do you have a loader with you?' asked Mann.

'No, but I will have one by the time we start tomorrow. The other thing is, do you mind if Mario Scaglietti also joins me in the butt? He's just made me a new pair and he's desperately keen to see how they perform.' Doyle was thinking hard.

'Anything wrong with our loaders up here, James?' Mann asked a little sharply.

'No, absolutely not, it's just that my man Tony Dyer is up in these parts, he's been loading somewhere else, and we're used to working as a team.' Doyle lied with ease.

'Have it your own way James, and it's fine about your Italian friend. In fact I'd like to meet him as I wouldn't mind a new pair myself. Does he need a room here?'

'No, he's fixed with his sister who married a Newcastle surveyor, but thanks. By the way these new guns have a few interesting refinements which I'm sure Mario will want to take you through if you are serious about a new pair.'

Doyle was shown to his room by Mann's ancient butler. He was pleased to see that it wasn't right next door to Lutin's.

Then he called Dyer.

'Dangerous places, sir, grouse butts, even with sane people either side of you.'

'That's why I want you here, Tony. More than ever before it would suit Lutin and his Russian masters if I was right out of the way. He's stubbed his toe on us at every turn, now he knows the size of the prize and he must be getting desperate to deliver the goods. Take a chopper but I want you here at breakfast. And Tony, I may need some decent transport on the way back to keep out of the way of Lutin and his gang.'

Dinner was a festive occasion. Doyle couldn't believe how the quality of food and wine in the average grouse lodge had risen since the moors had changed hands. Chefs were imported from London for the season, wine cellars had been transformed. It was all, he reflected, a country mile away from the rather dire overcooked English food which had traditionally been inflicted on guests, and from the days of all male gatherings with an exclusive focus on shooting, and where whisky had been used as a general anaesthetic against all the discomforts of the then unmodernised, cold, damp shooting lodges.

Lutin was at his most charming and most conversational, going out of his way to draw Doyle out on his hobbies. On hearing about the new guns he observed that he hoped the draw would place him next to Doyle so that he could see the magic of the new technology at work. Doyle shivered despite the warm evening and thought to himself that he could think of nothing worse.

As Doyle was going up to bed at about midnight his host accosted him.

'Nothing wrong with that fellow Lutin,' Mann observed, satisfied. 'Seems like a regular chap. Glad we've got him, livens up the party.'

Doyle muttered something about him seeming alright.

The next morning dawned dry and bright with a steady breeze from the South West – perfect conditions for the layout of many of the drives on the moor.

When Doyle went out to his vehicle after breakfast he found Tony Dyer waiting by it.

'Interesting times last night, sir,' opened Dyer.

'Really, Tony? We had a pretty peaceful evening.'

'I came up in the Porsche, sir, as you said you wanted something special for the return journey. Anyway I had a very fast trip, left at about eleven and got here just before two thirty this morning.

I knew the lodge wasn't going to be open so I thought I would doss in the Range Rover – I've got a spare set of keys for it as you know. I didn't want to create a disturbance on the gravel drive late at night so I left the Porsche in the village and walked up the verge of the lodge drive with my kit. Well, as you know, there wasn't much moon last night; it was pretty black with quite a wind and a lot of cloud.

I identified your car and then something made me stop in my tracks. There was a fellow, sir, all dressed in black, lying down under the car with his feet sticking out. I could hear the odd muffled noise as if he was trying to spanner something. I quickened my pace. Then I saw his hand come out from under the car and it seemed to have a small pair of bolt cutters in it.

Well, that was enough for me, so I jumped the guy and whipped some cord, which I had in my pocket, round his legs and dragged him out, wriggling like hell he was. I didn't want a disturbance so I took the precaution of laying him out with a blackjack, tied him up, carried him down to the bottom of the drive, stuffed him in the car and took him about twenty miles away. I removed all his identity papers and left him propped against a tree in a pretty remote spot.'

You have probably deprived Alexander Lutin of his loader, Tony,' said Doyle. 'Well done. Let's wait and see, shall we. I don't think we want to spoil the day's shoot with this little story just yet.'

'I checked the car as soon as it was light this morning sir. It seems to be alright. I must have caught him in the nick of time.' Dyer looked tired but pleased with himself.

They were joined by Mario Scaglietti who had insisted on looking after Doyle's new pair of guns overnight and now presented himself in a sharply tailored Italian shooting suit and an Alpine hat.

'This way for the draw please, everyone.' Alan Mann gathered the guests round and went round offering a silver cartridge from which each gun extracted the number of their opening butt which determined who shot where in the line for the rest of the day.

Mann's head keeper, Douglas, a magnificent figure with a great head of red hair and a luxuriant beard, clothed from head to foot in the estate tweed of light green check, stood to one side glowering and ruminating about the guns, who clustered eagerly around Mann.

'My loader seems to have gone missing,' said Lutin, looking concerned.

'Don't worry Alexander, you can have Bob, that'll be alright won't it Douglas?' Mann's wave acknowledged his keeper and indicated a jovial slightly raffish looking older man with a moustache and a twinkling eye, with an excited springer spaniel at his feet.

Lutin rather reluctantly handed his kit over to Bob.

Guns, loaders, drivers, keepers, pickers up, the proprietor and a myriad of dogs of all types piled into a rich variety of vehicles and, led by Douglas in an old Mitsubishi and closely followed by the guns, who generally favoured Range Rovers, they all headed for the moor and the first drive.

The cavalcade meandered up to the on top of the moor and parked in an old quarry. Doyle, Dyer and Scaglietti got out of their vehicle and stopped for a moment to take in the sensational view. The moorland, garlanded with heather, cotton grass and sedge, rolled away from them for miles. Apart from the odd stone hut and the lines of butts on various drives there was no sign of human habitation at all. Far away to the East it was just possible to see a dark smudge which indicated the sea and to the North Doyle made out the rise of the Cheviots. High above them a pair of hen harriers circled in the light cool wind which carried every scent imaginable. Until the spell was broken by the eruption of all the dogs from the beaters' wagon and the pickers' up vans there was almost no noise. To Doyle those surroundings, allied to the anticipation of the excitement of the shoot to come, were the purest magic.

They trudged off to the first line of butts. Doyle had drawn number eight. Dyer caught up with

Doyle and whispered urgently in his ear. 'Numbering from the right. You'll be drawn next to that Lutin, sir. You'll be alright until the last drive when you'll be on the end of the line again, and he'll be inside you. That's when,' Dyer growled, 'he might get up to some tricks.'

Lutin had drawn number seven and was on Doyle's right hand. Madeleine Fenwick, large, and jolly and relatively inexperienced, but desperately keen, had drawn six and would be on Lutin's right.

After each drive – there would be five in the day — each gun moved two up on his or her original butt number.

Doyle didn't share Dyer's views as to the predictability of Lutin's behaviour. He asked Mario to be his loader and told Dyer to keep an eye on Lutin throughout the day but especially to watch him like a hawk during the last drive of the day.

'If he makes to swing through the line, Tony,' added Doyle, 'just yell 'down'!'

Finally, after a long wait for the beaters to come in from a couple of miles back on the moor, the grouse began to come over. First there were birds coming in singly and in pairs, with the occasional crack of gunfire down the line indicating their flight paths, then the larger coveys came, sometimes two or three at once across the whole length of the line. The larger coveys were, paradoxically, harder to shoot. In the excitement and panic of the sudden arrival of a mass of fast moving quarry the inevitable temptation for the less experienced gun was to shoot blindly at the pack. The equally inevitable consequence was that nothing dropped. Doyle knew that, very early, you had to select a bird, a long way out, and shoot at it as soon as possible. Grouse were travelling, downwind, at about thirty metres a second, so, even if you identified a bird a hundred and fifty metres out, by the time you had mounted on it, fired, and the shot had reached the spot, the bird would be no more than fifty metres away, if that. An instant later and it would flash by overhead and be gone.

Doyle was thrilled by the performance of his new guns and cartridges. They shortened the time taken to get lead in the air, which meant birds were effectively taken earlier, giving more time to change guns and get off more shots in front. Their barrels were very precisely regulated which meant that the shot pattern stayed extremely tight over a long range. The result was that if you were accurate the bird was hit very hard and died; if you missed you missed cleanly and did not wound birds simply by hitting them with an odd pellet.

By lunchtime the little Italian gun maker was beside himself with joy.

'Eh, James,' he beamed, 'you shoot very well this morning, si?'

'Must be your wonderful guns, Mario,' Doyle grinned. He knew he had shot well.

Lutin had also been on form and on good behaviour. Because grouse fly so wildly there is no real shooting etiquette as to which bird can be rightfully shot by which gun, but Lutin had consistently not shot at birds which would be better shots for Doyle, and, according to Dyer, had never once looked like swinging through the line.

The party had lunch in an old stone hut high up on the moor. Lutin spent quite a lot of time engrossed on his mobile phone some distance from the hut – no doubt, thought Doyle, trying to locate his loader, whose mobile phone was switched off and in Tony Dyer's pocket.

Scaglietti, with a torrent of excitable comment and Italian gestures, was showing off Doyle's guns to a small group, including Bulstrode and Myers each of whom had large cigars on the go.

The other guns were lingering over coffee inside the hut.

Douglas appeared, his eyes rolling and with a face like thunder.

'Back in your butts by two fifteen, gentlemen please,' he barked – lady guns simply didn't exist in Douglas' mind – 'and it's quite a walk up the hill behind the hut,' he added grimly, immediately discarding the prospect of any physical fitness amongst the guns. He stomped off into the distance.

The two drives in the afternoon were 'back to back' – grouse would be driven over the guns one way and then back the other. Guns were lined out up a gentle slope and were to shoot over the valleys which fell away on each side. Doyle worked out that on the last drive he would be at the head of the slope with Lutin on his right hand side just beneath him. Further up the slope from that point was quite a pronounced hillock which prevented Doyle swinging through to his left, normally one of the few benefits of being at the end of the line.

The last drive of the day was in full swing. Doyle saw a pair of grouse coming in fast over the far lip of the facing valley, mounted on them and they both dropped. Scaglietti smoothly passed him the next gun, Doyle took one more bird in front and swung round behind to take one out of another rapidly passing covey overhead. Suddenly there was a great shout of 'Down'! from Dyer. He, Doyle and Scaglietti flattened themselves while shots whistled just over their backs. There were a couple of thuds behind them.

Dyer rushed across to Lutin, shouting at him. For some reason, Bob, Lutin's loader, was outside the back of the butt with a dead grouse in his hand.

'Did you see what your man did there, Bob?' shouted Dyer, 'damned near killed us all.'

Lutin had bent down to retrieve something and Dyer viciously elbowed him out of the way.

'I'll be keeping these, sir,' they heard Dyer say, 'and I think you should put your gun down now for the rest of the drive.'

After that the drive was quickly over although Doyle's concentration had gone.

Lutin and Bob had started to walk back down the hill when Dyer said to Doyle,

'Watch this, sir.'

Dyer opened his knife and walked towards the hillock above Doyle's butt. He searched the side of it closest to the butt minutely. Then he gave an exclamation and stepped forward. With a twisting motion he extracted two objects from the heathery slope, blew the sand and earth off them and placed them in Doyle's palm. Then he put his hand in his pocket and extracted two more objects from his pocket which went into Doyle's palm.

'Two slugs,' said Dyer triumphantly, 'and two brass cases.'

'Murder, sir,' he added, unnecessarily.

Nothing more was said about the incident. Dyer established from Bob that just beforehand he had been asked by Lutin to despatch a wounded bird a little way beyond the butt. Bob had therefore neither seen Lutin load the slugs from his pocket nor the actual shots.

The day ended up with two hundred brace of grouse shot, a good day for the moor. Mann was ecstatic and in the evening dispensed champagne with great good humour. Even Douglas, invited in for a dram, managed to crack a smile and thinly admitted that 'one or two' of the gentlemen could shoot a 'wee bit.'

The first course at dinner that night was a dish of escargots on a bed of polenta and roasted asparagus. Everyone was served except for Lutin. At the last minute the butler brought in a covered plate and placed it in front of him.

'A special dish for you, sir,' he intoned, lifting the cover.

The plate was empty except for the two slugs and their cases.

Immediately there was uproar.

Lutin sprang from his place, his hand went to his right hand pocket and he shouted,

'Doyle, you bastard.'

'That'll do, Lutin.' Mann's calm tones cut the air like a knife.

'If you wouldn't mind I think you should leave now. Your things have already been placed in your car.'

Lutin slowly stalked out, giving Doyle a last venomous glance.

There was an immediate loud buzz around the table.

'Fellow seemed to have got hold of the wrong sort of slugs,' japed Bulstrode.

'Ladies and gentlemen,' Mann rallied his guests, 'this incident is now closed. Mario Scaglietti will take Mr Lutin's place in the line tomorrow.'

The ancient butler cleared away Lutin's place and the offending plate.

The little Italian looked pleased – and excited. Really, he thought to himself, the goings on at these English shooting parties were becoming, well, quite Continental.

Nothing more was said. Bulstrode and Myers got hold of Doyle and quizzed him later that night.

'The things you do for us,' said Myers admiringly.

'Don't tell him that,' said Bulstrode, 'he'll want a bigger cut.'

The next day the weather changed completely and the moors were swept with rain showers and low cloud.

By lunchtime the guns, loaders, beaters, and pickers up were soaked and cold. The cloud was so low that it was hardly possible to see thirty metres in front of the butts.

Mann declared that they would finish the day at lunch and leave the birds for another day.

'You're all very welcome to stay,' he declared, 'or you can make an early start South.'

Dyer beckoned Doyle to one side.

'One of you is going to die,' he said. 'You've humiliated him and you're in his way on the oil. You're in acute danger from now on, wherever you are, until it's sorted one way or the other.

In terms of getting back to London in one piece you can't use the plane as we can't use Newcastle and there's no other runway up here that will take it. A chopper is too easy to shoot up. A crowded train, second class, would be good, and there are plenty of crowded trains. But you've still to get to Newcastle on some pretty back roads. That leaves a really fast car to London late at night. I've got Frank here to drive you in the Porsche if you want. I honestly don't think there's anyone can catch him in that.'

Doyle and Frank got some sleep and after a very late supper got on the road about midnight. Frank had been studying a route and was confident.

'Look, James,' he said, 'this is a Porsche Turbo, tweaked by Gemballa, with six hundred bhp. There's literally nothing which can live with it.'

They rapidly made their way undisturbed down Weardale and across the valleys to Bishop Auckland and the A1.

There was very little traffic about. Frank switched on the plethora of speed trap monitors he carried and within seconds the Porsche was cruising at a steady hundred and twenty miles an hour, no more stressed than if it had been idling through Hyde Park.

After twenty minutes Frank said: 'Something in the mirror, James.'

'Police,' said Doyle, unconcerned. 'You're for it this time my lad.'

'No,' said Frank, 'those lights, they're something else, I'm sure it's not police.'

'I'll tell you what,' said Frank, accelerating, 'nothing the cops have got is good for more than a hundred and fifty, especially on a road like this.'

The Porsche rocketed forward, Doyle watched, mesmerized, as the speedometer needle flickered to a hundred and forty and then rose steadily. The G forces, even on long sweeping bends, became intense. Frank kept consulting his mirror.'

'Still there,' he said. 'It's not police, it's them and I don't think I can get away from whatever they've got.'

There was a pause.

'Must be an Integrale, I suppose,' mused Frank, 'expensive bit of kit for these hoodlums.'

Suddenly there was a blaze of light in their mirrors which lit up the whole cabin of the Porsche. Simultaneously there was a burst of heavy machine gun fire from behind the rear quarter of their car. Frank slumped, the Porsche lurched madly, Doyle grabbed the wheel, there was a scream of tyres, a hedge appeared and disappeared. There was a huge impact.

Doyle knew no more.

Chapter 17

A CAPTIVE ASSET

It was a beautifully sunny mid August day on the balcony of Southwark Place but Matthew Fleming was worried. There was no sign of his chief and there were many issues to be attended to.

There was the process in Namibia where Barula's advisers, Harris Bank, were due, in three days time, to present their findings as to an appropriate split of value between the mineral and extraction rights. Immediately after that a major meeting was scheduled for the new Chairman and Board of the Field of Dreams Limited to meet Petersons, its own advisers, to discuss the bid for Rangoon. Then there was the financing of the Rangoon bid; it was all very well extracting promises from presidents, thought Fleming, but there was a lot of hard work needed to translate those into legally binding commitments. Meanwhile endless press and media speculation swirled around Rangoon, the 29.9 per cent stake held by the Sphinx and even the Sphinx itself. Takeover regulations in the UK had become so complex and so stringent that the slightest wrong move by the Sphinx, or even the wrong press comment, could put the whole enterprise at risk. Graham Makepeace and his team were working all hours navigating these and other shoals.

Fleming had made a comprehensive list of tasks for the Sphinx and the steps and professional inputs needed to achieve them in line with the bid timetable. This sat on his laptop and a hard copy was pinned above his desk. He sat looking at the tasks ; most of them, he thought glumly, involved Doyle.

Where the hell was he?

The door to Fleming's office opened and Dyer burst in. He looked tired and somewhat dishevelled.

'There's been a disaster,' he said.

'James's Porsche crashed on the way down from shooting and he's disappeared.'

Various scenarios flitted at high speed across Fleming's mind.

'What do you mean, he's crashed and disappeared?'

'The car was being driven by Frank,' said Dyer heavily. 'It was shot up by someone with a heavy machine gun, obviously when it was travelling at very high speed, and it went off the road out of control, rolled at least three times and had a tremendously heavy impact. I was there at first light this morning and saw it all. Not pretty sight. They cut Frank out of the wreckage and air lifted him down here. He's in a pretty bad way, in hospital, on life support. He also caught one of the machine gun bullets but, thank God, only in the right shoulder. Anywhere else and he would be dead. Both his legs are broken, but the air bag saved his upper body. But they think he'll make it.'

'What about James, though?' said Fleming, really worried. 'Presumably they would have had to cut him out too?'

'No,' said Dyer, '*someone else had already done that.*'

'Does that mean he's alive?' Fleming asked, by now really pale.

'That's got to be the assumption,' said Dyer, 'dead men tell no tales. But as to what state he's in – and even more to the point – where he is – we have no idea.'

'Don't the police have any clues?'

'They're working on it and I'm going to talk to them at midday. You probably don't know this Matthew, but James has a tracking device built into that Rolex he was wearing, together with a number of other things which were put into it which makes it a rather unusual watch. But there is nothing after the crash on the tracking record on the computer. Either the watch was damaged in the crash, or it's been removed from him or, since the crash, he's been in an environment where it can't pick up satellites. So for the time being we have to work on the other pointers.' Dyer rubbed his face and eyes.

'First of all the assault must have taken place at very high speed. The speedo on the Porsche was locked at a hundred and twenty miles an hour at the point of impact. Now, given that the car had come off the road, through a hedge, and had rolled three times it's fair to assume that its speed when it left the road was a good deal higher than that. The police reckoned it must have been doing about a hundred and sixty – they weren't too impressed I can tell you – and I wouldn't recommend to Frank that he regains consciousness if he can avoid it.

The thing is it was actually shot up at that speed which means that the people doing the shooting must have had one hell of a car. Don't forget that the Porsche was a tuned turbo.'

'Did the police find any evidence of another car at the scene?' Fleming's dismay was being quickly replaced by his analytical facility, seldom dormant for long.

Dyer hesitated.

'Yes, they did. They found some very faint tyre marks about three hundred yards further down the road where the attackers must have overrun and stopped, before going back to investigate the Porsche.

The tyre marks were really unusual. They were from an enormously wide tyre of a design the police had never seen before.'

Julie Walters put her head round the door and said: 'You two look as though you need some coffee. And the hospital has phoned. They said that Frank has just regained consciousness, they've finished patching him up, but he's still on life support.'

Thirty minutes later Dyer was being ushered to Frank's bedside by two rather attractive nurses.

Frank was not looking his normal happy go lucky self. Tubes and pipes invaded every part of his body, a very large oxygen cylinder stood at the head of the bed and an elaborate monitor flashed and blinked at the footboard. His face was ashen and his eyes were hollow and virtually unseeing.

At the entry of Dyer they flickered barely perceptibly.

One of the nurses said sharply: 'He's in a very bad way. You can have five minutes, Mr Dyer, no longer.'

Dyer didn't really do emotion but managed to utter some sympathetic words.

Then he said: 'Look, Frank, James has disappeared. Someone cut him out of the car and left you behind. We need to find him. Do you have any idea of what car it was that was following you?'

Frank's eyes dilated and his breathing faltered. One of the nurses quickly came forward and gave him some oxygen, with a warning look at Dyer.

'Hell.' The word rasped feebly out of Frank and he closed his eyes. A rictus of pain crossed his face.

'Right, Mr Dyer, that's all you'll be getting, he's very poorly. Out now.'

Dyer reluctantly made his way to the exit. 'Hell'. Was that part of a typically jocular Frank phrase — or did it refer to how he felt – or was it something automotive related?

A call to one of Frank's petrol head friends soon dispelled Dyer's confusion.

Integrale. Shelley Integrale. The most exotic automotive design vanity ever undertaken by a mass market car manufacturer, it seemed, according to Dyer's source. What, this source had wondered, on the phone to Dyer, was the reasoning behind a convoluted corporate strategy that would lead a European company which had started life by producing utterly basic and simplistic cars after the second world war to end up by developing a one thousand brake horsepower, two hundred and fifty mile per hour coupe, with a global sales potential you could identify on a dozen sets of fingertips?

While his source had pointed out that it was almost certainly the only car that could have done the job Dyer still couldn't make sense of it. A car like that, he thought, was ridiculously easy to trace. Lutin's men could only have got hold of one by buying a used car, or, less likely, by borrowing or stealing one, used it for that one purpose and then been planning to dump it or sell it.

But, he reflected, if it could be found it would tell a story, probably one the police would be better at getting at than he would.

Half an hour later he was in the Integrale sales offices in a discreet town house off Berkeley Square.

Prince Otto Gustav was quite unlike most car salesmen that Dyer had ever met. Immaculately dressed, in his early thirties, he explained to Dyer that his primary job was to know the automotive cognoscenti of Europe. He had five languages, which helped. Then he had to marry them with a marketing programme for the car which used the complete set of seduction tools common to that end of the market – technology, power, speed, and above all, exclusivity.

In his small but discreetly opulent office he angled a computer screen towards Dyer.

'Let's see,' he said, 'we have sold forty cars in the UK. Of those forty we know that thirty continue to be in the hands of their original owners. We know this because we are able to monitor all registration transfers through a special arrangement with the DVLCC dressed up as a part of the elaborate security package offered to purchasers. Two are on the market, one privately and the other through a specialist dealer, a car that currently belongs to a leading Formula One driver, both,' he added with a wide smile, 'at a premium to their original list price.

One other thing,' he continued, 'that forms part of this package is a GPS based tracking system for each car that it is so deeply embedded in the car that it is impossible for owners to remove or tamper with; in fact if they do it disables the black box which acts as the nerve centre for the car's electronic brain and the car immediately becomes completely inoperable. This system enables us to track the complete record of journeys made by any of our cars including their average and peak speeds.

Some of the results are pretty amazing, I can tell you,' he said.

He double clicked on one of the list of forty cars – Dyer noted, slightly disappointed, that the owners names were all in code – and a map of Europe came up on the screen with what looked like a colour coded spiders web crawling all over it.

'This is one of our most heavily used cars,' said Prince Gustav. 'There must be a girl in every port here, I fancy.'

He clicked on one of the spidery lines and a complete set of journey statistics came up – time of departure, time of stops and starts thereafter, average and peak speeds. Dyer was astonished to see that speeds of over two hundred miles per hour had regularly been recorded. He exited that screen and clicked on another icon and the present position of the car came up – it was in the NCP garage in South Audley Street.

'Just round the corner,' the Prince said with a smile.

Dyer left Prince Gustav having reached an understanding with him that Gustav would re-search the status and location of the Integrales which were or had been on the market and re-port to the police officer on Doyle's case with whom Dyer was liaising, and go through the confirmations needed to match the tyre imprints to the ones at the crash scene.

Doyle was very, very, cold. It was dark save for a very faint glimmer of light far above him, and it was completely silent. He was sitting on a floor with his back against a rough wall; he could feel drops of icy moisture running down into the thin casual shirt he had been wearing for the journey back to London after the shooting party. With difficulty he lifted his hands to find them bound with a chain. His feet were free but he was so cold he could scarcely move them. His whole body ached and he was in chronic pain.

His head ached in sympathy with the rest of his limbs. With difficulty he cast his mind back. He could remember two violent impacts, very close together. He dimly thought that the air bags exploding around him as the car started to roll would have been the first, and the second must have been the final impact after the third roll. He remembered the deep metallic rattle of the heavy machine gun fire and Frank slumping in his seat a split second before the car went off the road. Then he recalled voices and the brief sharp pain of a needle in his arm. Then no more.

He forced himself to roll his left wrist upwards, his Rolex said four fifteen am.

He knew he should get up and move his limbs to stay alert, possibly, even, alive. But he drifted off again.

He was woken by a trickle of light from the door. A voice barked to him to get up.

'You are wanted upstairs, quickly now,' it rasped.

Doyle tried to get to his feet and failed. He could no longer feel his feet, or his legs, or even move his arms much. He felt in a catatonic state.

Two young guards dressed in jeans and thick fleeces quickly came into the room and roughly dragged him to his feet and then to the door.

'Its two hundred steps up from here,' one said roughly,' and we don't want to carry you all the way. Get on! Walk!'

With intense difficulty Doyle toiled up the steep stone circular stairs, half supported, half dragged by the two guards. The air gradually became drier and, to his immense relief, warmer. They were clearly climbing up some kind of turret. There were no windows, just black metal sconces which had been converted to issue the dimmest electric light.

After about ten minutes Doyle gasped his way onto a broad landing lined with stag's heads, old, clearly Scottish, oil paintings with antique Persian rugs laid on oak boards, boards so old they were almost black. With guttural exclamations the guards pushed open a heavy studded wooden door and thrust Doyle inside, closing it with a bang behind him.

Doyle would remember the scene which greeted him for a long time.

The first thing he saw was Alexander Lutin, dressed in black jeans and a roll neck sweater, sitting at a table laid for breakfast in front of a large bow window. Out of that window Doyle saw the early morning sun warming a lightly cut rolling lawn which led down to some cliffs. Below them the glittering sea swirled and chafed at rocks and ledges which ran seawards for several hundred yards. On the adjacent wall of the room there was a massive Jacobean fire place with a crackling fire of roughly cut logs. Sitting by the fireplace, on a dark red high backed settee, was a woman, in her early sixties, dark haired and still strikingly beautiful, wearing an immaculately coutured black and gold trouser suit. She wore a gold filigree necklace and, on the index finger of her left hand, a very large brilliant white marquise diamond. Doyle thought she was probably Lebanese.

'Ah, Doyle,' said Lutin, 'good to see that you are still alive after your various experiences. I'm sorry that your quarters leave a little to be desired in comparison with your normal self indulgent lifestyle.'

Getting up, he crossed the room towards the settee and said: 'May I introduce you to my Mother, Maria Lutin.'

Doyle inclined his head and moved his chains confusedly. Lutin indicated he should sit in a chair opposite the breakfast table. He crossed to Doyle and fiddled with the combination lock on his chains until they sprang loose. He offered him a cup of coffee which Doyle eagerly accepted.

'You would probably like to know where you are,' he continued. 'This is my mother's house, known as the Castle of Gath. It was built in the early sixteenth century and acquired by my father for virtually nothing in the late nineteen seventies. It lies on one of the outermost islands in the Scottish Hebrides. There are no other houses and no one else on the island apart from our employees. Incidentally, James, no one knows where you are, and no one will be able to find you, until it's too late.'

Lutin poured them both some more coffee and continued.

'James, you probably don't know much about my family history. My father spent his life working for the KGB. He was fanatically devoted to the service of the Russian State and became one of the most decorated agents in the history of the service. He carried out innumerable missions internationally of immense value to communist

Russia, as it then was. In his prime, in the late nineteen seventies and early eighties, he was the KGB agent most feared by other secret services and he retained the confidence of every Russian Prime Minister until he died on one of his last missions in nineteen ninety. Killed,' Lutin's face darkened and his voice thickened, 'by a French agent in Algiers.

As you may know', he went on, slowly, 'I have retained the same political confidences as he. I have done what I can in London to serve the new Russian State and been well rewarded for it.'

Lutin got up and paced restlessly around the room, taking a cigarette from a silver box on a table near his mother's settee and lighting it abruptly. When he turned his face back to Doyle it had a glittering, febrile, intensity that Doyle had only seen in heavy cocaine users.

'But I feel that, compared to him, I have achieved nothing.'

'Nothing,' said Lutin, with added vehemence.

'That's not true, darling,' his mother's voice was soft and musical.

'No, mother, it is true,' said Lutin heavily.

'Now,' Lutin spoke deliberately and with gratingly precise emphasis on every word, 'I have the opportunity to do something for Russia, something really big. Something which could make Russia into a genuine global superpower.

Something,' he went on quietly, 'which would really make my Father proud.'

'Doyle, you have created a huge opportunity, for your own organisation, possibly for your own country, and I admire and respect you for that.

I want what you have created, Doyle,' Lutin spoke so quietly that Doyle could hardly hear him. 'I want it for Russia, and for the glory of my family.

I've been charged by Orlov with getting it. It's the latest in a long line of confidences placed in my family, and it's the first really big assignment for me. It's probably hard for you to imagine what this means to me Doyle, but let me tell you, I'd rather die than fail.

And, Doyle, 'continued Lutin, 'you, yes, you, are getting in my way.'

'Well,' said Doyle, 'you've done your best to get rid of me.'

'Frankly,' said Lutin, 'I concluded that that was the easiest option. With you out of the way the Sphinx initiative would collapse. None of your so called partners,' Lutin's tone was openly contemptuous, 'could carry on with your coup on their own for a moment. None have your charisma, your organisational skills, or your personal relationships with key political figures, above all with President Barula. They are just greedy jackals happy to eat whatever is presented to them.

If you were out of the way, Doyle,' Lutin went on, 'the Russian State could do the sort of deal they understand with President Barula. The sort of deal James, that doesn't involve level playing field deals, bidding for Rangoon and all that stuff which you and your kind are so culturally attuned to. The sort of deal we would do would leave your precious Sphinx holding nearly thirty per cent of Rangoon. When our Namibian oil came on stream, the subsequent oil price decline would produce for the Sphinx one of the largest losses in the history of hedge funds.

I can't imagine many of those bastards attending your memorial service, James,' Lutin concluded.

'The Russians don't like paying for anything, do they Alexander?' said Doyle. 'They'd much rather steal it.'

Lutin's face had become impassive.

'It's very simple, Doyle. I want, for Russia, half the Sphinx deal as a free ride. I can't be bothered with chasing you around any more and it's a much cleaner deal for Russia than beating up Barula. In public we'd look as though we were firmly in partnership with you — and all the other people you may have in tow – we'd look respectable citizens and we'd be the biggest oil producer in the world.'

'Sounds wonderful,' said Doyle lazily.

Lutin's eyes glittered.

'I'm not messing around here, Doyle. I have here a legal agreement which our lawyers have drafted. You can sign it and go free and finalise all your arrangements and we'll be silent partners along for the ride.

It'll be perceived as a brilliantly elegant deal, one you would be proud of. Russia will lose that kleptocracy tag I believe you use.'

'And if I don't sign it?' Warmth was creeping back into Doyle's limbs and his brain was beginning to work again at its normal rate.

'We have some wonderful science in Russia, you know. One of the many things they have perfected is a drug which kills brain cells. It's like a form of cancer except that it just targets the brain and not the rest of the body. It very slowly eats your brain. For a while you just appear to lose your mental edge, then it becomes more Alzheimer like, and finally,' Lutin was completely matter of fact, 'it eliminates all brain and control functions and you die. The whole process takes about a year. I have a supply of that drug here. I propose to inject you with it in twenty four hour's time unless you sign this agreement. You can either sign now, after which I will instruct my people to bring you breakfast and transport you to the mainland, or you can return to that delightful cell downstairs and the guards will ask you every six hours or so whether you would like to come up and sign.

It's up to you,' Lutin concluded blandly, 'but I do want you to know that I would be really unhappy to destroy a brain of such quality.'

Doyle didn't feel great but he felt better. He could move his limbs freely and was alert, even if his body hurt like hell after the trauma of the crash. He suddenly thought of Frank and a spasm crossed his face.

'Are you alright?' asked Lutin sharply.

'Desperate to go to the lavatory actually if you don't mind. Preferably without that chain,' he added hastily, as Lutin picked it up.

'Alright, you can go with Mikail, but no funny business, Doyle. And I shall want an answer when you get back.'

Doyle got up slowly and followed Mikail out onto the wide landing outside the room. Doyle knew that there was no question of signing Lutin's agreement and that once he was back in that cell, without food and in the bitter chill, life would drain out of him and he would once again be extremely vulnerable. Even if Lutin's drug didn't do everything Lutin maintained was written on the outside of its tin Doyle most certainly didn't fancy the experiment.

Seldom, Doyle thought, had so much depended on a visit to a lavatory.

He wasn't disappointed. The door was wide open disclosing a properly large country house establishment. It had a luxurious wooden seat, polished side tables, magazines, hairbrushes, mirrors and a gigantic cistern mounted high up from which dangled a long chain with a china handle. Doyle told the guard he thought he had diarrhoea, and might be some time, and noiselessly shot the bolt.

He made straight for the window and put his head out. He was over six metres up, too far to jump to be confident of no broken limbs. Nearly a metre above the top of the window was a projecting corbel about twenty centimetres wide, angled very slightly downward, which seemed to run to the corner of the tower. Apart from that there was nothing but smooth stones and flush masonry. It was impossible to read the shape of the building. It would be extremely difficult to climb up onto the corbel and even more difficult to remain on it, let alone walk on it.

There wasn't much choice. He had to use what was there, and he had to have some weapons. Doyle stood on the seat, reached up and detached the chain hanging from the cistern and then grabbed the heavy glass paperweight from the table and put both in his pockets. Finally he looked at his watch. Seven am. He breathed heavily. He knew he had missed a trick and he took the watch off and pressed a button at the back which re-set the energy saving device powering the GPS transmitter. Any help would now be at least six hours away.

He heard the guard getting impatient the other side of the door. Now, looking back the other way, he was delighted to see that there was a drain pipe on the side of the window which he hadn't inspected, just within reach, which presumably exited from the bathroom on the floor directly above. After his bathroom the drain made a leisurely descent until it went into a vertical downpipe at the corner of the building. Doyle thought of making an ape like descent by hanging from it but the pipe was too big to allow his hands a decent grip. However the bracket above the corbel, in line with the edge of his window, which supported the down pipe, and fastened it to the wall, made a possible handhold. He flushed the toilet, swung himself out onto the window ledge, let out an agonised cry as if he had fallen to the ground and started to see how he could mount the corbel. Seconds later he was standing on it, leaning slightly into the wall, inching his way along towards the corner of the building. A sudden gust of fresh Scottish sea air nearly blew him off the corbel but did more than anything else to revive him.

He reached the corner, hopeful of finding a means of descent. There was none. Another, exactly similar, wall and corbel faced him. This wall was fully exposed to what was now a considerable breeze which made keeping his footing doubly difficult. He was also now consumed with worry that he would be spotted.

He hoped desperately that the Castle of Gath was more than just a classic Scottish square. He reached the end of the second wall, feeling rather desperate. As he looked round the corner towards the third wall he could see a speedboat moored to a distant jetty. He looked up. So far as he could see there were two more floors. Above that he assumed the roof would be flat. The roughly cut lawns seemed to surround the castle on all sides. He could see an old Landrover parked by the front door.

Halfway along this third wall a massive rainwater downpipe descended vertically supported by large brackets every six feet or so. Doyle quickly made his way to it. It was made of lead and its smooth surface offered no grip or handholds at all. But the brackets stood just proud of the drainpipe and offered the slimmest toe hold. Once you had one foot on one the next was nearly two metres above. Doyle reached for his lavatory chain. If he could lasso that through the gap between the downpipe and the wall, above the next bracket, and clip the end back on itself he could use it a form of primitive rope ladder.

Up or down?

Then he heard some shouts which appeared to come from the side of the castle from which he had made his escape. Hopefully his captors must have assumed from his cries that he had made a mad jump for the ground, had somehow survived, and escaped into the woods. That was where they were putting their effort, at least for the present.

Doyle decided it had to be up.

He tried the chain lasso. It swung madly and the effort needed to lift his body up until one of his feet was just on the lip of the next bracket was intense. Doyle thought ruefully that it would all take too long and that his escape would soon be punctuated by Lutin getting busy with a rifle down below. He made a massive effort and within ten minutes was on the flat roof, sore and exhausted. The roof had a high battlement which, if he kept to the middle, ensured he was out of sight from any watchers on the ground. He made a very careful survey of all the aspects of the island visible from that point, noting again the route to the jetty. There was a very heavy, thick, studded wooden door in the middle of the roof area set into a small square structure which presumably gave headroom at the top of some stairs. It was locked. Doyle verified which side the hinges were on, positioned himself so that he would be behind it when it was opened, and settled down to wait. He knew it wouldn't be long. After about twenty minutes he heard shouts approaching the house and the bang of a distant door. He put his ear to the rooftop door and braced himself. Suddenly he heard the rush of steps on the stair and the door was noisily unbolted. Doyle kept close behind it, one of his hands firmly on the paperweight. It opened slowly and one of the guards made a cautious exit. A tactical error, thought Doyle, as he brought the paperweight down hard and silently onto the man's skull just behind his ear. He crumpled noiselessly and Doyle quickly relieved him of his automatic pistol, his knife and his mobile phone. Noting with satisfaction that the pistol was very heavily silenced, Doyle dragged the guard round the corner of the hut and returned to his post behind the door which he shut. He heard more rushing footsteps. The second guard was sharper, coming quickly through the door with his pistol swinging at the ready. Doyle shot it out of his hands, the gun making no more noise than a falling body, and quickly laid him out. He dragged him round the corner of the hut, took his weapons and quickly went inside the rooftop structure and made his way down the stairs, praying for some cover. After half a flight he reached a landing and tucked himself behind an unlocked door giving to a small room and waited.

A minute or so later Lutin came loping up the stairs shouting out to the guards to tell him if they had found Doyle on the roof.

Doyle followed Lutin up to the roof like a pan-
ther, and when Lutin had stepped through the
studded door swiftly closed, bolted and locked
it behind him and removed the key. Lutin, he
thought, was too dangerous to take on in a rooftop fire fight. Doyle went down the stairs very
circumspectly. He just didn't know how many
other of Lutin's people were in the Castle, while
he thought it would take Lutin a while to shoot
the door in. He made his way down to the first
floor and quickly checked his bearings against
the room where he had had that meeting with
Lutin and his mother.

His mother. She stood in front of him holding a
wicked little ladies gun pointed at his stomach.

'Tell me you haven't killed him and I'll spare
you,' she whispered.

Doyle thought it was no time for niceties.

'No, no, he's enjoying the sunshine out on the
roof,' he said guilelessly, waving his left hand up-
ward.

Momentarily distracted, her guard relaxed,
and Doyle knocked the gun out of her hands
with the butt of one of his guns. She screamed,
he picked her gun up and was on his way down
to the ground floor within seconds.

He reached the front door without further incident and went for the Landrover, praying that
the keys were in it, and roared off towards the

jetty weaving as violently as possible. A few shots, presumably, he thought, from the roof, kicked up around him but it was evident that Lutin wasn't carrying any heavy arms and that whatever he had was struggling at the range.

The twin two hundred and seventy five horse-power Yamahas fired up immediately. Doyle checked the extra fuel cans in the stern and cast off. Seconds later he was doing thirty knots in quite a rough sea, navigating by the seat of his pants towards the South East.

Two hours, and one conference with a fishing boat later, he was tied up in Ullapool and on the phone to Dyer.

'We finally got your GPS transmission,' said Dyer, 'and were just about to mobilise a rescue party.'

'Well,' said Doyle, 'if anyone would like some chopper practice they can get me out of here. Our friend Lutin is still at large and God knows what he'll do next.'

'How's Frank?' he asked, and received a brief report.

'One more thing,' said Dyer. 'You remember the Rangoon document storage house and what we found in the basement? Well you know the Chief Executive of Rangoon has been a very big spender on racing in recent years, and no one's been quite sure where his funding has come from. There's some thinking in the police that he may be linked to that basement operation. Apparently all the employees have been checked out and are very closely linked both to each other and to him. And his country house is only ten miles away.'

Chapter 18

THE TAIL OF THE SPHINX

The atmosphere in the Cabinet Room in the Presidential Palace in Windhoek was tense.

President Barula sat in the middle of the crescent table with his Private Secretary to his left and his Finance Minister beyond. On his left sat the Home Affairs Minister and Energy Secretary. Junior ministers spread out on either side beyond them. Most were wearing immaculate Savile Row suits and dark glasses. At one end of the table were a partner and two assistant directors of Harris Bank, the bankers brought in by Barula to advise on the split of value of the Field of Dreams.

Barula opened by welcoming Doyle and Fleming who were sat opposite the Cabinet phalanx. At the other end of the room from where the Harris Bank people were sitting was a large plasma screen.

'Gentlemen,' said Barula, 'welcome. We are very conscious that without the efforts you have made on behalf of the Sphinx partnership we would not be even contemplating exploitation of the Field of Dreams, as you have named it.'

At a signal from Barula the lights were dimmed, and Barula addressed the meeting:

'Everyone round this table knows of the exceptionally unusual circumstances which surround the mineral and extraction rights to this field. The mineral rights are leased to Rangoon but, according to an agreement which is not public knowledge, Rangoon is not permitted to extract more than twenty five thousand barrels of oil a day. Anyone wishing to extract oil to the full potential of this remarkable resource has first to do a deal with us, the Namibian Government, and secondly either to do a deal with Rangoon or to acquire it.

We, the Namibian Government, have to be assured that, in relation to granting any additional extraction rights, we obtain the best deal possible. We have therefore asked Harris Bank to carry out an exercise to determine the appropriate split of shares in the Field of Dreams which ought to be attributed to Rangoon, as owners of the mineral rights, and the Namibian State as potential grantors of the additional extraction rights. Now I am going to ask David Freeman of Harris to talk to us about the outcome of their work.'

Freeman was about forty five and one of the leading global experts in energy advice.

'This issue,' Freeman began, 'is less a question of rigorous financial analysis and more a question of politics. But we have endeavoured to begin by quantifying the value of the Field of Dreams. We have assumed that the figures supplied to us as working assumptions for reserves and production are fair.

You will all understand that the production capability of this field is so vast that it could have a most dramatic effect upon the global price of oil. There are two ways of looking at the outcomes here. If the Field of Dreams were simply to come on stream and pump at its maximum capability of, say, twenty million barrels a day, that would, even allowing for the decline in Saudi production, add some fifteen or sixteen million barrels a day to global oil supply and in our view the price of oil would simply go through the floor. That might seem a superficially attractive outcome but it would destroy the production economics of most other oil producers all round the world and of course remove any element of rationing of oil use imposed by a high price which would not only be undesirable from the environmental perspective but also mean your reserves would be used up quickly at extremely unattractive economic returns.

We believe a far more likely scenario is that Namibia will be encouraged by OPEC and others to pump at a rate which keeps oil prices in the region of sixty to seventy dollars a barrel. This would moderate demand while giving most other oil producers an acceptable economic return. We think this will involve Namibia pumping at about five million barrels a day, which would have to rise gradually over time in line with global economic growth, assuming of course that no other really major oil finds are made elsewhere in the future. On that basis we estimate the reserve life of the Field of Dreams to be over a hundred and fifty years.

Now Rangoon has about ninety years left on their lease and therefore on their ownership of mineral rights so they in theory will enjoy sixty per cent of the value of the reserves. However because near term cash flows are worth far more than longer term ones, even factoring in an assumption about the likely increase in the oil price over this very long period, we estimate that in terms of today's value the lease held by Rangoon represents well over ninety five per cent of the total value of the Field of Dreams. Gentlemen, we estimate that total value, after allowing for set up and production costs, and royalties, at about one thousand billion dollars.'

There were some gasps round the table.

Freeman laughed and put up a slide illustrating the bank note equivalent. It looked like an enormous warehouse full of double stacked pallets each containing ten million dollars.

'Yes,' he said, 'it's a truly unimaginable amount of money.'

Using computer graphics he sliced off five per cent from the warehouse.

'That's a generous valuation in today's money of the last sixty years of the reserves which are, effectively, not owned by Rangoon, gentlemen. At the end of the day that will revert back to the State of Namibia.

Now,' he went on, 'all we have to do is to decide what share of the remainder should be attributable to Rangoon for their ownership of the mineral rights and what share to Namibia to reflect the value of an extension of the extractive rights.

This,' he said, 'is where financial analysis leaves the room and real politick takes its place.

The blunt reality, gentlemen, is that Rangoon already has plenty of oil fields and has managed to operate very happily without the Field of Dreams for the last sixty years. Yes, Rangoon is constantly under pressure to find more oil and at some point would no doubt like to develop your oil. But it also has many other options – for instance Iraq, and especially Kurdistan, are opening up. There may be other opportunities – look what Twenty First Century have achieved in Brazil, for instance, and of course Rangoon already has big interests next door in Angola.

So, my point is that Rangoon is not short of options. It doesn't have that much immediate pressure to work the Field of Dreams. Of course, in the future, it will look at it more closely as it will want to utilise the time left on its lease.

But your situation, gentlemen, is very different,' Freeman continued. 'You have a most urgent need to see this field developed, to bring prosperity to your country and your people, and you don't have any other options.

So,' Freeman concluded, 'in terms of real politick Rangoon are the natural winners.

Taking all these factors into account we ascribe a two thirds of the value of the remaining lease to ownership of the mineral rights and one third to the extraction extension. So in our view Namibia is entitled to thirty three point three three per cent of the value inherent in the remaining term of the Rangoon lease.'

Joseph Barula thanked Freeman and turned to his Cabinet colleagues.

'Well, I must confess that that number is somewhat less than I had been hoping for but of course we must respect the professional judgement of Harris Bank.

I think,' he continued, 'that this analysis has also told us one more thing which is quite critical for our country. This is that, on its own, Rangoon may not develop this field anytime soon. As they own the mineral rights they can call the tune on this. Mr Freeman, am I right?'

Freeman nodded.

'In fact to ensure that this great asset is developed in a timely way for us, we, or someone else friendly to us, would have to control Rangoon?'

Freeman nodded again.

'The final reality is that the Sphinx partnership own twenty nine point nine per cent of Rangoon's equity and few companies, correct me, Mr Freeman, if I am wrong, please, would wish to counter bid against an original bidder with a holding of that size. So, gentlemen, my view is that the Sphinx partnership are our only realistic partner. To move forward on the exploitation of the Field of Dreams we have to do a deal with them and they have to acquire Rangoon. Mr Freeman, please confirm that view.'

'That's perfectly correct, Mr President,' said Freeman.

Barula turned smiling to Doyle.

'Do Sphinx's have tails Mr Doyle? And if so, may we tweak yours a bit?'

After two days of intensive negotiations and the drafting of some legal agreements which, to Doyle, seemed capable of growing at a similar rate to giant hogweed, and which tested Graham Makepeace's legendary affability and patience to the limits, Doyle, Fleming and Makepeace found themselves in the Cabinet Room again in the early evening.

President Barula looked around his cabinet.

'Gentlemen,' he said, 'I am pleased to tell you that we have reached an agreement with the Sphinx. I am pleased to report that they have agreed that the State of Namibia shall be entitled to a thirty seven per cent equity share in the Field rather than the thirty three point three three per cent recommended by Harris Bank, while the Sphinx they have indicated that they wish to be rewarded with a five per cent interest for themselves, with which I have agreed, and a pro rata share of this will come from our holding and that of Rangoon.

Rangoon will therefore have an economic interest of, in round numbers, sixty per cent, the State of Namibia thirty five per cent and the Sphinx five per cent.

However I am delighted to report that the Sphinx have agreed that the State of Namibia may have fifty point one per cent of the voting rights in the company set up to control the Field of Dreams even once Rangoon's interest in the

Field is amalgamated with it following the take-over of Rangoon. Once the takeover of Rangoon is complete we will auction a production sharing agreement which will mean that the field is developed on a tight timescale with no capital commitment from us.

So, gentlemen, our State will control its own oil and its own destiny, which I think is an incredibly important step forward both for us and for Africans everywhere.

I will now hand over to our lawyers to take you through the detailed provisions.'

As the presentation from the lawyers went on Doyle sensed a heightened tension in the room.

Finally the legal presentation concluded. Joseph Barula looked around his Cabinet colleagues and asked: 'Gentlemen, do I have your agreement to sign these documents? In addition to the detailed terms you have just heard it is of course conditional upon the Sphinx Partnership and their associates acquiring control of Rangoon within six months from the date of signing. Incidentally the Sphinx may sell on their holding in Rangoon provided it is to someone of whom we approve and who is able to meet that control condition.

This agreement gives us,' he continued, 'an incredible future for Namibia. The Field of Dreams will be fully developed, with all the appropriate infrastructure, free of charge to us. We will become one of the richest countries in Africa and the foundation stone of a second OPEC, which we will substantially control.'

The Home Affairs Minister, Benjamin Othello, a thin, tall, Namibian with a rather scarred and pinched looking face, said, 'Mr President, we hear a lot about 'we' and 'us' but to whom do these terms refer?'

'The State of Namibia of course,' said Barula

'This agreement doesn't do anything for the people around this table, Mr President,' said Othello.

'It is for the benefit of all our people, Benjamin,' said Barula. 'Do you have a problem with that?'

'No, of course not,' said Othello, 'but it's usual for the people who put such benefits in place to receive some direct financial recognition for their contribution in setting things up.'

'How do you feel about the payment of a commission, Mr Doyle?' asked Barula, going through a scenario that had been worked out between them the previous evening at his beach house.

'Normally I wouldn't have any problems with it,' said Doyle evenly. 'But in this case the Sphinx have to have backing to take over Rangoon and that backing is coming from debt and equity supplied by the US and British Governments.

They have made it quite clear that they will not provide it if commissions are paid to individuals.'

'Then I, for one, will not vote for this agreement,' said Benjamin Othello.

'Are you saying,' said Barula, 'that you would rather deprive the people of Namibia, whom you represent, of these untold benefits simply because you are not personally receiving any cash from this deal?

Also, Benjamin, ask yourself what contribution to this outcome have you made personally to justify such a reward? Have you drilled at your own expense? Have you negotiated financing deals all over the world?

No, you have not. You have simply been lucky enough to have been born on a piece of valuable sand — like every other citizen in this country. This is the kind of philosophy, Benjamin, wanting something for nothing, that has kept Africa so poor all these years. Now we have an opportunity to break the mould. Don't you, Benjamin Othello, want to be part of that history?'

His tone softened.

'Look, Benjamin. Before you entered this Cabinet you were a successful businessman, but on a small scale. Have you any idea of the business opportunities that will flow from the development of the Field of Dreams? I assure you they will be huge, and you will be in pole position to take advantage of them. The Namibian Government will provide backing to help such businesses become established.

Isn't it better,' Barula continued, 'to gain your rewards that way rather than from a simple hand out?'

There was a murmur of support around the table.

Barula said gently, 'Benjamin, will you come in with us?'

Othello looked dark but muttered assent. The documents were signed and champagne was wheeled in.

The next evening, en route for Heathrow, Doyle stretched his legs and said,

'Matthew, I must be getting old but these 747's really are very comfortable you know.'

Doyle hated large meetings. There were only six people in the room on the fifth floor of the London offices of Petersons.

There was Doyle and Sir Ratan Bata, the Chairman of the Sphinx bidding vehicle Field of Dreams Limited, Graham Makepeace and Suzanne Farr, an assistant lawyer, and lastly Daniel Romain, a Petersons' partner and the Head of Mergers and Acquisitions in London, and a Petersons' director, Harry Wrigley.

In a number of other rooms on the same corridor an army of people from lawyers, banks, governments, and accountants were working on a mass of financing agreements, press releases, offer documents, shareholder agreements, and submissions, both to competition authorities and to the European Panel on Takeovers and Mergers which regulated takeovers in Europe.

Doyle was supremely indifferent to all of this activity. Even though he was embarking on one of the biggest takeovers in history he was relaxed. He knew all the detail would get impeccably attended to and that routine issues and problems would get sorted with great professionalism. He also knew that he would contribute very little to that process.

Romain was speaking.

'So, Sir Ratan, James, we start with this letter,' he tapped a short document in front of him, 'to the Chairman and Chief Executive of Rangoon, and we see what the reaction is before we wheel out some of our more controversial and damaging ammunition.'

The 'letter' was the so called 'bear hug' letter which a prospective bidder often sent to the Board of a target company setting out an outline merger proposal. Very often, inexplicably, such letters, ostensibly private, found their way into the press, causing the shareholders of the target company to interest themselves greatly in the response of their Board to what was frequently a financially attractive proposal. Most bidders preferred to get the recommendation of a target board to their offer rather than fighting a hostile takeover.

The Sphinx letter was very simple. It was on Field of Dreams headed paper and read as follows;

'*Dear Sir Adrian and Lord Fettes,*

The Field of Dreams is a company owned by inter alia the Sphinx Partnership, itself an entity supported by a discrete group of international hedge funds.

As you are no doubt aware the Sphinx Partnership (the 'Sphinx') owns twenty nine point nine percent of the issued ordinary share capital of Rangoon, a holding which, if the proposals laid out below were to proceed, it would contribute to the Field of Dreams.

We are aware that you have persistently endeavoured to engage the Sphinx in dialogue as to its intentions and the future of its stake in Rangoon. Up until now we have not been ready to enter discussions but we hope that this letter will make our intentions clear to you.

We believe that Rangoon is a very valuable company which owns some unexploited assets from which significant additional value might be derived.

Accordingly we are willing to make a cash offer of seven hundred and fifty pence per Rangoon ordinary share against last night's closing price of five hundred and fifty pence.

We believe that such an offer, after years in which the share price of Rangoon has moved sideways, or declined, would be of the greatest interest to your shareholders.

We have all of our funding in place in principle and we do not perceive there to be any antitrust issues.

We would be concerned to, if possible, secure the recommendation of your Board to any offer we might make along these lines.

Our financial advisers are Petersons (Daniel Romain).

Yours sincerely

Sir Ratan Bata	*James Doyle*
Chairman	*Chief Executive'*

'It's a good letter,' said Doyle. 'It's ambivalent about whether we would bid or not without the recommendation of their Board, and the bit about valuable but unexploited assets will have them scratching their heads. It's always a trifle unnerving for a Board to feel that it doesn't fully understand its own company.'

Bata, the diplomat, said: 'Don't you feel the bit about the share price underperformance is too aggressive?'

'No,' Romain replied, 'at the end of the day their shareholders won't care whether the share price performance has underperformed because of or despite the efforts of the Board; they are just looking for a premium, especially given what they've lost in these terrible recent stock markets. We need it in because we're going to leak the letter.'

Romain picked up the phone and asked his personal assistant:

'Is Roderick Maguire here yet?'

'Just arrived.'

'Send him in would you.'

Maguire materialised, his slightly foppish appearance and floppy hair disguised one of the sharpest brains and best contacts lists in public relations.

Maguire nodded respectfully to Bata, smiled at Doyle and addressed his remarks to Romain.

'Well, boss,' he said, 'what are you rogues up to now?'

'Can we ask you a question?' Romain said. 'Are you conflicted with Rangoon Oil?'

Maguire said his firm was not.

'Well, that's what we're doing. Bidding for Rangoon.'

Maguire whistled long and low. Then he looked carefully at Doyle.

'You've already got a big stake, right? Who's funding the rest?'

The last thing Maguire wanted to do was to put himself the wrong side of the European business establishment on behalf of someone who couldn't deliver. Romain intervened.

'Listen to me Roderick. All that sort of thing is alright, otherwise we wouldn't be here either. This is big stuff, bigger actually than you know or might even imagine, and you'll be pleasantly surprised and pretty impressed when you find who is backing this.'

Maguire backed off.

'OK, boss,' he said, 'tell me the score.'

'This is the bear hug we propose to send.'

Maguire read it quickly.

'Seems pretty standard stuff. But what's all this about unexploited valuable assets? I thought their problem was just the opposite, that they haven't got enough oil.'

'Roderick', Romain spoke, 'this letter is just a starter for ten. These people don't know what they've got nor, apparently, do they know some of the limitations around it. The Sphinx have the keys to all that. We can make this Board look pretty incompetent and pretty silly if we have to — but if they fall into our arms at seven hundred and fifty we won't need to. We also,' he went on, his voice low, 'have some spectacular dirt, if we need it.'

Maguire's eyes gleamed. He knew just how damaging judicious dishing of dirt could be in a takeover. He had built part of his career on it.

'But that's not for now,' Romain was brisk.

'This letter is going in to Rangoon at eleven this morning and I think we can take it that you know what to do.'

Maguire asked a few more questions and left the room looking hugely pleased with himself.

A final version of the letter was signed by Bata and Doyle and hand delivered to Rangoon's London headquarters.

Twenty four hours later those headquarters were in turmoil.

A full Board Meeting had been hurriedly convened and was in progress in the Boardroom on the twentieth floor. The doyenne of City brokers, Anthony Fothergill, together with three bankers from Marshall Hall sat at one end of the table and the senior partner of Rangoon's lawyers, Cliftons, sat at the other with a junior partner and an assistant.

Rangoon's Chairman, Sir Adrian Melrose, asked if everyone had a copy of the Sphinx letter. Sir Adrian then asked Lord Fettes, Rangoon's Chief Executive, for his comments.

Fettes had been thoroughly annoyed about the Sphinx letter. He had been with one of his trainers, reviewing Desert Bloom, his best prospect for L'Arc de Triomphe, when the call had come from one of his personal assistants.

Fettes's racing mania had been steadily growing over the years and had now assumed something not far short of complete obsession. Long ago the cost of it, especially when added to his two divorces, had outrun even his generous rewards from Rangoon. The last thing Fettes needed was the threat to his personal position posed by a takeover.

Fettes hadn't known anything about the Sphinx before it had started accumulating its shareholding, and he had been angered by their persistent refusals to engage in discussions. As far as he was concerned hedge funds and their ilk were simply parasites which fed off entities which were the true wealth creators in society, such as companies engaged in manufacturing, mining, oil and agriculture. Such as Rangoon, he thought.

'I don't really think we can take this seriously, gentlemen,' Fettes launched his attack. 'Everyone tells me the Sphinx is just a loose collection of hedge funds. Although it has a twenty nine per cent plus stake most of that was in CFD's until a very short time ago and has just been converted into shares, probably on short term funding. I very much doubt whether they can fund a bid at this level. I think we should brush them off and put out some press chaff querying their bona fides.'

Anthony Fothergill looked a little uncomfortable.

'Chairman,' he said, 'if I may, I think I would urge some caution here. For one thing Sir Ratan Bata is a very serious businessman indeed and doesn't lend his name to any kind of flaky enterprise. For another they have Petersons as advisers — Danny Romain actually — and he only works at the highest level. Finally – as I am sure most people in this room are aware — the Sphinx made a stunning amount of money out of the Saudi oil crisis, which I believe would easily fund their stake.'

One of the Marshall Hall bankers spoke. 'The letter refers to valuable but hitherto unexploited assets. Can the company shed any light on what might be being referred to?'

There was complete silence around the table.

'Field of Dreams. It's an odd name for a company.' After a few seconds one of Rangoon's lady non executive directors chipped in. 'What kind of field is it referring to do you think? Does it mean an oil field – do we have something we've overlooked in the portfolio?' she concluded rather timidly.

'There's nothing of that kind,' Fettes ground angrily. He didn't rate female directors at all, especially non-executive ones. 'Otherwise we'd have found it and exploited it long ago. We've been short enough of the ruddy stuff.'

Sir Adrian said: 'Well, none of this is getting us very far. I suppose we should consider the price on the table.'

'Perhaps I could ask our advisers to opine.'

The Marshall Hall team eagerly distributed some thickish presentations upon which a vast team had laboured furiously overnight.

Sir Adrian looked at his copy with visible dismay. As ex head of the Cabinet Office he had the reputation of getting to the heart of matters with rapier precision and at lightening speed.

'Perhaps,' he murmured to the bankers, 'you would take us to the conclusion pages first of all; we are going to have to make a public response to this approach and the sooner the better.'

The junior members of the Marshall Hall team looked deflated but their leader said smoothly: 'Of course, Sir Adrian, perfectly natural. Our conclusions are on page sixty, may I suggest we all turn to that page. I'm afraid they indicate that the seven hundred and fifty pence offered by the Sphinx, the Field of Dreams, rather, is an acceptable offer, given all the factors we've looked at.'

He droned on about comparative companies and deals, reserves, discounted cash flows, historic share price performance, share price highs, the outlook and brokers forecasts.

'Yes, thank you,' said Sir Adrian drily, 'that's very helpful.'

'Lord Fettes ? Anything to add?' he asked.

Fettes looked really annoyed, and was attacking the wrapping on one of his habitual Monte Cristo's with a vengeance.

'Still think we should go for their jugular,' he muttered.

'I'm afraid,' Sir Adrian concluded, 'that I've also had, since this letter was leaked to the press this morning, some calls from two or three of our major shareholders who seem to be of a like mind to our advisers.' His mouth appeared to be sucking a rather bitter sweet.

'I think we should write back rejecting this, gentlemen, but knowing that we are on rather thin ice. More of a negotiating tactic really.'

'Chairman, I've got a funny feeling about this,' Fothergill spoke. 'I think there's a lot more to the whole thing than meets the eye.'

'Would you have any objection if I had a quiet informal meeting with Romain before we say anything which might end up in public?'

'Can you do it quickly please,' Sir Adrian said.

It was early afternoon of the same day. Romain and Fothergill were in a small ante room off Fothergill's old fashioned offices at the back of the

Bank of England. A doorman in morning dress had shown Romain up to the room with great deference and now, after another uniformed footman had served Earl Grey tea and ginger biscuits to them both, they were left alone. They were two men of very different ages with totally different personal and cultural backgrounds.

'The Rangoon Board are going to reject your proposal, Daniel.'

'I really hadn't expected anything else.'

'Aren't you bothered by that? Going hostile will be risky, even with your stake.'

'No, we're not worried at all.'

'Listen, Anthony,' Romain continued, 'we've known each other a while. Let me tell you, no bullshit, that your guys are dead meat.'

'Dead meat on two counts,' Romain went on. 'One, they've missed a really, really valuable asset. It doesn't make our valuation too low either,' he said quickly, 'as it has restrictive covenants on it which the Sphinx have managed to get around.'

'Two, there's some stuff on your Chief Executive. Bad stuff. It might come out anyway, but it'll certainly come out if this thing goes hostile.'

'It's your choice. If this goes hostile it's going to be incredibly damaging for the whole Board, especially for the top two. At worse they're going to look incompetent to a degree. And your chief executive could face criminal charges. I can't say more than that.'

Fothergill was stunned. This was scarcely a speech he expected to receive in relation to one of Europe's flagship companies.

He rallied.

'It's all very well, Daniel, for you and I. But the Board will want chapter and verse before they move on account of this.'

'They're not going to get it Anthony. You've had a gipsy's warning, we both trust each other.'

'We need a positive on this by midnight or we go hostile, full frontal.'

Chapter 19

A WAR WITHOUT DEATH

That was how he used to regard hostile bids, remembered Doyle, as he contemplated the telephone call he had just received from Romain.

Right now though, if anyone was going to be killed, Doyle believed it should be his lead adviser.

Why did Americans have so much, too much, testerone, he wondered?

Why did Romain have to tell Rangoon's bankers that there was some valuable asset they had missed, yet which, in the context of a takeover, didn't go to value?

Then he had put their Chief Executive on a black square of suspicion, probably the last piece of alienation the Board needed effectively to douse discussions. Had Doyle even wanted to use the issue, he thought bitterly, he would have sown the seed circuitously through Maguire, who was almost overcome with enthusiasm to use it.

Doyle thought there was no speech better than Romain's calculated to arouse suspicion and confusion, probably in equal proportions.

In Doyle's view it would at best remove any chance of getting a recommendation of the 750p from the Rangoon Board and at worst produce significant delay while Rangoon tried to work out the true position.

Investment banking, American style. Shoot first and think afterwards, he thought glumly.

He organised a conference call with the Field of Dreams Board.

Then he called Romain.

'Look, Daniel,' he said, 'your call this afternoon has made me very uneasy. If anything gets out publicly about some great store of hidden value in Rangoon no one will listed to the subtleties. The Rangoon price and shareholder expectations will go through the roof and we could get snarled up without control. If only we could get to fifty one per cent before any of that happens we would control the Board of Rangoon and can ensure it enters the conditional deal we've lined up with Barula.

The only way we can short circuit this situation is to get into the market and buy more stock. The downside to that is that we then have to make an offer under the Takeover Code with no conditions apart from getting that fifty one percent. I must say that apart from the risk of not getting to fifty one per cent I don't see many other issues, we have the agreements and funding we need and there isn't much that can go wrong.

You can atone for your sins, Daniel, by making a success of another buying operation. The Rangoon price is now 700p, a little off our rumoured price. Go to the top ten shareholders and say we are thinking of launching an unconditional bid at seven hundred and fifty pence but will only do so if they sell us more than half of their Rangoon stock. After you have got the best out of that go into every market still open after the London close, starting in the US, and buy all the stock you can up to that price.

I want control by ten o'clock tomorrow, Daniel, otherwise this thing's going to end up controlling us.'

Doyle gently replaced the receiver. He was taking a risk, but the alternative was worse.

The telephone rang.

'Hi, James, Persia here, darling.'

Bloody hell, thought Doyle, how long was it since he'd called her?

'I'm here to claim my reward.'

'What? What reward?' Doyle fumbled.

'My reward for all that money you made out of that Saudi coup! Surely even you can't have forgotten that so quickly – or me for that matter?' Doyle could almost feel the emotion coming out of the receiver.

'I'm really sorry Persia. Of course I haven't forgotten – I've just been very busy, fending off Russians and the like.'

'You mix with such bad people, James, you should spend more time with me.'

'Where are you, Persia?'

'At the Ritz, of course, all ready for you, James, darling.'

'I'm trying to take over one of the biggest companies in the world tonight, Persia.'

'You should take me over instead, James,' she purred down the phone, 'much easier, more enjoyable too.'

Doyle made a decision.

'I'll tell you what, Persia. I'll take you out tomorrow, I really can't do it tonight. But I might surprise you with a reward that goes beyond your dreams.'

'You do say the most wonderful things, James. Come round tomorrow night at six.'

For the rest of the night Doyle and Fleming were in more or less constant contact with the Petersons broking team.

But by eight am the next day they had only acquired an additional ten point one per cent of Rangoon, lifting their stake to forty per cent, but still ten per cent short of voting control. Doyle gloomily noted that another counter bidder would still be able to acquire fifty one per cent out of the remaining sixty per cent. It was highly improbable but an uncomfortable possibility.

Romain reported that some kind of rumour of a potential Chinese counter bid for Rangoon had started in Asia overnight and filtered into the London market by dawn, causing the major European institutions to hedge their bets and sell rather less Rangoon stock into the Field of Dreams offer than they otherwise might.

Doyle was disappointed but hardly surprised. He had expected the Board of Rangoon to indulge in some pretty crude counter measures and the artificial counter bid rumour, given the short time available to them, was one of the most obviously effective.

At just after midday the Field of Dreams issued a press release confirming both the making of an unconditional cash offer for Rangoon at 750p per share, the fact that it now owned forty per cent of Rangoon's equity, and a bland statement to the effect that it saw additional value in certain of Rangoon's assets. The announcement also contained the startling information that the financing of the Field of Dreams offer was being partly provided by the US and UK governments.

Immediately after that release the Rangoon share price leapt to nine hundred and fifty pence on massive and intensive buying by Chinoil, the Chinese State Oil Company, at prices of up to ten pounds. By the close the Chinese had accumulated a stake of twenty five per cent.

At an early evening meeting at his offices Romain summarised the position.

'There's no way the Field of Dreams can now get voting control of Rangoon if the Chinese go on to launch an offer, which they would have to do at ten pounds, the highest price they've paid. Equally even at ten pounds the Chinese would find it hard to get control out of the remaining stock, but it's certainly a remote possibility.

Of course they may not launch an offer but simply buy up to twenty nine point nine per cent and stop. That would be something a purely financial player might do, just to force you, as the original bidder, to pay up to get them out. But the Chinese are real long term strategic players in the energy game and so my guess is that they are in this for control.

But what I don't understand is why they are buying so aggressively – if they are doing so based only on the public information available about Rangoon it's hard to see why anyone in their right mind would pay anything like ten pounds for the stock.'

'That one's easy,' said Doyle. 'We know the Russians have spied on our Seismic X results and the Chinese spy on the Russians. They've probably got a deal together, as the Russians can't really afford to be big buyers. And don't forget they have every reason to suppose that Rangoon has unrestricted Namibian rights which means you could put pretty much whatever value you like on it and still come out ahead.'

Makepeace's brow was furrowed.

'I don't envy the Rangoon Board,' he said. 'I can see all kinds of charges being laid at them soon unless they clarify their position.'

'How can they?' asked Doyle. 'They are in the unfortunate position of not knowing what it is.'

Roddy Maguire was shown in, positively quivering with excitement.

'You boys really do know how to put on a show,' he said, pulling out a flamboyant yellow handkerchief and passing it across his flushed features.

'The media have gone absolutely mad, not helped, James, by your refusal to give the customary press conference after your offer was announced this morning.'

'Nothing we can say would do us any good, Roddy. We remain,' quipped Doyle, 'a mystery shrouded in an enigma, wasn't that what Churchill said about Joseph Stalin?'

'They're all desperate for stuff,' Maguire went on, increasingly agitated. 'They want interviews with you, James, with Ratan Bata, with the UK Prime Minister, the US President; they've all got so many questions. It's like a bloody powder keg.'

Maguire sank back into his chair. He had been right to be nervous about this assignment, he thought, but he had been right for the wrong reasons. Doyle had the money alright. But now Maguire had the professional public relation's man's complete nightmare — events without a story and a client who refused to speak. He swore to himself. It was, he thought, like being present at King Midas's feast, but without a spoon.

Romain had left the room to take a call. He returned and said: 'That was Fothergill. He wants a meeting with you and me, James. He says the Rangoon Board are in a frightful state.'

'Well, that's their problem and his problem, Daniel,' said Doyle. 'What on earth would we gain from meeting them now? We're not going to help them evaluate their assets – that's their job.'

'That's the point James. They've obviously done a massive amount of scurrying round over-night and fastened on the Namibian stuff as a missing link. But they either haven't found or bothered to look at the additional agreement.

So they've probably worked themselves up into a belief that they are sitting on a bigger gold mine than they really are.'

'I don't care,' said Doyle,' they've got no idea what there is there so what can they say?'

At this point Makepeace left the room to take a call from the European Financial Services Board (FSB).

He came back, looking pale.

'Guys,' he said, 'we're getting the book thrown at us. A big heavy book. That was the FSB Director General and he wants to see us all – right now.'

'And that means you as well, James, I'm afraid,' Makepeace added.

'What's his problem?' yawned Doyle, looking out of the taxi window at the lighters ploughing under Southwark Bridge.

'Use your imagination, James, will you,' scolded Makepeace. 'He's the Head Regulator of all European financial markets, he's got a one hundred and fifty billion pound bid backed by leading Western Governments, he's got massive buying of the same stock by a Chinese National oil company and he's got a target company Board who don't understand the value of their business and are having to ask the bidder what it is.

We're going to have to help him, otherwise all the professionals on this bid will have their firms put out of business,' concluded Makepeace.

Doyle had never seen him so anxious.

'Yes, put like that I can see his point,' conceded Doyle jauntily.

'Your Sphinx is bloody well FSB regulated as well, James, so you'd better take this seriously,' Makepeace said. He knew that to keep your nose clean with regulators you first had to have your client under your thumb and he wished in this instance that his client had been anyone else other than James Doyle.

They were shown into a room on the fortieth floor of the FSB's palace in Canary Wharf.

After a short while about twenty FSB and Takeover Panel staffers trooped into the room and after a couple more minutes the FSB Chief Executive, John McTape, joined them, together with the Director General of the European Take-over Panel, Maurice Duvalier. The FSB had over-all responsibility for the regulation of European financial markets while the Takeover Panel regu-lated takeovers. McTape took the lead. He was a rather gaunt, grey, gangling man, with a ner-vous facial twitch, who looked like and indeed was, by original profession, a corporate lawyer. At this moment he was also looking very stressed. He was light on introductions.

'Perhaps you'd care to explain yourselves,' he said.

Doyle said mildly, speaking on behalf of the Field of Dreams, that he didn't think there was much more he could explain. The facts were that he, on behalf of the Field of Dreams, had organised the building of a position in Rangoon, reached the mandatory bid threshold of twenty nine point nine per cent, bought more stock, gone through the threshold and announced an unconditional offer in compliance with all regulations.

'And that's it,' he concluded blandly.

He could see McTape seething with frustration.

'That's not what I meant,' McTape said heavily. 'I meant why are you so interested in Rangoon?'

'We see some value there,' Doyle was even blander than before.

'Everyone seems mystified as to what you can see, even Rangoon and its advisers.'

'Perhaps we've done more work on the potential of some of their assets.' Doyle thought it was time to toss an olive branch.

'Have you shared the results of this work with Rangoon?'

'Certainly not,' said Doyle. 'It's proprietary information to us.'

'Director General,' a youngish member of the Takeover Panel staff with a thinnish ginger beard spoke up. ' Under Rule 23 of the Takeover Code, in the interests of keeping all shareholders properly informed, the bidder has an obligation to release that kind of information, even where it is information which the target company would normally be expected to provide.'

'That's a very general rule,' said Makepeace. 'I hardly think it covers the extraordinary circumstances of this case. The information we have is exclusive to us, and has been obtained at our initiative and at our expense. It's commercially highly sensitive to us. We've made a general statement that we see more value in certain of their assets and that's as far as we are prepared to go.'

At that point, just as McTape was beginning to look distinctly testy, a secretary came in with a note for him to which was attached a print out of some kind.

He read it quickly and Doyle saw his features begin to relax.

'This, ah, is a press release just issued by Rangoon,' McTape announced, the confidence seeping back into his voice. 'I think I'd better read it'.

'*Rangoon announces that in connection with the offer announced this morning by The Field of Dreams Limited, it has concluded the rigorous review of its asset base which it has been carrying out for the last twelve months.*'

Doyle smiled to himself; this was vintage takeover- speak, he thought.

'*As a result of that review, and certain additional information made available to Rangoon by government officials in Namibia, Rangoon has concluded that the concessions it holds in Namibia, covering nearly half a million square miles, could be of immense value to the company. Rangoon believes that this acreage could hold one of the largest oil fields ever discovered anywhere in the world and, if so, would utterly transform the value of your company. Rangoon will proceed immediately to conduct all necessary tests on its own account, a process which it believes will take between six months and one year.*

In the meantime Rangoon recommend that shareholders take no action either in relation to the offer for your shares of 750p made by the Field of Dreams Limited or that might be made by any other party pending clarification of the position by your Board.'

McTape looked up, satisfied. At last, order had been restored to his markets, information had been provided by the target company. The threat of chaos had been averted.

His euphoria did not last long.

'What sort of information can that announcement be based on, John?' asked Makepeace. 'Rangoon has done no aerial, seismic or drilling work in Namibia in the sixty years they have had those concessions, you know.'

'Well,' said McTape, 'I'm sure those are the sort of questions that my staff will follow up with Rangoon.'

Another secretary came in, flourishing a substantial package which looked like a much lengthier press release.

McTape looked at it and a broad smile spread across his features.

'Oh dear,' he said, addressing Doyle, 'this doesn't look too good for your bid, I'm afraid. It's an offer by Chinoil for Rangoon at ten pounds a share, just this minute released.'

He read the opening paragraph.

'*Chinoil is pleased to announce, following Rangoon's welcome clarification of its asset position, that it is making a cash offer of ten pounds per share – etcera, etcera,*' finished McTape.

This was how markets should be working, he thought to himself. And, better still, it was one in the eye for the insufferably confident – and rather rich – James Doyle. These hedge fund people needed to be taught a lesson or two, including, he thought, proper deference toward their regulator.

'I wonder if we could have a word in a smaller forum?' asked Makepeace politely.

McTape looked discomforted.

'If you insist,' he said grudgingly and asked all his staff members to leave the room; only he and Duvalier remained.

'Thank you,' said Makepeace. 'I'm afraid this isn't all quite as simple as we might like. We have been working on this for a long time. We have had access to all the documents which cover the leases to these Namibian fields and I'm afraid there seems to be one piece of the jigsaw of which Rangoon, as the owner of the concession, is presently unaware. That is that while they have the undisputed rights to develop the field they may not pump more than twenty five thousand barrels a day.

We don't know why this side agreement was ever introduced but the original contract is in the Namibian Government files and is clearly signed by the then Chairman of Rangoon. We can only assume that the company have mislaid their own copy and are unaware of the existence of the restriction. It probably wasn't regarded as a big deal back then in the nineteen fifties when no one took the prospect of Namibian oil seriously. Maybe it was a smart Namibian politician seeing some scope to milk the situation twice if ever a large find was made.

It's certainly a pretty big issue now and I think you'd better take it up with them when you clarify the basis of the announcement they've just made. They obviously need to make a further announcement. That will be hugely embarrassing for Rangoon but at least from your perspective that further statement will reduce the impact of their rather controversial earlier message about the potential reserves at the Field of Dreams. And I imagine that the Chinese will definitely have something to say about it all.

Incidentally the Sphinx has signed a new agreement with the Namibians giving it, and the Field of Dreams, rights over all production in excess of twenty five thousand barrels a day. But the Sphinx cannot extract, so it needs to acquire Rangoon before it can make the whole deal work. In a way, Rangoon owns the treasure house, which is of almost unimaginable value. But,' concluded Makepeace, staring at a now white faced McTape, 'the Sphinx now hold the keys.'

'It's a horse trade, actually, as to how much those keys are worth,' added Doyle, maliciously, 'but I suppose it would be a good thing if the players in the trade were at least on a level playing field in terms of information'.

'We can give you copies of all the relevant papers', said Makepeace, 'and we look forward to hearing how you get on with Rangoon.'

Southwark Place was invaded that evening by the members of the Sphinx, jubilant.

Doyle's butler, Fred, poured vintage champagne, while Fleming ran over the figures.

'All in all, gentlemen,' Fleming summarised, 'we have invested some forty five billion pounds in eight billion Rangoon Oil shares. At the Chinese offer of ten pounds a share these are worth eighty billion pounds, a profit of some thirty five billion, less the six hundred million we have spent on all the Namibian exploration and drilling work and on James' expenses.'

'Yeah,' Bulstrode was never at a loss for a quip, 'get a cheaper plane next time please James.'

'It's all very well,' Weill was speaking, 'congratulating ourselves on the profit we may make on the Rangoon stock, but that wasn't really the original point of the exercise.'

Myers looked puzzled. 'Seems good enough to me, Michel.'

'No,' said Michel, 'the real value of this oil field is obviously so huge we can hardly comprehend it. Matthew, how do you value our participation under this new Namibian agreement?'

'Harris Bank estimates the value of the field at a thousand billion dollars and we have a direct interest of five per cent — so fifty billion dollars, plus of course our effective share via our Rangoon shareholding.'

'May I remind you guys that we cannot access any of that fifty billion unless we acquire control of Rangoon, and at present we don't have that. If we sell the Chinese our Rangoon stock control of Rangoon will pass to them and then we still have to do a deal with them on the value of our agreement with Namibia. They've been very canny in Africa, as you know, and I think they might outflank us yet by seeking their own deal with Joseph Barula.

Of course,' Fleming went on, 'they may not even proceed with their offer for Rangoon.'

'What do you mean?' said Doyle, 'it's an unconditional offer, same as ours.'

'Yes, it is,' said Fleming, 'but they will very shortly find it is based on incorrect information being issued to the market by Rangoon and my hunch is they may get the Takeover Panel to release them from it under those circumstances.'

'That's something that the Panel hardly ever do,' Doyle said.

'Yes, James,' said Weill, 'but look at the politics here. We're just a bunch of hedgies and count for nothing; the Chinese are a global superpower.'

Doyle left the room to take a couple of calls.

One was from Persia, which left Doyle pale beneath his tan and apologising profusely.

'I don't care how much money you've made, James, if my reward isn't exactly what I think it should be you may never see me again.'

The second was from Barula.

Almost immediately Doyle detected a tremor in his normally deep confident voice.

'Listen, James, a couple of things. First my Energy Minister was in Washington when he got hauled in by the FBI. Apparently they were acting for the US Securities Exchange Commission who were following up a call they had had from Rangoon Oil. Rangoon were maintaining that the Namibian Government had a body of knowledge about Rangoon's concession there which should be made public. Anyway, to cut a long story short, they gave him the third degree, he didn't really understand the rights and wrongs of our position so he gave them a copy of the various presentations and then they let him go.'

Doyle thought, that's what got passed to Rangoon and that's the basis of their press release. At least that was clear.

'The second thing, James, and you've got to help me here, is that this guy Lutin has turned up again. He came over the border three days ago with at least twelve trucks, bribed the guards not to inspect them, and I've just had a communication from him.'

'I'll read it to you.'

'*Dear President Barula,*

As you are aware Petrogaz is desirous of entering an agreement with you in relation to the oil concession presently held as bearer documents by Rangoon.

Rangoon have failed to take any action with regard to this concession for over sixty years, which Petrogaz believe to be an insult to the Namibian Government.

Petrogaz believe it would be appropriate if you were to cancel the Rangoon concession, citing this lack of activity as a cause, and issue a similar concession to Petrogaz. Obviously we would accept certain milestone and performance requirements.

You have persistently failed to enter into discussions with us on this matter which is of the utmost importance to the Russian and Namibian States.

In order to sharpen your focus on this matter it is my duty to inform you that twelve nuclear devices have now been buried in strategic locations in this concession. Were they to be detonated I am advised that they would effectively permanently destroy the geology of the field to the extent that it would no longer be of any significant economic value.

Unless you signify, within forty eight hours, your willingness to enter the attached agreement with Petrogaz, and sign the attached annulment of the Rangoon concession, these devices will be detonated.

I am also advised that under these circumstances significant collateral damage to the civilian population of Namibia could be expected.'

It's signed by Lutin on behalf of Petrogaz. He's given us a short wave radio contact and times when we may use it.'

Chapter 20

DESERT STORM

Doyle imparted Barula's report to the stunned members of the Sphinx.

'Jesus, James,' said Patrick Myers, 'I don't believe this. One minute we're counting unimaginable profits and the next minute we're looking at losing it all due to some mad Russian.'

'The Chinese can't know about this,' said Makepeace, 'but if they did it would vastly strengthen their case for withdrawing their bid.'

'No one knows about this,' said Doyle very quietly, 'except Barula, and I guess, his key security people, and us. And that's the way it's got to stay if we are to stand a chance of sorting this out before it all goes wrong. I've got an idea of how to do that and I'm going to see Prime Minister Singh now. Meanwhile I suggest you all go home and we all keep calm. It's not just our profits that are at stake here, gentlemen, it's the energy security of the West, and that's too big an issue for us to load entirely on our own shoulders.'

Doyle took a cab to Downing Street where Singh had invited him for supper in his flat.

'Well, James,' he said cheerfully, opening a bottle of Chianti, 'we seemed to be making good progress before the Chinese came on the scene and now I understand that they don't like Rangoon's latest announcement. I've had the Chinese Ambassador here breathing dragon's flames and I think we're going to find it very difficult to hold their feet to the fire. But presumably you're not too worried if they duck out. I assume your offer would carry the day and I that they would sell you their stock — hell of a loss for them though. Law suits everywhere I suppose.'

Doyle agreed.

'But, Prime Minister,' he said, 'there's a rather bigger problem.'

Doyle spoke for about five minutes.

Singh remained impassive.

'I suppose we'd better bring the Americans in on this,' he said eventually. 'They've got a pretty big vested interest.'

'It's your call Prime Minister, but I think we can sort this out without them. They'll be like bulls in the proverbial china shop you know, and they'll panic.'

'Tell me what you want to do.'

'I need the SAS, again, I'm afraid. I want one helicopter crew and detachment to go and see Lutin's mother first thing tomorrow at the Castle of Gath, and before that a team has to make a covert visit to the island tonight to check if she's there. Then I would like more units in Namibia, in sufficient numbers to storm and neutralise Lutin's position while I distract his attention. To do this I need a radio tracking expert to locate Lutin's base. And I need a Namibian army chopper to transport him back to Windhoek if I succeed in doing a deal with him. Finally I need, by midnight, a letter from you and Den Leopold addressed to the Sphinx agreeing to carve Petrogaz in on the Field of Dreams deal. I'll scribble a draft now. We'll have to persuade Den Leopold to let us sort this out on our own.

'You're not serious about the last bit of that letter, are you, James?' Singh was incredulous.

'Talk is cheap, Prime Minister, that letter may have a very short life.'

'Why a specifically Namibian chopper?'

'Don't ask.'

'Here's the number to call. Don't screw this up, James. I don't want my arse kicked to kingdom come by the Americans, the Chinese and every other oil dependent country.'

Doyle went off to a side room and called the number. He returned after twenty minutes.

'Not a good night for hot pasta, Prime Minister. But we're lucky to have those SAS boys. I've called President Barula and told him I'll be there tomorrow afternoon; the SAS team will be there late tomorrow morning.'

Very early next morning Doyle eased himself out of a helicopter and walked a little stiffly over to the front door of the Castle of Gath. He carried only the letter he had requested. The door was opened by a housekeeper who looked at him and the helicopter beyond. There was no sign of its SAS detachment which had fanned out of it into cover at lightening speed.

Doyle looked at her frightened face.

'Please tell your mistress that I have a letter for her. The name's Doyle. James Doyle,' he said.

She disappeared for several minutes and finally beckoned him up to the drawing room on the first floor.

Maria Lutin was in the same chair as at the time of Doyle's previous visit. He was distressed to see that her right hand was still heavily bandaged.

She waved away his apologies.

'I haven't seen Alexander for nearly two weeks,' she said, 'and I've not been at all well. Do you know what he's doing?'

'Yes,' said Doyle, 'he's about to blow up one of the most valuable oil resources the world has ever seen.'

Doyle spoke to Maria Lutin calmly for the next ten minutes.

'So, you see, Mrs Lutin,' he concluded, 'this resource is too big for any one country to own. It's going to be shared, by the Americans, the Chinese, the Namibians, probably even the Indians, in other words by many people who have a big oil dependency. And they are prepared to make the Russians part of this too, even though Russia has plenty of oil and gas. Look, here's a letter confirming that. I think you'll recognise the names on the bottom of it.'

Maria Lutin studied the letter, her hands shaking a little.

'What do you want me to do?'

'Mrs Lutin, your son Alexander has embarked on a course which could place him in very great danger. You are, I think, the only person he really listens to, the only person who can haul him back from this dreadful brink.

I want you to write him a letter, enclosing the letter you have just read, telling him that, in the circumstances, he has achieved everything possible for Russia. Perhaps you could add a little white lie and say that you have spoken to Prime Minister Orlov who also concurs and is looking forward to welcoming him home to Moscow a hero. Then, please, tell him how ill you are, tell him you need him urgently, and that you want him to come home.'

'Can you guarantee his safety?' she asked.

This wasn't a question that made Doyle very comfortable. People who held the civilized world to ransom with nuclear weapons didn't command the greatest life expectancy.

'No,' said Doyle, 'but he will stand a better chance if you write that letter than if you don't.'

Maria Lutin got up, crossed to her desk and drew some writing materials towards her.

'When we he get this?' she asked.

'I will be in Namibia tonight and will immediately try and make contact with him. He is promising to carry out this dreadful threat twenty four hours after that.'

From his glimpses of the letter she wrote Doyle guessed it was in Lebanese. He was going to have to take it on trust.

Doyle slept most of the way to Windhoek while the Blackbird rumbled steadily down the West African coast.

Alexander Lutin could still remember the last conversation he had had with Julius Orlov two weeks before.

It had taken place on the veranda in Orlov's summer palace. Unusually for a Russian Orlov never touched vodka and they were sipping a delicious Montrachet.

'I'm disappointed in you, Alexander. You've not produced the goods on this Namibian oil field. You've spied successfully on the potential – I had no idea it was going to be as massive as that. But you've not brought it home for us, you know, for Russia. You tried to get the detailed drilling records to back up the Seismic X data which we accessed. You've tried to steal the concession, you've tried to bump off Doyle, more than once, and finally you've tried to force the Sphinx to cut us in on their deal. None of your initiatives have succeeded.

I can't give you many more chances, Alexander,' said Orlov, sorrowfully.

'Chances to live up to what your father achieved.'

'I'll give you one more though,' said Orlov. 'You can have whatever you need but on condition that it all looks like your doing and nothing is traceable to the Russian State. Alexander, this is your last chance to show me what you can do.' Lutin responded and spoke while Orlov listened without emotion.

'You have a brother in the air force, don't you?' asked Orlov.

'Yes? I thought so. Well that will make it easier to spin the story as far as I'm concerned.'

'You do realise, don't you', Orlov was at his most avuncular, 'that doing what you propose carries a very high risk of losing your life?'

Lutin had had plenty of time to reflect on these things. The makeshift Russian tent that served as his HQ was hot despite the built in tropical flaps and ventilators. His small team of desperadoes were dozing in the heat in the smaller tents behind it. One guard was on duty, slumped in a canvas chair with his AK 47 cradled on his shoulder, just grazing his four day stubble.

There were two hours to go before the next six hourly communication slot.

Lutin wondered what the other side were doing now, wondered who would come after him. He wondered too at the morals of a man like Julius Orlov, happy to play each stage of a game in so many different ways. He supposed that, whatever the result was, Orlov and Russia would win from it. If they won the concession they would single handedly control OPEC 2. If Lutin blew up the Field of Dreams Russia's existing oil and gas supplies would give it progressively more global influence as the Saudi output waned.

Probably Orlov didn't really care what happened.

Lutin felt betrayed. He'd set things up now. It had been a massive struggle to source, transport and place the bombs in such a short time.

He'd had to endure a surfeit of the company of the mad bomb boffin he'd borrowed via Orlov's office. The logistics of transport, storage, bomb burial, fuse setting and time recording had been a nightmare, not really his bag at all.

No, he reflected, the die was cast and Orlov was right.

There was indeed a very high chance that he would die whatever happened.

He set his alarm for one hour hence and retreated to a rather dirty, torn, hammock in a corner of the tent, and toyed with a small glass jar containing a white powder which he kept for emergencies.

Joseph Barula had transformed one of the large rooms on the ground floor of the Presidential Palace in Windhoek into a war room.

At one end of a central oval table was a huge map of the Field of Dreams pinned to a board supported by some primitive trestles. Doyle's drilling team had marked the basic geology of the field. There were at least ten obvious sites where a bomb could be planted to do maximum damage but, unfortunately, they were all covered a large area and they were up to a hundred miles apart.

'We have to know the exact locations of these bombs, James,' Freddie Prior, the SAS's bomb disposal expert was talking, 'or even with the latest Geiger technology we could be looking for them for days.

We need that and we need the codes which were used to fuse each bomb.'

Doyle asked him rather sarcastically if he would like to be driven to each of them in an air conditioned limousine.

Prior laughed easily.

'The thing is James, is that we don't really know what generation of Russian nuclear devices these might be. My hunch is that this operation is only partly blessed by the Russian powers that be, and they stand ready to disown it at any convenient time. So I would guess that the bombs that have been made available to Lutin are pretty old. In that case they are fairly simple to arm and disarm; they will have minimal electronics which are integrated with the timing counters and set into a Perspex casing screwed to the surface of the bomb.

Apparently our diplomatic people have put some pressure on the Russians to send down an expert having looked at their weapons inventories to see what might be missing. I guess the Russians are waiting to see which way Lutin's little enterprise looks like going before they respond to that.'

President Barula was sitting at the big table drinking tea and asked Doyle how he thought Lutin would react.

'I don't know what I can get out of Lutin, until I try,' explained Doyle,' but I think he's nearly at the end of his tether. I think I know what buttons to press on the political front and I'm certain I know his weakest link on the personal side. What we mustn't do is frighten him. I want to warn him I'm coming and be put down by one Namibian Army chopper, not one of a whole posse of them, and I'm just going to go to him on my own. What we need is a counter movement from the rear which takes out his guards; then if he turns nasty we can rush him if need be.'

Some photographs of Lutin's encampment were screened; its location had been traced from the last six hourly radio transmission and had then been physically verified by a spotter plane.

His camp was pitched in a good strategic position on the top of a long ridge of dunes, scrub and stunted trees about five hundred miles north west of Windhoek. It commanded uninterrupted views in every direction over territory for about twenty miles around.

Doyle, the SAS commander and the Head of Barula's Special Guards studied the enlarged photographs closely.

'Is there anything else moving out there?' asked Mike Alcock, the young SAS lieutenant-colonel, 'any tribesmen, animals, anything which to him will form a natural part of the landscape?'

'Sure,' replied Jonathan Obutu, Barula's commander in chief, 'there are the Damara who keep goats and cattle.'

'Can we get one or two men from each of the Special Guards and the SAS moving up towards his rear over the next few hours,' asked Doyle. 'You know, something that won't give him cause for thought? Perhaps with someone from the Damara and some animals? Need some make up for the Hereford guys, I guess,' he added playfully, 'and, more seriously, a three way radio link for that party, for you and for me when I'm facing up to him.'

Obutu and Alcock went off to confer.

Within an hour a plan had been made and Doyle prepared for the imminent six hourly radio contact.

At 6pm the Namibian radio operator looked up and said: 'He's on air, Mr President.'

'Mr. Lutin,' said Barula neutrally, 'I have a friend of yours here, who would like to talk to you.'

'Who is it?' The reply was metallic and strained.

'James Doyle,' the President's deep voice was confident and relaxed.

'He's got some important information for you.'

'Okay.' Doyle could almost feel the reluctance in Lutin's voice.

'Good evening, Alexander,' said Doyle. 'I have two pieces of information for you. First of all we have decided to share the ownership of the Rangoon Oil concession, which we now call the Field of Dreams, amongst several countries and we will include Russia in that. I have letters to you to that effect from both the US President and the British Prime Minister. You have to understand that this resource is too big, too important for the world, for any one country to own it all. You have to think about whether it is best for Russia to have a piece of it or whether you will go on with your plans to destroy it and have Russia cast as a political pariah on the rest of the world for evermore.

Secondly I have a letter for you from your Mother, Alexander. She is not at all well and she wants you to go to her.

Will you let me bring these letters to you and have a talk?'

There was a long silence.

The radio crackled briefly.

'Alright.' Lutin's voice was more emotional.

'But come on your own. Midday tomorrow. I know you know where I am.'

The radio went dead. It was very, very hot.

Doyle had a mile to cover to reach Lutin's encampment which he could see indistinctly in the heat haze on top of the distant ridge. Doyle wore a t- shirt, shorts, dark glasses and a sun hat. He carried no weapons, just a water bottle. The two letters were tucked in his shorts. His radio mike was hidden in the shark's tooth he wore on a leather lace around his neck and the receiver was hidden in the curved frame of his sunglasses. He could see no sign of life at the camp. There seemed to be no one there. As he drew nearer he raised one arm in greeting but he was fighting the sensation of being duped. He spoke briefly into his microphone to a pre arranged code. Then at last he saw Lutin, sitting on a canvas chair in the shade to one side of his old army tent. He seemed rather a crumpled figure.

Doyle reminded himself, for about the millionth time in his varied career, never to underestimate opponents.

When Doyle got to within twenty metres of the tent Lutin raised an arm and beckoned him to the canvas chair's brother. Lutin was unshaven. Periodically he wiped his face and nose with a none too clean white handkerchief. He certainly didn't look like a man who held the future of the world's oil supplies in the palm of his hand.

Doyle strained his eyes into the darkness. Yes, there were two heavily armed guards at the back of the tent, who seemed at least awake, if not alert. Some rather halting pleasantries followed. Doyle sensed that Lutin was pleased he had come on his own, pretty much naked. Lutin seemed to be deriving some sense of obeisance from it. Without further ado Doyle handed over the two letters.

Lutin read the Field of Dreams letter first, and nodded to himself at the end. Then he read his Mother's letter. Towards the end he slumped in his chair and put his head in his hands.

'I've been to see your Mother,' said Doyle gently, 'she's really anxious to see you, you know.'

Then Lutin sat up and looked at Doyle. For the first time Doyle could see his eyes properly. Doyle almost drew back, Lutin's eyes burned so brightly they almost seemed on fire.

'Either it's heavy cocaine use,' thought Doyle, 'or he's gone slightly mad.'

The sight forced Doyle to divert his own eyes and his gaze shifted to the back of the tent. A goat, or some other animal, seemed to be eating the back of the tent. A larger and larger hole was appearing in it while the sounds of vigorous mastication continued. The guards seemed comatose, almost as if they had been drugged. Doyle watched fascinated as one of them seemed to be drawn out of the tent by an unseen hand.

He forced his gaze back onto Lutin.

'Yes,' said Lutin. 'I would like to go to my Mother.'

'But,' he continued, 'on the other matter you are too late. You see, even as I was bringing in these bombs, I became convinced that even they wouldn't get what I wanted for Russia. So I decided that I would leave behind a little firework display to compensate me for all the disappointment I have had in not meeting my father's expectations. At least, I thought, people would remember that.'

He wielded the handkerchief again.

'What do you mean?' asked Doyle, who felt the pit of his stomach beginning to crawl.

'Just this,' said Lutin. 'These bombs are primed to go off. To stop them you have to find them and disable them.'

'But,' he continued, 'they are primed to go off in series, at one hourly intervals.'

Doyle looked at him, horrified. A slight whistle in his ear piece gave him the signal that all Lutin's guards had been disabled. Now all he had to do was incorporate the word 'rush' in his next dialogue with Lutin.

Doyle found difficulty in speaking.

'When is the first one due?' he asked.

'In just under one hour,' Lutin's voice had a cackle to it.

'And where is it?'

'Underneath your chair,' Lutin cackled madly again and Doyle jumped.

'I'll make sure you get to see your Mother, Alexander. In fact I'll lend you my plane.'

'But, 'Doyle continued, 'I need the exact locations, the firing order, the bomb types and their priming codes.'

'That's no problem,' Lutin said, indicating a tin box under his chair, 'but you won't have enough time. It's my firework display, you know.'

'We'll have to rush,' Doyle concluded.

After that things happened very quickly.

Lutin was overpowered and the chopper was brought up from its lair a mile off to just outside the encampment. The contents of the tin box were checked by Freddie Prior and the bomb disposal team.

Another group of six helicopters was brought in from twenty miles behind the encampment and Alcock and Obutu conferred with furious urgency. A large scale map was unrolled on the sand and all the bomb positions marked.

Alcock summed up.

'The biggest problem is logistics. Most of these bombs are a hundred miles apart and these choppers cruise at a hundred and thirty knots. With a one hour interval between bombs that leaves barely twenty minutes to find, uncover and disable each bomb. And there are refuelling issues over that distance. It's too tight, we're going to have to have more than one chopper and that means we're going to have to spread the bomb disposal expertise pretty thinly.'

Doyle suggested with a straight face that they might like to start with the bomb under his chair and Alcock grinned.

A plan was formed, nothing more was wanted of Lutin and he was bundled roughly into the original helicopter.

'Barula's boys will put you in my plane,' Doyle promised.

The helicopter whirled up in a cloud of heat and dust and rose steadily into the sky silhouetted against the early afternoon sun.

Doyle didn't want to look but couldn't help himself.

When the chopper reached about fifteen hundred feet it suddenly disgorged a wildly spinning figure, like a kind of mechanical stick insect. It span down and down and down in a never ending spiral until it crashed into the desert about a mile away in a slight pother of dust.

No one moved or spoke for what seemed a very long time.

Last thing that evening Doyle and President Barula and his wife Michelle were sharing beers on the State House verandah in Swakopmund.. Barula had gone inside for a moment.

'Have they found all the bombs, James?' she asked, looking first at the sea view and then, more lingeringly, at Doyle.

'Yes, all of them,' he replied, 'but the last one was with ten minutes to spare. Those guys have been incredibly brave.'

Barula re-appeared.

'Making love to my wife again, I see James,' he said, jovially. 'Well I've just been invited by your good Prime Minister to a summit to, as he put it, 'sort things out.''

'Really,' said Doyle, 'you know I'd thought we'd done a fair bit of that on our own.'

Chapter 21

BRANKSEA CASTLE

Doyle, dressed in torn and faded jeans and an old t-shirt, his deck shoes parked on the grass beside him, dangled his feet into the water lapping at the harbour wall. The late afternoon September sunshine gleamed on the flood tide swirling and chafing at the harbour entrance and made a picture of a very pretty little gaff cutter which was easing back home on the dying sea breeze.

For a man in control of forty per cent of one of Europe's largest oil companies, and a stakeholder, albeit contingent, in one of the largest oil fields ever discovered, Doyle had to admit to himself that, bizarrely, he no longer felt in control of events.

All day heads of state had been being shipped in to Branksea Castle with much fanfare and security. Doyle hadn't seen them all but he had caught a glimpse of the Indian and Chinese premiers. His friend Joseph Barula hadn't yet arrived. Nor had Julius Orlov. Doyle wasn't looking forward to that meeting.

The summit hadn't actually been Singh's idea. It had been the inspiration of Den Leopold.

He wasn't there yet either. Doyle's mind boggled at how the normal US Presidential security entourage could be accommodated in the confines of the old, elegant castle which had guarded the entrance to Poole harbour for nearly two hundred years. Normally used as a holiday home for a retailer's employees Doyle felt that it would relish a return to the status and glamour it had enjoyed under some of its earlier, wealthier, and distinctly eccentric, owners.

Leopold had apparently issued strict instructions that only Heads of State, and one adviser each, could attend the meetings scheduled for the next day.

Singh had given Doyle the details. Leopold had decided that the Rangoon situation was a mess and that he needed to put together what he called OPEC Two. Since the Chinese had announced their unconditional offer of ten pounds a share the Indians had entered the fray and bought over ten per cent at prices of up to twelve pounds a share. Now there was less than twenty per cent of Rangoon shares left in public hands. The Sphinx held forty per cent and the Chinese thirty per cent and the Indians just over ten per cent.

No one could get voting control without buying stock held by the others or without increasing their offers to the, by now, stratospheric levels which the remaining public shareholders, faced with a buying bun fight being carried on by some of the richest nations in the world, would want to tempt them to part with their stock.

As a consequence no one could agree the composition of a new Board for Rangoon, and without a new Board no one could cause Rangoon to progress a deal with the Field of Dreams which would enable the Namibian oil to be actually produced.

For Doyle, and the Sphinx, there was a real risk that the situation would drag on past the six month window of the Namibia agreement, which could then lapse – taking the Sphinx's valuable interest with it.

Eventually everyone had arrived and an informal late night supper was served in the spectacular drawing room overlooking the harbour entrance. Doyle was intrigued to note that Singh had laid on a particularly avant garde young Indian chef.

Julius Orlov had been courtesy itself, brushing aside Doyle's commiserations on Lutin, and congratulating him on playing a difficult situation in just the right way.

'James,' he said, 'Alexander was always going to self destruct one day. He carried too much baggage I'm afraid. Stupid thing he did at the end, though. It was never going to work.'

After supper Doyle was smoking one of his Egyptians in the rose garden between the castle and the sea when he felt an arm go round his shoulder.

It was Den Leopold.

'Hey, Doyle, you schmuck,' he said, 'put that damn thing out and come with me.'

Doyle followed him. Leopold, in a black leather jacket, jeans and sneakers, loped easily along towards the jetty and hopped down into one of the Castle's motor launches. Two secret servicemen fell quickly in behind them and one of them told the helmsman to make for 'Egret'.

Minutes later they were bumping against an old black cutter moored in very shallow water in the bay the other side of the South Deep channel which ran south west from Branksea Island. She was showing no riding lights and only the very faintest glow percolated from the cabin.

Leopold told the launch and the secret servicemen to stand off and await his call to return.
He led the way below to the rather faded saloon. There was a coal fire burning in the grate,
on either side of it two comfortable looking arm-
chairs, and on the table glasses and a bottle of
Jack Daniels.

Leopold splashed some whisky into the tum-
blers, pushed one over to Doyle and flung himself into one of the chairs.

Doyle sank into the other one. Suddenly
he felt tired. It really had been one hell of a
journey.

He looked across at Leopold who, although a
few years older, didn't evince the slightest trace
of fatigue or stress.

'Doyle,' said Leopold, 'you've played an absolute blinder right through this you know.'

'But,' he continued, 'long term, the Field of
Dreams, and whatever Rangoon metamorpho-
ses into, they're no places for you and your gang.
Together they are going to turn in to a sort of
OPEC 2, that's my vision, and that's going to have
to be controlled by a mix of the world's leading energy dependent nations and Namibia itself. That's delicate diplomatic work, James, not
something for you and that bunch of greedy
hoodlums you've got in tow behind you.'

Leopold took a swig of whisky.

'What's more I don't think you deserve the enriching and priceless experience of negotiating with all the interested parties here, James. You've done your bit, and the world should be damned grateful for it. To be frank, I'd also like to have the whip hand tomorrow for the US and at the moment we're laagered up in some kind of contingent convertible which only gives us a small chunk of Rangoon and of course nothing in the Field of Dreams.'

Leopold turned his famously direct stare onto Doyle, who felt himself being sucked in inexorably by Leopold's charisma.

'My proposal, James, is this. The Sphinx has a participation of five per cent in the Field of Dreams. We're happy to see you keep that. You've earned it. But we want control of your Rangoon stock and we'll pay you twelve pounds a share for it.

You guys are better off to take the cash and play again, though God knows what you'd do for an encore after this.

Well, whaddya say?' Leopold's smile flashed at him, lighting the dim cabin.

He got up and recharged their glasses.

As soon as he had returned from Namibia Doyle had spent the best part of a day with the members of the Sphinx in a long and at times painful discussion about the end game, a game which Doyle had seen coming from a long way off. It didn't seem to matter to some of his members that they had made a profit equal to the gross domestic product of many emergent economies; they just wanted more.

'We're not sellers,' said Doyle, deadpan, to the American President.

The smile on Leopold's face instantly disappeared.

'Just kidding,' Doyle added.

'We've thought about this,' said Doyle evenly, 'but your Rangoon stock proposal doesn't begin to address the real value of Rangoon with its holding of sixty per cent of the Field of Dreams attached to it. Harris reckons that's worth six hundred billion dollars, that's three hundred and seventy five billion pounds. That means that Rangoon altogether is worth more than five hundred billion pounds. That's at least twenty five pounds a share.'

'James,' said Leopold,' now you're living in a dream. Nothing in this world is ever quite as good as it may appear at first sight. Unless you want to be a very public part of one of the biggest securities scandals of all time and irrespective of the purely legal rights and wrongs of what has gone on here, you have to accept that the Rangoon shareholders who sold their stock in the last few months are going to have to be compensated. There's just too much shit around to do anything else. Believe me, by the time that's all finished, a clean twelve pounds a share now and a get out of gaol free card will seem like a damn good deal.

I want to make life simple for you by taking you and your Sphinx guys right out of this. We'll even indemnify you against all future legal actions. Think about it. You'll need to square your rogues, of course. They'll do this if they know what's good for them.

And I need an answer by nine tomorrow morning, James.'

Leopold got out of his chair and came round to Doyle and extended his hand.

'You have my word,' he said.

'And at that price we might even chuck in an update of that ridiculous plane of yours, at least it'll be a bit easier on fuel costs after this.'

'I'll talk to them, Den. They're not easy people.

But there's one more thing, Den,' Doyle spoke with feeling. 'I don't want Joseph jerked about. That's why he wanted us to be involved. He wanted to keep some control. He's a straight guy, one of the best in Africa. He's got to come out of this with a decent position.'

'Well, you have my word on that too,' said Leopold. 'I'll give him a complete carve out on the choice of operator and he's got overall voting control of the Field of Dreams anyway. If we can't show the best guys in Africa a good deal there's no hope for any kind of global leadership by us.'

They shook hands again and went up on deck. There was a half moon just visible through the clouds. A fresh little wind had got up after the languor of the evening lull. The buoys in the great harbour flashed their symphonies of red, white and green.

Doyle took a deep breath.

It was going to be alright. The Field of Dreams was going to be alright.

Doyle took a sudden decision. He turned to Leopold.

'I'm not going to have much to do tomorrow,' he said. 'Do you mind if I invite a friend?'

Persia arrived in time for lunch. She looked, if possible, even more ravishing than ever before. She was wearing a beautifully cut pair of white jeans with a shocking pink top and a pair of jewelled sandals.

None of the statesmen had brought partners and she was quite a distraction in the dining room.

'It's been a long time since you managed to have dinner with me, James,' she said, 'and you've been woefully short changing me in one or two other departments as well.'

Doyle said he thought he could at least put that right even if he wasn't being allowed to deal with anything else remotely important.

After tea he led Persia on a tour of the island. They walked up past the tiny church, and up through meadows dotted with peacocks. Persia said she didn't know how such a beautiful bird could make such a dreadful noise. Doyle said he didn't find it so hard to understand.

Finally they reached the upper woods where they drifted along through the pines, their bare feet being caressed by pine needles and cool sand.

They reached the North end of the island and were looking down through the woods to the glimpses of the harbour below.

Doyle turned to Persia and gently turned her face up towards him.

'Persia, darling, will you come away with me?' he asked.

She pressed herself against him.

'Is this my reward?' she whispered.

'It might be just the first instalment, if you're good,' said Doyle.

She tipped her head back and smiled gloriously at him.

'Of course I will,' she said.

When they got back Singh sought them out.

'Well,' he said, 'we're all agreed but we didn't want to issue a communiqué until you were happy and we haven't been able to find you. What have you been doing, James?'

'I've been doing a deal of my own with Persia, actually, Prime Minister.'

Singh rolled his eyes and thrust a document into Doyle's hands.

It read as follows:

'*Rangoon Oil agrees to be acquired by an international consortium and acquires a sixty per cent stake in the Field of Dreams Limited (2010), a company established to hold certain rights to the extremely valuable Field of Dreams concession in Namibia.*

Rangoon announces that it is to recommend a cash offer of twelve pounds a share, to be made by an international consortium comprising the Governments of the United States, China, India and Russia. The Field of Dreams Limited has agreed to sell its stake of forty per cent in Rangoon to the consortium at that price. At the same time it has been agreed that Rangoon and the State of Namibia and the Sphinx Partnership will, subject to various conditions, own stakes of, in round numbers, sixty, thirty five and five per cent respectively in the Field of Dreams Limited (2010) conferring the rights to substantially all future oil production from the Field of Dreams prospect in Namibia which is believed to be, by a very substantial margin, potentially the largest oil field in the world.

Rangoon will have a new Board of Directors comprising representatives of the Governments concerned and including Mr James Doyle, who heads the Sphinx Partnership and who has played a critical role in the development of the Field of Dreams.

Further announcements will be made as appropriate.'

'Is that alright?' asked Singh of Doyle. 'It was Joseph Barula who was especially keen to keep you involved and he also wants you on the new Field of Dreams Board.'

'That's fine,' said Doyle.

Dinner that night was festive. The old castle's rooms were decked out at their finest. Persia was at the centre of male attention.

Finally President Leopold got to his feet.

'Gentlemen and lady,' he started, 'this is a unique occasion. Today we have all agreed to share in a new energy resource of almost unimaginable size. Not only will this resource, when on stream, underpin economic prosperity throughout the world, but the fact that we have agreed to share the resource and to co-operate in its development, management and conservation surely sets us on a new path of global co-operation.

None of this would have been possible without the skill and entrepreneurship of James Doyle combined with the statesmanship of Joseph

Barula and we are very happy indeed to be moving forward in this great development with both of them so heavily involved.

I'd like to thank Prime Minister Singh for laying on this very special venue and for the outstanding contribution his own commercial flair has made to our success.

Finally, I'd like to remind everyone here to tell their friends that James Doyle is now an exceedingly rich man, and, if they have any foundation which needs filling up, to pass their begging bowl across the schmuck, he's got plenty!

However I understand that Doyle, who gets bored quickly, ceased to interest himself in our deal this afternoon and disappeared with the very beautiful Persia Mansour.

Gentlemen, please raise your glasses.

The toast is — 'James Doyle and Persia Mansour'.'

Thank you. Again, and finally, the toast is – 'The Field of Dreams.'

THE END

About the Author

Philip Swatman spent nearly thirty years in investment banking. He lives in London. This is his first book.

Made in the USA
Lexington, KY
30 September 2010